I0611283

THE FACES OF DOCTOR RICHARDS©

The Faces of Doctor Richards

The Faces of Doctor Richards
A SUSPENSE THRILLER

By
STEVE JAFFE
A Weaver of Tales Press
www.weaveroftalespress.com

The Faces of Doctor Richards

Copyright © 2020 by Steve Jaffe ISBN 978-0-9819410-7-3 (Paperback) ISBN 978-0-9819410-8-0 (eBook)

The Faces of Doctor Richards

<u>Other works by Steve Jaffe</u>

The Haven House Chronicles, The Conspiracy
ISBN:978-0-9819410-0-4

Children with Invisible Faces
ISBN:978-09819410-4-2

God's Looking Glass
ISBN: 978-0-9819410-2-8

The Stranger I Came to Love
ISBN:978-0-9819410-3-5

The Invisible Enemy
ISBN:978-09819410-4-2

The Architect's Manifesto
ISBN: 978—0-9819410-5-9

Review all books at <u>www.aweaveroftalespress.com</u>

The Faces of Doctor Richards

Dedication

To my wonderful wife and best friend, with your support and encouragement, you have helped keep my passion for weaving tales for my loyal readers.

The Faces of Doctor Richards

Prologue

One month ago, Doctor Todd Richards, a world-renowned biochemist, and plastic surgeon did not have a care in the world. Now he was running from the FBI. Two of his patients had turned up missing, and only he knew why. He was not ready to be questioned by the authorities.

Running at a fast sprint, he was out of breath as he ducked into a public restroom at the bottom of La Jolla Cove, just north of Seal Beach. He turned his aqua blue reversible sweatshirt inside out, turning it bright red. Then he unzipped his travel pant legs he was wearing, converting them to shorts.

His heart was making so much noise that he could not think clearly. The news of the disappearance of his patients' had been plastered on every local and national news channel. These women were high profile celebrities who were being investigated by the FBI.

Now, Todd Richards was not prepared to talk with the authorities or the media who had started to hover at his office. It was not the FBI that scared him, but the CIA. He knew The Central Intelligence Agency wanted him more than the FBI.

When he started running, he knew he needed a new identity, just for the time being. It seemed like the only smart solution. What he had created and what the CIA wanted, allowed him to keep himself young and healthy, while allowing him to transform into numerous identities.

Sitting inside one of the restroom stalls, he tried to catch his breath, but the putrid urine smell from the homeless people who use the restroom as shelter late at night filled his throat with bitter bile. His hands could not stop shaking. *"Get a grip Richards,"* he scolded himself.

He pulled from his wallet a nude full-body photo of a man who had died a few years back. It was a picture of a handsome young man who had committed suicide. This photo, like dozens more, he had used while practicing his transformation abilities. This one, he believed, would give him some needed time to plan his next move. He wanted to disappear while the FBI and reporters feverously searched for Doctor Richards.

He stood up, holding the photo at arm's length and stared at it, concentrating on initiating the transformation process. Tonight, what he had done a million times before, was not working. *It must be stress*, he told himself. He took a deep, cleansing breath and slowly let the air escape, feeling his heartbeat slow down. While still focused on the photo, he felt a tingling engulf his entire body. Within seconds, his face and body had begun reshaping itself. After five minutes, he stepped out of the stall, looked in the mirror, and was pleased he looked identical to the man in the picture.

As he stepped out of the restroom, he sucked in a deep breath. He filled his lungs with the sweet ocean air he had always enjoyed during his daily jogs around the cove. Richards knew he might not have a chance to do again unless he came up with a feasible plan and explanation about his two missing patients.

He heard sirens coming from Prospect Street. The pulsating sound whisked him back to four weeks ago when a medical error changed his life forever.

1

Four Weeks Earlier

Doctor Richards dropped to the floor, his hands cupping his head, while his body shook wildly. He had made a careless error by allowing himself to get distracted. Angelica Rathburn, a famous actress and one of his beloved patients had started convulsing after her bi-monthly injection. She, like all his other female patients on this unique protocol, trusted him. For the last eight years, there had never been a mistake, especially like the one that was happening right now.

These women, like Angelica, all came to him for his experimental elixir with the promise for eternal youth. They needed to be at this office every fourteen days. No deviations were permitted. For his program to work, each of his special ladies had to receive their injections on time. Earlier today, they all came in together before their scheduled time. He was feeling rushed and stressed.

He struggled to get up off the cold marble floor, unable to take his eyes off of Angelica. Her contorting body, her gasping for air, left him paralyzed. He cradled her in his arms, rocking her back and forth, tears cascading down his cheeks. He was having flashbacks to the day his wife Molly died in his arms, carrying his unborn son. *"I'm so sorry. I've failed you, Molly,"* he whispered.

Richards jumped off the exam table, releasing Angelica. He slapped his forehead hard, a loud wail spewing from his lips. *"Angelica, please don't die, not today, not ever."* 911 was out of the question. What he had been doing with her and the other women patients was a secret, an illegal secret. He was between a rock and a hard place. For the first time, he was all alone with no friends or family to turn to for help. He took a shuddering breath and realized he and only he had to survive.

"This isn't happening," he kept screaming at himself. A million thoughts swam inside his panicked mind, and they scared him. He was friendly with over a dozen doctors in the La Jolla area, but calling them for help was out of the question. Not even his office manager and head nurse, Miss Hollister, could know what he had been doing.

If doctor Richards could not reverse the reaction Rathburn was having, the horrible result could not become public knowledge. If it did, the FBI would lock him up, as well as his other four patients in federal prison. They would never receive their shots, and death would come quickly.

Richards helplessly watched Angelica continue to struggle for her life. Her eyes were bulging, screaming at him to help her. His mind had begun running over scenarios on how to conceal this tragedy.

He considered many scenarios. None of them were positive for Angelica.

Richards was unable to think clearly as a doctor and as a scientist. All he had worked for, all he had accomplished, was about to go up in smoke unless he could make this tragic accident disappear. He was deep in thought as the solution to this immediate problem flashed inside his mind.

He left his dying patient and walked over to his patient file cabinet. He had to change his identity to make his plan work. He pulled out a file that contained over ten aliases he had accumulated over the last eight years. He sorted through the papers until he found the full-body photo he had taken at a morgue many years ago. He glanced over his shoulder at Angelica. Her breathing had become shallow and slow.

Another perk from his serum was that it was possible to change his body and appearance with his thoughts. He began focusing on the full-body photo he held in his hand. Within seconds, his face and body were remolding itself, as if they were a large mound of clay.

2

He walked back toward Angelica, again staring helplessly over his dying patient. Rathburn's loud cry snapped Richards back to the problem he was facing. Just then, he remembered he had created an antidote. It was untested.

"You won't die on me, not today," he said with an air of confidence.

Richards did not have any windows inside his exam room; privacy was a priority. It had only been thirty minutes since he made this fatal mistake. Inside a locked metal cabinet that contained his vials, he searched for his antidote. He smiled when he found it. He wasn't sure if it would work, but he had no choice but to try it. If it did not reverse what was happening to Angelica, he was all out of options to his problem.

His thoughts were spiraling out of control while he stared at Angelica's lifeless body. He looked down at the life-saving antidote in his hand; he looked at Rathburn and realized he was too late. He wanted to go back to his life with Angelica and his other four female patients but knew that was never going to happen after today. His mind was becoming irrational, and his will power to control what he was about to do evaporated.

Until today, everything he had accomplished was flawless. He had honed his new transformation skills, as he walked through La Jolla every evening, meeting people at different happy hours, as a different person.

He estimated he'd need another year or so to have the ultimate combination of genome editing and fetal stem cell modifications that would make him unstoppable and hidden from the FBI forever. Now with Angelica gone, he had to figure out what to do with the remaining women in his program.

His mind was going over everything that had happened before Angelica walked into his exam room. He remembered that the waiting room at his medical office building had closed at five o'clock. All his regular patients had gone. His nurse and office manager, Carolyn Hollister, was wrapping up some paperwork and getting ready to head out the door.

Richards recollected how the afternoon sun slowly sank at the edge of the Pacific's deep blue waters witnessing a rare "Green Flash." The outside temperature had dropped ten degrees. Unbeknownst to him, the temperature inside the waiting room had begun to rise.

He remembered before Angelica stepped into his office, that he was in his exam room preparing for three bi-monthly injections his patients needed. Again, he recalled that it was unusual that these three women would be at his office at the same time. Their demands to have their injections today, all at the same time, caused him unnecessary stress. He was a stickler for keeping to his daily routine, no deviations at all, and what his special ladies had done today made it difficult for him to adjust.

They had told him five days earlier they had scheduling conflicts and needed to get their two-week shot before they went out of town. Today, the three women did not leave him much choice. Little did he know that Angelica would turn his world upside down.

Rathburn had been his first female patient who had agreed to his program of eternal youth after she had a near-death car accident that had disfigured her beautiful face.

He had the first human phase of his formula created after his wife and unborn baby died. He had been perfecting his transformations on himself; however, he was running out of his serum. He needed a way to get fetuses with his DNA.

It was Angelica's fetuses that moved his research to its current stage. Richards knew she appreciated what he had done for her after her horrible car accident, and that she owed him her restored beauty and her career.

Once Angelica had her photogenic looks fully repaired, their doctor-patient intimate relationship went to another level. Falling in love, or getting married again, was not going to be in the cards for Richards.

Angelica was a very fertile woman. It was not difficult getting her pregnant. It had become more than just a clinical job for him. For the first time since his wife died, he was enjoying himself.

What Richards had learned with Angelica had transferred over to the other female patients in his program. After their shots, they would retire to his upstairs bedroom for hours of stress, releasing intimacy.

Today, Richards knew that was not going to happen with all the women being there at the same time. Having these women in his life, helped him produce his serum, over the last eight years.

Like a drug addict, he needed fetal stem cells to enhance his research. He was becoming obsessed with his transformation abilities and what he could do with them. He was driving himself crazy, searching for the perfect mixture, the right combination that would make him indestructible. Now, nothing else mattered. Creating more and more aborted fetuses so that he could build a better hybrid mixture had become his obsession.

He had begun to experiment with a crossbred blend of serum from each of his patients. Since using the new combination serum, he was unable to focus clearly. Mistakes within his work environment were happening. Panic set in.

Richards laid down on the cold exam room floor, in a fetal position, mumbling to himself. His thoughts strayed back to the moment he knew something was wrong in his waiting room.

It was when the loud cacophony of voices from the women had stopped. Rathburn had always been her friend's cheerleader. It was not happening today.

Trish Morgan, a popular talk show host, jumped in first with a direct question. She flung her long black hair with a twist of her neck—then combed her slender fingers through her bangs. "Angelica, you seem a million miles away. What's the story, girl?"

Angelica sadly shrugged her shoulders. "I can't talk about it," she replied sadly. Her response only made everyone's curiosity boil even hotter.

That answer wasn't going to keep the nosy women from dive-bombing the friend they've known for a couple of decades. While Angelica had been the veteran of Doctor Richards' treatments, she had been the positive force that kept everyone in line—until today.

Lea Strong, an international model, interjected herself into the conversation. She spoke with her jaw clenched, feebly attempting a British accent she had been practicing for her next modeling role. "We're all friends here, my good ladies. Your troubles are our troubles. It's jolly good to talk things out. We'll understand."

Trish Morgan could barely control herself. "Lea, you'd do better sticking to your normal voice. The Brits will have a field day with you if you attempt to speak like that."

Lea either did not hear her or was ignoring her and focusing on their friend.

Angelica raised her head slowly, exposing two swollen red eyes. Then, her emotions had gotten the best of her. She looked over her shoulder, then left, and then right, making sure they were alone. Without warning, she broke down into a spasm of sobs.

Trish and Lea popped up and were by her side. They were both kneeling, each holding one of Angelica's hands. The circle had been formed, providing their upset friend a sense of security to speak. Neither of the women saw nurse Hollister listening by her office door that was conveniently ajar.

Rathburn took a deep breath—her voice cracked. "I can't agree with another abortion. I want to be a mother."

"It can't be done. You…no…we all signed an agreement that could never be broken. Abortions were the price we had to pay. Also, Doctor Richards won't permit it. We can't permit it. If anyone got a hint of what we've been doing here, we'd all be locked away for the rest of our lives, rotting away in some jail cell. And I do mean rotting if you get my drift?"

"I know, I know. I can't be part of this anymore," Angelica cried. "I would never reveal what we've done. You know it would affect me also," she said, her voice a low whisper.

Lea jumped in. "Without your shots, you'll begin to lose your youthful appearance. How will you explain that to your fans, your friends, and your family?"

It was apparent that Angelica had not thought of that, shrugging her shoulders. "I don't know. I'm feeling so guilty about killing my babies, that I guess, I don't care how I'll look," she said, sucking in some air. "I want to be a mother. Have a normal life. I have enough money that it won't matter if I ever work again."

The women had become silent. The alternative that Angelica had thrown in their faces had not occurred to them. They feared not having their youthful appearances more than being mothers. Vanity and deception had become their addiction.

Lea spoke. "You signed an agreement. He'll keep you to it."

Angelica looked at Lea with an icy stare. "Girl, how's he going to enforce our contract? It wasn't drawn up by an attorney anyway," she said. "He won't sue me. What reason would he tell the courts? He'll have to be reasonable, and trust that I will keep my silence."

No one had a response for what she had said, as they all sat back in their chairs, an eerie silence filled the room. They wanted their injections and to go home. What had been a room of high-pitched chatter turned into a cold silence—only their pounding hearts filled their heads.

Within moments when Doctor Richards stuck his head out from the procedure room, the women had become very animated and agitated.

Richards noticed the seriousness on everyone's face when he opened his door. "Who's going to be first today?" he said, his voice upbeat. He felt the cold chill his ladies projected. "How about you, Trish?" he said, exposing his perfect white teeth.

The Faces of Doctor Richards

Todd Richards looked more like a surfer than a doctor. Brown glowing skin, long blonde hair with deep ocean blue eyes, and a square chin. He was boasting a thirty-two-inch waist that completed the perfect V-shaped torso that he loved to show off. He was beautiful to all these female patients.

When Todd saw Angelica with a sad expression on her face, it had brought him back to when they had first met. The hair on the back of his neck was at attention. He sensed trouble was about to come his way. He forced a big smile before Trish walked into the exam room.

* * * * *

Nurse Hollister quietly closed her office door. Shock stamped on her face. *"What's been going on with Doctor Richards?"* she asked herself. Carolyn shook her head, not wanting to believe her boss was breaking the law. She went outside unnoticed by Lea and sat in her car, her hands shaking.

4

Richards stared at Trish Morgan, sucking in a deep breath. "Are you ready?" he asked, noticing the tension on her face.

"Sure," she said.

"You look down in the dumps," he said as he twisted his head, causing his long hair to fall gently down the back of his white lab coat.

Morgan tried to hide her concerns for Angelica. She loved her vanity and didn't want to lose it. With what Rathburn wanted to do, was putting them in legal jeopardy. She pulled out her vacation photo and prepared herself for the transformation into her secret identity, Lisa Beverly.

"I don't feel this is the right forum to talk. I think after you see Angelica this evening, you'll have a clear picture of what's bothering Lea and me," Trish said, forcing a smile.

Doctor Richards looked confused. He wasn't in any mood to listen to her, so he changed the subject back to the task at hand. "I see you have your vacation picture. Going on a trip?" he asked as he prepared her injection.

"Bermuda. I haven't been there in a while and have a friend who'll keep me occupied while I take in the nice rays on the beautiful face and body you've given me," she smiled as her hands rubbed her hips and waist.

"Okay. You know the rules about changing your appearance. Don't try to meet 'Mister Right'—it won't work. Just have fun and get home within fourteen days. Remember, you're Cinderella and will turn into a pumpkin unless you are back here for another injection."

The Faces of Doctor Richards

Trish whipped out her false passport, driver's license, and social security card with her Lisa Beverly alias. "Thanks, dad. I know the rules. I'm only going for a week, possibly ten days at the most. I'll be fine."

He smiled and patted her firm buttocks as she laid down on the examination table. He slipped the full-body photo she handed him, inserting it into the metal frame above her. He then adjusted the metal arm so she could see the photo without straining her neck. Doctor Richards remembered how he found this new identity for her.

It was a while ago at a local morgue while visiting the coroner, who was a friend. One day he came upon a beautiful young woman who had died from an overdose of heroin. She had no name, no family, and was not in any of the police databases. She was a perfect Jane Doe.

His friend, the coroner, did not know the real reason Richards was always taking photos. Only the doctor knew that he was building a database of aliases to use for himself and his patients later. The coroner believed Richards' story that he was interested in various body types for his cosmetic surgery practice and building a photo album for future clients.

That day he found the alias for Trish, he took photos of her naked body and her pretty face, as well as her fingerprints. Little did the dead woman know that she would be resurrected as Lisa Beverly.

As he injected the solution into Trish's neck, he watched her jerk from the pain. It was normal. Then once the fluid was in her system, she would relax and concentrate on the women in the metal frame. The transformation process started quickly. Her face had begun to twist and stretch like a glob of silly putty. Then, her naked body began to transform into Lisa Beverly. The final transformation came when she stared at the photo of two female hands with visible fingerprints.

In a matter of minutes, Trish Morgan had become Lisa Beverly, an advertising executive. She needed five minutes of rest, something that was required for the body to adjust to the transformation. Then, she was up, and heading out the side door, not wanting her friends to see her other identity.

* * * * *

Nurse Hollister, his office manager, was still sitting in her car, shaking from what she had heard the women talking about earlier. "Doctor Richards doing abortions," she kept muttering. "It can't be. He's a wonderful man."

She saw the side door to the building open, and a woman, she did not recognize, briskly walk out and open the driver's side door to Trish Morgan's car. Hollister did not know what to make of this, as she watched the stranger drive away. Carolyn tried snapping a picture of the women, but she was speeding off down Prospect before she could document what she had seen.

Hollister was confused about everything she had heard and seen that evening. Confronting Doctor Richards was out of the question. She liked her lifestyle and decided to look the other way and pretend she had never seen or heard those horrible words from the three women.

5

It had taken Doctor Richards over an hour to complete Trish's and Lea's serum procedure before he could see Angelica. He noticed she was anxious and asked her to go into his office first so they could talk. He watched her sit down on the leather couch that faced a large picture window that opened to La Jolla cove. He walked over and sat beside her.

He put his arm around her and gave her shoulder a gentle squeeze. "Something's bothering you. I can see it. I've known you for a long time. So, spill the beans," he calmly said.

Angelica was his favorite. She was his first patient to use his new serum, and it bothered him when she didn't show off her beautiful face with a smile. Richards could tell she had been crying by her swollen eyes. She tried to speak, attempting to catch her breath.

Richards put his steady hand on her thigh and, with his other hand, turned her chin toward him. "I can't do the procedure unless you're calm, and by the way you look, relaxed is a million miles away."

"I can't abort my baby," Angelica blurted out. "I know we have an arrangement. Isn't there a way for me to be a mother?" she sobbed.

Todd could not believe his ears after all he had done for her. Her words bothered him. His mind was spinning out of control.

"I am a little alarmed and at a loss for words," he said. His friendly smile had vanished. "How long have you been thinking about this?" he asked, his tone resonating an icy edge to it.

"Since last year, after the last abortion. I read that women who have had too many abortions have a high risk of not ever having children. I don't want to be that statistic," she said, rubbing her hands nervously.

"Please understand. Our secret will be safe with me. Please say yes?" she pleaded, holding his hands tightly in hers and kissing them gently.

Todd pulled away and stood. He had begun pacing around his office deep in thought. He was getting close to perfecting the miracle serum he needed, and losing Angelica's fetus she was carrying was going to set his research back a few years. Different scenarios had begun flashing inside his mind. Most of them scared him. Without warning, he clapped his hands, and his smile returned.

"Everything will be all right," he assured her. "I have a year's supply of your serum. I'm not sure how this will work for you and your baby."

Richards was now wondering if what Angelica wanted to do would be a benefit for his research. He tried to picture that when her baby was born, he could use some stem cells from the newborn to create the right formula he needed. His thoughts kept spinning like a fan on high speed. *"If this works, no more abortions,"* he nodded his head.

We can try to give you your shot every three weeks. This schedule might provide us with enough serum to last you two years. Then we can get you back on your routine. It's possible, no guarantee, that the degeneration will go slowly or that your baby won't be affected by the new infusion schedule or by the serum. I can't guarantee that this alteration to your regimen will allow your body to adjust and gradually revert to your normal aging process. If it works, then we can restart your injections after the baby's born and hopefully go back to the way things were."

Angelica jumped up and put her arms around him. "I love you, Todd. I do, you know. Yes, just one child. That's all I want." She looked up at his six-foot two-inch frame and bit her lower lip. "I can't wait to see what our baby will look like." She noticed that her slip of the tongue upset him. She knew how tormented he was about losing his wife while she was carrying his son. "I didn't mean it the way it sounded. I won't ever expect anything from you, as the father. I'll have time to think of a believable story to tell my child about his or her father."

Richards turned away, opening the door to the procedure room, unable to control his shaking hands. He had not anticipated the complications of being a father with a woman he was not married to, even though he felt some love for her.

He noticed her full vial and empty syringe on the tray where he had left it. He realized he had not prepared it. He was preoccupied, his thoughts a million miles away, as he pulled back on the plunger, his thoughts were only on what Angelica had said to him.

He was in a trance, unable to think clearly. He was not looking at Angelica, as he slowly pushed the warm fluid into her internal carotid artery.

He was startled when he heard Angelica moan. He stood there, unable to move or react as he watched her body convulsing. He looked at the empty vial of her serum. He then knew what he had done. He had given her three times her usual dosage by accident. He needed to counter the side-effect with a solution he had created for just this situation. He tried to move but remained frozen as he stared at his patient.

Richards was now moving in slow motion, holding the syringe with the antidote. He was helplessly watching her die on his examination table. He remembered how his wife Molly had died. He got on the exam table and held her in his arms. He was now crying uncontrollably.

He turned his head, his lips almost meeting hers, as two final gasping breaths were released from Angelica's lips.

Richards had never anticipated having a patient die in his office. He got up and carried her body to his operating room, unable to control his emotions. His throbbing heart was drowning out his thoughts.

"What have I done?" he muttered. He was again back to the same feeling he had for not being able to save his wife and son. This time he had killed his second unborn child.

He couldn't stop torturing himself, as he placed her still warm body on the cold metal surgical table.

His mind was a slide show of "what if's," and none of them called for doing the right thing. His mind seemed to snap. He was in survival mode. Without hesitation, he made his decision. He had become an expert criminalist from all the research he had done, as his hybrid serum mixtures gave him the ability to absorb tons of data.

6

Richards tried to calm the voices inside his head. His brain, like a super-fast computer, had begun laying out a sound plan to cover his tracks. Like a computer sorting data, the steps he'd take to handle his problem were now in numerical sequence.

First, he had to salvage Angelica's fetus, and place it in one of his liquid oxygen tanks, freezing it until he was ready to use it. He gasped when he saw it was another boy. *"Shit, I've lost a second son,"* he cursed.

The next, he had to get rid of the body and all traces of Angelica. His eyes grew wide as he fixated on her body and how fast she was aging on his surgical table. He knew it would be a side effect that would happen by missing a serum injection. He never had an opportunity to test his theory if a patient died during the serum protocol.

"Shit, this is another predicament I didn't predict." Richards did not like losing control.

One of the crime stories he had read a while back was about a sadistic serial killer who disposed of his victims in suitcases. Transporting them was very efficient.

Remembering that scenario made what he was about to do easy physically, unfortunately, not psychologically easy. When he snapped Angelica's left leg at the knee, the sound echoed inside his surgery room so loud it brought shivers up and down his spine. What he was doing to the woman he had a deep affection for made him jump every time another of Rathburn's bones snapped. It had taken him one grueling hour to break Angelica's legs and arms. Each snap of her bones gave him the shivers.

Once every bone in Angelica's arms and legs had been broken, she easily folded into a softshell suitcase. He had cut open her chest cavity and made four thin slices on both her lungs so they would not inflate, as her body decomposed. Again, he had read this in the crime story. He knew this last action would allow her body to sink deep off the coast of California.

The one part of his plan he was conflicted with was how to dispose of her car. Since he had already changed his appearance, he was no longer Doctor Richards, and if he allowed his face to be recorded on every security camera on his route to dispose of Rathburn, he'd not be a suspect.

Transforming to Charlie Stokes, a successful import/export businessman from London, who had died in a horrible car accident five years ago, was a perfect disguise, as well as the perfect alibi.

Next, he had to get Angelica to the Nordic Tug 54 trawler boat one of his patients allowed him to use. Richards loved to deep sea fish when he had time. This time he'd be feeding the fish.

Richards carried the suitcase out the side door of his clinic and dropped it into Rathburn's car trunk. He did not notice nurse Hollister was still in her car, watching his office.

* * * * *

His office manager could not believe her eyes when she saw one of her patients who had died years before, walk from Doctor Richards's side door carrying a suitcase. She rubbed her eyes, believing she was hallucinating.

"What's going on?" she mumbled. "First, a strange woman leaves the office and now a dead man. Did I hear that Angelica, Trish, and Lea have all let Doctor Richards perform abortions on them?"

Hollister started her engine and sped away from her office. She was confused, needing to talk to someone to help her make sense of what she had witnessed.

7

Richards had gotten to the boat in the Oceanside marina in thirty minutes. He parked Angelica's car in the member parking lot and lifted the heavy suitcase out of the trunk. He passed a young couple who held the gate open for +
him. "Good evening," said Charlie Stokes with a big smile as he rolled the body toward the boat.

The couple replied. "Have a nice evening."

Richards made sure he had made eye contact with the two boaters. If they ever were questioned, he wanted them to remember Charlie Stokes.

It did not take him long to untie the boat from its mooring and get out of the marina. Once he was five miles off the coast, he took Angelica out of the suitcase and tied three sandbags around her neck, torso, and legs. He stood there like a zombie, as the last sandbag sank and disappeared. He didn't understand why he had begun saying a prayer and whispering something spiritual about the woman who had trusted him with her life.

He felt a little piece of himself *disappear, as Angelica's body sank.* "You murdered your favorite patient," he screamed at himself.

After wiping every area of the boat, he had touched and then hosed it down. Once he was satisfied, he did a thorough cleaning, then he turned and walked to Angelica's car. He began wiping down the entire interior and trunk. He left her keys inside her bright red Mercedes SL 560. The only thing that would appear on the security footage was Charlie Stokes, driving Rathburn's car to an Oceanside marina parking lot and leaving it there.

Inside the marina restroom, he transformed back to Doctor Richards. Charlie Stokes had to disappear forever. He would burn that identity when he got home.

He walked up to a long pathway that led him to the Coaster commuter train. He'd take it to Solana Beach, and then call UBER to get him back to his office.

It had been almost five hours since Angelica had died, and her body laid at the bottom of the ocean floor. Once home, like a dead man walking, he shuffled back to the operating room, connected a hose to a water spigot, and began washing down the entire room with hot soapy water. Then, he attached a chemical spray container to the hose and covered the room with an eye-burning solvent that would remove any trace of Rathburn's DNA or her fetus's DNA.

After sanitizing the operating room that evening, he retired to his apartment above his clinic, a bottle of Jameson in his hand, satisfied he covered his tracks. He thought of turning himself in to the authorities and letting his life wither away in some dark, cold prison cell.

He knew it was too late for him to cleanse his soul. No one would comprehend that what happened to Angelica was an accident from an unthinkable experiment. He knew no one would understand that he had no other choice than to dispose of the body the way he did.

Richards rationalized to himself that he had unique abilities now that justified what he had been doing and would continue to do until he found the perfect formula. In the eyes of the authorities, he had become a criminal years ago doing his abortions and working on fetal stem cells. Now he had added to his list of crimes, murder.

His mind was spinning out of control; he tried to figure out how he had gotten to this point in his life. His thoughts were back to the time right before his wife Molly had died, and how helpless he had felt.

8

Two men sat in a black Suburban with puzzled expressions on their faces. They were part of a covert team that had been monitoring Doctor Richards's office since he left UCLA eight years ago. They worked for CIA Special Agent Ralph Bingham.

When Richards had left UCLA, after the top-secret project he was part of was dissolved, he had become a national security threat. He was the only person outside UCLA who knew about the CIA's secret military program. After he quit, his research had come to a complete halt.

Keeping an eye on Richards over the last few years confirmed that he had continued working with fetal stem cells. And now they suspected that he had created the serum the government wanted.

Until today, they believed he had not progressed past his previous testing results at UCLA. His lab chimp, "Pretty Girl," had performed close to the initial results they had wanted. With Richards gone, however, no one working in his laboratory was knowledgeable enough to give her the correct dosage of her shots. She aged quickly and then died seven months later.

Bingham knew that Richards's private practice was booming. The CIA agent knew about the female subjects testing his serum and suspected that those women were able to keep themselves young, just like "Pretty Girl" the lab chimp was able to do until her serum ran out.

CIA agent Leroy Todd had called Bingham with their observations. "Ralph, the doctor never left the building. What's strange is that an unknown male carried out a suitcase from the doctor's office. He drove off in Rathburn's car. We've sent his photo to our face-recognition database and should have the results by the end of the day," Todd said. Also, Rathburn has not left Richards office since her appointment."

"What's so strange about that?" asked Bingham.

"About the unknown male? Well, nothing right now. It's Rathburn that's bothering us."

"Have you seen Rathburn at all?" asked Bingham, sounding impatient.

"No. Richards had appeared five hours later in an Uber car. The unknown male subject never returned Rathburn's car," Agent Todd said, frustrated. "Sir, what would you like us to do now? My butt is getting a little numb sitting here, twiddling my thumbs."

Bingham sighed. "I'll send another car in an hour to relieve you. I'll put a trace on Rathburn's car and check on the results from your mystery man," Bingham said. "I'll be calling the Director with an update."

* * * * *

"No, sir. They are not mistaken," Bingham told CIA Director Kramer. "I believe Richards transformed himself into this unknown male subject. Once I get back the results for our mystery man, I'll know for sure."

Director Kramer paused before replying, his breathing heavy. "I'll run this by the President. Don't do anything without clearing it with me first," Kramer ordered.

Bingham held back his frustration with his boss, as he listened to his orders. "Copy that, sir," he replied and ended his call.

9

It had been forty-eight hours since Angelica had died. Doctor Richards could not shake off his depression. He was relapsing into the farthest corners of his mind back where he was eight years ago after his wife died.

Up in his apartment above his office, he'd sit at Molly's piano playing all of her favorite musical pieces. After cancer had destroyed the woman he loved, he began reading every piano lesson books he could lay his hands on, and to his surprise, he was able to teach himself how to play classical piano. As his serum formula mixture became more potent, so did his ability to master anything he put his mind to learning—one negative side effect from the new hybrid serum was the angry voices inside his head. Paranoia was blanketing his mind.

Richards would spend most of his evenings and early hours of the morning stroking the keys on Molly's piano, feeling the pain of losing the only woman he had ever loved. She was his rock, his calming force he so needed right now. He knew she would have been ashamed of what he had created with his research. She was a devout Catholic, and abortion was something he knew she would never condone.

With Angelica's death on his mind, he was not ready to see Meg Cummings and Beth Thomas, the last two women who were part of his secret program. Richards knew they needed their shots, and he prayed he'd not make any more mistakes.

He took a deep breath and got ready to see his first patient. He didn't want to raise any suspicions about what had happened with Rathburn and was unable to get himself aroused and ready to have the intimacy that they expected after they received their serum shots.

Both women respected Richards's privacy and infrequent mood swings, so they did not question what was going on with him during their office visit. He promised them that by their next appointment, he would be back to normal.

After they had gone, Richards went up to his apartment to think about how to deal with Angelica's disappearance. Like he had done many times before when he had sunk into his depression, he poured himself a stiff drink.

That night he drifted back, remembering his friendship with Professor Franklin, his close friend, and mentor and how they had parted ways. He thought about the research program he had once headed up for UCLA and his contract with the CIA.

Back then, it was a top-secret program, which needed his theory on DNA editing and his fetal stems for their secret military program. He had lost track of Franklin and was not sure if his old project had continued without him. He had become nostalgic wishing he was back there, and Molly was still alive. He imagined how different his life might have been.

His melancholy had never subsided after his wife's death. He blamed himself for his failure to cure his Molly's cancer.

After losing his wife and child, his cosmetic surgery practice had almost vanished due to neglect. When he found time to see patients, he was tired, old looking, and worn out. Being a doctor had become boring. The wealthy patients he cared for were spoiled, as well as hung up on their vanity. Nevertheless, he kept helping them as he needed the money to fund his research.

After losing his wife, progress with his serum had hit a brick wall, as it was becoming impossible to find fetuses legally. His local morgues were being watched closely by a new task force that focused explicitly on anyone thinking of buying fetuses. SACU, the Special Abortion Crime Unit, at the FBI had over a thousand agents across the country, all trained and ready to arrest all violators of the new Federal Anti-Abortion Law.

He'd miss appointments, or when he would show up, he was unshaven and dirty from not showering. He was a mess. It didn't take long for his practice to dwindle to just a few loyal patients.

The FBI's new task force had interviewed Doctor Richards on numerous occasions as each hospital's morgue filed complaints about him looking for fetuses. Since it wasn't a crime to ask for fetuses, they still needed to ask him questions. Each time he'd lie to them, and each interview would end with no charges filed.

The time he had available to work on his research was in the early hours of the morning, keeping him from eating properly or getting enough sleep. His short supply of serum, from his lab chimp, *Pretty Girl*, that he had taken from the UCLA laboratory had shown promise on his new laboratory chimps. While he still had not found a cure for cancer, he did stumble upon a formula that was able to trigger the brain to stimulate the body's cells and slowly reverse the aging process.

His new formula using a specific combination of fetal stem cells combined with the subject's modified DNA reproduced younger, healthier cells inside the brain. Then, with visual stimulation, like a photo from a more youthful period, triggered the brain to send signals to regenerate new healthier cells, allowing the body to transform back to a point in time before it had any diseases. The serum had become a sort of human time machine.

He now needed to create a serum for himself to test. His desperation had made him irrational. He knew that testing on himself would be foolish and risky. He was no longer coherent. If he could not create his miracle serum, he did not want to live any longer. He understood that the risk was worth taking.

Inside a liquid oxygen storage container was the fetus of his son Richards had harvested after his wife Molly had died. Using the same protocols he used on his chimps, he created his first human formula.

Within a week, he had his first batch of vials to test. He wasn't sure what dosage he could tolerate or how it would affect him. He just proceeded without fear. If it worked, he'd be a new man. If it didn't, then death would be a welcome relief.

His injections into his internal carotid artery had gone on for six weeks. He believed that for his serum to work inside his brain, this was the fastest route to take. Giving himself an injection was not easy.

In the beginning, he had not seen any change in his overall body chemistry by using his thoughts. He tried every mind over matter technique he knew.

Then, one evening, after eight hours of testing, he was dejected. He closed the lights to his laboratory and walked upstairs to his bedroom. On his dresser was a picture of him and Molly on the day they had gotten married. It was the happiest day he could remember.

For the first time since Molly's death, he took the photo to bed, with tears in his eyes, causing his eyes to well up. He stared at the picture, holding the sides of the pewter frame tightly above his face. He cried as he gazed at his young face, wishing to go back to that time.

As those thoughts flowed through his mind, a strange tingling had begun to wash over his entire body. At first, he thought he was having a stroke. He was in severe pain. His heart was racing wildly.

He jumped up and gently placed the photo back on its spot on the dresser. He slowly moved his head and stared at the mirror above his chest of drawers.

He could not believe his eyes. He was staring at the same man in the photo. "It works," he muttered. He immediately removed his clothing. He was disappointed when he saw an aged out of shape body attached to his new, more youthful face. He looked around the bedroom.

"*I need other photos,*" he told himself. "*In the closet,*" he slurred.

He began rummaging through a box of old photos until he found the picture he wanted. He held up the memory of him and Molly on their honeymoon, both in bathing suits. He again stared at himself in the photo, and within five minutes, his body began changing. This time the pain was worse, lasting around ten minutes. As if someone was molding a lump of clay, he had transformed back to the slim muscular body he had that day on that tropical beach.

He looked inside his briefs and laughed. He remembered he had a photo of him and Molly without any clothes on. It was during their courtship, when they both were experimenting, and falling in love. He stared at the photo and watched his youthfulness magically come back. For the first time since Molly died, he had a big smile on his face.

10

During the early stages of his experiments, Richards injected himself three times per week. He began varying the dosages after a near-fatal heart attack. After weeks of testing, he determined that a dosage of twenty CC's twice a month was the highest levels of the serum that a body could handle without going into cardiac arrest.

Over the next few months, he was learning to manage his newfound fountain of youth. He kept reading all the current medical literature on stem cell research, DNA modification, human regeneration experiments, and Genome editing. In addition to being able to transform his appearance, he also discovered he was able to absorb thousands of pages of research materials on every subject. His ability to recall everything he had read was amazing.

Richards was absorbing as much data he could get his hands on turning his brain into a human-computer. He had always had an interest in police work, mostly with investigative techniques. After processing everything he could get his hands on, he had become an expert in all fields of interest. When he read instruction manuals on martial arts or weapons, or sports, he found it easy to become a seasoned expert in those sports with the natural moves of someone who had studied each activity for years.

He had a fourteen-month supply of his formula. He was addicted to his newfound fountain of youth and knew he'd need more. The problem he faced was getting fetuses that would have his genetic DNA. But where?

The Faces of Doctor Richards

When all hope had begun to evaporate, he received a phone call from a friend, Doctor Steven Fleming, in Washington, D.C. He had a patient, a famous actress, Angelica Rathburn, whose face had been disfigured in a horrible car accident.

The actress was beyond repair. Fleming knew that Richards had had some remarkable results with his cosmetic surgery practice and stem cells.

Doctor Fleming did not know about Richards's new serum, or what Richards had accomplished with his research. He wanted to help his patient Angelica, and Richards was her last hope.

Richards was over-joyed with the request. He hoped this patient would overlook what she'd have to do to regain her beauty. He agreed to do the initial consultation.

If Angelica Rathburn agreed to go along with what it would take to create her unique serum, he knew he'd be able to harvest what he'd need for himself.

During their initial session, Richards reviewed her case and her prospects to regain the beautiful face she once had. His hands gently caressed her distorted bone structure, turning her head from left to right. He smiled, nodding his head deep in thought.

"Angelica, if I can promise you a way to give you back your beautiful face, would you agree to let me try?"

She sat up straight and leaning forward, her hand's palms down on his desk. "Doctor Richards, if you can make this mess," she pointed to her face, "look better than it does right now, then I will agree to anything you want to do to me," she said, forcing a smile on her deformed face.

"Wonderful. Then, what I am about to tell you cannot leave this room. You cannot tell Doctor Fleming, your friends, or your family. You have to promise me you will not tell a soul," he said, his expression serious. "I can promise you I can give you back your youthful features." He watched her struggle smile. "But, let me be clear, if you agree to let me help you, we'd be breaking federal laws."

Angelica stood up from her chair, removing her wide-brim hat that covered her scars and disfigured face. "If you can give me back my looks, then, I am in one hundred percent," she said. "I don't want to look like this. I do not want to play wicked witches or zombie characters anymore. If I have a chance to look beautiful again, then fuck the law," she said.

They talked for over two hours. Doctor Richards asked her how she felt about abortion? If she was very religious?

Angelica was a pragmatist and believed that she came first in her life. She had never wanted children, only her career. She thought religion was too controlling.

Richards liked what he was hearing. "What I am about to show you might shock you." Right before her eyes, he changed his appearance.

Angelica was amazed. Then, a smile spread on her face. "How do I get this magic potion?" she asked, clapping her hands.

"My process requires the stem cells from a fetus that we've created. Then, I take blood samples from both of us and edit our DNA and combine this solution with our fetal stem cells. This process takes about four to six weeks after we have our fetus. And, if all goes well, we have what you called your *magic potion*."

"What's my next step?" she asked.

"We have to get you pregnant," Richards said, noticing a confused look on her face. "I do not have the In-Vitro-fertilization equipment to create an embryo or a way to get you pregnant artificially. The government has closed down all of those facilities," he said, his tone had become somber.

She squeezed his arm, letting a loud giggle explode from her lips. "When can we get started?" she said.

"I will need some old pictures of your face, preferably at a period when you looked your best. Also, I will need to take photos of you with all your clothing removed. If we are going to re-create Angelica Rathburn, it must be complete, down to every detail," he said, his tone clinical.

As he looked up from writing something in her file, his eyes grew wide. She was standing in front of him naked. He was getting very excited, as he could not stop staring. She was beautiful in every aspect, except for her facial injury. She had proportioned breasts for her body size, a narrow waist, and as she turned around with her arms spread out, her buttocks were firm and rounded.

"What do you think? Should I send you some of my younger nude photos?" she said, smiling.

"I can't imagine those would be any more beautiful than what I am looking at right now," he said, his face flushed.

"Can we get started right now?" she asked, clapping her hands.

An ambulance's siren coming from the street startled Richards back to the present. His sadness had returned.

11

Doctor Richards could not liberate his remorse about how he committed his first murder. He drifted back to the time of Angelica's initial treatments. His decision to have her live with him at the beginning of her treatments provided him some needed happiness of not sleeping alone. He stressed to Angelica that she was not going to be his surrogate wife. She agreed to remain his patient while he created her serum. However, the months they lived under the same roof, their doctor/patient relationship changes, and they become sexual playmates.

It was a complicated business relationship that had grown into something more. Intimacy for Richards had always needed a warm emotional side to it. He was surprised it was happening for him with Angelica. At times he thought he was falling in love again.

He knew it was wrong, but he was unable to control his years of bottled-up emotions. It had taken Angelica four weeks to get pregnant, and six weeks later, Richards had their first fetus. Then it took three weeks to create Angelica's serum.

Two months after her initial injections, she learned how to transform herself. Angelica was back looking like her youthful self. At first, it had not been easy for her to let her mind take over and concentrate on the photo of her younger self. Learning to focus her mind on her photos was frustrating, as the transformation did not happen immediately. During her learning process, the pain of her face remolding itself from her injury was excruciating. In the beginning, Richards thought she would not be able to control her mind long enough to allow the serum to do its job.

However, Angelica was a strong, determined woman and never gave up. She praised Doctor Richards for giving her back her career. When she reconnected with her friends, they were amazed at what her doctor had done for her. They wanted Richards to help them. They were wealthy and would pay any price for the procedure.

Angelica had told Richards that four of her very close friends were interested in having him as their doctor. Two were media personalities, one a world-renowned model, and the fourth woman a cosmetic CEO.

"I told them you were not taking new patients. These ladies are like me, unable to take no for an answer. They insisted to at least meet with you so that you could hear them out," Angelica pouted. At first, Richards objected. However, Angelica was very convincing.

"While I did not tell my friends how you helped me, I am sure they would go along with your program. They, like me, want to stay forever young and beautiful. Our vanity is our only drug."

"Okay. I will only help your friends if I am sure they can be trusted," he said.

"These ladies will do anything to keep their fan base."

After agreeing to bring these women on as his additional test subjects, he began to realize that a variety of serum blended with his DNA could be a way to create a more potent formula he knew existed. Working intimately with four more stunning women sounded like a dream come true. Little did he know how complicated five dynamic and liberated women could muddle his life. He knew what he was about to embark upon was very risky.

Richards realized these five new patients were all he could handle, and they were an excellent solution to his financial problems. He'd now have time to work on his research.

One evening working late in his laboratory, he experimented with a different serum for one of his lab chimps. He had been working on a theory. He thought a new combination that did not have fetal stem cells have exciting results. He used the mammal's stems cells, and it's edited DNA. What happened next surprised him. His lab animal had taken on a more youthful appearance, without having to change its appearance or look at a photo of itself.

Two months later, he had tried this procedure on a woman who did not want to go the Botox route. After two injections, each costing $5000 per shot, her wrinkles on her face, the bags under her eyes, and her double chin tightened up, giving her a youthful appearance. The injections lasted for thirty days, which made this new venture very profitable. Unfortunately, this new approach only worked on a person's face, not other parts of their body. That was a minor problem for his older wealthy clients. They kept coming back each month to revive their tired and wrinkly faces.

Once the word got out, Doctor Richards's office was overflowing with very wealthy patients of all age groups. One problem he had not thought about was the Food and Drug Administration. How was he going to explain his procedure and get them to clear it for public use? He did not have the energy to jump through all the hoops the government agency required.

Richards decided to classify his new health serum, for these patients, as a natural health product avoiding having to get approval from the government. As it turned out, using a person's DNA and stem cells turned out to fall within the guidelines as a natural health product.

Meg Cummings, one of his unique patients and TV newscaster, interviewed Richards promoting his new practice. She had pushed her story, titling it as *The Faces of Doctor Richards*.

Richards was enjoying his notoriety. The money he was bringing in was making him filthy rich. His serum was over-the-top priced so high that only a small elite group of wealthy patients could afford his procedure. He had clients from around the world flocking to his office.

He remodeled his office to include a thirty by twenty-foot room, setting up recliners like an infusion center. He was able to move two-hundred men and women through the procedure every month. He was bringing in around $1,000,000 per month. He had hired an office manager/nurse, a Carolyn Hollister, who he trained to safely administer the serum, leaving him enough time to work in his laboratory.

His business was clearing twelve million dollars a year. Richards' life could not have been any more perfect.

A military jet from Miramar flew over his office, creating a sonic boom that snapped him out of his daydream.

As Richards contemplated his current options regarding Rathburn's death, he decided his new cosmetic serum business would have to close. He did not want it to happen.

With Angelica gone, he'd have to figure out what to do with the other four women once they discovered their friend had disappeared.

He hoped he'd figure out a logical solution and have enough time to get his life back on track. He had no clue when the disappearance of Angelica Rathburn would hit the news.

It had taken him five days to remove most of his frozen fetuses he used from his patients. He still needed his lab equipment and brought it to an emergency location he had rented in Santa Monica, under his alias Chad Green. No one knew of this identity. Unlike his other aliases he had used during his intimate moments with his female patients, Chad Green had to stay a secret.

Before the authorities started searching for Rathburn, he felt it would be prudent to close his practice and remove any evidence of what he had been doing in his La Jolla office. He wasn't sure how these women would react or if they would put two and two together and realize he had murdered Angelica.

Nothing was making sense anymore. Richards's irrational actions were escalating, causing his mind to think of cutting all ties with these ladies, and starting over somewhere else under a new identity. That option had too many unknowns.

"I don't like where this is leading," he told himself. *"Angelica's friends are smart. If she had told them about not aborting her baby...shit, they would suspect I killed her or made her disappear."*

His brain was on overdrive. He did not like the solution or where it was telling him to go. "Take a breath, Todd," he scolded himself. "Wait until the shit hits the fan first before you panic and run like a guilty murderer."

12

Trish Morgan had landed in Bermuda the day after her infusion at Doctor Richards office. She was worried about what Angelica had told her. She kept playing the scenario her friend wanted to do in her mind, and there was no good outcome for all of them.

She could not stop visualizing all of them being arrested because of Angelica's selfish whim. She wanted to text her friend and find out how her conversation had gone with Doctor Richards. She looked at her phone and realized the cellphone she had was Lisa Beverly's, her current alias that she needed to remain her secret.

She sighed, shrugging her shoulders as she walked off the plane, refocusing on her well-needed vacation as Lisa Beverly. She started fantasizing about her lover and how he'd watch her walk toward him in her ocean view room, wearing her sheer floral robe draped over her naked body. Morgan loved teasing men, especially in her Lisa Beverly persona. Especially the frequent lover that always joined her in Bermuda.

She forced herself to remember she was not Trish Morgan now as she departed her plane. In the States, she was a celebrity and was sad that no paparazzi were looking for her in Bermuda.

She knew she had twelve days' max to get back to Richards's office, so she would not miss her next shot. Her thinking was interrupted when she saw the man holding a small white sign that had her name *Lisa Beverly* handwritten on it. She smiled, then handed him her luggage tickets and proceeded to walk with him to baggage claim.

The entire process had taken only thirty minutes. They were soon on their way to the Princess Hotel. Lisa noticed the dark, ominous clouds coming from the East toward the island and scowled.

"Are we going to have good weather?" she said, pointing toward the blackness that was fast approaching.

The driver, a polite black man with a strong British accent, sighed. "There was a hurricane yesterday heading toward the Caribbean, madam, it made a turn, and is now heading toward my island. They say it is losing its strength and should be nothing more than a tropical storm by tomorrow. The weather should pass in a day or so," he said, turning his head. "I'm no weatherman. I've seen our weather come and go in a flash. Just listen to the TV lady, and the local weatherman should have a better idea of what you could expect."

She leaned her head back, feeling the soft leather headrest. She was unruffled, knowing that most of her days would be in bed with her man-toy. As the car made its turn up the long driveway of the Princess Hotel, she sighed at the majesty of the facility. Seeing the bright pink buildings gave her goosebumps.

There was a message waiting for her at the front desk. She laughed, startling the clerk who had been checking her in. "Sorry," she giggled, covering her mouth with her hand. The note was from Eric Landers, a New York Stockbroker, who was her lover for the next week.

13

It had been seven days since Angelica's death. Doctor Richards was still unable to think or regroup. He was a nervous wreck. It was turning out to be impossible for him to remove all the equipment and serum he had stored at his office without raising suspicion. He still had patients to see and supervise their infusion procedures.

Carolyn Hollister, his office manager, had noticed her boss's abnormal behavior. She tried to hide her worry about what she had heard and witnessed a week ago. She asked Richards if there was something wrong.

Richards tried to look into her eyes to figure out why she was so concerned about him. He sensed she might suspect something by the way she was asking him questions. He brushed it off as his paranoia over Angelica's untimely death. He was confident he had not been careless that night.

What made matters worse was that Lea Strong had been calling him every day, ranting about not being able to find Angelica. Richards had become agitated at all the phone calls he had been receiving from her. She had always been an insecure, needy woman. Her constant non-stop phone calls, her incessant worries about her friend, was bringing a rage to the surface he could not control.

Lea was easy to read from her questions, and Richards guessed she knew about Angelica's desire to stop her abortion and raise her baby on her own. His mind was now spinning out of control. He thought if there were any logical solutions to his current situation, he would have figured it out already. Unfortunately, he couldn't concentrate on any alternatives. He was able to imagine how easy it would be to fold Lea's slim body into a suitcase and dump her in the ocean so she could be with her friend.

Today, Lea would be with him for their weekly lovemaking. Her non-stop questions had caused him to lose control, showing a side of himself that Strong had never seen. Lea's high shrill voice over the phone was like fingernails on a chalkboard, and she did not hear his anger at the other end of the call.

"I'm so worried about her. I've been calling her house, the studio, even her mother's," she whined. "No one has seen her or heard from her. We had a date to go nightclubbing in Beverly Hills five days ago," Lea ranted, not taking a breath.

Richards had no time for Lea's need to talk. He barked back at her. "Maybe she's gone off without telling anyone. Perhaps she needed to get away from you…and everyone for once. Get a grip. You're driving me nuts with your nagging. For once, try not to be so helpless," he heard her suck in a quivering breath and knew what was going to happen next.

He heard her start crying, which only triggered her to further go on about how she hates being alone and having to work such long hours. She was not making any sense, which again was another of her unpleasant habits.

Her self-pity triggered a mood he had never felt before. "Look, I'm not your shrink, not your friend, or therapist, just your lover, and doctor," he barked. He heard her gasp. Then, a deep sigh. *Shit, it's not over,* he said to himself.

Her sniffling was subsiding. "You're right, Todd. I'm a real butt. "I know I've ruined your mood. Can I still come over later and try to change your mind…please? She begged.

Richards rolled his eyes, exasperated. "Fine. I cannot promise you I'll be in any mood to fuck you," he said indignantly. Before he could say another word, his phone pinged. He was receiving a Skype call from Lea.

Lea was now smiling, throwing him kisses. "Is there anything I can do to…" she said, pouting, letting her sundress fall to the floor. She was not wearing anything. "I bet you're getting excited now. Let's try to get me pregnant tonight." Her mood had changed, and her voice sounded surprisingly perky.

"Later? I'm not so sure I'd be able to perform," he said.

"I bet you're more than ready right now," she said giggling at the other end of their skype call.

Five hours later, she was at his bedroom door. She turned the doorknob slowly and walked in.

"You should not be here right now. I have a lot on my mind and can't do this right now."

She ignored his comment letting her dress once again fall off her body. This time, it excited him even more.

"I'm sorry for driving you crazy. When it's our night, it's hard for me to put it off," she flirted. "Even before I get here, I'm so wet… I could almost die."

Richards bit his lower lip and began removing his shirt. "Let's try and see if we both can enjoy ourselves," he said, pulling her toward him and falling back on his bed.

* * * * * *

Later that evening, after Lea left his house, he was exhausted from her wild lovemaking. He sat in front of his TV, a glass of Jamison's in his left hand. The eleven o'clock news had come on. The reporter, Meg Cummings, was reporting about Angelica Rathburn, and that she was missing. He could see she tried to control her voice; her exasperation had come across the screen loud and clear.

Richards' heart ached as he stared at the TV screen. His guilt returned.

"It has been seven days since Rathburn missed her shoot at Monarch Studio. The director is furious and calling for the police to put out a

BOLO for the actress," the reporter tried to control her smile at the ridiculous words she had just said. *"Excuse me,"* she said, turning her head away from the camera for a moment to regain her composure. *"I was told the studio is in the middle of a costly movie, and it has come to a complete halt by her absence. While her studio does not believe it is foul play, they have called the FBI to help locate the missing actress."* She could not control her laughter anymore. *"I guess having the President pro-Hollywood, helps in a big way. This is Meg Cummings, CBS News,"* she said, blushing. They broke away for a commercial.

It had not been more than thirty seconds after she reported the news that Meg was calling Richards.

"The studio asked me to call you. They know you're still treating Angelica since her accident. I'm trying to keep our relationship out of this story," she said. "Have you heard from her?" her tone edgy.

"No. Not since I had seen Angelica last week when she got her injection,"

Meg interrupted. "I'm being called back. Can we talk tomorrow? I want to talk about this. Trish Morgan told me about what Angelica wanted to do. Must go. Call you tomorrow, sweetie."

Todd's heart was pounding in his chest. He sat in front of the TV, staring, his mind a tornado of twisted thoughts. He knew that the FBI would realize he was Angelica's doctor. The entire world knew about him. He realized that if the FBI came to his office, he'd have to cooperate with them or raise suspicions.

Now with Meg Cummings wanting to ask him questions about that evening, put him in a panic. With all four of these women having a close connection to Rathburn, it had him paranoid. He had too many loose ends that had to be severed. He rushed to his operating room.

He knew it would be useless; however, that didn't stop him from going over every inch of the operating room one more time for any signs of blood or anything that might have Angelica's DNA on it. With Lea and now Meg, concerned about Angelica, he was freaking out. The once-safe world he had was coming to an end.

The Faces of Doctor Richards

Richards stood and looked out the picture window in his living room that looked down on Seal Beach in the La Jolla Cove. He couldn't end his relationships with these women. He needed his serum to keep him young, as well as continuing his research for the perfect formula.

He walked over to the river rock fireplace and stared at the picture of his wife. At that moment, he had promised himself that he would never fall in love again or have children. The pain of losing someone he loved had almost killed him once, and he wouldn't open his heart ever again to that pain.

When he first discovered his fountain of youth serum, it provided him some beautiful women with fringe benefits. His careless mistake had created a domino effect that he did not know how to handle.

The only alternative he kept coming up with was to rid himself of these women and start over. He needed to bide his time with the remaining four remaining women so he could come up with a workable plan for everyone.

He sucked in a deep breath. He decided he needed a walk by the ocean to clear his head.

14

Listening to the Bermuda weather channel, Trish Morgan had begun to panic as the hurricane turned toward Bermuda. Just yesterday, the weather front was a tropical storm. Now, it was forecasted to impact the island and was estimated to be more destructive.

Hurricane Fernando by morning had damaged hundreds of homes and office buildings on the island. A United Boeing 727 had crashed on the main runway of the airport while attempting an emergency landing.

Trish Morgan, aka Lisa Beverly, had been going out of her mind as day eleven had come, and it did not look promising that the airport would open for her plane to take off for another two or three days. She had never missed her serum injection, and it looked like it would happen unless she got help fast.

She frantically called every transportation service on the island, offering any amount of money to get her in the air and back to anywhere on the East Coast. It was not going to happen for her with all helicopters booked. She had only one last-ditch hope, and she made that call.

"Todd, you have to do something now," she screamed. "I can't get off the island. You must come to me and bring my shot. Rent a helicopter. Do something. I'll reimburse you," she begged. "I've tried every possible way to get off this goddamn island. Everyone else with money wants off as bad as I do, not for the same reason—shit, which doesn't matter. I need your help now," she was out of breath as she pleaded with Richards.

He had pulled the phone away from his ear. He had not gotten over Lea's and Meg's irritating phone calls a few days earlier, and now this. He felt lightheaded.

"I'm up to my eyeballs with problems," he thought of telling her. His first thought was to rid himself of these women systematically.

"Calm down. Have you called your employer?" he asked.

"Very funny, she said. "You know perfectly well why my employer won't come for me. I'm Lisa Beverly, not Trish Morgan. What would I tell them?" Her sarcasm almost melted his phone. "Please stop trying to calm me down and get your ass down here…please," she begged. "You have a lot to lose, too, if I begin to revert to my old self or whatever will happen if I do not get my injection on time."

Richards was unmoved by her threat and didn't respond. A solution to this predicament suddenly popped into his brain. It was one that he had not thoroughly thought through.

He reached for one of the crime books he had read a few months back, remembering how ingenious those serial killers were under pressure. A plan began formulating inside his brain for Trish.

"I'll see what I can do. I have a friend in Washington, D.C., a colleague who owns a long-distance, eight-passenger helicopter. If he can help, then I can be there…" he paused… "in no more than two days. That will be your thirteenth day. So, stop worrying," he said, trying to act sweet to her. "I can't come as myself. So, don't panic when I knock on your door. Then, once I give you your shot, we can leave the island together," he said.

15

Richards had packed a small bag and left for Lindberg Field for his flight to Washington, D.C. His friend, Doctor Steven Fleming, the maxillofacial surgeon who sent him Angelica Rathburn, owed him big time and agreed to loan him his pilot and helicopter for his day trip to Bermuda. Richards had told him he had to see a prospective patient.

"She must have plenty of money to get you to fly out there?" Doctor Fleming teased.

"Something like that." He hated lying to his friend. He knew he had no choice.

Steven Fleming was one of the leading maxillofacial surgeons in the world. He had more money than he knew what to do with, and helping his friend was something he felt he had to do. "If you get the job, I want a helicopter service fee," he joked.

"All you'll get is a new bow tie, a case of the best Cab, and some illegal Cuban cigars," Todd shot back.

"Right, I'm still waiting for my referral fee for sending you, Angelica Rathburn. You must have made a mint on that job. What you were able to accomplish was so remarkable. Let's have dinner when you get back from Bermuda so that we can catch up," Fleming said. "I still want to know how you transformed her back to her younger self. Does that miracle serum you are making a fortune with work that well?"

"Let's talk after I get back from Bermuda," he said. *You're right about transforming her; you just wouldn't believe me on how I did it,"* he thought. Now, he had more important things on his mind: Trish Morgan and how he was going to resolve her problem.

16

Trish Morgan was startled by the loud knock on her hotel door. She put her eye up to the peephole. Standing outside her room was a man she did not recognize.

"What do you want?" she said.

"Open the door, Trish. It's me," he said in a low whisper, "Todd."

She had forgotten that he had told her he would be coming to her as one of his aliases. She opened her door, doubt showing on her face as she stared at Jeff Peters.

"How do I know it's you?" she asked, a little grin on her face.

Richards was in no mood for her games. He pulled out his photo and began transforming back to himself.

Five minutes later, he looked like Doctor Richards. "There. You satisfied now? I need to give you your shot. I have to get you and the helicopter back to my friend today," he said curtly.

Morgan clapped her hands. "I can't believe you made it on time," jumping into his arms like an excited little girl. "I was so nervous. Tomorrow would have been too late."

Richards looked at her and forced a smile. "I told you I'd get here. I couldn't let my favorite talk show host turn into a pumpkin, now, could I?" he said, gently stroking her cheek with the back of his hand.

Trish read body language well—it was her job. She looked at him—she could tell something was bother him. "Something's wrong. I can tell," she said, taking his hand. "I know you too well. You can't fool me."

Richards tried to put on his charm. "I've never been in a helicopter before. I guess it unnerved me. I'll be okay in a minute. Let's get started, I've got to get this aircraft back tonight, or he'll have my head. Now, it's Lisa Beverly's time," he said with a shrug of his shoulders.

"This can wait a few minutes," she said, pointing at her syringe. "Can't we talk for a while before we have to leave? I heard on the news that Angelica is missing. Have you heard any more about it?"

He shook his head—he looked downcast. "I'm beginning to worry too. It has been almost two weeks since we all had seen her. Angelica had told me that she had told all of you about wanting out of the program," Richards said. "She had been very emotional that night. Once I told her she could leave and have her baby, she seemed to calm down."

Trish's face twisted in disbelief. "I thought none of us could leave the program. We all signed an agreement."

"This was different," he tried to hide his lie. "Angelica was the first patient in my *Fountain of Youth* program. I told her it might be possible for me to alternate her injections and see if her body would adjust. Perhaps go back to a normal aging process." He could see Trish wasn't buying his bullshit.

"That's not what you told us when we started. Has something changed?"

He could see she was not going to let up and tried to change the subject. "It's a theory I have. If it didn't work, she understood there could be a risk to her and the baby. She was desperate and wanted to try anyway."

Trish pursed her lips and tried to digest what he had said. "So, if I ever want to start a family, I too can leave the program?"

Richards' heart was now pounding. He couldn't have everyone leaving him. A frown formed on his face. "I thought you never wanted to have a baby, let alone be a mother?"

"Just kidding. I like the idea of staying beautiful and young."

"Can we get back to what I came here to do?" Richards asked, his tone getting edgy.

Trish blushed. "I'm sorry. I guess I can't get the talk showgirl out of my head. I'm sure Angelica is off somewhere thinking about being a mother."

She flopped down on the bed, her firm breasts bouncing like Jell-O inside her small bikini top. She was gorgeous, like a Playboy centerfold.

He tried not looking into her eyes as she kept chattering about her wonderful vacation with her friend.

"Now that I'm getting my injection, I don't have to leave now. The weather is clearing up and a few extra days in the sun, might do me some good," she grinned, raising her hand. "Maybe you can spend a few days with me now. We've never had a vacation before. You do know that vacation sex is the best?"

Richards nodded, trying not to let his anxiety to show, as he filled her syringe. Unlike Angelica, who died because of his carelessness, this time, he knew what he was doing. His hands began shaking—doubt consumed him. He thought of pushing the extra serum back into her vial. Then, something inside his brain was telling him something else. *"An accident was one thing,"* he said to himself, *"premeditated murder of Trish?"* was something foreign to him.

"Sorry. I can't stay," Richards said, tapping the syringe with his finger and releasing some fluid. "I told you the helicopter has to be back tonight."

Trish pouted. "Okay. We do need to go on a vacation sometime."

Richards took a deep breath as he pushed the fluid slowly into her neck. It did not take long for the liquid to take hold and put her in cardiac arrest. Unlike Angelica, she did not heave or convulse. She stared at him, her eyes frozen with fear. She was dead instantly, frozen in the body of Lisa Beverly, an advertising executive.

His eyes welled as he stared at the photo of Jeff Peters. He had abandoned Doctor Richards for the drive back to the air terminal. In the taxi ride back, he began reviewing all that had happened in less than fourteen days. He had murdered two of his patients. He saw his reflection in the taxi's window and realized that this would be the last time he could use this alias. He had displayed his face for every hotel security camera, as well as the airport security systems.

At the air terminal, he hurried toward the restroom at the airport hangar. He pulled his ball cap down, covering his face. Inside one of the stalls, he changed back to Doctor Richards for the short flight back to Frederick, Maryland. Making sure he kept his ball cap pulled down, he hoped the security cameras would not pick up that he had changed his appearance. Then, once at the airport in Maryland, the final part of his plan had to be flawlessly executed. He needed to turn back again to Jeff Peters without being noticed.

On the helicopter, he wondered what the authorities would think of the dead Lisa Beverly and her cardiac arrest. Two down, three to go, he thought. He felt a peculiar change engulf his body, as the adrenaline rush of killing started to excite him.

The flight back from Bermuda took two and a half hours. Richards had returned the helicopter to the private airfield near Fredrick, Maryland. He called his friend and told him he'd take a rain check on the dinner invite.

"Todd, you sound upset. Everything okay with your new client?"

"She was a real bitch. Only interested in my fees. She was shopping around. Go figure," he said, unable to sound upbeat.

"Never heard that one before. Let someone else handle her. She sounds like a real piece of work. If she's worried about price, she's not good enough for you," Fleming said. "I'm going to be in Newport Beach next week. Let's meet halfway and have that dinner?"

"Sounds great. I'll come up to see you. Let me know time and place."

On his plane ride back to San Diego, Todd couldn't stop thinking about what he had done to Trish Morgan. "I can't murder all of them," he whispered, his lips almost pressed against the small window in first class, "can I?" He was startled when the flight attendant called out his name.

"Mr. Peter's, would you like another cocktail?" The Flight Attendant asked pleasantly.

He nodded and handed her his empty glass.

17

FBI Agents Matt St. Claire and Jill Emerson were the lead agents for the Angelica Rathburn missing person case. They were annoyed they needed to find a spoiled celebrity who was probably in seclusion somewhere far away from all her annoying fans.

They both told their boss this case was in the LAPD's jurisdiction. Their opinions didn't seem to matter because POTUS had made the Angelica Rathburn situation a top priority.

The attorney general had gotten the necessary search warrants fast-tracked. Rathburn's agent was waiting for them at her home.

The actress's beach house was a sloping tri-level that rested above the sandy beach off the coast in Malibu. The house boasted floor to ceiling double pane windows on every level. There were no curtains or blinds to block out the sun or provide any privacy.

The sparse Angelica Rathburn file contained a brief resume of her past movies, her accident she had almost a decade ago, and that she was an exhibitionist. The tabloids lived on the beach twenty-four-seven. Today was no exception, snapping pictures of the two FBI agents, entering her home and from the beach, taking photos of them roaming through every room.

The white living room couch, with eight floral throw pillows, faced the beach. Slightly to the right of the sofa was a twenty-foot high rock wall that framed her fireplace. Her furniture was all art deco white.

Agent St. Claire was first to comment. "This doesn't look too comfortable. I'd rather have a leather recliner with cup holders and a sixty-inch smart TV to look at right above the fireplace."

Jill Emerson laughed. "Only you would want a TV to look at, instead of this beautiful view of the Pacific."

Matt shrugged his shoulders. "Whatever."

They walked upstairs to her bedroom that had a sprawling deck that wrapped around the upper third level of the house. Her master bedroom was minimalistic. She had white furniture and one extremely enormous bed that faced a twenty-foot wide sliding glass door that led to an oak stained deck. Like everything in her house, privacy was not the issue.

"A little disgusting how the rich and famous live," Agent St. Claire said, sounding envious.

Agent Emerson gave him a scornful look. "Hold in your jealousy. If you could live this way, you'd do it in a heartbeat," she saw him shaking his head. "Oh, I forgot, you'd probably want a leather recliner in your bedroom and an eighty-inch flat-screen TV?"

Matt rolled his eyes. "The only way I could ever dream of a place like this would be to find some drug money evidence nobody needed or win the lottery," he laughed. "I'd rather be working on our drug cases than looking for a spoiled actress."

Jill tried to ignore him. They had been partners for over eight years. She was finally getting used to his whining attitude.

She was rubbing her index finger along the top of her dresser. "It doesn't look like anyone's been here in at least two weeks. The dust is thick, and by the way she kept her house, I don't think she'd allow it to get this out of sorts unless she wasn't around. I wonder if she had a regular house cleaner. Maybe she'd know where Rathburn is?"

"Great detective work, Emerson. Didn't you notice two weeks of newspapers on the driveway and mail stuffed in her mailbox?" St. Claire liked busting her chops.

Jill kept walking around the bedroom, ignoring her partner. "I agree. Would you have thought she'd have a housecleaning service coming in weekly? Let's find an appointment book or a computer with a calendar or any other clue as to where she might be hiding. I want to get back to some real investigative work."

Matt was searching in Rathburn's dresser when he saw that Jill was waving a book.

"Seek, and ye shall find, my good Watson," Emerson said, holding up what looked like an appointment/address book.

Matt rolled his eyes at her attempt to be cute. "Find anything?" Matt asked.

"Nothing since she turned up missing. The last notation was exactly two weeks ago." Jill read it out loud. "D.T.R., La Jolla, 5:00 P.M., injection."

"Well, that's fucking great. Three initials, La Jolla, and an injection. Could it be Botox? Anything in her address directory that matches those initials?" he said impatiently.

She turned the pages until she found the "R's" and thumbed down a two-page list. Nothing matched D.T.R. The closest name was a Todd Richards with an 858-area code. "He's in San Diego." Jill was already searching on her phone. "Bingo. It could be Doctor Todd Richards. Her file says he was her doctor that rebuilt her face after her accident.

"Are we done here for now?" Matt asked.

"Let's go visit this doctor. He might know where she's hiding."

18

Agents Emerson and St. Claire chomped on the burritos they had gotten at Jose's Mexican Cantina, a few blocks North from Doctor Richards office. They waited across the street, hoping he'd show up.

They had already spoken to Richards office manager, Carolyn Hollister, who had told them he was on his way. Something about the way she acted in front of them, her mannerisms, raised the hair on St. Claire's neck. She appeared overly nervous and edgy, a signal to the FBI agent that she was hiding something.

"Did you notice how nervous Hollister was behaving? All we did was show our FBI badges, and she almost fainted."

"You're such an intimidating man," Jill said, elbowing him in his ribcage.

"Right. Me intimidating," Matt smiled. "I get a sense something's going on at this office."

"Calm down. We're investigating a missing person, not a murder victim. Let's finish eating and wait for Doctor Richards to show up."

Matt would not let it go. "Did you notice how Rathburn lives? She has too much money and time on her hands. Why are we helping her studio owner?"

"You need to get out of your apartment more," she said. "Rathburn might be a rich drop-dead beauty; what I've read about her is that she's a genuinely nice person."

"I don't agree. These types of women are spoiled and rich," he said.

"You need a nice woman in your life. You could learn something by dating more. Women like men who listen and understand their ways. It's not buying us dinner, and then as a favor, we'll jump into bed for the free meal," she said.

"I don't want a relationship. I want sex, and no obligation to have a second date, something like you do after hours," Matt returned the dig. "A nice friend or friends with benefits would be perfect."

"Funny. I'm serious, you jerk. You must become charming. Never be aggressive with a lady like you did with Hollister. Show some degree of sensitivity," she poked him harder this time with her elbow. "She could be having a bad day."

Before he could respond, Jill glanced down at the photo in her hand and confirmed it was Doctor Richards walking toward the red brick two-story building. "That's our man. Let's go. Let me do the talking. He's not a suspect since we don't even know if we have a crime on our hands."

Matt wiped his greasy chin with his coat sleeve and tried to speak with his mouth full. Glued to his gums and teeth were his black beans and cheese. Jill turned her face away from the sight, feeling like she wanted to throw up her meal.

"Look in the mirror. Make a smile. That's what I'm telling you needs to change before you can even expect to get a dinner date," Jill said, slapping him on the back of his head. "You're a real slob, St. Claire."

He flipped the visor down and opened the mirror, exposing his teeth. "Shit, that's disgusting," he laughed, rubbing his index finger over the food waste that clung inside on his top and bottom teeth. He forced a big smile and turned his head toward Jill. "Better?"

Emerson shook her head. "As good as it gets, you bozo."

Hollister pressed a button on her phone and spoke softly into her mouthpiece. "The two FBI agents are back. Yes, I'll send them in." She pointed toward a narrow hallway.

"Straight ahead and stop at the door that reads Dr. T. Richards," she said, her tone icy cold.

They walked down a walnut-paneled hallway to a door with a brass sign that had the doctor's name on it. Agent Emerson was first to notice.

She smiled. "DTR. Same initials that were in Rathburn's appointment book. Good, we confirmed the appointment was with Richards?"

Matt knocked firmly and opened the door. He didn't wait for a response. "I'm FBI Agent Matt St. Claire, and this is FBI Agent Jill Emerson. He held out his identification. He plopped down in front of the doctor's desk, unsmiling. He could see Richards was getting a little nervous with his attitude.

Jill extended her hand. "Agent Emerson. You're Doctor Richards?" She tried to catch her breath. She had not expected him to be so handsome, as she sat down in the chair next to her partner, her heart panting.

The doctor stared at Jill, not saying a word. She had become uncomfortable, as his eyes scanned her face. Then he spoke. "How can I help you?" he said, keeping his eyes on Jill and ignoring Matt.

"We're investigating the disappearance of Angelica Rathburn. We know she was a patient of yours. You did an unbelievable job on her face after her accident."

Richards sat back in his leather chair and smiled. "Yes, she is, not was, a patient of mine. And, yes, her recovery was quite remarkable."

Matt interjected himself into the interview. "Any clue where she might have gone? Any relationship problems in her life?" he asked.

The doctor shook his head. "I had seen her two weeks ago for an ongoing infusion treatment she needs for her healing process from that accident she had years ago." He tried to read the agents' faces. He didn't want to lie. He didn't know how far he should go with his answers. "I don't get involved with my patient's personal life and did not know if she was having any relationship problems or even a relationship."

Agent Emerson got control of her composure. She had never met anyone that radiated such electricity as this doctor did. "Since her appointment, had you spoken to her?"

He shook his head. "She left my office around six that evening. After she left, I was up to my eyeballs with a ton of paperwork. I honestly cannot tell you what she did after she left my office. I do remember she said she was going out of town. Sorry, she did not say where," he smiled sincerely. "Should I be worried about her? She's been on the news. You've been on the news too…at her home, you know. Everyone seems so upset. Now you're here. I'm getting very concerned about all of this. She was very nice, you know, for an actress. I hope she's all right?" he said. His eyes had become moist as he spoke.

"We're not sure if there is a problem," Agent Emerson said. "If there is anything you can think of that might help us, or if you hear from her… here's my card," she leaned across his desk, "it has my office number and my cell. Call me anytime." She felt her face get flushed, realizing how forward she had sounded.

Doctor Richards stood and extended his hand, gripping Jill's tenderly. "I'll pray that everything is going to turn out fine for Ms. Rathburn. I'm sure she's hiding away as most famous people do."

Matt stood, looked at his flustered partner, and handed the doctor his card. "You can call me anytime, too," he grinned. He gave Emerson a little push on her back when they were out the door.

* * * * *

"He got you wet, didn't he?" Matt teased.

"Don't be an ass," she said, slapping the back of his head again hard. "But he was a handsome hunk." she chuckled.

As St. Claire made a U-turn, heading out of La Jolla, neither he nor Emerson noticed the black Suburban CIA issue, idling a half a block away from Richards office.

Matt wouldn't stop teasing her. He had caught her unable to control her emotions. "Are you going to see him again. You know, to ask more questions?"

Jill stared straight ahead, her jaw muscles flexing as she ground her teeth. "Drive ass-hole. You say anything to the guys when we get back, your dead meat."

During the rest of the drive back to Los Angeles, their Ford LTD had a cold silence. They both understood each of their moods very well, and the silence in the car didn't mean either of them was angry. They respected the quiet space they both needed.

Matt had never shown an emotional side to anyone. He recognized that Emerson had that characteristic to her too, and this was the time for him to drive and be quiet.

St. Claire had an uncomfortable feeling about the doctor. He didn't know what it was, but he had always trusted his gut, and this time, it told him to be cautious.

* * * * *

The two CIA agents in the Black Suburban made some notations in their logbooks. They knew the FBI was getting involved in their case. They did not like that it was Emerson and St. Claire.

"Sir, Emerson, and St. Claire are the agents on the Rathburn case. They now know she was Richards patient," Bingham said.

. "Keep your distance," CIA director Roger Kramer said. "If those two agents get wind, we are watching the doctor, well it will send up flares. Remember, we're there for Richards only. We cannot afford to have the FBI looking into our business or why we need Richards."

"Copy that, sir," Bingham replied. "Director Kramer, shouldn't we pick up Richards now and get him off of the FBI's radar and move forward with our project?"

There was a long silence at the other end of Bingham's phone. "No. As I said, we do not want to have their investigation looking into the CIA," he said, sounding irritated at his agent.

Bingham stared at his phone. "That asshole hung up on me. "Let's get our dinner," he told his partner.

* * * * *

Todd rushed up to his apartment after the two FBI agents left. He had to look at Molly's photo. His heart would not stop racing. The memories of a past life a long time ago had rushed to the present like a speeding train.

Except for her short hair, Agent Jill Emerson was the spitting image of his departed wife. A warm rush blanketed his body, something that had not happened since her death. He knew he had to see the agent again. Could he start over? Would God forgive him for his recent horrible deeds?

That night he was unable to sleep. His thoughts kept focusing on what he had done to Trish Morgan. After being questioned about Angelica, he was happy Lisa Beverly had no connection back to him.

Richards got up and went downstairs to his office. He pulled Angelica's file that had all her photos. He had an idea that he needed to plan out.

19

The loud hysterical screams from the chambermaid caused every hotel guest on the fourth floor to rush out into the hallway. Seeing the scurrying around of hotel security, frightened the other chambermaids that something terrible had happened.

The door of Lisa Beverly, AKA, Trish Morgan, was open, revealing her stiff body clad only in her bikini. She was lying on her bed in the same position Richards had left her.

The security guards had come to a halt, frozen with terror. Seeing the decomposing body, engulfed by thousands of flies feasting on the corpse, had one guard ready to throw up his guts.

Lisa Beverly still had her do not disturb sign on her door, and the windows fully opened. It had kept the smell of death from alerting the daily cleaning crew, or any other hotel employees.

The hotel's protocol, with a *'Do not Disturb'* sign on the door, required all the hotel's staff to give their guests the uninterrupted privacy they wanted.

The dark-skinned maid, her hand covering her mouth, would not stop sobbing. Her eyes fixated on the decomposing body, and Beverly's mouth that was in a state of frozen shock.

One of the guards escorted the maid out and told her to go back to their housekeeping office and wait for the police. She looked up and, with a shiver, nodded, and left the room. The guard in charge had already called the hotel manager before calling the police. It was a hotel procedure.

There had never been a murder or death at the hotel. The guards were inexperienced in matters like this and didn't know what to do. Their hands touched the walls, dresser, and even the TV, which had been left on. They covered the body with a sheet so the flies would go and find another food source before the police came.

Alfred Stern, the hotel manager, was staring at the body for the longest time. He was deep in thought, unable to move. He was brought back to the task at hand by the guard's voice.

"Sir, we need to call the police," he said in a whisper.

Stern gave him a queer look. "Why are you whispering," he said, his voice trembling. He saw the guard shrug his shoulders. "Yes, call the police, and secure the room until they get here. If any of the guests ask, tell them someone's ill. No, tell them a snake had entered the room, frightened the maid. It is common and believable," he said, and marched out, holding his hand in front of his mouth.

An hour later, the police had arrived, along with the coroner.

"Might be an overdose or coronary event," the coroner said upon his first observation. He was emotionless after giving the body a quick exam. He ordered his men to bag the corpse and gave directions to the two police officers to check the room for any evidence that she had a visitor.

"Right away," the young officer replied, clicking his heels together.

"Let's check the security cameras on this floor to see if she had a visitor." He saw the officer nod his understanding.

Thirty minutes had passed, and the officer was wrapping up his evidence gathering when homicide detective Gilbert Smith strolled in. "What in hells name are you doing?" he shouted.

"What I was told to do, sir," he said embarrassed. "The coroner gave me orders."

"You've bloody contaminated the scene," detective Smith cursed. "Didn't you learn in your training to wear gloves when bagging evidence?" he barked. His face twisted with disgust.

"Didn't bring them," he said, his head dropping to his chest.

"Get out of here and let me do my job."

"The coroner suspected it wasn't foul play. I was told it might have been an overdose or heart attack," the police officer said smartly.

Detective Gilbert Smith was a paunchy man of small stature. He waved his hand at the irritating officer, signally him to leave him alone. He closed the door, not wanting any further intrusions so he could do his job. The room, except for the body, looked like it had not been serviced up in a few days. Old room service trays, with crusted leftovers, four bottles of champagne lay on the floor, as well as soiled towels piled up around the room.

He noticed the stains on the bedsheets. He assumed it had come from sexual activity. He found two sets of hairs on the bed's pillows, and inside the oval bathtub.

He had begun to package all the evidence, for Gilbert's forensic lab. He called down to security to get all videotapes when Lisa Beverly checked in to the present.

"What do you mean you gave it to one of the officers?" he barked at the female clerk.

"He had come down earlier and demanded them. He only took the tapes for the last two weeks. I can go back as far as you'd like," the woman said, nervously.

"Can you tell me when Lisa Beverly checked in?"

"That would have been sixteen days ago."

"I want every tape from the day she checked in and the tapes of the downstairs lobby area, too," Gilbert ordered. He knew he had been acting impolitely. Now, it didn't matter. He hated having his crime scene corrupted.

"You want every tape from the lobby?" she asked, surprised.

"Yes, and include the valet area for those dates. I want to see if any of her visitors came in a car." He lowered his tone and thanked her for her cooperation. He told her he'd be down to collect the videotapes within the hour. Next, he needed to interview the housekeeper who found the body.

Gilbert was inside the maids dressing quarters interviewing the shaken chambermaid. "Is it normal for you to not check a room after the scheduled check out time?" He didn't look at her, as he stared at his notebook, ready to write her answers down.

She was behaving upset at his question. "Normally, if a hotel guest is not out of their room on the scheduled date, I call the front desk, and ask if the guest has checked out."

Gilbert had a puzzled look on his face. "Why wouldn't you knock on the door? If there was no answer, then let yourself in?" he said, scratching his head.

"I remember that day. One of our other girls had called in sick, and we were all doing extra rooms to pick up the slack. Ms. Beverly had a *Do Not Disturb* sign on her door, and with the TV on, our rules are that we give our guests their privacy," she said, her arms tightly crossed, resting on her oversized bosom. She rocked back and forth, acting annoyed at these questions. "I even called downstairs, and they had told me Ms. Beverly extended her stay, and she would be checking out today. That's why I found her. I do my job good, and find your questions insulting," the maid lashed back. Her eyes had started to get moist as she defended herself.

Detective Smith, in a cold monotone, apologized. "I'm just doing my job. It requires me to ask all sorts of questions. If what you say is correct, then there is nothing to concern yourself with," he said, closing his notebook. "I'm done. You can go."

Detective Smith had one last stop at the front desk. He had met the hotel manager early and had asked him to get the clerk that had checked in Ms. Beverly.

The front desk clerk was English, with an alabaster complexion. She had a turned-up nose, red hair in a tight bun, which complimented the uniform all the front desk clerks had to wear. She looked unremarkable as she removed her black-rimmed glasses.

"This is Monica Fellows. She has been with the hotel for five years. She knew Ms. Beverly, the best of all our staff," Alfred Stern said, his British accent strong.

"Ms. Fellows, what can you tell me about Ms. Beverly?" Gilbert asked.

"She's one of our regular guests. We see her perchance twice, sometimes three times a year. She checks in alone and usually stays in her room most of the time. She's a strange one. That is, she's so beautiful with perfect skin. I never could understand why she didn't utilize our beaches?"

"Interesting," Detective Smith said, taking notes. "Anything else?"

"She ordered lots of room service, and kept the TV on to all hours, sometimes disturbing our guests. We'd get complaints. I'd see them usually in the morning when I got in," Fellows answered in a mild leveled tone.

"This staying inside her room. You never saw her leave, not even once?"

"Yes, she would leave, but not often, unless she went out the side doors. If that were the case, I would not know if she had vacated the hotel. Will that be all, detective?"

"One last question. When did Ms. Beverly call the front desk to extend her stay?"

Ms. Fellows rubbed her chin, deep in thought. "She hadn't. I spoke with my manager Alfred Stern, and since she was a regular guest, he approved an extension."

Gilbert closed his notebook and stood, thanking her for her cooperation. He had enough for now. He needed to analyze all the evidence, including all fingerprints collected, and see if the Beverly woman had visitors.

His drive down the winding driveway toward the city office in Hamilton gave him time to relax. The blue ocean and the cotton-ball puffy white clouds were mesmerizing. He had never gotten used to the quaintness and the relaxed pace on the island. Compared to London, where he previously worked, Bermuda was too tranquil. The pastel colors of each building were far from what he had back home. The dirty, and in need of repair apartments that occupied his old neighborhood in London, seemed like an old black and white photo, compared to the vibrant colors that dotted the island he now called home. He would have liked to be lying on some white sandy beach before going to the city morgue.

20

Detective Smith was at the Bermuda Coroner's office an hour later. Frederick Simons, the coroner, had been working on Lisa Beverly's body. He had been talking into a ceiling microphone, reciting her vitals, and terminology Gilbert didn't understand. The room's foul smell forced the detective to grab a surgical mask as he tapped Simons on the shoulder.

The coroner jumped, startled by his visitor. "Bloody God, Gilbert. You want me to be a customer in my morgue? Don't go sneaking around like that," he grimaced. "You here about the Beverly woman?"

He nodded, not wanting to taste the smell of death. The last time he did that, he couldn't eat for a week. He backed away and motioned for Frederick to talk to him outside in the corridor.

"Any signs of foul play?" he asked, his voice tired.

"No bruises, nothing to think it was rape or a drug deal gone wrong," he said, dropping his surgical mask around his neck. "Only one small needle mark by the carotid artery. Very strange," he said, shaking his head.

Smith tried not to stare, but it was hard not to when the coroner talked. His teeth were in such disrepair inside his mouth as well as stained with brown tar from smoking.

Gilbert tried to look past his shoulder, but it was like a beacon on a lighthouse—you couldn't miss it unless his mask covered it. "What makes you think it couldn't have been foul play? Or rape?"

"She had dried semen on the inside of her thighs, and inside her vagina wall. Whoever she had sex with, was gentle, there was no bruising. She must have known the person well enough not to practice safe sex. Which currently is like playing Russian roulette," he said, poking his finger inside his mouth and prying a speck of something he sucked into his mouth. "Leftover lunch or from one of my customers," he joked. "Something I don't want to think about," he grinned with a shrug of his shoulders.

Detective Smith had a puzzled look. "Any drugs in her system? Any residue at the puncture wound? Could she have been drugged so the rapist would be able to be gentle?"

Simons had a queer look on his face. "That's the curious part of this whole drug thing. I could not find any other old needle marks on her body. That's a possible theory. Won't know until I get her blood work back," the coroner said.

Simmons continued with his analysis. "On the other hand, if she was a drug user, she didn't have the normal track marks on her arms or between her toes like most addicts. When I found the fresh needle mark on her neck area, it was not from drugs. I was able to get a small sample of the crust inside the puncture wound. I'll have the results in a few days."

"Do you think it was murder?" Detective Smith asked. "

Gilbert shook his head. "I can't say. She died of a massive heart attack. What caused it is unclear. She appears to have been a healthy woman in her mid-thirties, per her passport. I might have a better idea after I receive the results from my sample."

Smith extended his hand. "Please, first thing, get me those results. Now, I better get back to my office. I have a lot of security tapes to review. If she had been meeting someone at the hotel, it would be on those bloody tapes."

Simons touched Smith's jacket sleeve pulling him back toward him. "There's one more peculiar element about this woman. Her passport shows that she is thirty-six, however after a bone density test, and examining a piece of her skin under my microscope, this woman was pushing almost fifty. I'd bet my career on that one."

Gilbert laughed. "I've seen women who come to the island from New York after they have their cosmetic surgeries, and I couldn't tell if they were thirty or sixty. What's your point?"

"This woman has never had any plastic surgery. Her epidural, her shell, is as if someone glued her a new outer body. I know it doesn't make any sense. I don't have the foggiest idea on how, to begin with, this crazy theory. I'll let you know if I turn up something that can be useful for your investigation," said Simons.

"Thank you," Detective Gilbert said, tossing his surgical in the hazardous waste receptacle.

Before Smith was out the door, Simons called out to him. "One other thing that has me baffled. After a person dies, the body decomposes. That's normal. But this Lisa Beverly woman is decomposing faster than normal. It's not typical," he said.

"Figure it out and get back to me," Detective Smith said. He was out the door before Simons could tell him something else.

* * * * *

Detective Smith sat at his desk and spilled out the contents of Lisa Beverly's belongings. She had a home address in Los Angeles and a business card where she worked. Her Rolex, as well as her jewelry, told him she had money—a lot more than he earned. What he had been looking at was probably worth two years of his salary. He eliminated the theory that her death was not a robbery gone wrong.

Smith flipped through his stack of business cards he kept wrapped with a rubber band until he found his friend at the FBI. "Bingo," he said, holding up Matt St. Claire's phone number. He needed a favor, and Matt owed him.

79

21

Matt St. Claire had been called into his field office at midnight. He could not believe that another high-profile celebrity had been reported missing. He tried to block it out of his head, but serial kidnapper/celebrity/stalker kept flashing inside his brain.

Trish Morgan had never made it to her afternoon talk show on Monday, and with it being Wednesday, all the California networks had the same headlines: Has a *Serial Abductor of the Stars Struck Again*?

He seemed relieved that the reporters were holding back with what everybody had thought that Angelica Rathburn and Trish Morgan were somewhere lying dead or held captive by a crazed fan.

The entire team at the FBI's Los Angeles Bureau in Westwood, California, had been put on high alert. Emerson and St. Claire had been put in charge of the investigative unit for the two high profile stars.

Matt had tried to get a hold of Jill, but she was not answering her phone. It had been normal for her to be out of reach when she clocked out. Their boss had been chewing out Matt's ass for over an hour about him not knowing where his partner was hanging out.

"What the fuck do you mean you don't know where she is?" deputy director Miller shouted.

"I'm not her babysitter," St. Claire barked back. "We both work damn hard, and long hours, if you'd ever notice. When we can take some time to chill, the world of the FBI will not come to an end when we clock out. I'll find her before she goes to sleep and bring her up to speed.

There's nothing we can do now anyway until we get the warrants to search Morgan's house," he said, unable to hold back his irritability.

"You find her and get her ass in here pronto. My boss is pressuring me, and he's being pressured by the Director to solve these cases immediately. So, don't give me any of your bullshit about not knowing where your partner hangs out. Go to her normal dance clubs and get her back to my office in two hours."

Brian Miller was the biggest ass kisser at the FBI. Everything he did was political, and he drove all his agents crazy, especially St. Claire and Emerson.

Matt did not say another word. He was out the door before Miller could get in another jab. He waved his arms in the air, and when he was out around the corner, heading toward the elevator, he cussed at him under his breath.

* * * * *

After rambling through three ear-splitting acid rock dance clubs on Sunset Boulevard, Matt finally found Emerson sitting in a dark corner trying to hold a conversation with a handsome, well-built sweaty guy that wouldn't take his eyes off her. He pushed his way through the crazed dancers, passing a tall booming speaker, which caused his heart to vibrate out of his chest. *What the fuck does she like about this stuff?* He thought, his hands cupping his ears.

At first, Jill had not noticed him standing off to her left. She acted enthralled with her new man-toy. If he didn't know her so well, he'd think his partner was another party-girl out on the town. He had known that she did not use any illegal substances, only an occasional good night of drinking to let off some steam.

Matt could see she was not going to look his way, so he tapped her shoulder. She didn't respond at first, so he poked her shoulder harder.

Without turning her head, her hand quickly grabbed St. Claire's, and twisted it hard, causing him to cry out. The club's loud noise muted his scream.

The Faces of Doctor Richards

When she saw it was her partner, she loosened her grip. She stood facing her partner. She was shouting at him. "Sorry. What are you doing here?" she yelled above the noise.

Matt signaled her, pointing to his ears, that he could not hear a word she had said. He pulled her toward the restrooms, where it was a decibel quieter.

"We've got another missing celebrity. Miller wants every agent in his office now," he screamed, straining his vocal cords until his throat hurt.

She held up a finger and walked back to her new boyfriend, or whatever he was for that night. Matt watched them exchange business cards and then saw the guy give her a light kiss on the cheek. She blushed and said goodbye.

They went out the rear door to a deafening quiet. Matt's ears would not stop ringing as he followed her to her car. "I'll see you at the office," he shouted. He laughed as she took out her earplugs and smiled.

She pretended to respond with sign language, as she sped out of the parking lot. All Matt could do was try to read her lips, as the ringing inside his ears would not subside.

As he walked toward his car, he was talking to himself." How the fuck can she take it?" he said, shaking his head. He did not notice the strange looks he had gotten from two people he passed in the parking lot. They looked like they were from a Dracula movie set, smoking something.

22

Deputy Director Miller was pacing up and down the conference room as Emerson and St. Claire walked in. "Agent Emerson, so nice of you to give up your night off to join us," he said, his sarcasm coming across loud and clear.

"Matt said you had a burr up your ass and wanted to see me." She felt her partner elbow her ribcage—St. Claire gave her a stern look, which did not slow her down. "What's so fucking important that it can't wait until my shift starts tomorrow?" she said unmoved by his tone.   She found a seat in the back of the room. "You do have other fine agents capable of handling a missing celebrity?"

Miller ignored her insubordination and spent the next two hours briefing his two agents about Trish Morgan and how long she had been missing. He tied both Angelica Rathburn and Trish Morgan together as one possible crime.

"Both women now appear to have gone missing right around the same timeframe. This case has become a top priority for this field office," said Miller.

Matt could sense Jill was about to lash into Miller for his ludicrous theory. Everyone knew he had been an inept agent since leaving Quantico. Nonetheless, his political skills had landed him this job in Los Angeles ahead of a lot of more qualified agents, including Emerson. The tension had become thick. St. Claire knew how Jill would react—he'd seen it before. He held his breath.

"Don't do it," St. Claire leaned over and whispered.

She acted coy, tapping his thigh, pretending not to understand what he meant. "Do what?"

Matt turned his hands over, palms up. "Be respectful. You do know everything in this conference room is taped and reviewed? Remember, you still have a career to think about."

"What career. It might be happening around the country that a female agent can move up the ranks, but in this fucking office, it won't happen." She let her body relax and leaned back in her chair.

Miller had been watching his two agents whispering, and like he did so many times, he foolishly put himself right in the middle of Agent Emerson's mood.

"Anything you want to share with me, Emerson?" Miller asked.

A big grin exploded on Jill's face. "Well, if you want to know. I was curious about how you find similarities to these two disappearances. Did the two women have a common connection? Did they know each other?" she rattled off her questions as if she was firing a machine gun. "Or are you quoting the tabloid news and using them for your facts?"

Miller's face drained of color. He had started shuffling his notes, searching for some logical answer to her bombardment of questions. He looked up, a blank stare on his face. He tried to avoid eye contact with Emerson.

"I assumed that since they were both high profile personalities, it was a good hunch," he said, shrugging his shoulders.

That's all Jill had to hear to let go with one of her famous insulting phrases. "Assumption is the mother of all fuck-ups. You should know that. Tomorrow we'll get started on our investigation, and if there are any similarities, you'll be the first to know."

"Emerson, we have two personalities within days of each other. There's something about it that bothers me, and I'd think it would bother you. I want to be briefed by day's end tomorrow," he demanded.

Jill gave him a queer look. "Sir, it's after midnight. Do you want your briefing end of today or tomorrow?" she said with a grin. Matt yanked her out of the conference room and pushed her toward the elevator.

"Don't you ever give up? Can't you just let him be?"

Emerson gave him a wink. "He's a jerk, and I'm who I am," she said matter-of-factly.

Matt was pressing the down button feverishly, wanting to get out of the building. He needed to be in his bed for some needed sleep. "We all know how he is, please keep it to yourself for a change. I'm your partner. What you do reflects on me too."

They both stepped into the elevator, and before the doors could close, they burst out laughing. "That was a good one," Jill said, drying her moist eyes with the back of her hand.

St. Claire had finally gotten control of himself before they reached the garage level. "Who was that guy you were talking to at that ear-splitting dance club of yours?"

"Just a new guy. Hadn't seen him around before, but he was a good looker," she said.

"How do you do it? Strangers like that. He could be a rapist or some pervert?"

"I have a good sense about people. He felt good. If you hadn't interrupted, I might have found out how good," she smiled.

"You gonna call him?" Matt asked.

"I'm thinking about it," she replied, holding his business card and looking at his name.

"Your sex toy got a name?"

"Chad Green," she said.

"Is he a dimple Chad, a pregnant Chad, or hopefully for you, a big hanging Chad" Matt teased.

"I hope the last one," She nodded with a big smile. "I need a quick cup of coffee. We'll go over our strategy there."

Matt agreed as he enjoyed her company better than his cold and dreary one-bedroom apartment in Studio City. They met up at their favorite all-night restaurant at Olympic and La Cienega Blvd.

Matt had his notebook out, ready to map out what had transpired over the last two weeks with their two potential victims. On the job, they were by far the best team Miller had, and they knew it.

"All I see is that we have two high profile women missing. They're both celebrities. Rathburn was a patient of Doctor Richards, who, by the way, gave me the creeps," Matt said, as chill radiated over his body.

"You suspect something about the doctor?" Jill asked, puzzled. "I had okay vibes from him."

"You were smitten," Matt replied.

"That's bullshit. Let's get back to the task at hand."

Matt rolled his eyes. "Okay. Here are the things we know. We do not have a body on the first victim. No signs of any foul play at her home and nobody is demanding a ransom. Until we get into Trish Morgan's home, we don't know shit, or if the two cases are related. For all we know, these spoiled women are hiding somewhere away from the pestering press."

"Here's how I see it. I believe that there are no coincidences. I'll bet my next paycheck that both these women are dead, and the murderer is one crazed fan or some run of the mill nut case. Let's check every database and see if any of these women had stalkers on Facebook, Twitter, or any other social media sites. Maybe they got some inflamed fan mail. Then we should look for any similar M.O.s around the country. Maybe our guy has recently come to California? My brain's toast. Pick me up at eight tomorrow, have coffee with you, and a croissant with egg, cheese, and cream cheese," she gave him a sexy grin.

St. Claire gave a disapproving look. "I'll do coffee and bring some donuts. That girly food I won't go near," he protested.

"See, that's why you'll never find the right woman. You must spoil a lady first, so she'll want to spoil you. Ever hear the phrase, ladies, first? We fussy women like it when a man does our bidding. It gets better when he's trained, and thinks for himself, and stays one step ahead of what we want. But that's probably asking too much from you. You're still in the stone age of knowing what a girl wants." She could see she had hurt his feelings. She leaned in closer and gave him a soft kiss on his cheek. "Where's that hard-callous skin of yours?"

"I'm fine," he said, rushing out of the restaurant.

"Then, I'll see you at eight."

23

At the far back corner of the parking lot under a broken spotlight, a dark Mercedes, its windows tinted, was in a perfect location to observe Jill Emerson and her partner. He had followed her from the dance club and then to her FBI office. His obsession with the FBI agent that looked identical to his dead wife made him irrational and unable to think clearly. He was feeling a pang of jealousy as he watched her at her early morning rendezvous with her partner.

Doctor Richards could not get her out of his mind. While he didn't like how she flirted at the three clubs, she danced at—he was happy to have spent some time with her as Chad Green. This alias was his go-to one to meet women. He slipped the photo back in his pocket to use at another time.

He had found this identity as he had for all his other aliases while searching the obituaries at the local library. He had come across four deaths a few years back that intrigued him. While the photos were grainy and of poor quality, he was able to with some google searches find excellent color pictures of the men he planned on using during his experimentations with his transformations.

Green was his alter ego. He was handsome, with European features, and had been dead since nineteen-seventy-seven, with no family listed. The other men, while they had family, those connections were in other countries far from La Jolla.

Like all his secret identities, they came with some risk. He knew he could not get into trouble with the law, or his aliases would be exposed.

The Faces of Doctor Richards

Since he first laid eyes on Emerson, his wife Molly preoccupied his thoughts non-stop. He was acting overly emotional. He was unable to think clearly. Making time for a new relationship with two murders to cover up, did not make sense, particularly a relationship with an FBI agent.

He was confident that as Chad Green, he'd be able to win over the heart of agent Emerson. He fought with the idea of starting a life with Emerson. He knew how dangerous it might be, especially with the ongoing investigation into Angelica and now Trish's disappearance. However, he wanted his wife back so much that any control of rational behavior evaporated.

He watched Emerson drive off. He followed her, staying far enough back, blending into the early morning traffic that never died in Los Angeles.

Think fool, he told himself. *Emerson's a damn FBI agent investigating Angelica and now Trish. She'll spot you.*

He tried to assure himself that what happened in Bermuda would not come back to bite him in the ass. "There's no way she'd be able to tie Lisa Beverly's murder and match her up with Trish," he muttered, shaking his head. "I have to think," he said. "Chance favors the prepared mind."

He saw his new Molly turn off Wilshire and drive to her apartment at the corner of Gayley and Le Corte. A metal gate slid open, and she drove down into an underground garage. He wrote down her address and got back on Wilshire and headed West toward the 405. He took the on-ramp south toward La Jolla.

Richards was talking to himself, trying to convince himself that what he was planning on doing was a good idea.

"Soon, Agent Emerson, you'll be mine. We'll have a son, possibly two, all with special abilities, and then we'll live happily ever after with you as my new Molly. First, I have to deal with my other three patients."

24

Matt had gotten back to his apartment, forty-minutes after he left Jill. He knew he had to wake up in a few hours to avoid the early morning commuters.

He checked his voicemail. There were three. The first one had been from his mother, who lived in Clifton, New Jersey. Her message, like most of them, was frustrating.

He regretted getting her a cellphone so she could save on her long-distance calls. She was eighty, and using her new phone had become a struggle. She didn't understand she had to keep the phone by her ear and speak softly.

Teaching her how to use her speaker feature was next to impossible. Listening to her message, he pictured her holding the phone in front of her mouth and shouting into it. When she was able to speak to him on his cell, their conversation sounded like a shouting match of him telling her to put the phone to her ear, and his mother shouting I can't hear you. To his partner, their verbal exchange was cute, but to Matt, it was exasperating. He had wished he had never gotten her the phone.

Today's message, she sounded hysterical like always. Matt had never changed the pre-recorded message that came with his phone system. It had a pre-recorded female voice on it. His mother would ask the digital voice for permission to speak to her son. *"Hello, whoever you are. I want to talk to Matt St. Claire. My son. I'm his mother calling long distance. Are you hearing me?"* Her silly shouts screeched out his machine. *"I don't know if you can hear me, but please have him call me. I am his mother, Betty."*

Matt shook his head and saved her message. He then listened to the next call. It was from a recorded telemarketer—he usually never got messages, except from his partner or his mother. The third message had been from a police detective he had met years ago, Gilbert Smith from Bermuda.

Smith's British accent was usually hard to understand but was clear and concise on his message machine.

"Hey, St. Claire, I know it's been a while. I need a favor. I faxed over a crime scene report to your home fax line you had given me. It's of a woman who I believe was murdered on the island a few days ago. The victim's name's Lisa Beverly. I sent her home and work address, along with her fingerprints. Our computers can't pull her up. She's come back as if she doesn't exist. It's a strange case. Even our coroner is stumped. Call me in a few days, old boy."

Matt went into his bedroom. Next to his computer was the fax machine with the documents his friend had sent. He took them off and folded them and slipped them inside his coat pocket.

"Tomorrow, Gilbert," he said, falling back on his unmade bed, too tired to disrobe from his dirty clothes.

He never needed an alarm. The apartment's walls were paper-thin. The bus driver that lived next door woke up to loud radio music every morning at five-thirty, except on the weekends. While his bus driver neighbor slept on Saturday mornings, his kids were up bright and early, blasting their morning cartoon shows. If he got five hours of sleep any day of the week, he felt blessed.

25

Jill had just stepped out of the shower when she heard a loud banging on her door. "Just a minute," she shouted, cinching a towel around her wet naked body. It barely covered her butt and clung tightly around her breasts, squeezing them like a Victoria Secret model wearing a push-up bra.

Matt's eyes bulged when she opened the door. "I think you should wear that today. It would stop the rest of the guys at the office from speculating about your body," he said with a seductive grin. He handed her a cup of coffee and a white bag.

"Sit your butt down and behave." As she turned, she could feel his stares, and wiggled her half-covered buttocks, as she headed back toward her bedroom. She laughed, hearing him yell, "More, shake it more," as she kicked the door shut with her foot.

She took a sip of the hot coffee and peaked inside the white bag. "You remembered," she smiled. "St. Claire, maybe there's still hope for you yet," she hollered. She lifted the croissant and took a savory bite. "Thank you, Matt St. Claire," she mumbled.

Fifteen minutes later, Jill was dressed and ready for another workday. She knew today they would be looking for evidence at Trish Morgan's house. Uniform of the day: denim jeans, New Balance running shoes, a white oxford shirt, and a thin silk tie, as well as her faded blue FBI hat that had seen better days.

In the car, she leaned across and kissed Matt on his cheek. "Thanks for remembering," she said. He just stared straight ahead, beaming.

"I need to stop at the office first. I need to do a favor for a detective friend from Bermuda. You remember, Gilbert? He's got a murder on his hands and can't find out anything about his victim. He thinks she came to the island with a false ID. It's on our way. I won't be too long. I'll get her in the system and check on it after we finish at Morgan's house."

"That's fine. I thought of something that I want to run through the computer about Angelica Rathburn and Trish Morgan. I want to see if there are any connections recently. With Morgan being a talk show host, maybe Angelica was on her show recently. It's worth a try."

They had gotten to their field office early. Miller was not there. The entire division looked like a ghost town, except for the clerical personnel. That suited St. Claire and Emerson.

Matt gave the paperwork he had from detective Smith to Peggy Lynn Matson, their mother-protector at the field office. If something had to get done, she knew the system after thirty-six years working for the Bureau. She liked Los Angeles. It allowed her to see her daughter and three grandchildren regularly since transferring from the Hoover building seven years ago.

"What you got for me this morning, my big cupcake?" she asked. Her cheeks puffed out from her smile.

Matt was too tired to smile. She understood him and could care less about ever getting one.

"I see it must be Tuesday—pink floral dress," Matt commented, as he dropped Gilbert's papers on her desk. "You look very…" he searched for the right words… "Like a beautiful garden."

She blushed and waved her hand at him. Matt might not be the most charming man, but Peggy liked him over all the other agents who treated her like she was a low-level clerk. Matt gave her respect no matter what the situation.

"If I were only twenty-five years younger, your love life would be just the way you'd like," she said, slapping him on his buttocks.

"That's sexual harassment," he protested, giving her shoulder a soft pinch.

"That's invading my personal space," she jabbed back at him, laughing

"Can you run this victim through all of our databases? Do you remember my friend Gilbert in Bermuda? He called last night. He needs a favor for a case he's working on."

She took in a big breath and then let it out slowly. "Ah, Gilbert? Anything for my little round furball," she said excitedly. "How's he doing?"

"Don't know. I haven't spoken with Gilbert in a while. I got a message early this morning after Miller's damn waste of time meeting a few hours ago. I never got to speak to him. When I do, I'll send him your regards."

"Call me before you come back from the Morgan house. I should have something by then. Oh, here's the warrant you'll need to enter her house. Good luck. I liked that woman. She had a great show."

"We don't know that she's dead yet," he frowned.

"I've been doing this for too long. I know the signs. First Rathburn, and now her. You've got a serial killer on your hands."

Matt walked away, knowing she was probably right. He saw Jill getting up from her desk, a grin on her face. "Find anything?"

"Yeah. Morgan had Rathburn on her show two months ago. I've ordered the tape, and the one they take of the audience. It might not mean anything, but it's a few dots that might get connected?"

"Great. Peggy is running my stuff. Perhaps we'll both get lucky for a change."

26

Doctor Richards finished his phone call with Meg Cummings. She was a reporter, a very nosey one, that had him on edge with what she said to him yesterday.

She had asked him too many questions about Trish Morgan turning up missing also. Her barrage of questions rattled him. He knew things were getting out of control, and it had to stop.

Cummings tossed her questions at him about Morgan, as well as Rathburn, and they sounded accusatory. It was strange behavior for her, with the kind of relationship they had. Richards was becoming defensive.

Meg was now talking fast. She told him she was driving down to see him that evening. She needed a face-to-face and an on-the-record interview. His heart began to race, feeling like it was ready to burst out of his chest.

He could not get her badgering out of his head. *"Doctor Richards, do you find it odd that two of your patients, both high-profile celebrities, are missing? Have you spoken to the FBI about this?"*

He began questioning himself. He thought he had covered his tracks. *Was she recording this conversation? Did I miss something? How could I be linked to any of this?* He was beginning to second guess his recent actions.

He remembered the adrenaline rush that he had after he overdosed Trish. It returned within seconds after he hung up the phone. He was feeling threatened, cornered, and didn't like where his thoughts were going. Meg was one of his patients who could ruin everything for him.

Richards was in survival mode, unable to control his urges. He had begun to question whether he was going mad. He had let loose an explosive sinister laugh as he walked toward his laboratory wondering if Igor would come shuffling out of the shadows, all hunched over, dragging his deformed leg, yelling at him *master, master*.

He knew he had become the maestro of creation—a forbidden role that only God was supposed to have the power to perform. He approached the door to a sterile room, and without thinking, he put on his hygienic yellow lightweight safety suit, shower cap, and a surgical mask. Confusion engulfed his brain. What was he going to do about Meg Cummings?

She had to talk. That's what she said. What did she want to discuss about Angelica and Trish? His curiosity had been piqued. What other surprises would pop up and cause him to terminate another life? A thousand scenarios flooded his mind—they had the same ending—overdose.

He needed a distraction before Meg would arrive. Working in his lab was a logical choice. He had two projects that needed completing since returning from Bermuda. Richards kept repeating his favorite motto out loud: *Chance favors the prepared mind.* He knew he had to implement a sound plan within the next week or so. He needed to escape with his serum inventory. Choose one of his other identities, one he could remain in incase the FBI got closer to tying him to his crimes.

First, he checked his current supply of vials. He had over two-hundred serum doses, most of them his, and the others for his special ladies. He calculated that if he kept blending vials from his five ladies with his, he could survive for five years. He knew it wouldn't be hard finding more women who would want to keep forever young. He knew if he had to start over again, then he'd have to do things differently.

He opened the 69 cubic foot chromatography refrigerator. He checked the temperature gauge that read four degrees centigrade.

The Faces of Doctor Richards

He knew that five years might seem like a long time, but it wasn't. That wasn't his immediate problem. He needed to create the formula that would give him the powers he believed he could achieve with the right hybrid mixture to extend the time interval between injections.

He took out eight of his vials for his current patients and began to blend them with his serum. Once that was done, he needed to test it on himself.

Richards was a genius on many levels. He had always had contingency plans, but murder had not been one of them. He scolded himself for being so impulsive after Rathburn died.

Richards flipped on the intercom speaker in the lab so he could hear when Meg arrived. He moved to his liquid nitrogen unit and extracted Angelica's fetus. He had another experiment he had to try.

He had done this a million times, and with the instincts of a brain surgeon. He gingerly carried the tubes of serum, placing them carefully with the Rathburn/Richards Fetus. They were organized between his Saybolt Viscosimeter and a Multi-Tube Rotator that mixed his blood, with Angelica's blood and the stem cells from the fetus. The process would take one hour, as the shaker speed stayed at a constant 30 rpm. He liked the flexibility of this unit. It was portable and could hold up to twelve test tubes. Once this mixture finished, he was going to add it to his hybrid vials.

He hated waiting, but impatience would cause the solution he created to fail. He looked around the lab, remembering how he had almost gone bankrupt, spending hundreds of thousands of dollars on equipment. Back then, he did not know if the investment was for a crazed scientist with a compulsive hobby or a doctor who had found the real fountain of youth.

The timer on the tube rotator startled him and snapped him alert. The next step was to put the solution inside the Viscosimeter to allow the solution to circulate. It was a fifteen-minute process and, then the final solution would be placed inside an air jacketed automatic CO_2 incubator for one week. This new supply, combined with his existing vials, he calculated, would create an additional two-year amount of his new formula.

His original goal was to have a twelve-year supply, but with only three patients left in his program, it looked like he'd have no more than eight years. He thought that disposing of the last three ladies right now might not be the right thing to do.

The second timer had gone off, right when Meg had arrived. He pressed the intercom button, telling her to come in.

"Sweetie, I'm finishing up some work in my lab. Give me ten minutes. You can wait in my office."

He removed his sterile lab outfit and tossed everything into a metal receptacle, locked the eight-inch thick laboratory metal door, and forced himself into a positive mindset for his meeting with Meg.

27

Being a reporter by trade, Meg had become antsy, as well as curious, waiting for Doctor Richards in his office. She couldn't stop pacing around. She pulled out books from his neatly organized bookshelves and scowled. "I hope he reads some entertaining fiction at night. These books seem boring," she grumbled. "Why so many crime books?"

Unlike the organized bookshelves, his desk was another story. Files and loose papers lay scattered. A plane ticket had caught her eye.

"Washington D.C.?" Then, she saw under the ticket stub a brochure for the Princess Hotel in Bermuda. "That's Trish's favorite place," she muttered. Her curiosity had peaked even more. *"He wouldn't go away with her, would he?" she asked herself. "That's not part of our agreement,"* she scowled. *"I've invited him on trips before which he's refused."* A jealous emotion flooded her body.

Meg heard his footsteps echoing on the ceramic tile. She quickly stuffed the brochure back under the disheveled papers. Her heart was pounding out of control.

"Sorry to keep you waiting," Richards said with a big smile. He saw that her face was flushed as he entered, looking guilty about something as she tried to shuffle away from his desk. He knew she was very nosey. *"What did she find?"* he thought.

She tried to speak. Her voice had a nervous edge to it. "After the two-hour drive down from Los Angeles...I couldn't sit anymore," she said, sheepishly patting the papers she was trying to organize. "You have the most boring library," she said, pointing at the bookshelf.

The Faces of Doctor Richards

Doctor Richards closed his eyes, deep in thought, as he exhaled a deep breath. "It's a nice night. Let's go for a walk down by the cove. I need to clear my head. I want to be attentive to your questions. You sounded so downcast over the phone...you have me concerned."

Meg was petite. Her five-foot-four height made her appear excessively thin, except for the firm muscles that showed through her short sleeve blouse. Her long flowing auburn hair seemed to float lightly, as her animated head bobbed, while she spoke.

On their walk, Meg was shivering as she talked. "I think you're right. This walk is making me feel better. Trish and Angelica are big news items."

Richards's body had become stiff. He realized that Meg was going to interview him for her story. "Why are you here?" he asked, turning around, and walking backward so he could look her in the eyes.

"I've been assigned to cover Angelica's and Trish's disappearance. They are, you know, connected to you, as their doctor," she said, her body continuing to tremble from the cold night air. He helped her slip on her dark brown leather jacket. "I'm scared...Todd...scared for them and me. Am I next?"

Richards tried not to react to her question, as he checked his pocket for the syringe he had brought in case he needed it. "Next for what? You do not believe this crap about a serial killer, do you?" He now realized why she came to see him. She was terrified.

Meg shrugged her shoulders, unable to respond.

While they walked, an eerie quiet had come over them. Cummings grabbed his hand, and like the other loving couples who strolled along La Jolla Cove at sunset, they tried to blend in. The only sounds different than the waves breaking on the shore were the crying seals lying at the edge of the breakwater.

As they walked further toward the marine sanctuary, they noticed the divers snorkeling, as well as the scuba divers entering the water. They all had patches on their wetsuit with the La Jolla School of Oceanography logo.

The Faces of Doctor Richards

Meg could not keep silent any longer. "The buzz I hear from local authorities is that Morgan and Rathburn are dead. I had finished listening to a press conference in Los Angeles about the two cases. While they are not saying it is a serial killer, we at the media believe it is," she said, still shivering.

"I'm nervous too. I loved them, just as I love you. I don't know what evidence the authorities must have to think they are dead. Do you have any specifics?" Richards asked, hoping to get something useful. "Why did you say they were connected to me as their doctor? Have you said something to the authorities?"

"No. I'd never talk about our special arrangement. It's bound to come out sooner than later that we are all your patients. We know the FBI had come to see you about Rathburn. It will only be a matter of time when they tie you to Trish as her doctor too. They could have seen all of our photos hanging on your hallway wall."

"Is the media beginning to think I had something to do with their disappearance?" Richards asked, stopping abruptly. He placed his two strong hands on top of Meg's shoulders, squeezing them firmly.

Meg grimaced. "You're hurting me," she said, pulling away. "Shit, you know how the media works? We throw the shit against the wall and hope something sticks."

Richards put his hands in his pants pockets, trying to hide his nervousness. "The FBI had come to my office to see me. They had found the connection Angelica had with me. I hope when they search Trish's home…" he took a deep breath… "They don't find a similar connection. Also…" he sucked in another deep breath, "I hope you've followed our rules about any notations, or memos on your phone, or computer that ties you in with my clinic or me?"

Meg was quiet, lost in thought, and started to giggle. Without warning, she spun around, her hands stretched out, skipping backward. "I've been meticulous. My appointment calendar doesn't have a notation about our bi-monthly shots. It was very careless, and irresponsible what Angelica had done," her mood had quickly changed, as she said her friend's name. "I've been thinking that Lea, being very close to Angelica, could be a problem and could connect herself to you." She saw Todd thinking, his face twisted with concern.

"You could be right. I'm going to have to call Lea."

"Maybe I should ask her?" Meg said. "We girls know how to ask questions without ruffling any feathers. If Lea thinks you're upset or concerned, she might clam up and not tell you the truth."

They made their way up the steep grade from the seawall toward Prospect, the main road in town. Richards noticed how she kept looking at her watch. "Is it time for you to get to the studio?"

"If we walk back a little faster than our current pace, I'll make it back on time."

As they passed Georges at The Cove, Meg's name had been called out by a few people waiting out front of the restaurant for the valet to bring their cars around. Richards went into a panic, as he had not anticipated being seen with Meg. He scolded himself on how stupid he was, thinking he could walk with a local personality like her, and avoid having a loyal fan recognize her and snap photos.

Cummings tried to ignore the shouts, pretending not to hear her name called out. Then a hand reached out and caught her sleeve. She turned, embarrassed, and put on a relaxed smile that she had practiced a thousand times when she'd get cornered in public.

She whispered in Todd's ear as they stopped. "I should have used my alias... sorry," she said.

The male voice was not a fan, but her old boyfriend of five years ago. He had a gorgeous woman draped all over him and was drunk as usual.

"Well, if it isn't the famous Meg Cummings," he shouted a bit too loud, causing other heads to turn and recognize her. More cellphone flashes went off, while others videoed the encounter.

"You're looking great. Been under the knife a few times, I see," he slurred his words, as the booze controlled his rudeness.

"No, trying to live a healthier life since we broke up. I see you've not changed," she said with a sarcastic tone.

He belched, putting his hand in front of his mouth. "Excuse me. You still have that razor for a tongue," he said, slurring his words. "Aren't you going to introduce me to your new boyfriend?"

His girlfriend pulled him away, as their car stopped in front of the valet. "I know him," she whispered in his ear. "Get in the car. I'll drive," she said, pushing him into the passenger side.

Doctor Richards had started walking fast, trying to get away from the commotion in front of the restaurant. He could not afford to be recognized or associated with Meg. It was too dangerous for what he had planned for her. He glanced back and saw Cummings signing autographs and posing for her fan's cameras. As her ex-boyfriend's car passed, the horn blasted, and his girlfriend waved. Todd thought she looked familiar, but his mind could not focus.

"Shit, this is not good," he muttered. He wondered how many photos of his face made it on social media.

Meg had caught up to him, breathing heavily from her short jog. "Sorry about that, jerk. He had always been an ugly drunk when we dated. I guess things never change," she said, shaking her head.

As they got to her car, Richards realized that tonight would not be the night he got rid of his third patient. He needed her fetus first. His body shuddered, as he went over every scenario on how he'd get rid of Cummings. Nothing made sense. He had to find the right moment when it could look like an accident. He knew he had at least two more weeks before she had to abort. He had confidence that an opportunity would appear if he kept calm.

She got up on her tiptoes and pulled on his neck so her lips could reach his mouth. She planted a juicy kiss, and then let go. "I've got to run. We'll talk soon. I know it almost time."

He watched her bright red 328I BMW convertible pull away from the curb. She had her hand extended high above her head, giving him a wave good-bye. He didn't see her wave and headed inside his office. He was looking through his records to see if he could trigger his memory about Meg's ex-boyfriend's girlfriend, who acted as if she recognized him.

After an hour of searching, he had found her picture. She was Carla Palmer, who needed some facial work and breast enlargements around three years ago. He wrote down her address. He knew she had recognized him. Why else would she have beeped the horn? He now knew where she lived, but would not do anything to her, unless she tried to contact him.

Richards was now in a full-blown panic. His comfortable life was now spinning way out of control. He wanted more time to think things out. He went back to his bookshelf and found the book he'd been reading.

Within five minutes, he had his solution. He understood that his survival was the only thing that mattered.

28

Jill and Matt had gotten to Trish Morgan's house in the stately hills of Pasadena. Compared to Beverly Hills, this section of town smelled of old money. The house, by Matt's unqualified estimates, was in the mid-seven-figures range, he had told Jill. He also had a sarcastic comment about it being on three to four acres of land, with a panoramic view of downtown Los Angeles.

"Does anyone need this much money?" he complained.

Jill gave him a skeptical look and pressed the intercom button on the left side of a ten-foot polished, solid bronze mechanical gate. "How the heck can you tell how many acres this house is on and its view?" she said, pressing the button a few times.

"I know things like this. It was in detective training 101," he smiled, holding out the property description of the house he had gotten from the county recorder's office.

"You're the biggest dumb ass— "she couldn't finish her sentence when a voice squealed over the speaker box attached to a post just right of the gate. "Shit, that's loud," she shouted.

"Who there," the Spanish accented woman said.

Jill thought of scaring the holy shit out of her by answering ICE but thought they'd never get in without ramming down the front gate. "FBI. We have a warrant to search the house," she said.

"Policia? Dios Mio," the voice cracked across the intercom.

"Senorita, open the front gate, understand? comprende?" Matt shouted over Jill's shoulder.

"Si, si. Un Momento."

They got back into their car and waited for the gate to open. The massive double metal frame parted slowly in the middle. It did not make a sound, as the hydraulics that controlled it did its job.

"I can't get my bathroom door not to squeak," Matt whined as they drove on the long circular driveway.

"You live in a shithole apartment on an FBI agent's salary. What do you expect?" Jill said sarcastically.

The grounds were pristine and manicured. The massive lawn was a healthy green. The driveway had tall palms on each side, with a blanket of red, white, and purple begonias filling a planter that ran the entire circumference around the lawn. "Geez, another rich woman with too much money on her hands," St. Claire protested.

"Let's try to be nice for a change. Morgan might be rich, but I have a bad feeling she's not going to be spending any more of her money," Jill said.

The eight-foot-high teak front door opened, as they stopped their car. A short, stocky, heavyset woman dressed in a black and white maid uniform greeted them. She acted nervous, and anxious, as she swept her arm in a gesture welcoming them go inside.

"Senorita Morgan? You have bad news?" she asked in her thick accent.

Matt waved the warrant in the maid's face. He rushed past her and into the foyer that had an inlaid black marble floor. Jill could see the concern on the maid's face and tried to relieve her tension.

"We are here to look around. We don't know where Ms. Morgan is at this time." Jill wasn't sure if the woman understood. All she did was nod her head as she closed the wooden door behind them.

Jill had taken the warrant from Matt and handed it to the maid. She called out for Matt, who had disappeared. "St. Claire," she shouted.

"In the living room," he shouted back. "Morgan's damn entryway is bigger than my apartment," he groaned.

"Please focus. Let's get started on our search. It's a big house, and I don't want it to take us all day to look around. You take the first floor, and I'll go upstairs. If you don't hear from me in a few hours, send out the hounds to find me," Jill joked.

It had been two and half-hours, and Matt had finished his search. He had ten plastic bags of evidence he thought might prove interesting.

He had taken hair samples from three bathrooms downstairs. Then he lifted several prints from cabinets, doorknobs, and tools inside a toolbox he found inside the garage. He found an appointment book in the kitchen and another in the maid's quarters that was next to the laundry room. A search of her calendar and address directory had not found any clues they had seen at the Rathburn's house. He hoped that Jill had been luckier.

He had been sitting in what appeared to be a game room with a sixty-inch digital TV monitor. He had turned it on and found a baseball game. He had begun to doze when Emerson slapped the back of his head.

"Shit, Emerson," he cussed. "What's your fucking problem?" he said, leaning his head back, his greasy hair making a deep impression on the soft white couch.

"I'm working my ass off upstairs, and you're sleeping on the job in front of a TV. Typical guy," she scowled.

He waved the numerous bags of evidence he had gotten. "Did you do better?" he said in a challenging tone.

"I've got enough DNA samples, so when we find the body, we'll know it's hers. I can't believe she didn't keep a paper calendar of some sort. Her only calendar was with Gmail, as was her contacts. I must assume her smartphone had the same information. No leads reflecting where she would have gone. Shit, no current entries for three weeks?"

"Sixteen days," Matt corrected her.

"Sixteen, twenty-one, it doesn't matter. We have diddly-shit on where Trish Morgan has been or might currently be."

They had not noticed that the maid had been listening. She must understand English better than she spoke it, as she answered their question.

"Ms. Morgan leaves for regular vacation…" the maid was struggling for the right words to say… "Let me see," she scratched her head, pulling out her own Smartphone. "Ah, here it is. She leaves for Bermuda on the sixteenth. That seventeen days ago."

Matt pulled the phone from the maid's hands and looked at it. "Do you know the airline or flight number, or where she was staying?"

The maid shook her head. "I only make a guess. A long time ago, when Ms. Morgan returns from one of her trips, I see matches from a hotel in Bermuda. Then, when she leaves another time, she returns with something else that says Bermuda. I think this is the favorite place Ms. Morgan like to go."

A bell had gone off in St. Claire's brain when he heard Bermuda. What his friend had sent him about his murder victim, might not be a coincidence.

Jill, unaware that her partner was deep in thought, began to speak. "I found an interesting photo array of five women. I recognized all of them. One is a Lea Strong, the international model. You know the one you love in your collection of Victoria Secret catalogs," she teased. "The other is Meg Cummings, a TV anchor. She used to be up in Los Angeles, as the weather girl until she got her big break in San Diego."

Matt blushed. "The other two you recognized?" he asked, confused.

"Wake up. It's our two women we're investigating. The fifth one in the photo is Beth Thomas, the CEO of Thomas Cosmetics."

They both left Morgan's house, thanking the maid for her cooperation. Matt was still digesting the connection Trish Morgan might have to Bermuda and his detective friend's unsolved case. This mysterious woman might just be the person they are looking for.

Inside their car, they sat dumbfounded. Then their voices blended as one.

"Doctor Richards?" They both said.

Matt shook his head. "I hate it when you do that. You've got to stop listening to my thoughts."

"Could he be connected to all of these women?" Jill asked.

Matt's slammed his file on the dashboard. "Is it a coincidence that Gilbert's murder victim has a false identity, and Morgan's favorite vacation spot is Bermuda?"

Jill started nodding. "Interesting. It's a good lead. Let's check it out."

29

Back at the FBI field office at 11000 Wilshire Boulevard, Matt kept busy checking all flights on or about the time the maid thought Morgan had left for Bermuda. He scrolled each manifest until his eyes almost fell out of his head. Then, he saw on a Delta passenger manifest that a Lisa Beverly had left for Bermuda on the sixteenth from Lindbergh field in San Diego.

He meandered over, deep in thought, toward Peggy's desk. "How'd you make out with the Lisa Beverly search?"

Peggy frowned as she handed him the information she had found. She saw him look down befuddled.

"This is it?"

"This Beverly woman has no past, present, and by the look of her morgue photo in Bermuda, she's not Trish Morgan. I did a deep search and found a record of a Lisa Beverly from Missouri who died over thirty years ago. I ran everything I could on her and came up with zilch. No family. No children." Peggy was not one to give up, but this one had stumped her.

"Do you think this Lisa Beverly had stolen this identity and was traveling with forged papers?" asked Matt, staring at the photo of the corpse lying on a metal table in the Bermuda morgue. "If this woman is not Trish Morgan, then who is she?" he whispered to himself.

Peggy patted his thigh, looking defeated. "I agree with you. If this woman's death was a murder, then Gilbert has a bigger problem on his hands."

"I'll let him know. You didn't happen to get into the facial recognition database, and review the security cameras at both immigration checkpoints to see if they caught Morgan or Beverly on video?"

"I requested it. It will be here tomorrow," Peggy said, frustrated. "But there is something else that you might find interesting. Doctor Richards has been all over Facebook, and the local news channels in San Diego. He got caught walking with a newscaster, a Meg Cummings. They acted friendly. They were confronted by a nasty drunk guy and a pretty woman who acted like she knew the good doctor too," Peggy said.

"Interesting. Not sure what that might mean? But, you're the best," he said, kissing her on the cheek. "Can you do one more thing for me? Can you get a DNA sample from the Beverly woman? I have a hunch about something and want to put it to rest."

Matt filed what Peggy had said about Richards being on Facebook in the back of his mind. He had more important things to focus on than a bunch of social media gossip.

Jill caught up to him. They decided to take over the conference room with all their evidence. Matt walked with her while he talked to Gilbert on his cell. He brought his friend up to date on his findings. I should have more for you tomorrow, but I wouldn't get your hopes up. You've got a difficult case on your hands."

"Thanks for trying," Gilbert said, showing his disappointment.

"Sorry, old buddy. I wish I could do more. I will review the tapes on the day Lisa Beverly left for Bermuda. Perhaps we'll get lucky and see that she had flown in with somebody." As soon as he hung up, he saw Peggy running toward him.

"I almost forgot. While Beverly's prints didn't turn up anything, the other set of prints in her room did. An Eric Landers, a stockbroker from New York, was with her. It seems he's a frequent flyer to Bermuda," she said, catching her breath. "That's all for now."

Matt pressed redial on his cell and got Gilbert back on the line. "Check your immigration records for Eric Landers. He's a stockbroker out of Wall Street. His prints came back positive that he was inside Lisa's hotel room."

Gilbert sounded relieved. "Thanks. I'll call you tomorrow with the time and day he arrived and where he had stayed. Thank god stockbrokers are fingerprinted," he said. "Oh, Peggy called about Lisa Beverly's DNA. It's going out tomorrow."

Jill looked up at her partner. "I guess someone's case just got more interesting. Sit. Here's what I found out about Trish Morgan. She has never been on a plane to Bermuda, going back five years. Either her maid is crazy, or she's getting there by private jet or boat. I want to see if her maid has any hard copies of her calendar or any other dates that might prove Morgan had gone to Bermuda. Did you ask Gilbert if he can get a record of all private planes and boats that entered Bermuda?"

Matt shook his head. "No. But that's a good idea. I'll ask him if he has any Jane Doe's in his morgue."

"How are you doing with our case?" Jill asked.

"Not much better. But Peggy gave me something about Doctor Richards. He's been tagged on Facebook with a Meg Cummings. She's in that group photo array with Rathburn, Morgan, Strong, and Thomas."

"Interesting. Do you think Cummings was talking to Richards about Rathburn and Morgan?" Jill asked.

"Not sure. Cummings is a reporter. Why wouldn't she? We should bring it up when we talk to her?"

"Good idea."

Matt had a confused look. "Not sure if this means anything, but there was some altercation Richards had, or Cummings had, with a drunk guy who appeared to know the reporter. Also, there was a woman with a drunk guy who acted like she knew the good doctor. Not sure what it all might mean? It's breadcrumbs on a very dismal trail. Let's see if we can get the name of the drunk guy and the woman?"

"Interesting. We've got an appointment tomorrow with Meg Cummings to see what her connection to the two missing ladies is. Wonder what she might say about her friendly relationship with Doctor Richards?"

Matt nodded. "Can't wait."

Jill raised a finger to say something. "Found out, Lea Strong is on a shoot in the Caymans and will be home in three days. I have forensics running all the fingerprints I found inside Morgan's home. This case is getting more intriguing by the minute."

* * * * *

Richards never paid much attention to any social media sites. After listening to the news last night and seeing his face plastered on his TV monitor with Meg Cummings, and his ex-patient, Carla Palmer waving at him, he had to see what Facebook had of his crazy evening. He moaned. There were photos of him walking with Meg.

"Shit, how could I be so stupid. I've got to re-think my plan," combing his hair with his fingers. "The FBI will be connecting a lot of women to me. Think," he moaned.

He slammed his laptop shut. He pulled off his bookcase one of his reference books on serial killers. He thumbed through to the page he had dog-eared a few days earlier. He smiled.

"That's it."

30

Emerson and St. Claire had gotten to Meg Cummings studio ten minutes early. The receptionist could not find her. After waiting for thirty minutes, the two FBI agent's frustration was ready to explode.

Agent Emerson walked over to the receptionist. She slammed her ID badge on the petite young Hispanic woman's desk. "See this," she pointed at her badge, "We're FBI. We do not like waiting. Find Ms. Cummings now, or we'll go get a warrant, bring ICE with us, and investigate everyone at this studio."

The young woman started shaking. "I'm an American," she replied, her voice trembling. "Please, give me a moment. I'll find Ms. Cummings. She must be getting ready for her show." She jumped up and ran toward the back of the studio.

Within thirty seconds, Meg Cummings was walking toward the two agents. "I'm so sorry for the delay. My staff did not tell me you had been waiting," she said. "When they are prepping me for my show, they know I cannot be disturbed for any reason," she said, forcing a smile.

Emerson looked around and asked. "Is there a more private room we can use to ask you a few questions about two of your friends?"

Cummings looked confused. "My friends? I thought you wanted to talk to me about one of my investigative pieces?" she said, acting surprised.

St. Claire was getting irritated. "We left a message that we were going to talk to you about Angelica Rathburn and Trish Morgan. You do know that they are both missing?" his tone harsh.

Meg nodded. "I did know that. But I thought they were off on one of their secluded vacations. We girls like to do that a lot," she said. She could see that both agents were not buying her response.

Inside a small conference room, Emerson started her questions. "How well do you know both ladies?"

"We're casual friends. We see each other occasionally for a drink to talk about our lives. You might probably not believe this, but we have very stressful careers. We give each other support."

St. Claire noticed how young and fit Cummings looked. He kept staring at her wrinkle-free face. He was now thinking about her relationship with Doctor Richards. Her bio said she was forty-nine, but she looked twenty-five. "Like Ms. Rathburn and Ms. Morgan, is Doctor Todd Richards in La Jolla, your doctor? Based on the video and Facebook photos of you and the doctor, you seem to be more than a patient?"

The two questions had rattled her. She had started rubbing her hands nervously. She had not seen any of the Facebook photos or the news piece of her and Richards the other night.

"My relationship with my doctor is none of your business. You said you wanted to ask me about my friends. I've done that. I think you should leave now. If you have any more questions," she said, writing something on a notepad, "here's my attorney's number. Speak with him," she said, standing and storming out of the room.

Emerson looked at her partner. "What's she all huffy about? You made her uncomfortable when you mentioned Doctor Richards. Do you believe she didn't know she was plastered all over Facebook with him? We need to dig a little deeper into the relationships Doctor Richards has with all of these women?" Jill said.

St. Claire smiled. "I'll call Peggy Lynn. She'll love to dig up some shit on the doctor."

"I want some more time with Cummings. I think she knows more than she's telling us," Emerson said.

31

Doctor Richards was not handling Meg Cummings hysteria well. "The FBI was at my studio. We're going to get caught. I know it," she sobbed. "They must've found the picture at Trish's house...shit...she had all of us right on her dresser. I had forgotten she had it. They're going to put all of this together and figure out what we're doing," she screamed. "I can't go to prison."

"Meg, take a breath. You need to get a grip."

"Get a grip? I can't be associated with Rathburn and Morgan. I have to lie low for a while," Meg said, her voice cracking.

"I can tell you haven't seen the photos of us from the other night?" Richards asked, trying to stay calm.

"Photos...shit, they mentioned photos," she replied, looking at her phone. She clicked on her Facebook Icon. "Damn. We're all over Facebook," she wailed. "We have over forty-thousand hits. What are we going to do? They'll for sure discover what we've been doing now."

"Let's not get ahead of ourselves. All the FBI know is that Trish and Angelica were your friends and that I'm their cosmetic surgeon, and yours. It makes perfect sense that all of you would know each other. You're all celebrities. And that I am the doctor for famous people. There was nothing wrong with us holding hands that night in La Jolla. We're friends. If you hold it together, they'll never figure out what we're doing," he tried to assure her. "And, if they do connect all of us, remember it's not a problem. I'm a successful surgeon that has

115

thousands of high-profile clients. So, relax, and answer their questions if they come by again," he said.

"They asked me if I knew you. How am I going to get my shots if they begin to watch me?"

Todd had become silent and withdrawn as he listened to her.

"If we act united, you can still come to your scheduled appointments. There is nothing suspicious about you being treated by me," Richards reminded her again. "So, settle down."

He knew she was correct about seeing him at his office. They needed a new place to meet. He expected Lea, and Beth would be next on the list for interviews.

"I'll bring the shots to you and the others for a while...until I can find a new location for us. I'll use one of my other identities. Everything will be fine. In a few weeks, when Angelica and Trish turn up, they'll get tired of watching you and the others. Then, we can go back the way it was."

"I'm not so sure. Maybe we could all go to Bermuda as you did. It would be far enough away so we could all think of a logical solution to our problem."

Hearing her mention, Bermuda had put his mind in a panic. *"How did she know?"* Then, he remembered she was inside his office the other night. She must have seen the helicopter manifest and the brochure on the Princess Hotel. Shit, I'm am getting too careless.

"Are you free later tonight? We should talk before you speak to the agents again," he asked.

She sucked in a deep breath before responding. "Midnight. After the eleven o'clock news. Let's meet at the rock jetty by the Hotel Del. The beach is very secluded at that time of night. I'll have a small flashlight. You'll find me, okay.

"Okay, see you then," he replied.

Richards pulled out the phone number he had been given the other night at the dance club. He knew he had to find out more about the FBI's investigation into Angelica's and Trish's disappearance, and Jill Emerson was his only lead.

The Faces of Doctor Richards

* * * * *

Jill Emerson had gotten undressed and jumped into the shower. "Shit, ice cold." She detested waiting for anything, especially her shower to warm up.

Her phone rang, pissing her off even more. With uncontrolled fury, she lifted the phone and brought it to her ear.

"Who the fuck is calling at this hour," she cursed. The other end of the line had gone dead, or so she thought. Then she heard a nervous sigh.

"Is this Jill Emerson's number?" the voice asked timidly. "It's Chad Green. Remember we met the other night?"

"Oh shit," she said under her breath. *He's the hunk from the other night.* Her demeanor changed. "Hi, Chad. Sorry for the greeting, but it's been one of those days."

"I have them myself, more than I'd like to admit. Probably not as bad as an FBI agent."

"I'm glad you called. I was going to give you a call at the number you gave me. I'm on a big case, and my time gets away from me."

Richards was now smiling. "I wanted to see if we could get together soon, only if your schedule has some playful openings. I did enjoy dancing with you the other night," he said. "I'm glad you didn't try to call. It would have been embarrassing. The company I worked for had just announced layoffs. I got the ax. I hope that won't make a difference, you know, us going out sometime?"

How about tomorrow evening. Pick me up around eight. Here's my home address. You decide what you'd like to do," she said.

"Tomorrow at eight will be just fine. Sleep well," Richards said sweetly, hanging up his phone. He looked at his watch, realizing he had to go. He had some unfinished business that needed his attention.

32

Doctor Richards, aka *Jeff Peters*, saw a flashlight blinking. He knew it had to be Meg playing a stealthy game. He, like Meg, had been feeling the pressure of the last few weeks, but for different reasons. He didn't think he'd be using this alias so soon, but for his plan to work, Jeff Peters was the answer.

He had not fully worked out his strategy for Meg, which scared him. He was feeling out of control, unable to get a grip on his actions.

He had brought something for Meg. Now, severing another relationship the way he had done to Trish, would be tricky out in the open. He knew he needed another way.

Richards had ground thirty, one-milligram tablets of Xanax and dissolved them in a bottle of water. Getting her drugged and unable to fight back, would make what he had planned easier.

His heart was racing, as Meg's dancing light beam pierced his eyes. His chest pounded, feeling like a caged animal was trying to escape. Illogical thoughts spun inside his brain. He was frantic. He told himself one more or possibly three more murders would not make any difference if he got caught.

Richards wanted these women out of his life so he could start over again. He justified it was best for all of them to die quickly instead of the slow death they'd experience without their shots.

After tonight, he had a plan to distract the FBI and get them to close their missing person cases on Angelica and Trish. Part of his scheme involved Doctor Richards disappearing temporarily. He was not ready to burn every link to himself and what he had been doing. He needed more time and more money from his practice

He walked toward Meg, his mind racing. *"No,"* he told himself as he shuffled toward the light. *"Think. Is there a better solution?"* he racked his brain. *"So far, the FBI has no evidence that Angelica and Trish are dead. An overdose of Xanax would be believable."*

The beach area by the rock jetty, illuminated from the hotel's bright floodlight beams, exposed the loud breaking waves. He looked toward North Island Navy Base relieved, with just a hundred-yard walk, they would be in total blackness.

He watched Meg stand, brushing sand off her buttocks as she walked over to greet him. "Oops, I thought you were someone else," she said, embarrassed.

"Meg, it's me," he said in a calm tone. "I told you I'd be in one of my aliases."

Doubt etched on her face. "How do I know this isn't a trap?"

"You have a butterfly tattoo on your left butt cheek, as well as a smaller one on your upper thigh, a place only someone very intimate with you would know," Richards said.

"Well, someone could have told you that," she replied, walking backward a few feet. "Tell me something that you and I would only know," she said, her hands on her hips.

Richards was getting irritated with her little game. "You're ten weeks pregnant," he blurted out.

Meg let out a long breath. "Thanks for coming," she said, relieved.

Richards had leaned forward and kissed her cheek. "It's my pleasure. I've given what we talked about some more thought, and I've come up with a reasonable solution for all of us."

She had let go of a deep sigh, grabbing his arm as they started to walk. "Let's go south. I love how nice the beach is alongside the apartments. The darkness by North Island frightens me."

Todd frowned as his mind twisted with the change of direction he wanted. He needed the darkness, as well as the seclusion. "Let's go toward the Naval Base. I don't want us to be recognized...like what happened in La Jolla, remember?" He squeezed her hand as he gently pulled her with him. "You'll be safe with me," he said with a reassuring smile.

She shrugged her shoulders—despair had crept on her face. "Make sure you hold me tight," she said, her hands shaking as she pulled a plastic bottle with some pills out of her purse. "It's something that will take the edge off," she said, reaching for the water bottle Richards had in his hand.

. "What are you taking?" Richards asked.

"Just something my psychiatrist prescribed for those stressful days I have." She had started the conversation, her words a staccato of sounds, while sipping slowly on the bottle of water Richards had handed her.

He did not hear a word she had said, as he watched her gulp down his laced bottle. They walked at a relaxing stroll by the edge of the ebbing surf, jumping at times when the water rushed toward their shoes. The night air was brisk, and the sky a dark blue, with a million tiny lights beaming down on them from space.

Doctor Richards held her left hand in his right and supported her back when her legs had become rubbery. Meg's slurring words had rattled him, as she told him she wanted out of the program, and to get back to her regular life.

Meg whined about being a criminal. She told him how frightened she had become with Angelica and Trish missing, and did not want to be next. What shocked him was that she wanted to drop out of sight and retire on her secluded ranch in Montana.

"I can't handle this anymore," she said, stumbling on some soft sand. "The FBI, my friends possibly dead…the thought that some maniac is out there trying to kill me too. I believe this madman knows all of us and knows what we've been doing. He will not stop until he kills everyone, maybe even you," Meg said as she fell forward, her face impacting the sand.

Richards tried to control his grin. *How right she is,* he thought. He watched as Meg tried to roll over but had no control of her body. The high dosage of Xanax and whatever she had taken were kicking in.

She had begun sobbing out of control. She fumbled for her flashlight; the explosion of light startled Richards.

With his hand over his eyes, he asked her to turn it off. "You're blinding me," he laughed strangely. "Meg sweetie, you're overreacting," he said, in a low whisper. He handed her his bottle of water. "Here, finish this, your lips are dry. If you keep your cool, everything will be just fine. In a few days, the FBI will be out of your hair. Also, you can't stop cold turkey. Your body would degenerate at an accelerated rate, and you could be dead within months."

Her crying stopped as fast as it had started. She was now combing her sandy fingers through her scalp. "Damn. That's not what I had in mind. Maybe I can," her words were slurring as they spewed out of her mouth. "to take my shots on my own?"

Richards was getting exasperated. He knew the amount of Xanax he put in the water would have put a horse to sleep. He was surprised she was still awake after taking what she had in her purse. "It's too dangerous. If you make a mistake, you could overdose and be dead. However, I have a better solution."

Meg's eyes started fluttering, ready to pass out, but she struggled to ask questions. "What solution?" She had not noticed the syringe in his left hand as he knelt beside her. He put his right arm around her shoulders. He started telling her how he had come up with a workable plan for Angelica, and how he would agree to try it with her. His other arm was preparing to plunge the phenobarbital in her thigh. From out of nowhere, a bright spotlight engulfed the two of them.

Richards was startled. It did not matter as the needle penetrated her jeans, and the fluid instantly flowed into her bloodstream. She yelped. With a look of horror on her face, she clenched the moist sand with her fists.

The spotlight from the military jeep had lit up Jeff Peters' face as he stood up over Meg's body. Richards was unable to see that the soldier had on his chest a body camera.

"Halt. You're in a restricted area," the deep burly voice called out. When the military sentry had seen Meg lying lifeless on the sand, he shouted out once again. "Stand fast, hands in the air."

Jeff Peters finally understood they had drifted too far down the beach. "Shit," he muttered. Now a military guard, possibly a Marine, had caught him. Without hesitation, he ran at an angle toward the retainer wall that would take him into the quiet residential area on Coronado Island.

He looked back and saw that the guard was trying to attend to Meg first. The sand was soft and deep, making it hard to run fast. He had made it over the wall, startling an older couple that had been walking hand-in-hand. Richards did not try to shield his face from the elderly couple. He sprinted into the poorly lit residential neighborhood.

Richards hoped they could give a good description of Jeff Peters, confirming what the military man saw. He needed his alias to be the prime suspect on Bermuda and now Coronado Island. It would make the next part of his plan more confusing to the FBI.

After a few minutes, he stopped near an unlit alleyway. He turned on Meg's flashlight and put the beam on the photo of himself. He panned the area to be sure no one was walking by or looking out a window. In five minutes, Jeff Peters was no longer on Coronado Island. Richards hailed a taxi, tossed the empty bottle of water Meg drank from, and his windbreaker, in an old trash receptacle. He needed to get back to La Jolla.

* * * * *

The Marine knelt over Meg's body. At first, he could not find a pulse, but then a faint beat appeared. "Woman attacked, she's down. Send medics, a hundred yards west of beach security checkpoint fifteen. He then called the Coronado police and had them initiate a BOLO for a white male, short black hair, around six-foot-one or two, who attacked a white female five minutes ago, on foot. He should still be on the island.

He was wearing a blue nylon windbreaker, and khaki slacks. Close the Coronado bridge, and the Silver Strand," the guard ordered.

The police dispatcher responded. "Copy that. We'll get him pronto. There are only two ways off the island. He can't get far."

"Roger that," the Master Chief said. "I'm on duty all night. Call me to identify our perp."

As a taxi sped by the empty tollbooth at the beginning of the Coronado bridge in the direction of San Diego, Richards noticed the flashing lights up ahead. *They're fast,* he thought. The taxi inched its way toward the checkpoint, and a young police officer directed his flashlight beam on the Doctor's face.

"Sorry, sir," he said, re-reading his BOLO. He waved his hand and let the taxi go through the roadblock. Richards leaned back and smiled. He twirled his long blonde hair on his finger. He had finally understood how he could commit the perfect murder and never get caught.

33

Meg Cummings had been airlifted to Scripps Mercy General, still clinging to life. The Coast Guard physician and nurse that attended to her on the short flight to the hospital had determined she had overdosed.

The protocol called for them to use intranasal naloxone. The doctor tilted her head back and injected the spray into her left nostril. Nothing happened. They now hoped she would live long enough until they could get her to the trauma room.

The young nurse at first didn't recognize her, but then she spoke with a surprised expression. "She's Meg Cummings, the news gal on CBS. I saw her do the eleven o'clock news earlier. She did not look like she was a drug addict."

The Coast Guard doctor didn't look at the nurse as he kept working on keeping his patient alive. "There are millions of recreational drug users in every profession. She must have made a mistake. Let's get a blood panel first before we jump to any conclusions."

＊ ＊ ＊ ＊ ＊

Doctor Richards had the taxi driver drop him off at La Jolla Village Drive and Prospect. He walked down a path toward the cliff that overlooked the cove and sat on some rocks, still shaken by what he had done. He pulled out the empty syringe ready to toss it down onto the rocky bottom when he noticed that he had not given Meg the entire dosage. A cold chill engulfed his body.

The Faces of Doctor Richards

He took out the photo of Jeff Peters and stared at the picture. This time he did not try to transform back into him. This identity had to vanish. This alias had committed two murders, Lisa Beverly's and now Meg Cummings. Richards tore up the photo.

He then took out his picture of Chad Green. He waited for the transformation to take place. This time it took longer. The second change of appearance within hours had been more painful and took more time. He knew that multiple transformations had to be limited to only four in a twenty-four period. Anymore, and his skin and his bone density could become corrupted. It was an imperfection he'd known for some time with his current serum formula that needed to be corrected.

He felt his bones twist and stretch, forcing his skin to remold itself into the correct features of Chad. After ten minutes, he stood, a little wobbly, but stable enough to walk back to his rental car.

Before he got into his car, he needed to revise his plan to eliminate his last two patients: Lea Strong, and Beth Thomas. He understood he had been careless and clumsy with Meg. The FBI would be on high alert, and if they were doing their due diligence, they should put his other patients in protective custody. He was now driving to Chad Green's apartment in Santa Monica to think of his next move.

34

In the ER trauma unit, three teams of doctors worked on Meg. She had gone into cardiac arrest two times and brought back. They had her hooked up to three IV's to counteract the overdose of Xanax, and phenobarbital they found in her bloodwork.

She was stable for the moment. She was in an induced coma to allow her body to fight off the drugs in her body. If she made it through the next twenty-four hours, she would survive. The doctors were not sure if there had been any brain damage.

San Diego PD had two officers sitting outside her room. They had orders not to let any unauthorized personnel near her. They were handling this as an attempted murder case that involved a high-profile celebrity.

The Marine sentry who stopped the attack had been working with a sketch artist at the Coronado Police station. Even though it had been dark, the intense beam from his military jeep's spotlight allowed the experienced SEAL officer to give a full and accurate description of the man who had run away.

San Diego PD Detective Bradley Connors and his partner Scott Nicholas were the lead investigators on this case. The facial sketch streamed over the entire police network system in the three Western states that bordered California, as well as Mexico. Every patrol car, every smartphone, had the sketch, as well as the BOLO bulletin, as their immediate priority.

Tomorrow detective Connors would send their sketch out to every law enforcement unit around the country, as well as to the two FBI agents handling the Rathburn and Morgan missing person case. It was only a hunch that their victim was connected to their investigation.

It was two-twenty in the morning, and he was tired. Detective Connors knew everything could wait. All the roadblocks had not turned up a suspect who came close to the marine's description.

35

Matt St. Claire had just started locking his apartment door when his phone rang. He looked at his cellphone. It had been off all morning.

"Shit. It's going to be one of those days," Matt moaned. "St. Claire," he shouted out of breath.

Peggy Lynn from his office had a worried tone. "Glad I caught you. I tried Emerson, but she too had her cell turned off. You know how Miller feels about that?" she scolded him.

"Did you call to admonish me, or do you have something for me?" His harsh words upset her.

"Got up on the wrong side of the bed?" she lashed back. Her voice had hurt coming out of it.

Matt felt terrible how he had spoken. "Look, you know I think the world of you. My moods are not to be taken personally. I'm very sorry," he said.

Peggy tried to hide her sniffle that she muffled in her Kleenex. "That follow up appointment you and Jill have with Meg Cummings, well I think it's going to get canceled. She was on the news a few minutes ago. The SDPD says she had been attacked on the beach in Coronado. She had an overdose of Xanax and phenobarbital in her system. She's a coma and struggling to stay alive. We have a sketch of the guy that assaulted her. It's on your desk. Better get in here now. Miller's having a shit-fit since she's the third celebrity that has gotten herself in the news."

"Thanks," Matt said and hung up the phone. "Shit, another Doctor Richards patient. Who did the doctor piss off?"

He rushed down to his garage. He had to pick up his partner. While stuck in the regular stop and go rush hour traffic, he had time to think. Matt racked his brain and thought of his friend Gilbert's murder victim in Bermuda, and what had happened to Cummings in Coronado. "Did Lisa Beverly have a connection to the five women in the photo?" he pondered, recalling the picture they had found at Trish Morgan's house.

Matt hated coincidences. Their case was getting stranger by the minute. The preliminary information from Bermuda had indicated Lisa Beverly died from a massive heart attack. There was a puncture wound by her neck, but the coroner's report was inconclusive. His thoughts bounced back and forth through the evidence they had, and nothing was making sense.

It appeared that Eric Landers, the stockbroker in New York, had become an active suspect in the Lisa Beverly murder case. Matt had gotten the security video from the Hotel, and the FBI's crime lab was analyzing it to see if any other person or persons went into Beverly's room. He hoped that Peggy had gotten from Gilbert the security videos from the airport he had requested, as well as the DNA sample he wanted.

He thought of Lea Strong and Beth Thomas, the other women connected to their two missing celebrities, and now assault victim Meg Cummings. He pounded the steering wheel hard, as the stop and go commuters were driving him crazy.

Matt started talking to himself out loud. It helped him understand the puzzles he investigated. Hearing his voice utter the logical and illogical facts helped get him closer to solving his cases. *"Damn, we have two women who are missing…if not dead, and another is clinging to life, all connected to Doctor Richards."* His cell rang, startling him.

Peggy Lynn was whispering. "When are you planning on getting into the office? Miller won't stop ranting. He's driving everyone crazy. Get your sorry ass here and quiet him down," she whispered.

"Is Attila the Hun close by?" he joked

"Get in…" she said in a low voice. She covered the mouthpiece on her phone with her palm. "No, sir, that's not St. Claire or Emerson," she lied. "Please get in here," she pleaded.

* * * * *

On the way to the office, Matt filled Jill in on everything he knew as well as his suspicions about Lisa Beverly and Eric Landers. He wasn't sure if that case had a connection to Doctor Richards or the doctor's patients, but his gut was telling him it did.

"We need to get Lea Strong and Beth Thomas into protective custody before we have two more of Doctor Richards patients disappearing or dead."

Jill could see how distraught Matt had gotten. Their case was moving at the speed of light these last three weeks, and they had no definitive direction to go in. "Let's first hope that Cummings wakes up from her coma so we can talk to her. We only have one victim in the flesh right now, Meg Cummings."

Matt seemed perplexed. "Do you still think we're dealing with one serial killer?"

Jill shrugged. "It's looking that way to me, but I won't be sure until we have the scattered pieces of this puzzle laid out," Emerson said, patting Matt's shoulder. "We should have everything back from forensics today. Let's wait and see what that shows us.

36

Miller had been standing in the middle of the lobby reception area, his hands on his hips. His posture exhibited anger, as Matt and Jill got off the elevator.

"Where the hell have you two been? You know my rules about turning off your cells," he said, his jaw clenching.

Emerson put her hands to her ears. "You're one decibel away from having every dog in Los Angeles coming up here," she taunted, walking past him.

He yelled at the backs of their heads. "In my office in five. Bring everything you've got on the Angelica Rathburn and Trish Morgan cases. We've got another attack or attempted murder…whatever, on another high-profile celebrity," he yelled. "Just bring everything."

They both gave him a boat wave and nodded as they got to their desks. Peggy had made duplicates of everything she had done for them. They had three files. Each labeled with the three women's names.

Jill pushed her sketch of Meg Cummings attacker across their adjoining desks, stopping in front of Matt's face. "We've seen this guy before. Right? But where?" she asked her partner.

Matt squinted with a silly-ass grin. He had his smart-ass look that Jill hated. "Yes, we've seen him before," Matt said, scratching his head. "I'd say my original theory that we're dealing with a man is still number one. My gut instincts still work," he said, pinching a few inches of fat around his waist. Matt looked at Peggy. "Where are the security tapes from the Bermuda murder?

Peggy pressed the play button on his computer screen. "Already uploaded for you. I've checked it out, and I think both of you will find what's on the tapes interesting," she said, patting Matt on the top of his head. She turned and walked back to her desk.

Jill slid her chair closer to Matt. They both leaned in closer. They looked at a man getting off a private helicopter in Bermuda, wearing a baseball cap with the brim pulled down covering his face. They watched him walk into a restroom, and fifteen minutes later, walkout, the baseball cap now on backward, exposing his face.

Emerson and St. Claire looked at the sketch of the man who attacked Cummings, and the man on the security camera feed. They were not saying anything until they watched more footage of tape.

They watched the guy from the airport restroom enter the Princess Hotel and enter *Lisa Beverly's* room. Forty-five minutes later, he leaves in a rush. They rewound the security tape sixty-minutes verifying that Eric Landers had been with Beverly first.

Emerson was first to remark. "This last guy," she said, poking her finger on the sketch, "I'll bet one month's salary it's the same guy who attacked Cummings."

St. Claire was rubbing his chin, shaking his head. "Is it possible that Eric Landers murdered Beverly, and our other suspect found her and rushed out?"

"I don't buy it. Why would the second guy, the one from the airport, stay in Beverly's room for three-quarters of an hour with a dead body? Maybe this second guy is a jealous lover. After he saw Landers leaving Lisa's room, he confronted her, and murdered her," Jill said.

Matt was shaking his head. "Let's do facial recognition of this guy and see what we come up with." Matt was holding up the sketch of the suspect who attacked Cummings. "It's a pretty poor sketch, but it does resemble the second guy. We now need a timeline for this guy, and Eric Landers," he said, dropping the sketch on the desk. "Can't make suspect two good for the murder just yet, but he's looking perfect for it."

They found Eric Lander's photo on his New York driver's license. Their case had just gotten weirder.

Matt spoke first. "Even Landers looks like our guy in the sketch. Could this case get any crazier?" St. Claire slammed his file closed.

Miller had buzzed for them to get in his office. He sat like a pompous ass, his arms crossed behind his neck, and his small feet up on his desk. His jowly pockmarked face looked like a used golf ball that had seen better days.

"The Cummings woman just died. The amount of Xanax she ingested was too much for her heart. The hospital said she was pregnant too. Shit, what type of asshole would do this to a woman with a kid on the way," Miller complained.

Jill had a bewildered look on her face. "Pregnant? She did not look like she was expecting. We need DNA from the fetus, ASAP," she said, "and determine who's the father."

Miller was tapping his pencil on his water glass. "Let's stay on point here. We now have two missing celebrities and one dead one who was pregnant. What have you found out so far?" the deputy director said, sitting upright in his chair.

Matt spoke first, giving Jill a dirty look, pointing to a chair for her to sit. "The DNA on the fetus could be an important clue. Maybe the killer was the father? Now, we have a lot of clues, but none that lead to any definitive suspects or conclusions. We have a suspect who's in Manhattan, but I'm not sure about him. We'll need to interview him and find out his whereabouts for the last few days."

Miller's face knotted; he was confused. "New York? I don't understand."

St. Claire had begun to tell him about his friend, detective, Gilbert Smith, and his murder victim, Lisa Beverly. It appears this Eric Landers might have been the last person to see her alive. He looks like the suspect in the sketch from the Cummings crime scene," he said. "This Lisa Beverly murder might be by the same perp. It's probably a dead-end, but the crimes seem similar. We have two suspects that resemble the guy in our sketch. We need to rule one of them out. We're going to put the other suspect in our facial recognition database and hopefully get an ID."

Miller had been shaking his head. "It won't take both of you to interview the guy in Manhattan. Agent Emerson, you're going to New York. You can check out this Eric Landers. St. Claire, you'll work the cases here while she's gone." He stared at Jill, his eyes glowing with hatred for her. "You'll leave this afternoon and be back here within forty-eight hours. Notify the local authorities you're arriving, and that you'd like their cooperation. Don't embarrass me while you're back there."

"That would be impossible, sir. Everyone from coast to coast knows what a fine deputy director you are. Nothing I'd do could change that," she said, storming out of his office.

"How do you stand her?" Miller asked, frustrated.

"Once you know her, she's a lot of fun to be around," Matt replied, leaving the office.

Jill looked pissed. "He's one arrogant bastard."

Matt scowled. "You don't make it easy. Try to lighten up. It could work wonders."

She scooped up all her files and headed to the conference room. She looked back. "Are you coming?"

He took a deep breath, as he tagged along like some lovesick puppy.

Before I leave you with these cases, we need to look at all the evidence we have so far. I'm beginning to think these women all have a similar connection, even this Lisa Beverly. Have we gotten Beverly's DNA?"

"Oh. I forgot to tell you. My friend called me earlier. Since Lisa Beverly looks American, even with her forged ID's, he's shipping her back to our forensic lab. She'll be here when you return from Manhattan. He said that something bizarre is happening to her body. It's decomposing rapidly, and her facial structure is changing. Bermuda's forensic people don't have the tools to figure it out. They want us to do it. Oh, one other detail, she was pregnant too."

Jill slapped her forehead. "Great, another case to work. We need to find a link these ladies have to each other and these two men. They're all beautiful and well-maintained. I'll try to hook-up with Beth Thomas while I am back in Manhattan."

Matt nodded his head in agreement. "You need to get her into protective custody and see how she reacts."

Jill was now deep in thought. "Is it possible Doctor Richards is their cosmetic surgeon too? Do you think he'd volunteer the information? Maybe his DNA? I doubt we'd be able to get a warrant on what we suspect," said Jill, as she took her plane ticket from Peggy. "I've got to get home and pack."

"You need me to drive you home, and then to the airport?" Matt asked.

"Remember, my car is downstairs in the garage. We left it four days ago."

"That's right. You did drink a little too much that night. How'd you get around without your car?"

"Big secret. A bus. I love taking public transportation. Real people are on them. I like grounding myself occasionally, especially after some of our hideous cases." She slapped her forehead again. "Shit. I've got a date tonight. I hate having to cancel. He's the hot one."

As she dialed the phone number Chad Green had given her, she got a recording. The voice sounded like someone else she'd spoken to recently. She had an ear for voices and could place a voice and face. It sounded like Doctor Richards. *You've got Richards on the brain, girl*; she scolded herself. "This is Jill. I'm sorry, tonight is off. I have to go out of town for a couple of days. I'll call you when I get back. Can I have a rain check?"

Matt had noticed her confused look. "I've seen that face before. What's up?"

Jill furrowed her brow and pressed her eyelids tight. "I must be working too hard. That guy I met the night you found me at the dance club, well, we had set a date for tonight. The strangest thing happened when I heard his voice on his answering machine. It sounded like Doctor Richards. I must be losing it."

Matt laughed. "It's about time you came off your pedestal and made mistakes like us peasants."

She pressed her lips tight. "It sounds crazy. If I hadn't met this Chad Green, I would have bet the voice on his answering machine was Doctor Todd Richards. Perhaps a few days in the big apple will do me some good."

"Have a good trip. I'll call you if anything breaks on any of the cases. Also, I'm doing a full background check on Doctor Richards. Maybe he has an interesting past?" Matt said.

37

Richards drove back to La Jolla after he listened to the message from agent Emerson that their date was off. He wasn't sure why she had to cancel, except that it had something to do with her case. His paranoia kicked in, and it was causing his irrational behavior to consume his thoughts again.

He decided he needed to use this time to work on the next part of his plan. He had lost two of his fetuses with Trish's and Meg's death. Getting Lea's and Beth's fetuses would be even more difficult now. With Emerson out of town for two days, it would give him enough time to distract the FBI from looking at him as a suspect for Rathburn's and Morgan's disappearance. Richards needed some quiet time to work out all the details.

He had not been home for more than thirty minutes when his phone rang. It was agent St. Claire. The agent said he wanted to ask him a few questions about Rathburn, Morgan, and Cummings. Richards tried to postpone the meeting, but the FBI agent was persistent.

"You know there's doctor confidentiality I have to deal with," Richards protested.

"I don't want to know about what procedures they've had or any of their medical information. I only want to get an understanding as to why two of your patients are either missing or, as in Meg Cummings's case, dead. I'd think you'd want to help us find out what's going on?" Matt asked. "Maybe there is a disgruntled ex-patient that is angry at you. Your cooperation will be a big help to the FBI."

"I guess so," Richards said. "You know I am just their doctor. I know nothing of their personal lives, or how they spend their free time."

Matt was rolling his eyes, listening to Richards bullshit. "I'd appreciate a little collaboration. I'm sensing you're a little defensive. I'm not the enemy here," Matt said, his impatience resonating over the phone.

St. Claire heard the silence at the other end of his call. He was wondering if he had pushed Richards too far. Matt had a hunch after seeing the Facebook photos of the doctor and Meg Cummings that maybe the doctor had a similar relationship with the other victims. Perhaps he was the father of the dead babies and wanted to stay as far away as possible from a scandal that would ruin his reputation.

St. Claire took in a deep breath and spoke. "I do appreciate that you are taking the time to meet with me," he said, trying to tone down his frustration. "I need to wrap up some loose ends to our case and eliminate you as a suspect." He held his breath, realizing he had slipped up with those words.

Richards fell back in his chair. He realized St. Claire was coming out to try to trap him into saying something incriminating. "I'll give you thirty minutes, no more. Do I need my lawyer?"

"It won't be necessary, but you have a right to have him present. I should be at your office in a couple of hours."

* * * * *

After his phone call from agent St. Claire, Doctor Richards was climbing the walls. He had tried pills and alcohol, but the pain of killing the women he had come to love, the only family he had, plagued him. Since Agent St. Claire had pushed for an interview, he was going off the deep end. Panic filled every nerve ending in his body.

"How could they think I murdered my patients? What evidence do they have?" he asked himself. Then, it hit him. *"Meg and Trish were*

138

pregnant," he moaned, gulping down more booze from his whiskey bottle.

He thought of running and leaving with the rest of his serum and his equipment. He knew he did not have enough time to remove everything before he met with agent St. Claire.

After he had heard the news about Meg Cummings dying, he felt some relief. Seeing the sketch of Jeff Peter's identity on TV, he prayed that the hotel security cameras in Bermuda, as well as at the airport, had captured that image too.

Richards knew if the FBI started focusing on Peters, then the final part of his plan would free him from suspicion. He could then get back to his research and making fetuses with other women.

"Stop worrying," he told himself. *"You've covered your tracks."* He knew they only had him connected because he was their doctor. Nevertheless, he could not stop agonizing.

Horrible thoughts exploded inside his brain again. "Shit, Trish, and Meg's fetuses might have my DNA," Richards remembered he had used his hybrid serum when Meg and Trish had gotten pregnant. But he never verified that the DNA would not match his. *"Stupid mistake,"* he scolded himself.

Richards was losing it. His foolish thoughts had him believing that killing the FBI agent was his best solution. His world had begun to crumble faster and faster. His head spun like a top—he was not making sense. The guilt of killing another human being had twisted his soul, throwing him into a whirlwind of despair.

He had gone into his operating room and prepared three syringes of tranquilizers for the nosey FBI agent. He kept imagining the questions St. Claire was going to ask him.

How long had Angelica Rathburn been a patient? Did she know Trish Morgan and Meg Cummings? Did the three women know Lea Strong and Beth Thomas too? Did you have an intimate relationship with them? Did you get them pregnant?

It had been, as if a tornado had entered his head and was lifting him off the ground, twisting and throwing him about, making him powerless over his situation. Now the final question bounced back and forth like an old game of Pong.

Where were you on the nights that Rathburn and Morgan turned up missing, and where were you last night when Meg Cummings was attacked?

He let loose a loud howl, like an animal dying in horrible pain. Under his white lab coat, he had soaked his oxford shirt, from guilty sweat.

As fast as his panic exploded inside his head, a calm blanketed his body. He had come to an obvious conclusion on what to do about Agent Matt St. Claire.

He believed he had it all planned out. The sedative, dumping his body in the ocean. He honestly thought he could kill a trained FBI agent after reading all the self-defense books he memorized.

However, whatever sanity he had left overruled that course of action. He decided to call his attorney and have him deal with the agent's questions about his patients.

38

When Matt entered Doctor Richards' office, his receptionist took his card. Her cold icy confused stare didn't make sense to him. There was nothing friendly about her. With her arm extended, and her index finger stiff, she pointed to a chair gesturing for him to sit down.

"You need to take a seat. I will let Doctor Richards know you are here," she said, a nervous edge pasted on her words.

She was not gone more than thirty seconds, and escorting St. Claire back down the same long hallway he and Emerson had walked done on their first visit. This time it was brightly lit, illuminating a photo array of famous men and women patients. He stopped at three photos, two of his missing ladies, and the recently departed Meg Cummings. Then he saw Lea Strong, as well, and Beth Thomas on his wall of fame, both ladies were smiling with Doctor Richards. He turned and asked the receptionist a question.

"Why are Lea Strong and Beth Thomas photos grouped here and not with their friends?" Matt asked the receptionist. He saw her expression and understood she was not going to tell him anything. He filed his question in the back of his mind for another time.

She gently touched his arm and ushered him into Richards's office. Seeing a slender man in a three-piece pinstriped suit sitting in front of Doctor Richards desk, caught him unaware. He knew his interview would be a waste of time. *"Idiot, you spooked the doctor with your dumb ass questions."*

The Faces of Doctor Richards

The slender man extended his hand, holding a business card. He introduced himself. "I'm Charlie Feldman. You can call me Chuck. I'm Doctor Richards's attorney. He asked me to be here to help answer some questions you have. I'm only here to advise him when the questions fall within his doctor-patient confidentiality. He wants to cooperate. He also doesn't want to break the law and jeopardize his medical license," he said in a soft melodic tone. Feldman looked at Richards and gave him a wink.

Matt wondered if the attorney could see his rage. He tossed a note to Richards, who was sitting behind his desk, with his arms folded across his chest.

St. Claire cleared his throat before speaking. "I know the women named on this piece of paper are patients of yours. I noticed their photos on your hallway of fame. Why aren't Lea Strong and Beth Thomas grouped with their friends?" He then continued to direct his questions to Richards, ignoring Feldman as if he was not in the room.

The attorney grabbed the piece of paper. "I will have to advise my client not to divulge any information that exposes who his clients are. Most of those photos are from fundraising events for which he has been a major donor. He's a very prominent cosmetic surgeon, and some of his clients like to keep private..." Feldman paused, "certain improvements they at times make to their bodies. I'm sure you can understand their need for confidentiality. He has other celebrities that are not on your list. If it got out that they had cosmetically enlarged their breasts or did a nip and tuck, or other modifications, you get my drift, it could be embarrassing, let alone costly to their careers and their sponsors. You do remember the scandal with Suzanne Summers, who advertised her thigh exerciser? When word got out that she had cosmetic surgery, some nip and tuck surgeries, her creditability dropped like a broken elevator. I'm sorry we can't be of any help in that area," he said patronizingly. "Are those the only questions you have?"

Matt bit his lower lip, holding back his frustration. He did not like Richards's demeanor from the beginning, and now he put him on top of his list of suspects connected to his missing women.

142

"I'm not here to invade your patient's privacy. I am investigating two missing celebrities, and now one dead celebrity, who coincidently are, or were, your patients. I believe that these ladies have a stalker, who might be after more of your patients," Matt said, his icy voice and unblinking stare made Doctor Richards squirm in his chair.

Richards leaned forward, his elbows on his desk. "Are you saying that I am a suspect?"

Matt let a small smile crack on his face. He knew he had rattled Richards.

He too leaned in a little closer and spoke. "I do have a few other questions? Doctor Richards, where were you last night say around, midnight." St. Claire never took his eyes off the doctor's face, watching his eyes twitch and dart back and forth.

Richards turned his face toward his attorney, afraid to look at his interrogator. "I was fast asleep," he pointed up toward the ceiling. "Upstairs in my apartment. I was alone and do not have an alibi. I'm assuming you're asking about the tragic death of Meg Cummings?" He sat facing his lawyer cracking his knuckles.

"Are you always this nervous when asked questions?" Matt shot the query at him.

"I'm a timid person, and only deal with my patients. Most of them do the talking and pointing at where they want to see improvements. Having to be involved in some way with a murder investigation does make me nervous, especially when it involves one of my patients. If it leaked to the media that I might be a suspect, it could ruin my reputation and business."

"Unless you have something to hide, you should not be nervous," Matt said, leaning in a little closer. "I have more questions I want to ask," he said. "How close were you to Ms. Cummings? Were you in an intimate relationship with her?"

"Are you referring to those Facebook photos? Meg is, was a very passionate woman. She was very touchy-feely with everyone. She wanted to hold hands on that cold evening. Nothing more," he said.

"Don't you think it's strange that bad things have been happening to your patients these last few weeks?"

"Why am I feeling you think I had something to do with the other women on your list who are missing?"

Matt was pleased his questions continued to rattle the doctor. "I don't make assumptions. *Assumption is the mother of all fuck-ups*, and I don't screw up on any of my investigations," he said with a menacing grin. *"Thanks, Jill. You'd be proud of how I used your phrase."* "One last question. Was Lisa Beverly ever a patient of yours? Or related to any of your patients?"

Richards, as soon as he heard Trish Morgan's alias float our of the agent's mouth, his face drained of color. He fell back in his chair. "Who? Lisa Beverly? Never heard of her before," he stuttered.

Matt saw an opening and took it. "Have you been to Bermuda recently?" he asked.

Richards was now noticeably shaken by the question. He hesitated before he spoke. "Bermuda? No, not recently. I've been there on previous occasions, but, no, not recently," he said, his voice trembling.

"I think you've helped me enough today," Matt said. "I'll be in touch if I have more questions."

Matt stood and extended his hand to the doctor and then the attorney. He was happy with what he had seen today.

Before he left the doctor's office, he looked back. "I'm looking into your past. It's part of my normal investigation so I can eliminate you as a suspect." He looked at Richards's attorney. "I hope you do not try to interfere or hinder our investigation?" St. Claire turned and left the building without saying another word. He watched Richards face turn bedsheet white.

Outside he adjusted his coat, feeling proud of the way he handled himself. Except he knew he wasn't any closer to solving any of the cases.

* * * * *

Feldman looked at his client. "Are you in any trouble?" he asked cautiously. He knew any admission of murdering someone would require him to go to the authorities. "I don't want details. If you know something about Angelica or Trish, or where they might be hiding, you should let the FBI know," he said. "Attorney-client privilege does not work if I know you committed a crime. Withholding evidence can make you an accessory to the crime too."

Richards was off in another time and place. However, he did hear his attorney covering his ass. "Chuck shut the fuck up. I didn't kill anybody or do I know where these spoiled women are. Thanks, a heap for even thinking I could kill someone after all the years I've known you and Marge." He saw that he had embarrassed his attorney. He wasn't lying, except it was Jeff Peters who murdered two of the ladies.

"I didn't think for one minute you could do something like that. I had to tell you the law, just in case," he winked. "Marge would love to have you over for dinner one of these nights. You can't keep hiding away in your work."

Todd smiled and patted Feldman's shoulder. "Okay, next week. I'll give Marge a call and set a date."

That evening he drank himself to sleep. For the first time since losing Molly, he had again fallen into the dark pit of despair he had during the years after her death. He knew he had to prepare himself for the worst, and that his practice might have to close sooner than later. He hoped the FBI would go on the wild goose chase he had set in motion with his Jeff Peters identity. He needed Lea and Beth to go a few more weeks with their pregnancies.

Before he passed out, he thought of his next plan to get the FBI off his back. It involved Angelica and Trish. As he fell into a deep sleep, dreaming of Agent Jill Emerson, as his wife and mother of his children.

39

Matt had no sooner sat down on his couch when his phone rang. He cursed at the phone, feeling the exhaustion that blanketed his body. The interview with Richards and his attorney had his wheels turning. He now believed the doctor was involved in some way with these cases.

He looked at his phone screen and saw it was his friend Gilbert from Bermuda. "Hi, Gilbert. How are you?" He struggled to get his words out.

"Matt, old chap, you sound tired."

"I am. These cases are confusing and exhausting. We seem to be going nowhere."

"I know the feeling. This Lisa Beverly case has all of us stumped," Gilbert said. "I don't want to make you any more frustrated than you are, but my forensic team noticed something strange on the security tapes I sent you. Particularly, the one from the airport."

"My partner and I looked them over. Nothing out of the ordinary about them."

Gilbert, sucked in a deep breath, expelling a loud sigh. "You and Jill should look at them again. I know this might sound crazy, but the man who entered the restroom at the airport, you know, the guy with his face shielded by his ball cap..." Matt interrupted.

"Gilbert, get to the point. I need to get some sleep," he begged.

"Sure. We don't think the guy who went into the restroom was the same guy who came out. We estimated that the first man was around six feet four inches, and the man who came out ten minutes later was four inches shorter?"

"That's crazy. Is it possible the first guy went out another exit?"

"We thought that too. There isn't another exit, plus how do you explain that whoever this person was, came out wearing the same clothes as the first man, and the cuffs of his pants are dragging on the ground?"

Matt moaned. "Thanks a lot, friend. You added more confusing shit to my crazy cases. I can't explain it but will let my forensic team look it over and call you back."

Gilbert nervously coughed. "Thanks. Also, look at the last part of those tapes, and tell me if the second guy came back out as the first guy again, and explain how his pants fit him perfectly again. That's it. Sorry to mess up your evening."

"It's okay. My partner's in New York following up on your Eric Landers lead. He might be involved in a murder case back here, too. Talk to you soon," Matt said and ended the call.

Matt wanted to call his partner to update her on what Gilbert had told him but looked at his watch and realized it was three hours later in New York. "Shit, she's probably up drinking and flirting."

40

The taxi ride from Kennedy had been uneventful, as Emerson pulled into the JW Marriott driveway at Forty-sixth and Broadway. She checked in and rode the glass elevator up to the forty-eighth floor. She tossed her bags on the bed. Without changing or putting on a fresh face, she rushed downstairs for a gin martini.

She was tired and irritable. She had connected with Eric Landers. He agreed to have dinner after the market closed tomorrow.

She had found out that Beth Thomas would be in Manhattan while she was there. The cosmetic CEO was at first reluctant to meet, but after a little bit of pushing on Jill's part, she agreed to breakfast the next morning. She was one of their pieces to a confusing puzzle.

Emerson sensed something strange about the woman that made the hair on her neck stand at attention. She called Peggy.

"Can you get a printout of Beth Thomas's travel schedule? I need to see how many times she comes to the West Coast. It's just a hunch."

Peggy, like she always did, was one step ahead of her two favorite agents. "Already done, and waiting for you," she said. "When you told me that you were seeing her, I thought it would be helpful if you knew if she was seeing Doctor Todd Richards."

"You're the best," Jill said. "So, tell me what you found out?"

"Thomas has been coming to the West Coast, mainly San Diego these past few years, every two weeks. She seems to stay one day and then flies back to JFK. Any thoughts on what that might mean?"

"Not sure, but you can bet I will ask her tomorrow at breakfast. Thanks again, Peggy. I don't know what we'd do without you," she said.

Jill knew that once she completed her interviews, she planned on catching an early flight back home the following day—that was her promise to herself. She did not like New York. Never did, and never would. It brought back painful memories of Alex, and the time they had both spent on a romantic weekend in Manhattan. It was on that trip he had popped the question to her.

Sitting at a small cocktail table in the lobby bar, she had become mesmerized by the changing colored lights that illuminated the large bottles of liquid pleasures the hotel had to offer evenly stacked behind the bar. She thought of her fiancée, while the bubble elevators raced each other to their floors.

She snapped back to the surroundings of the lounge when the barmaid lowered her drink. "Will this be charged to your room?" the petite Asian accented woman asked.

Jill nodded. "Room forty-eight-forty-eight, last name Emerson." She slowly began sipping the drink. During her third martini, she had a buzz that had her almost falling asleep on the soft armchair.

Her phone rang, startling her. It was St. Claire. "Miss me already?" she said.

Matt ignored her comment. "How was your flight?"

"Boring. I'm having a martini in the hotel bar before crashing upstairs. You're calling for business or pleasure?" she asked, her words slurring a bit.

"Business. I had gotten a call from Gilbert a few hours ago. His forensic team found something none of us can explain. I've got our guys looking at it to confirm," he said.

"What are you talking about?"

"Right, sorry for rambling. I'm exhausted. "You remember the security tapes at the airport of our suspect entering the men's room his face shielded by the brim of his baseball cap and then coming out, exposing his face to the security camera?"

"Yeah," she replied.

"Well, it looks like the first guy…"

"What do you mean, the first guy? There's a second guy?" she asked.

"That's what we don't know. The guy who comes out of the restroom ten minutes later is a different guy. He's shorter by around three or four inches. Even his pants don't fit him right," Matt said, his voice sounding tired.

"I think you and Gilbert have been smoking something. It's impossible," she said.

"I know. But you need to see it yourself. Get back here as soon as you can. I need your help," Matt said.

"I will. Make yourself a stiff drink and get some sleep. Things might look different in the morning."

41

Jill took her time drinking her martini after hanging up on her partner. She needed to let her mind and body chill, so she'd be able to get a good night's sleep.

Sitting behind her had been Eric Landers. He had been intrigued about her visit, and why the FBI wanted to talk to him. He liked having an advantage before any meeting, and one with such a beautiful woman had him enthralled. He knew he had done some insider trading, advised some clients to get out of a holding or two with some confidential backdoor information, but everyone he knew had done it at some time in their career. He was puzzled why the FBI, and not the SEC wanted to talk to him.

He watched her closely as she wobbled up from her chair, steadying herself on the small round table that held her empty glass. He smiled as she regained her balance and headed toward the elevators. He stood and quickly read her room number on the signed bill. He rushed toward the elevators. She got into one as he arrived. He decided to wait until the next transporter came.

As he got off the elevator, he noticed that she was still staggering toward her room. He thought about grabbing her and dragging her into her room for some drunken fun, but he liked his women more alert to his sexual calisthenics.

He saw that she had dropped her room keycard and quickly bent over to pick it up. "Here, I think you'll need this to get in," he said with a seductive grin.

Jill never looked up and grabbed the plastic key and opened her door. As she stepped in, he started to move toward her, but before he could get his hand on the door, she had kicked it shut in his face.

"Maybe tomorrow after dinner, my lucky lady," he said with an arrogant smile.

She had carefully dusted the card key, then affixed a clear tape over his thumbprint. She thought he looked familiar. His phony mustache and amateurish wig did not fool her. After making enough impressions of his thumb and index finger, she used her portable fax machine to send Peggy the fingerprint and find out who this jerk was that had been following her.

Emerson called her partner to tell him about the jerk and to find out how his interview with Richards had gone. She had forgotten to ask earlier.

Matt picked up on the first ring. "He had his attorney there?"

"Yes. Something about this guy is bothering me. You should have seen his hallway of shame. He had photos of the three women patients we are investigating. They all seem to have a unique relationship that goes beyond him being Richards being their cosmetic surgeon," Matt said. "His attorney said those photos came from charity events the doctor attended. I'm not buying that bull-shit," Matt said.

"It does seem strange. Something like a small club, with a big secret," said Jill. "Let's see what I can get out of Ms. Thomas tomorrow. She appears to come to San Diego every two weeks. I need some rest. I'll call you before I fly home."

"Okay. Be safe. Peggy gave me some detail on Lander's character. He's a real piece of work," Matt said.

"I know. I think scumbag followed me up to my room. Landers had a ridiculous disguise. This moron, after I dropped my keycard, picked it up. His prints are on Peggy's desk."

"This whole case is getting weirder and weirder. Sleep well," Matt said before disconnecting the call.

As Jill undressed, she looked in the mirror and noticed a few extra lines on her face. The crow's feet by the corner of her eyes had become more noticeable. "This job is killing my looks," she nit-picked to the reflection while standing there naked. "The body is still in good shape for thirty-nine-years. One more year to the big Four-O," she shook her head, thinking of her loneliness. Her tired thoughts only triggered her memories of the day Alex died.

It had been Jill's birthday, the magic number, thirty. Alex called that his DEA unit was taking down a drug smuggler, Alejandro Munoz. She had waited for an hour past the time he promised he'd be there. She knew in her profession, keeping appointments were impossible when you're on a case, and with Alex and the DEA stakeouts, often get postponed.

It had become so late that she told herself they could celebrate her birthday another day. When her cellphone rang at two in the morning, she thought it was Alex calling and forgot to look at the time.

With her voice gravely, she said. "You get tied up at your bust?"

"Agent Emerson, this is Assistant Director Connelly…"

Her heart sank, her eyes fluttered. She knew right away why Director was calling.

"I am sorry to inform you at this hour…" his words trailed off.

Jill fell back on her bed and waited for the formal words to tumble out of the Director's mouth. As she prepared to listen, her entire body started trembling.

"Agent Emerson, are you there?" he called out.

"Yes," she replied, sucking in a deep breath.

"There's been a horrible accident. The bust our team had gone on had been a trap. We lost four agents. Agent Alex Martin was one of the casualties. I'm very sorry for your loss," he said, trying to sound sincere. She understood in their business that death was part of the job.

"Thank you," she said, holding back her pain, and hung up.

Every birthday since then had become a constant reminder of Alex's death. Ten years later, the pain felt like it happened yesterday. The memory of Alex had painfully lingered inside her heart. It had become impossible for her to get close to any other man since then.

The Faces of Doctor Richards

She needed her rest. Breakfast was ordered from room service and scheduled for six-thirty in the morning. She looked at her watch. She thought that the four hours she had to rest would be more than enough. However, she didn't trust her internal alarm, and set-up her wake up call for five-thirty. She needed her one-hour and thirty-minutes to make herself presentable. The rest of the time, she'd check on how California had been holding up without her. She glided under the sheets and pulled the blanket up to her chin. She fell into a deep dream instantly.

42

Beth Thomas had been sitting at a table reading the Wall Street Journal when Jill arrived. She smiled at Emerson, extending her hand.

Emerson felt the firm handshake and returned the smile. "Thank you for taking the time to meet with me. I know you must have a busy schedule?" Emerson said congenially.

Beth folded her newspaper. "I'm more than happy to help the FBI. With all the corporate scandals rocking our financial world, I hope this meeting hasn't anything to do with my business practices. I run a tight ship and oversee all the accounting methods. My background is a CPA. So, if there were any shenanigans, I'd know about it first," she said. "Now, what can I do for you?"

Jill had begun to size up the woman. She never made assumptions or took anything for granted. She had to consider her a suspect until it could be proven otherwise.

"I'm sure you're aware of what has happened to three of your friends these last few weeks?" she stated, her tone relaxed and casual. "Two are presently missing, and one is dead."

Beth's face turned bedsheet white, as droplets of sweat accumulated on her forehead. She looked like she had sprung a leak. "Friends?" she said, rubbing her hands together, trying to act unaware.

Emerson could see Thomas was trying to play dumb. "Angelica Rathburn? Trish Morgan? Meg Cummings? Why do you think I know these women?"

She could see that Ms. Thomas had her gears moving at lightning speed, as she pursed her lips deep in thought. "I read about the two of the missing women you mentioned. Who'd you say was attacked? A Meg Cummings? Why would you be talking to me about this? I've been out of the country for the last nine days, cosmetic shows, and speaking engagements."

Jill knew she was lying about not knowing the women. She didn't know how to approach her about it without getting her to clam up. What Matt had told her last night about Richards, and the apparent relationship he seemed to have with all of them, it had alarm bells going off. Also, what Peggy had told her about Thomas' frequent trips to San Diego every two weeks was sending up flares.

Emerson kept her composure while she thought of more questions to ask. "In a search at Trish Morgan's house, we found a photo of five women with a tropical beach setting for its background?" she said. "Does that help your memory?"

Thomas was now rubbing her hands faster, looking like she was going to faint. "What photo. Tropical beach?"

Jill could not take it any longer and raised her voice. "Look, let's cut the crap. You're in the photo. I saw it. You know you're in the photo, so stop trying to play dumb." Emerson was ready to grab her by her throat.

"I'm not sure what photo you're talking about? I've been in a lot of pictures. I can't keep track of who takes one. I'm sorry I can't be of help," she said.

"Are you saying you've never met the women I've mentioned?" Emerson shot back, her tone harsher. "Please think a little harder. You do know that the FBI doesn't ask questions we don't already know the answers to," she said, leaning in closer. "Lying to the FBI can get you arrested."

Jill had noticed that Thomas had begun to sweat. It didn't take a rocket scientist to figure out she had gotten caught in a trap.

Emerson had begun sorting the questions she wanted to ask Thomas inside her mind. *What type of web had Thomas spun for herself that forced her not to be open about her relationship with these women? Was she hiding something? Was there a secret all of these women were hiding about Doctor Richards?* These were just a few questions that were bouncing around inside Jill's head.

"You seem jumpy and distracted, Ms. Thomas," Jill asked pointedly. "Let me continue making you feel even more uncomfortable. Why do you travel every two weeks, for the last three years, to San Diego? Each visit seems to be for only one day."

Thomas was now sweating profusely. "I'm disturbed you'd fly all the way here to harass me about your three victims and the model Lea Strong in some photo. I've told you I don't know these women, and can't help you any further," she now had gotten belligerent. "And, about my travels? It's none of your goddamn business," she cursed.

Jill stared at the angry CEO and smiled. She respected her for trying to throw her power around; it wasn't working on her. "Let's stop with your lies and begin telling the truth. I've got two missing women; I fear they are dead, and one that just died after she was attacked. You could be next?"

Thomas's face looked like it was about to explode. "How dare you accuse me of lying? If my life's in danger, then you should be talking to me about that, and not harassing me. You'll hear from my lawyers…"

Before she could continue her tirade, Emerson stopped her dead in her tracks. "You might be good at your job, but so am I. I never told you that Lea Strong was the fifth woman in the photo. So, can we start over, and get to the truth. I'm here because you have a connection with all of this, or you're on a hit list, and could be next."

Beth cupped her hands, trying to stop them from shaking, as she tried to bring her coffee cup to her rosy red painted lips. For the first time since Jill had sat down, she had seen a strong, self-confident, beautiful woman lose her composure. Her face had become moist, as the beads of sweat on her brow started to cascade down her cheeks like a raging waterfall. It had been evident that Beth Thomas, the CEO of one of the world's Fortune Top Fifty companies, had been trying hard to keep her emotions in check. The floodgates had started to leak, and her eyes filled with tears.

"I assure you that I had nothing to do with Meg's death or the disappearance of Angelica and Trish. Yes, we're all friends, and I like to keep our private lives just that, private. I'm sorry I lied, but you can check my itinerary, and see I wasn't even near California during the dates you asked me about." She had begun talking incoherently, her face writhing with fear thinking that her name could be on some killer's list.

Emerson looked down at a printout that Peggy had sent her about Beth's itinerary. "You might want to correct your last statement. It seems that you were in San Diego two weeks ago, right? I need you to level with me. You might be next. You have something in common with all these women: Doctor Todd Richards. Is there something about Doctor Richards someone would kill for?"

Her head slumped forward, hearing Doctor Richards name mentioned. "Doctor Richards? Sure, I know of him. Do you think I go to him?"

Having her face on his wall of shame was close enough for Emerson. "Your photo's hanging in doctor Richards's office."

Beth could not catch her breath. "Yes, I'm one of his patients. Now, I'm more concerned about being on a hit list? Is that the correct term?" she asked while her hands trembled.

Jill's eyes narrowed, wrinkling her forehead. "It's a guess, and yes, you can call it a *hit list*. Have you had any death threats recently? Can you think of anyone that would want to see you or any of your friends dead?"

Beth shook her head, deep in thought. "No. I have no enemies. Also, I've never heard any of my friend's talk of any." She had become very animated, pulling her long black hair tight behind her head and wrapping it in a ponytail. She then stood and removed her bright red blazer, revealing a soaked white silk blouse. "Damn, I'm a mess," she said, calling over the waitress, and asking for a Bloody Mary. "I hate drinking this early. But, today, I'll make an exception."

Emerson looked at her notebook. "If someone is targeting you, and your friends—there is only one common connection each of you shares: Doctor Richards. It might help with the other evidence we already have," Jill paused as she was not ready to press her about Doctor

Richards, and his relationship with all five ladies or that two of her friends were pregnant.

"Other evidence?"

"I can't talk about an ongoing investigation," she said.

"I understand. I can't think of a connection, except that we sometimes frequent the same parties. Angelica always invited us to her grand bashes. I've been on Trish Morgan's talk show, and once Meg Cummings had someone from her network interview me. That's about all I can think of at this time," she said, glancing at her watch. "I've got to go," she said, rubbing her hands on her blouse. "Can't talk about looking your best when I look like I just had a workout."

"Just one last question and I'll let you go. Did you know that Meg Cummings was pregnant? And, did you know who Lisa Beverly is?" The questions made Thomas gasp. She had begun rocking left and right in her chair.

"I'd rather not say at this time. I do not want to start a rumor. Furthermore, I do not want my name associated with Doctor Richards. I promote products that slow down the aging process. How would it look if I helped it along with a little nip and tuck? I'll talk to my lawyers and see what they will let me say about our relationship."

"Are you saying you are not a patient of Doctor Richards?"

"The whole world knows Doctor Richards. He's one of the best cosmetic surgeons in the world."

"Yes, he is, and very handsome too. Did you say you knew Lisa Beverly?" Jill asked again. Thomas looked like she was going to faint.

"Lisa Beverly? It doesn't ring a bell," she said.

"She was murdered in Bermuda two weeks ago, about the same time Trish Morgan went missing. She, too, was pregnant and could have a connection to all of you, as well as Richards. Could she have been a patient sharing some secret all of you seem to have?"

Beth jumped up, almost knocking over her chair. She was off-balance. She extended her hand, said goodbye, and marched toward the elevators.

159

Jill finished writing her notes and looked up. She had found out a lot of things, unfortunately for her case, nothing concrete. Beth Thomas knew the name Lisa Beverly and decided that pursuing that matter would be for another day.

She opened the plastic folder that contained her bill. She laughed when she saw that Thomas had stuck her for the breakfast and the drink she had.

She decided to spend the rest of her day in her room. She needed to make some important phone calls. Her first was to Matt to see how he had been doing. She looked at her watch, and it had been four hours since her breakfast meeting with Beth Thomas.

"St. Claire," he barked, concentrating on the TV monitor near his desk.

"Hey Matt, it's Jill. Miss me yet?" she teased. Then she heard him cursing.

"What the fuck," he shouted. "Are you watching CNN?"

"No. What's happening. Another terrorist attack?"

"Turn on your TV. You won't believe who just turned up."

43

When Thomas got to her room to change her blouse, she called Doctor Richards. She did not realize how early it was on the West Coast when she called. "Todd, we're fucked. The FBI knows we're all connected...even to Lisa Beverly," she said, unable to control her nervousness.

Richards looked at his clock on his dresser. "Calm down. Do know what time it is," he said, trying to comprehend what Beth was saying. "What are you talking about? Who at the FBI told you this?"

She looked at the card she had in her hand. "An agent Jill Emerson. She grilled me today about Angelica, Trish, Meg, and tied in Trish's alias, Lisa Beverly, who she says is dead. What's going on. Three of my friends, your special patients, are dead? Am I next?"

Richards didn't know what to say, or how to calm her down. "Let's keep our cool right now. If she knew about us, she would have said something. Let me think about all of this. I'll call you in a couple of days."

"You better. I'm thinking of hiring a bodyguard," she threatened.

"Don't do anything until I talk to you. Now go about your business, and stay composed," Richards said, ending the call.

His hands had started to shake. He needed to move ahead with his plan he was going to implement later today. He hoped it would get the FBI off his back.

44

Doctor Richards could not go back to sleep after the wakeup call from Beth Thomas. He had to get himself in the right mood for his next plan to work seamlessly.

He bounded out of bed. He thought this idea was genius.

After he got dressed, he went down to his lab and pulled out Angelica's full body nude shots. The before and after photos he had taken when she first came to him. He knew it would be perfect. He had never transformed into a woman before. His current situation called for drastic measures, and once again, he recited his favorite motto. "Chance favors the prepared mind."

If this worked, he was going to do it again as Trish Morgan. Then he realized with what Beth had told him about Lisa Beverly; he'd be foolish to become Trish while Beth was in the picture. He'd have to wait and deal with his Morgan problem at a later time.

Richards placed Angelica's photo inside the metal frame attached to the examination table. He laid back naked, ready to transform into Angelica Rathburn. He slowly injected a combination of his serum and her serum into his body, using a plastic neck cuff he had created for his self-injections. The needle opening on the mold was in the perfect location to enter his carotid artery.

Concentrating on her photo, he could feel the change taking place. After fifteen minutes, he stood, his balance unsteady. He looked at himself in the mirror.

"Perfect," he said, smiling, giving himself two thumbs up. "Now, he had to listen to Angelica's recorded voice so that he would sound like the actress."

She bounded upstairs to his bedroom, where Angelica and the other women kept extra clothing they'd need after their regular scheduled intimacy. Richards found a Victoria Secret push up bra and thong panties. He fumbled with the bra clasp but finally succeeded. Her panties were another story; Todd did not feel comfortable having an undergarment inside his butt cheeks. After putting on a White pantsuit and black leather flats, and a white large brim sun hat, he was ready to be Angelica Rathburn.

Before his office opened, Richards slipped out unnoticed wearing Angelica's clothing she had on the night she died. He had her handbag with all her items inside, including her house keys. Flagging down a cab and gave the driver to take him to Lindberg Field. He had gone to the commuter terminal for the puddle jump flight to Los Angeles.

Before he could get through the terminal at Lindbergh Field, Angelica's fans had noticed her. They started screaming her name. Richards buried his head, pulling the large white sun hat over his eyes, his hands feeling his new female features, and pushed his way from the taxi area and through the crowds of adoring fans.

A security guard had noticed the commotion. When he recognized who it was, he radioed for some help. He escorted Rathburn through a security door. The guard politely asked her to sit in a dingy unremarkable office until she could be escorted safely to her plane.

"Right. Yes, sir, good idea." He turned and faced Angelica and told her about the plan. She nodded. They were both moving toward an emergency exit where a security patrol car waited.

"Thank you so much, officer," Doctor Richards said, pleased with how much he sounded like Angelica.

As they walked down the metal stairs to the tarmac, the guard in a whisper, asked for her autograph. "It's for my wife. She's a big fan and will be so happy that you're not dead. You know, with all the news about you being missing?"

"You're cute," Richards said, touching the guard's cheek with the palm of his hand. Thanks for coming to my rescue."

Less than an hour later the same thing happened at LAX, this time airport security was able to get her away before she walked through the terminal. Richards got to Angelica's Malibu house in a limo. The driveway was mobbed with television network vans, reporters with cameras, and two police officers. The officers ordered everyone to move, and the crowd parted to both sides, letting the long black Mercedes enter her driveway. The police slid wooden barriers behind the limo as it parked in her driveway.

The hum of the reporter's voices blended into one loud buzzing as if she had stepped out next to a hive of swarming bees. Richards waved his arm and held up one finger, signally for all of them to give her a minute.

Raising his voice, he shouted to the reporters. "I'll talk to all of you in a quick moment," Richards shouted over their cacophony of sounds. He was so enthralled with how exact his voice was to Angelica's. "I need a moment to freshen up," he patted his face as Angelica would.

As Richards put the house key into the lock, a cold chill swept over his body. *Her fucking alarm. I don't know the password.* He had started searching through her wallet, tossing photos and miscellaneous papers about, as panic had set in. All her junk went to the bottom of the purse, and then he found it. *How stupid*," he said, glancing at the security company's business card. On the back was her numeric security code and password, in case the alarm went off accidentally, and the security company needed verification that the person they would be speaking to was, in fact, Angelica Rathburn.

He turned the key and pushed on the door. He heard a beeping sound that was not near the front door. He headed toward the sound of the rapid beeps, not knowing how many seconds he had before the alarm went off. Breathing hard, he finally found the keypad by the garage door entryway. He pressed in zero-four-two-zero and was relieved when he heard the digital voice repeat, *system disarmed.*

He was in her house for the first time. He scanned his surroundings to get the lay of the floorplan. Inside her bedroom was a double door walk-in closet. He found a green summer dress and a pair of sandals. He looked at his…no Angelica's gorgeous body. He decided not to put on any undergarments. Again, something he knew she would have done.

Looking at Angelica in the mirror, totally naked, had gotten him aroused. He looked down to see if he had an erection. He had forgotten that his penis had disappeared during the transformation. Nevertheless, he felt stimulated, why he did not know, as he was a nervous wreck.

He walked out of the closet, touching wetness between his legs. He noticed all of Angelica's adult toys by the nightstand. A strange thought flashed inside his brain. Then, he reprimanded himself. *First, handle the press, and then check things out*, as weird ideas consumed his mind.

He opened the front door and prayed his performance would go over convincingly. He gracefully walked toward the clicking cameras, letting the sundress flow against his naked body. The dress was sheer, and with the sun's rays beaming on his partially covered female body, it revealed he had nothing on underneath. He wanted every male reporter focused on Angelica's nakedness, not her face. The cameras snapped incessantly, sounding like a swarm of crickets.

"I know how concerned everyone has been about my going into hiding. I love that all my fans were concerned for my safety, but this will be the last public appearance I'll be making for some time. I needed time to think about my future. I've accomplished everything I've ever wanted, and by the grace of God, I thank the wonderful people who had given me the magnificent roles I was fortunate to play. I will not give any of you my reasons for this abrupt retirement at this time. I hope you'll respect my privacy. I'll pose now for your cameras, so take your best shots, because I won't permit any further intrusions into my life. I'm tired and burnt out." In typical Angelica fashion, she waved, and spun around, giving them one last look at the movie industry's most beautiful body.

45

Richards had collapsed on Angelica's super-king size bed. He was amazed by how his body had fully become female. He had never imagined his serum could do a gender change. He was happy it worked so well for his plan.

His brain was on overdrive wondering if his hybrid serum, combined with a female hybrid, had made the change possible.

He opened his eyes, letting his thoughts swim with what he was feeling now. Angelica's bed pointed toward the ocean and beach. He noticed the cameramen had taken to that position, snapping photos at the house, hoping to get a great picture of the famous actress.

He stood, realizing he had no privacy. "Damn, no curtains. Shit, she's an exhibitionist."

He might have the body and voice of Angelica, but he still had his modesty. He rushed away from the bed and went inside her large walk-in closet. He was pleased it had a semblance of privacy away from her *open for public viewing* master bedroom. He went inside her all-glass bathroom and was relieved when he noticed there were no windows.

"Thank god. I can take a shower in private." He wiggled his shoulders, and the loose dress fell to the floor. He kicked off his sandals, feeling very feminine. He started the shower. His mind was still that of a man's, but his mannerisms were that of a woman. He was baffled, as well as curious about what had happened to him.

The shower stall was in the middle of the bathroom, surrounded by clear glass that didn't seem to fog as the hot spray from the showerhead pounded his back. No matter how he turned, he could see Angelica's lean curved body in the mirrors that bordered her bathroom. Her breasts were firm, and her nipples hard. As Richards washed his body with soap gel, it created a strange but pleasant sensation he had never felt when he showered as a man. He was becoming aroused again.

He began to slowly massage Angelica's breasts, lightly pinching her nipples with enough pressure to radiate goosebumps over his entire body. He knew that she had liked it when they made love, but he never understood why until now. As he moved his hand between his legs, the lubrication from the gel touched his clitoris, causing his knees to buckle. His legs felt like rubber.

He was enjoying what he was experiencing. He kept gently rubbing, increasing the rhythm with each stroke of his middle finger. Again, he recalled how Angelica like how he had aroused her, but he never imagined it was this good.

He had watched many times Angelica's facial expressions while they made love, but now he was on the receiving end of what she might have been experiencing. Richards had loved sex with her, but never felt as good as he was feeling right then.

Richards had to lean against the glass wall to hold himself up as an explosion of pleasure blanketed his body. He kept rubbing and felt another burst and then another. "Shit," he gasped for air. "Women are fucking lucky."

After another five minutes, he had lost count of the orgasms he had had. He slid slowly to the shower's basin. He could not catch his breath from what he had just experienced. Finally, he was able to stand, and he turned off the hot water.

He patted his body dry and wrapped himself in a thick cream-colored terry robe. He stood over the bathroom sink looking at Angelica's beautiful face. For the first time since she died, his conscience got the best of him.

"I'm so sorry," he said. He watched Angelica's head nod and believed she had forgiven him. His body was unsteady. He flopped down on a leather recliner inside the walk-in closet.

After thirty minutes, he got up. He had begun searching for things. Anything that he thought a person like Actress Angelica Rathburn would take on a long trip.

Richards nervously started grabbing whatever clothing he could find and stuffed them in a hard-shell suitcase. In one of the drawers of her nightstand, he found her jewelry and a life-size vibrator shaped like a penis.

He gave it a light squeeze, and it had begun to vibrate—startling him letting it fall on the thick, light gray carpet. To his surprise, the dildo stopped vibrating.

Holding his manly part was one thing, but playing around with another, even though it was fake, gave him the shivers. He had recalled the shower incident and decided he had to see what some women think is better than the real thing.

He dropped his robe and laid back on the settee in the closest. He was nervous, as he placed the rubber device gently on his thigh, moving it slowly up toward Angelica's vagina. He started with slow circular movements until he felt the moisture between his legs return. He slowly inserted the tip and felt a reflex that caused the dildo to vibrate. The same sensation he felt in the shower rushed over him faster than the first time. As he inserted the rubber penis deeper, he had instinctively started moving it in and out, increasing the speed, never allowing the tip to pop out. After thirty minutes, he was exhausted and dropped it in her small suitcase.

He put on some denim shorts and a tank top and fell asleep inside the closet. "Let's remember why we're here," he scolded himself. "Enough experimenting."

Before he dozed off, he started planning on how he'd bring Trish Morgan back. Beth Thomas was an obstacle that he needed to resolve before his second resurrection took place. If his plan worked then, Jeff Peters would be on the FBI's most-wanted list.

46

"Are we wasting our time or what?" Jill shouted into her cellphone. Next thing, we'll see Trish Morgan turning up somewhere."

Matt grunted as he looked at their three files, and the evidence he had on his desk. "I guess that changes this whole serial killer theory. Perhaps Meg Cummings was just a drug deal gone bad?"

"Give me a break, Sherlock," she said. "What drug dealer would use Xanax to kill a client? Right now, we still have the Meg Cummings murder case and a sketch of a suspect. Also, Trish Morgan is still missing."

Matt understood his partner's frustration. He saw it frequently in many of their cases. He, too, was perplexed about all of this. "You're forgetting," he said. "We still have the American woman Gilbert had shipped off to us. Similar MO to Cummings. We have photos of the two men entering Lisa Beverly's room. Maybe we can connect the dots and find that killer?"

"Remember what I told you about Beth Thomas, and her reaction when she heard Lisa Beverly's name. There's something there. I'm sure of it, but what?" Jill said.

Matt was wrapping up his conversation with Jill when Peggy dropped a thick file on his desk. He looked up at her and thanked her. The bio she handed him was on Doctor Richards. "Peggy just dumped a big file on my desk. Let me read it over. I can brief you later," he said.

Jill sighed. "Great. Also, can you go over and talk to Angelica and find out where she's been? She might know where Morgan might be too.

See if she'll talk about her relationship and her friend's relationship with Doctor Richards. Something fishy is going on at his office. I can feel it in my gut. I still think they all have a little secret they don't want to go public. Maybe it's for free cosmetic surgery for sexual favors? Richards is a hunk," she said.

"Better idea. I'll hold off on Richards's file. It can wait until we both can look it over together."

"I should be back on the West Coast tomorrow late morning," Jill said.

"What else did you find out about Beth Thomas? What did she say about the connection they all have with Doctor Richards?"

"She's cagey. She won't say anything until she talks to her lawyer. Something about her reputation, you know, being in the cosmetic business. I hate talking to spoiled bitches with too much money and power. I'm meeting with Eric Landers today over dinner. Might be nothing more than a fling with Lisa Beverly. I want to see what's up with this guy. I'll call you this evening with his story. Have fun at Angelica's," she teased.

"Yeah, right," he answered.

47

The drive to Malibu to interview Angelica Rathburn took under an hour using Sunset Blvd to the coast. He got there at six o'clock. A handful of media trucks were still outside the actress's house. The police had gone. Matt noticed a black Lincoln Limo jutting out of her driveway.

Before Matt could get to the front door, he heard a man's voice from the back of the house shouting profanities. Pushing open the front door and stepping inside the foyer, he drew his gun. He followed the loud voices toward the back of the house, his revolver in his right hand, pointing down at the floor.

He called out, identifying himself, "FBI," he shouted. He remembered when he, and Emerson had been searching Angelica's home, the kitchen, and a small sitting room occupied the part of the house where the yelling was coming from.

He heard a woman's voice talking, as the loud man turned abusive with his words. As Matt stepped into the kitchen, he saw two men, both in dark suits and Angelica.

Rathburn was seated at the kitchen table, and the obnoxious short chubby man was standing over Angelica shaking his finger. The other man that was standing had his arms crossed. He must have been at least six foot six, two hundred eighty pounds of solid muscle—bodyguard Matt thought.

The bulky man saw St. Claire and reached inside his jacket. Matt pointed his pistol at the Mack Truck, who he imagined could break him in half like a twig. He waved his ID shaking his finger at the bodyguard,

171

signaling the man to show his hands. He wished Jill was there for back up. He looked at Angelica. She was acting upset.

St. Claire raised his voice and commanded. "Slowly get your fucking hands over your head," he ordered the man yelling. "Little man, with the big ugly mouth, step away from Ms. Rathburn," he shouted. Matt's veins on his forehead were bulging. He continued to flash his FBI badge with his left hand at the two men while pointing his gun at the unsmiling linebacker.

"Who the fuck are you?" the short obnoxious man yelled back.

"FBI. Are you deaf and blind too? I've identified myself already," he said, folding his badge. "Miss Rathburn, are you all right?" He could see that she was beginning to calm down.

"I'm Joseph McMillan, the owner of McMillan studios where this bitch has three years left on her contract," he said, his face puffing out like a bright red balloon.

Matt looked at Angelica and spoke. "Do you want these assholes to leave?"

She nodded. "I told this terrible man that my lawyers would be in contact with his lawyers…they can work things out. But he doesn't take no for an answer. Please make them leave, now," she said, holding back her sobs.

St. Claire kept his gun pointed at the bodyguard, giving both men a command. "When a lady says no, she means no. Now get the fuck out of here, and let the lawyers do all the shouting."

McMillan got in the last word, as he and his guard stormed out. "You'll never work another day in Hollywood, or anywhere in the world with this stunt you've pulled. By the time we're through with you, every penny you have will go to your attorneys."

She looked up at Matt and touched his hand. "Thanks. You're my hero. Can I get you something to drink?" Richards was seething having to be sweet to the bastard who had caused him grief the other day. He had to keep the charade going for a little while longer so his plan would work.

"Just water," he replied. "I need to ask you some questions if you're up to it?"

"Oh, that old frump. His bark is worse than his bite. Ask away. I'm sure I know what your questions are going to be."

Matt sat down at the kitchen table and looked at his notes. "Since you disappeared, your studio called in some presidential favors. I've…I mean, my partner and I have been handling your case."

She put her hand to her forehead and feigned a shocked look. Richards knew his acting abilities wouldn't improve because he looked like Angelica. "I have a case. Oh, my goodness," Richards said dramatically.

"Can you tell me where you've been for the last three weeks?

"I'm sorry to say I can't. I wanted to see if I could stay away from all my crazy fans and the pesky media. I found the perfect location. Unless it's a crime not to tell you, I'd like to keep my secret hiding place. You know a secret." Richards's thoughts went to Angelica's burial at sea. I hope you understand.

Matt nodded, his eyes focusing on his notebook. "One last question. We found some photos of you with Trish Morgan. I assume you two are friends? Would you know where she might be? She's been missing a little over three weeks now. She's not at your secret hideaway too?"

"No. I had last seen Trish right before I left. She didn't tell me where she was going. I know she's been under a lot of pressure like me. It's not easy being a successful woman in today's world," he said. "It's feasible she's found a secret hiding place somewhere too?"

St. Claire stood and thanked Angelica, enjoying the feel of her slender hand. He was surprised when she stood and gave him a wet kiss on his lips. Then, she pulled away.

"I'm so sorry. I felt grateful you had come when you did. I loved how forceful you were with your gun pointing at McMillian. It's so big and powerful," she swooned. "Are all FBI agents as macho and strong like you?"

Matt was now blushing. "I've got to go. Thanks for your time. I'm glad you're okay. I'm disappointed I won't be enjoying any more of your films."

"If you stay awhile, we can pretend we're making a movie," Richards said seductively.

St. Claire was in his car, speeding back to his office. His heart wouldn't stop pounding until he was back in his office. His excitement would not subside either, as he kept adjusting his seatbelt.

* * * * *

Richards couldn't stop laughing. That was so perfect. He hoped the media, camped out on the beach, got all the action. "He's going to have some explaining to do tomorrow," he roared.

Doctor Richards wanted to lay out his next plan for how to bring Trish Morgan back into the picture, but first needed to deal with Beth Thomas? He knew it would be tricky since the Bermuda authorities had the body of Lisa Beverly.

48

Jill glanced at her watch as her phone rang. It was Matt calling. She had fifteen minutes before she met with Eric Landers. She couldn't believe her ears about what her partner was saying.

"She did what to you, and you didn't stay. You're a fool?" Jill teased.

"Rathburn is still a victim on our case we haven't close yet. It's totally against FBI rules. Also, she's too much woman for me. I was afraid I wouldn't be able to perform like the studs in her life. Please, let's forget about this. Will you keep it to yourself? Right?"

"Sure, Casanova. I guess you haven't read a newspaper or watched the news yet?"

"What are you talking about?"

"Oh, I don't want to spoil it for you. Find a TV, and have a stiff drink in your hand," she said, laughing. "Now, tell me what you've got?"

Jill listened intently to what he had to report about Angelica's whereabouts, and her refusal to disclose her secret location. She was disappointed that Doctor Richards was not turning out to be a viable suspect.

Matt filled her in on the file that Peggy had put together for him. "Yes, Richards is that smart. He was one of the leading biochemists in the world. He was working with Professor Franklin at UCLA ten years ago. There's nothing this guy can't do," Matt said. "It seems that when his wife, Molly, was diagnosed with cervical cancer, he had become obsessed with finding a cure for her, using fetal stem cells. Then, when

Congress passed legislation banning all forms of abortions, as well as any research using fetal stem cells, Richards went off the deep end."

"Deep end? What do you mean?" Jill asked.

"The project he was heading up at UCLA was for the CIA and Defense Department. They, without any reason, dissolved his research and closed his lab. The reason he had to resign was that he wouldn't back off using fetal stem cells he took from his lab monkey's fetus. Richards left angry and broke all ties with his friend and mentor, Professor Franklin."

"Why is his leaving relevant to our investigation?" Jill sounded puzzled.

"I'm not sure, but listen to this," Matt said. "While on his own, he turned his attention to cosmetic surgery and bought his mixed-use building in La Jolla. He's petitioned Congress numerous times to allow him to use fetal stem cells from fetuses at morgues. He asserted he was close to finding a cure for cancer, as well as other diseases."

"Why would a brilliant bio-chemist turn to cosmetic surgery?" Jill asked.

"I don't have an answer for that, but he kept up his research he had been doing at UCLA," Matt took a deep breath. "He's a persistent guy. He kept doing his experiments and was interviewed numerous times for pestering coroners in the greater San Diego and Los Angeles counties for fetuses. He was never found guilty of breaking the law, so no formal charges had ever been made. Now, he practices his cosmetic surgery on celebrities," St. Claire said. "One thing he did create was a serum he uses on his regular patients, the affluent ones. This magic potion takes away all the wrinkles they have. It's better and safer than Botox. He charges $5000 per monthly infusion."

"What about our five celebrities. Do they use this new serum?"

"Not that I can see. All these appointments are after hours," Matt said. "Very secretive."

"This case does not make any sense. Five women, all celebrities, one dead, who was pregnant, and all of them seeing Richards outside his normal business hours. Do you think he created a different serum for these ladies? Maybe one that requires fetal stem cells?"

Matt signed. "I hope not. I don't want to think about what he might be doing with these women. I'm exhausted from all of this. Nothing's making sense."

"Let's do a paternity test on Cummings' fetus," Jill said. "I have a hunch Richards' could be the father. He could be aborting these pregnancies and using their fetuses for his research?"

"No way," Matt said. "I can't believe any woman would get pregnant and intentionally abort her baby for free cosmetic work. Shit, no fucking way. They would be arrested and locked away."

"I don't think so either. Nevertheless, it's a lead we should pursue. It's possible these women, for the promise of eternal youth, would break the law? It's just a theory we can explore," Jill said. "Let's get the paternity test done, and then we can go from there. Also, do the same for Lisa Beverly's fetus."

"No way I can get that to happen. It will take a court order from a judge. What reason should I give?"

"Think of something," she said.

"Look, I'm wasted," Matt said, releasing a chest full of tension. "Let's talk tomorrow when you're back. Meet at your place?" he said while clicking on his TV. "Oh, shit. I'm on TV with Angelica Rathburn. You knew about this?"

"Yes. It will be great for your image. Now you'll have tons of women running after you."

"I don't need this crap. See you tomorrow."

Jill could not contain her giggles. "Fine. You know where I hide the key. Let yourself in and leave me some Gin to drink. I'll need it."

Matt sighed. "This case is getting to you too?"

"I hate this case. Nothing's making any sense. We have no solid leads; we have nothing," Jill said.

"Spoken like one of the guys. I'll bring some chips and dip. We'll have a party, and figure things out," Matt said, sounding tired.

"I'd like that," she replied and ended the call.

49

Eric Landers had gotten to his interview with Agent Emerson early. He had been seated for over thirty minutes at Henry's Bar & Grille in SOHO. The restaurant-bar had an after-work crowd who were loudly chattering about their day.

Jill knew that if she were not on the clock, this place would be right up her alley. She was curious about how this stockbroker would handle himself since their first awkward meeting in her hotel hallway.

She had seen him wave at her, realizing he was an idiot. *He's acting as if we've met before.* She had him pegged as an egotistical blowhard. Jill ignored his erratic waving arm and checked out the large L-shaped bar that had drinkers three deep. The colorful art on the walls and the rough, unfinished ceiling reflected the quaintness of that section of Manhattan.

Jill walked gracefully toward the hostess, slid her body left, then right, and then right again, weaving her way through the mob of people waiting to be seated. Her target the woman who had been taking names for the dinner crowd. She turned her head away from Eric, and his ridiculous animated gestures he kept making trying to get her attention. She showed the hostess a photo of Eric. When the woman checked her list, she found the name Landers on her reservations sheet and pointed toward his table.

Only then did Jill look up and acknowledge the foolish actions he had been making. With a casual wave of her hand, she moved toward him, unsmiling, and ready for business.

"Miss. Emerson?" he asked, puzzled.

Jill flipped open her FBI badge before she spoke. "Yes. And you must be Mr. Landers. Thanks for agreeing to meet me on such short notice. I'll only take a few minutes of your time, and let you be on your way," she said, noticing the disappointment on his face.

His brow had wrinkled. He was acting out of sorts. "I thought we were having dinner?"

With icy eyes, Jill spoke. "You thought that? I only wanted to talk to you about an active murder case. If you assumed…" she hesitated, thinking better of her response. "Well, I'm sorry for the misunderstanding. I have to get packed and back to Los Angeles in the morning."

"Can we at least have some appetizers and a drink?" he asked, putting on some bullshit charm.

She nodded, forcing a smile. "That'll be fine. I'll have a…" He interrupted.

He remembered the martini she had been drinking the other night. "I bet I know the drink you want? Let me guess," he said, pressing his index finger to his lips, "a Gin Martini?"

"Hate them," she said. I'll have a beer, a Blue Moon." She loved the puzzled look he had on his face.

Landers acted bewildered. He signaled for the waitress and ordered their drinks. "First time I'd been wrong," he bragged.

"Maybe you should hone up on your stalking skills," she said, tossing him three photos she had taken of him, as he sat in the Marriott bar with his phony mustache and wig. "Next time you follow an FBI agent to her room, you might get shot," she said, opening her jacket and exposing her holstered gun.

He looked like he was about to faint. He had begun to tremble. "How…?"

"I'm that good. That's all you need to know. Now for my questions." She watched his body go limp as she rattled off what was on her mind.

"First, tell me about your relationship with Lisa Beverly?"

He almost fell off his chair at hearing her name. "Lisa Beverly? Murder case? What the fuck?"

"Don't play dumb. I have your fingerprints, and I'm sure your DNA from her hotel room in Bermuda where someone killed her. You, by all indications, are the last person to have seen her alive."

"You think I did it? We're only lovers. We meet a few times a year at the Princess Hotel in Bermuda. When it's over, we go our separate ways. That's the truth. I know nothing more about her than what I could discover during our romantic interludes."

"Where were you two nights ago?"

"Shit. I don't remember."

"Were you in San Diego?" she asked. Jill could see he was ready to pee in his pants.

"Yes," he replied, his voice trembling. "I was visiting my sister in Hillcrest. How did you know?" Beads of sweat pooled on his forehead.

"Just a lucky guess. Do you know, I mean, did you know Meg Cummings?" she asked without taking a breath. By his reaction, she had pressed a button.

He stood, rage exploding on his face. "Now, you're going to pin that murder on me too. I'm leaving," he sprang up, his chair almost knocking over their server carrying their drinks.

Emerson was not impressed at his outburst. With a snap of her finger, she signaled him to sit back down. "I'm not moved by your melodramatics. I'm interviewing you about two murder cases you seem to have been in the general vicinity of, and close to the time, these women had died. She thought it best not to tell him too much about the FBI's involvement with Lisa Beverly.

Landers' hands were still shaking as he stood frozen over their table. "Do I need a lawyer," he said, his voice trembling.

"You can do that," she said. If I were you, I'd sit my ass down and answer my fucking questions before I drag you down to our local field office. I think this environment is more conducive to the line of questions I have. Once I log you in at the field office, it could take days, maybe weeks, before you're out of there. Processing is a bitch with our ongoing active terrorist alert programs, and all the material witnesses we're hauling in by the truckloads." She knew most of what she had said was bullshit. He didn't, and that's all that mattered to her.

He moved his chair back and flopped down. He looked like a guilty man.

"Did you see Meg Cummings during your stay in San Diego?"

"Yes. We had coffee. We're High School friends. Nothing more. We've always kept in touch, reunions, and things like that. I've been distraught ever since I heard about her murder."

"Then you must know her parents?" Jill kept writing in her note pad while she asked her questions.

"Her father died a long time ago. I never knew him. Yeah, I know her mother. She lives in Pacific Beach with her new husband." Eric's trembling body was losing all degree of control. He kept looking around the restaurant, his eyes bulging, darting left and right.

"You did call her mother and offer your condolences?" she asked coldly. Jill's expression was emotionless as she listened to the pathetic man she had been interviewing for the last thirty minutes.

He had started to stutter, searching for the words to say. He hung his head, shaking it slowly. "No. I've been busy with the fluctuating stock market. I was planning on going to the funeral," he said, trying to act convincingly remorseful.

"How would you know when and where the funeral would be held?"

Landers was hyperventilating. "I'm done here. Am I under arrest? If not, then you can talk to my lawyer. I feel you're trying to entrap me. I didn't kill anyone. I might be a bastard, but I'm not a killer," he stood, this time knocking over his chair as he stormed out of the restaurant.

Jill made a few more notes. Then she lifted his empty beer bottle and placed it inside a plastic evidence bag. She had gotten the DNA she needed. It might be possible that he's the father of Beverly's dead baby? If so, she knew Richards would be off the hook for that murder too.

The appetizers had come. The waitress had a puzzled look on her face as she placed the stuffed potato skins, a second beer, and Jill's second Blue Moon they had ordered. The waitress looked sympathetic to

Jill's uncomfortable situation, as she organized the drinks, and food on
the small table

"I couldn't help noticing him storm out. Relationships have their ups
and downs. If he's worth it, try to work it out," she said, her head tilted in
a consolatory pose, as her fat lower lip drooped.

Jill gave her an icy stare. "Not a boyfriend. Just business. And, yes,
he's a bastard."

Emerson looked at the bill and grinned. *Second time today I've been
stuck with the tab. Miller's going to be pissed.*

She needed to understand Landers' relationship with Lisa Beverly and
Meg Cummings. It was essential to her case so she could rule him out as
the murderer.

She paid her bill and flagged a taxi. She decided to go to the FBI's
field office in Manhattan and have them run a DNA test on Eric Lander's
beer bottle. She had a bad feeling about the guy. Maybe, he wasn't right
for the murders of Lisa Beverly, or Meg Cummings, however, after what
he had done the other night in her hotel hallway, he might be right for
some other crimes against women. She knew of many older unsolved
crimes with coincidental DNA could get solved. If nothing turned up,
then she'd move on with what she still had with her existing files.

* * * * *

Back at her hotel room, she had started to pack as she talked to Matt
about what had transpired with Eric Landers. He praised her for checking
him out for other crimes, but really couldn't see him as a suspect for the
Beverly and Cummings murder.

"I should be back at my house tomorrow late afternoon around five.
See you then," she said, a sad tone in her voice.

"Hey, wait a minute, partner. You can't leave me like this.
Something's wrong. Spill it." Matt could be, at times, sensitive to her
moods and knew her better than anyone.

"It's an Alex thing. Something tonight triggered a few memories. I'm
fine now, just tired and wanting a good night's sleep. I promise I'll tell

you all about it tomorrow, over drinks. You can become my shrink again."

50

Inside an interview room at the San Diego FBI field office, a short petite woman waited for two FBI agents, who were part of the new Strategic Abortion Crime Unit, to arrive. She sat sipping the strong coffee they had given her, her hands trembling, shaking drops of the hot liquid on her fingertips.

She had started to have second thoughts about what she was about to say. She considered herself a good Christian. Her religious conscience put her in a horrible position with her employer and the doctor she respected. Ever since the new federal abortion law was legislated, making fetal stem cell research a crime, she felt proud that she was instrumental in its passing. Her protests at abortion clinics, she believed, had been rewarded by God and the United States government. It was a blessing for her when she became a nurse for a cosmetic surgeon, Doctor Todd Richards, in La Jolla.

She kept mulling over what she had heard and how she would present it to the agents. She was sure about what she had overheard in the reception room a few weeks ago by the three patients of Doctor Richards and felt it was her civic and religious duty to file a report.

The FBI bulletins were explicit. It required people to anonymously file a complaint to SACU, Strategic Abortion Crimes Unit. If a report proved worthy and credible, they would investigate. She had prayed every day that God would guide her to make the right decision. After the disappearance of Angelica Rathburn and Trish Morgan, what she had heard still had her worried, even though Angelica was now back home.

Now, with Meg Cummings being murdered, it was her sign from God that she had to say something. Doctor Richards kept missing appointments, could not account for his whereabouts when asked ever since Rathburn and Morgan had gone missing. It was not his normal behavior, and she had to tell someone of her suspicions.

She put her coffee cup down when the two agents carrying yellow pads entered the room. Carolyn Hollister wanted to jump up and run out of the building after seeing the two FBI agents walk into the small cubicle. She bowed her head as the agents sat down across from her.

Hollister could not muster a smile or speak. She prayed that they would guide her.

"We're happy you've come down to our office. It's tough to find people as brave as you, who'll put themselves on the line for something as serious as illegal abortions," said FBI agent Amy Verduzco. Her partner agent Forrest Patch sat silent, his arms crossed, his eyes riveted on the plain woman in the yellow-floral print dress.

Carolyn answered, her voice cracking as she looked down at her sweaty hands. "I hope I'm not overreacting. I have been thinking about what I overheard, and maybe I might have misunderstood what the women were saying." Ms. Hollister's eyes were focused only on the female agent. She had found the male agent's unsmiling demeanor uncomfortable.

Agent Patch had no patience for people like her, and sat up straight, startling Carolyn. "Either you have something to tell us, or you don't. We don't have time to listen to exaggerated stories. If we go out, and what you've told us proves to be false, it could be embarrassing, even damaging to people's reputation." His harsh tone had caused her to start crying.

She tried to control her sniffling, using a Kleenex from the box agent Verduzco pushed in front of her. "Thank you," she said, her voice trembling. "I don't want to hurt or cause anyone any trouble. I am a good Christian woman, and my conscience won't let me turn my back and look the other way when babies' lives are at stake. If the doctor I'm working for is contributing to murdering innocent babies, well, I have to say something."

Agent Verduzco leaned forward. "Miss Hollister, you haven't told us who you think has committed a crime?"

"Oh, I'm so sorry. I'm very nervous. My employer, Doctor Todd Richards, might be doing abortions at his medical clinic. I'm sure I overheard Trish Morgan, you know the TV celebrity who's missing, tell Angelica Rathburn, who was missing, but now she's not," she paused, holding up her finger. "I have something to tell you about that also," Hollister was now rambling. She took in a deep nervous breath before continuing. "Ms. Morgan said that she was pregnant and that after her serum injection, she was going to have an abortion."

"What gave you the impression that Doctor Richards was going to do the abortion?" Agent Verduzco asked, confused. "She's probably off somewhere having the abortion. Maybe another country?"

"I might be mistaken. However, I am sure I heard the ladies talking that Doctor Richards needed the fetus for his research with their serum experiments. It has something to do with their bi-monthly shots. I'm horrified. Since these patients come in every two weeks for their serum injections, a hideous thought popped into my head," she paused again, almost hyperventilating. "Perhaps all of the other women let Doctor Richards abort their babies for free cosmetic work."

Verduzco rolled her eyes at her partner, shaking her head incredulity. She saw Patch making circular motions with his finger up near his ear.

"What women? If it's not Trish Morgan and Angelica Rathburn. Who else?"

Hollister acted rattled. "I'm not making any sense, am I? Maybe I should go now? I might have misunderstood everyone?"

Agent Patch was losing his patience. "Can you tell us the other women you think are having abortions?"

"Well, Trish Morgan, for sure. I think Angelica Rathburn, Lea Strong, Beth Thomas, and…" she paused to blow her nose. "Meg Cummings. So sad, she's now dead."

"What makes you believe that these women are aborting their fetuses for free cosmetic surgery?" Verduzco asked.

"I do the billing for all of the doctor's patients, and none of these five ladies have ever paid Doctor Richards any money since I've worked for him. It's been well over eight years. Right after his wife died of cancer, she had terminal cancer and was pregnant too," she said, acting as if they knew. "It affected him losing his wife, and their baby boy Mrs. Richards had been carrying."

Agent Patch needed to move on with all of this. He stood pacing around the table where Hollister sat. "Do you have anything to support what you're saying?"

She pulled some folded papers out of her yellow straw purse with a big Sunflower on the front flap. "Here. I've made notations next to the women that are dead or missing." She again spoke, as if they understood.

Agent Verduzco sat up, as agent Patch had stopped talking.

They both spoke in unison.

"Dead? Missing?" Patch deferred to his partner to ask the sixty-four-thousand-dollar question, his hands stuffed inside his pant pockets. "When did this all happen?"

"It's been on the news almost every day," she said, puzzled. "I thought that all FBI agents communicated with each other?"

"There are other agents on this case?" Agent Patch raised his voice. He was at the end of his rope with this woman and lost control. "So why the fuck are you here and not talking to the agents working on those cases?" he said, frustrated.

"You have a foul mouth, Agent Patch. I'm a lady and do not like your language. I should forget about all of this. I thought I was supposed to call you so I could talk anonymously. That's what the news bulletin said on the TV."

Before she could say another word, Verduzco took control of the interview and the volatile situation. "Forrest, go grab us all a fresh cup of coffee," she said sweetly. He had seen her that way many times and knew he should leave the room immediately.

"I don't like him," Carolyn said, pursing her lips tight.

"He's a good agent. He needs help with his manners. I'm sorry about his behavior. You did do the right thing coming to us. I'm very much interested in what you have to say. Tell me about the other FBI agents. Do you know their names?"

Miss Hollister fumbled again inside her purse, looking for something. "Here it is," she passed it over to Verduzco.

"I know them. Those agents mostly deal with kidnappings and abductions. Why were they talking to Doctor Richards?"

"They appeared right after Angelica Rathburn, and Trish Morgan were reported missing. Then, they came by to see Doctor Richards after Meg Cummings was murdered. I guess they figured out that Doctor Richards was their doctor," she said, shrugging her shoulders.

Agent Verduzco still appeared puzzled at all of this. "I'm only familiar with Angelica Rathburn's case. Now she's back safe and sound. Why do you have a question mark next to her name?"

"She didn't have her new tattoo. Before she had disappeared, she showed me this delicate, but tastefully drawn tattoo chain that went completely around her waist. The Angelica Rathburn that was at her house the other day did not have that tattoo. You can see it plain as day through her sinful dress she wore while the media took pictures of her. One other peculiar thing. She had a weirdly shaped birthmark on the lower portion of her back. Ms. Rathburn…" she took out a photo of her she had taken from her file… "see, she doesn't have a birthmark in this photo."

"It has now become popular for people to remove unwanted tattoos with laser surgery and add birthmarks to their bodies. Something I'm sure Doctor Richards is qualified to do?"

"She had gotten the tattoo only sixty days ago. After all the pain she said she had gone through, I don't believe she'd have it removed," Carolyn said. "Why would she put such a hideous birthmark on her back like that? It does not make any sense."

"Who do you think it was at Rathburn's house if it was not her?"

"I don't know. When all of this started, you know hearing about the abortions, well, while I was outside in my car crying and trying to calm down so I could drive safely," she paused to catch her breath. "I saw a woman I didn't recognize leave by the side door at Doctor Richards office."

"Another patient?"

"No, not a patient, I know. I've never seen her before." Hollister had begun combing her fingers through her hair. "She had on Ms. Morgan's clothing, or what seemed like her clothing, but it wasn't Trish."

Agent Verduzco was beginning to believe Hollister was crazy. She stood, extending her hand. "Thank you so much for coming forward. I think we've got enough to start a quiet investigation. Thanks for your sincerity."

Right before she left the room, Carolyn Hollister turned toward Agent Verduzco. "Don't forget about his laboratory. The fetuses might be there. Please remember to keep my name out of this." She had almost knocked into Agent Patch, as he juggled three cups of hot coffee. With a flip of her head, she turned her nose up and marched out of the office.

"That loony bird finished?" he said, putting the coffee on the table.

"Close the door. We've got a bigger problem on our hands."

51

Agent Patch could not believe what his partner had told him what Hollister said to her that there might be aborted fetuses inside Richards lab. When Amy mentioned the bi-monthly shots for five of the doctor's patients and that they were free and the revelation that Angelica Rathburn was missing a new tattoo and showing an odd birthmark she did not have before, had him shaking his head. He burst out laughing when his partner told him about the unknown woman wearing Morgan's clothes.

"I think she's a disgruntled employee, trying to get even with her boss or maybe is crazy," Patch said.

"Maybe so. We still have to investigate," said Verduzco.

They had both been briefed three years ago regarding all the genetic research using fetal stem cells, and why it was a sinful act. Verduzco could care less about the religious reasons. She was an excellent agent and wanted to follow the law. If Richards was doing research using fetal stem cells, then he needs to be brought in and investigated.

It was common knowledge within their department about the far-out theories, the experiments that went beyond reason, and moral conscience. Those researchers were all locked up now.

They were unsure of what to do since two other FBI agents had active cases that included these women and Doctor Richards.

"We need to open an investigation so we can put Hollister's claims to rest," agent Patch said. "I can't believe any woman would get pregnant and abort their fetus for free cosmetic surgery."

Verduzco did not seem so confident. "There had been speculation that fetal stem cells could reverse the aging process. I know about Doctor Richards and his success with his proprietary anti-aging serum. He's getting wealthy from it. Our labs had tested it and found no fetal stem cells, just human stem cells."

Patch seemed puzzled. "You think these women are getting a different serum with fetal stem cells in it?"

"I'm not sure. Richards has been investigated before, and nothing illegal came up. Understand that some abortion clinics, before it had become illegal, had made abortions a profitable business," she said. "It's possible this doctor, and the women are breaking the law?"

Patch had doubt etched on his face. "To get a warrant to search the doctor's home and business, we will need to show probable cause. What we have on Richards is the word of a fundamentalist Christian spewing crazy unsubstantiated gossip that five women are trading their fetuses for free serum shots."

Agent Verduzco shook her head. "I find it hard to fathom any of what that weird lady had to say. I don't believe there is a shred of truth to it, but, by our department rules, we have no choice but to investigate."

Patch shrugged his shoulders. "Yeah, but what if she's right, and the doctor does have a laboratory with stored fetuses...there might be some truth to what she's told us?"

"Here's my take on this doctor. He's trading favors, sexual ones, for free Botox treatments." She leaned back in her chair with a smug look on her face.

Forest laughed at her silliness. "Good one. However, I've seen some of these ladies and their beautiful line-free faces are not from Botox. If the doctor shot them up on their entire face with Botox, well, they'd all look like the Joker from Batman. I want to run a lengthy background check on Richards. If we find any information that he had been accused before of illegal abortions, or even doing abortions before it had become illegal, I'll push for a warrant to search his office and laboratory. I want to verify what Hollister said about Angelica's missing tattoo," he said, as he put down his notepad. "Not sure where all of this will lead.

Rathburn might have gotten one of those fake tattoos for an upcoming movie part."

"How about talking to..." she paused to look at the business card she had in his hand, "Agent St. Claire, the agent who is working the current case."

"You call him, and I'll get started on Doctor Richards."
We do nothing until we have all the facts?" Patch said.

"Look, this is our first case in almost two years. The last one we had, shit, we were too fast and aggressive. I've learned my lesson. I'll take this one real slow. See if you can dig into Richards's work history, marriage, childhood, if possible."

52

St. Claire had arrived at Emerson's Westwood Village apartment at Le Corte and Gayley. He had to park four blocks away, which only made his mood worse. He would not stop cursing at the uphill hike, struggling with the massive "Banker Box" of files he had to carry.

As he stood in front of her apartment dripping from sweat, he craned his neck, getting madder as he had to schlep his way up the fifty steps to her front door. He dropped the box of files. He lifted a flowerpot that rested on the edge of her windowsill and found her spare key.

Inside he laid the evidence box by her wrought-iron glass top kitchen table and flopped down on one of the kitchen chairs. He had been breathing hard as he glanced around the oversized room that made up the living room and kitchen. Off to the left of the front door, he assumed it was her bedroom. He found it strange being in her place alone. He wished she would have arrived before him.

He needed to take a leak. He was uncomfortable with the thought his partner had only one bathroom, and that he would have to go in her bedroom. His bladder was ready to burst when Jill busted through the front door.

She had one of her infectious smiles she exposed only after working hours. Jill dropped her small suitcase by the front door. "Been here long?" she asked, rushing toward her bedroom. "I'm busting," as she crossed her legs. "I'll be right out."

"I'm next," Matt yelled, feeling the pressure press against his swollen bladder.

With a cordial sweep of her arm, she pointed to the second bathroom that was behind a closed door left of her bedroom.

She glanced at the stuffed banker box, nodding. "I see you're ready to work. I'll pour us some wine after I relieve myself. You going to join me?" She could see her partner nod with a painful expression as he rushed to the toilet.

Jill sipped her glass of Cab very slowly, as Matt laid out the evidence, he had accumulated on her kitchen table. Her mind drifted to her two interviews in Manhattan, which did not turn up anything of importance for their cases. She pulled out her notebook and held it in her hand.

"I'm not going to have much to contribute. Manhattan was a waste of time with Beth Thomas, but Landers is showing some promise," Jill said. "Surprisingly, the guy looks similar to our murder suspect."

She had not told Matt that she had turned Lander's beer bottle over to the NYPD Sex Crimes Unit. Her hunch about him had proven correct. They had matched his DNA and linked it to three open rape cases that were still unsolved in Manhattan.

That result had been rewarding in more ways than one. First, Jill didn't like the man, and two, it had improved the FBI's relationship with the NYPD by sharing evidence. She held the wine glass with both hands, lost within her happy thoughts, as she panned her unremarkable Westwood apartment.

She had moved into her new apartment right after Alex had died and had no desire to make it look like a home. All the furniture and artwork they shared had been sold or given away to Goodwill. She did not want any reminders of their life, even though each day, he'd still creep into her head unexpectedly, as everything in her world reminded her of the love of her life. Her thoughts tumbled back to Eric Landers, as she heard her partner call her name.

"Hey Emerson, you still on this planet?" Matt said, shaking her shoulder. She snapped alert, ready to work.

"I'll tell you later," she smiled contently. "It always makes me feel great when our justice system works fluidly."

St. Claire's face twisted with confusion. "We need to focus here. Miller wants a full report in the morning."

She had put her glass down and moved her chair closer to her partner, rubbing her shoulder next to his. "I'm all ears."

Matt had gotten goosebumps as he felt her soft body next to his. Her sweet perfume filled his nostrils.

"First, I want to go over the Lisa Beverly case. The coroner has concluded his findings, and they scare me. The decomposing rate is abnormally fast for anyone being dead a little over two weeks. Look at these photos. Ever see anything like it before?"

Jill sat up straight, held one of the photos at eye level, and shuddered. "She looks like she's a mummified woman."

"Exactly. The coroner and our forensic unit said that would be impossible. They did have a theory I thought was bizarre."

She elbowed him softly in his ribs. "These cases are all strange. What did they say?"

He took a deep breath and pushed his chair back so he could look at her. "Around ten years ago, when stem cell research, using aborted fetuses, was not illegal, scientists and doctors had been experimenting, and believing that fetal stem cells could lead to a non-surgical way of reversing the aging process..."

"You're not suspecting that this woman had been part of an experiment?"

"No. The forensic team says that nothing ever came of that research. Now, hold on to your seat. Here's the strange part. Right after we searched Trish Morgan's home, we put her DNA in our computer database. Our forensic lab had Lisa Beverly's DNA from her corpse already there, and here is the twilight zone result. Beverly's DNA matched up with Trish Morgan's. They are so similar that they are either sisters or possibly twins."

"You're shitting me," Jill's eyes were wide with disbelief. "Now, this is getting creepy."

"That's not all. The security cameras at the Princess Hotel have determined that the other suspect that went into Beverly's room after

Eric Landers left matched the facial ID from his passport photo. We now have another piece to our puzzle that I am not sure how it fits.

"Does this mystery guy have a name?"

Matt flipped a few pages in his notebook, looking for the name he had jotted down. "Jeffrey Peters. The airport security cameras show him leaving a restroom at the private plane terminal about the same time that a helicopter left for Washington D.C... Now, hold on," Matt said, "that's not the strange part. Doctor Richards was on the manifest for that helicopter," Matt said.

"Doctor Richards? What the fuck was he doing there?" Jill asked.

Matt was scratching his head. "I don't know. We don't have any video of him at the Princess Hotel, linking him as a suspect with this Lisa Beverly case. I do know a Doctor Steven Fleming, from Bethesda, Maryland owns the aircraft. I've got a call in to speak to that doctor. Right now, he's traveling, and expected to get back to his office tomorrow."

Jill smiled as she sipped the last of her wine. "Do we know anything about this, Peters guy?"

Matt shrugged his shoulders, showing his exasperation. "He's a non-entity just like Lisa Beverly. His passport and ID's are phony."

"Shit. First, Meg Cummings is dead because of an overdose and was pregnant. A similar MO happens to the Beverly woman who we know was pregnant. I need ASAP, those paternity tests. We need to find this Jeff Peter's character. Maybe he's part of that secret CIA project you mentioned earlier? If Peter's is the father, it could be a motive for killing these women?" she blurted out, pouring herself another glass of wine. "Shit, I forgot about Richards and why he went to Bermuda. Do we have any answers to that question?"

St. Claire had gotten up and flopped down onto the soft couch in her living room. His tired body sank into the soft cushions. His hands had crossed behind his neck. He looked exhausted from all the confusing evidence he had uncovered.

"You look like you have more to add?" she asked.

Matt nodded. "Here's the real fly in the ointment. Since doctor Fleming had signed his Whirlybird out to Doctor Richards, we now need to talk to the Richards again. Perhaps he knows Jeffrey Peters? Or perhaps he's working for the CIA again?" St. Claire threw his arms in the air. "I wish we never caught this case."

Jill ignored her partner. She had more on her mind. "Could it be possible Jeffrey Peters was on the chopper and flew with Richards to Bermuda? Maybe Richards hired a hitman to clean up some secret business he's doing? Like abortions? Like getting women pregnant for his research?"

"Damn. We've got a dead body, a missing person whose DNA is identical to the stiff in our morgue. Doctor Richards borrows a helicopter from a doctor Fleming, which he gives to a Jeffrey Peters, who's probably a murderer for hire, to fly to Bermuda where he's the last person to see Lisa Beverly alive…"

Jill cut him off. "It seems clear to me, this Beverly woman is a patient of Doctor Richards too, and possibly the sister of Trish Morgan. Richards hired Jeffrey Peters to kill Morgan's sister for what reason I can't say right now. Just give me some latitude. We have to find a connection between Richards, Morgan, Peters, and Beverly and possibly Cummings?"

St. Claire picked up the police sketch of Cummings attacker. "Shit, Jeff Peters looks like our suspect too."

"I'll bet Doctor Richards is hiding something he doesn't want to be made public. I feel it," Jill said. "Beth Thomas was very defensive with me during my interview, especially after I mentioned Lisa Beverly's name. I'm beginning to believe that all these women are hiding a dirty little secret about Doctor Richards and all the illegal things they are all doing. Maybe doctor Fleming could shed some light on all of this?"

"You're as confused as I am. I'd feel better if Charlie Chan was here helping us. This one's right up his alley," Matt said, throwing his arms in the air, signaling surrender. "We need the security camera footage at the airport where Doctor Flemings helicopter took off from? My friend wants us to look at it. It's another weird piece to our already confusing puzzle."

"Maybe we need to get some fresh air. Let's go for a walk around the Village, and clear our minds," she said, gulping down the last of her wine.

Matt's cell rang. It was their boss, Miller. "No, we haven't listened to the news. Are they sure?" he asked. "Okay, we'll see you in the morning."

Jill had a puzzled expression on her face. "What's up? You look like you lost your best friend?"

"A body was dredged up earlier this evening. It appears to be Angelica Rathburn," he said.

"Then, who was the woman that kissed you at Rathburn's house?"

53

Jill was ready to close her front door when she heard her phone ringing inside her apartment. "Shit, I bet its Miller again," she cursed. By the time she had reached the phone, the answering machine had kicked in. They both stood there listening, as the male voice identified himself.

"This is Agent Forrest Patch from the San Diego FBI Field Office. We're in the Strategic Abortion Crime Unit. It has been brought to my attention that you and your partner are working a case that might involve a person of interest in one of our cases, A doctor Todd Richards…"

Jill and Matt did a double-take. They looked at each other, disbelief on their faces. "We were talking about abortions and fetuses a moment ago. How would they know?" she said.

She picked up the phone before the agent could finish his message. "Hey, this is Agent Emerson. You caught me leaving. Your message, can you explain it?"

Patch had brought them up to date about his case, and what Doctor Richards' receptionist, Carolyn Hollister, had told him and his partner. Jill had put the agent on speaker so that Matt could introduce himself. Then, agent Amy Verduzco introduced herself, and the four of them carried on a convoluted four-way conversation.

Agent Verduzco had changed the subject with a surprising question. "Agent St. Claire, have you seen the National Star that had come out today?"

Matt knew what the question was going to be. He looked at Jill, rolling his eyes. "That's one of those tabloid papers. I don't read them. Why?"

Agent Verduzco tried to hide her giggle, but it had come across loud and clear. "You're on the front page getting a very provocative kiss from Angelica Rathburn. I liked the headline: *The FBI is once again deeply involved with one of their cases.* You want me to read what the article says?" she asked.

Agent Patch interjected, trying to hold back his laughter. "Is she as good as they say she is?"

Matt had turned beet red as he looked at his partner, who tried to control the outburst that was ready to explode through her hand that covered her mouth.

"It was an innocent kiss for helping her with the son-of-a-bitch studio boss that wouldn't leave her alone," Jill said, holding back her laugh. "I guess you guys hadn't heard, but they think they found Rathburn off the coast early this morning. We're going to check it out tomorrow."

Verduzco, acted like she had not heard a word Jill had said. "It doesn't look that innocent."

Matt barked at her. "Did you guys call to talk about your case or my most embarrassing moment," he snarled at the phone Jill was holding.

"Sorry. Just having a little fun," Amy said. "So, what's this about Rathburn, you said?"

St. Claire replied. "We just heard from our boss that a fishing boat had netted a body earlier this morning. Female. First examination, points to it being Rathburn."

Forest jumped into the conversation. "I think we need to meet. It's obvious we have overlapping cases. Can we compare notes."

Jill replied. "Why's SACU involved in a missing person and murder case?"

"We're not. It's Doctor Richards who we're interested in at this moment. Our tip from his office manager forces us to check the doctor out to see if he's doing illegal abortions for five of his patients," Agent Verduzco said. "I need to stress to both of you that our informant needs to remain anonymous. Richards's name at this time can't be linked, under any circumstances to abortions until we have definitive proof."

When agent Verduzco told Emerson and St. Claire, the women's names, they were checking out, their mouth dropped to their chests.

Matt spoke. "These women are part of our case too. Can we meet tonight? Let's say halfway, somewhere off Interstate 5?"

"How's Costa Mesa at a coffee shop off of Bristol and the 405?" Agent Patch suggested.

"We'll leave right now. We should be there within the hour," said Jill.

"Make that an hour and a half. The restaurant's called 'The Mesa Cafe.' It's seven-forty. We should get there a little after nine. Bring all your files, and we'll bring ours," Amy said.

54

It had not been easy, but after transforming back to Doctor Richards, he was able to sneak out of Angelica's Malibu house around two-thirty in the morning. Transforming from female to male was excruciatingly painful. The process took over two hours to fully become a male again.

He brushed it off as no big deal and made a mental note to take a Cat-Scan and compare it to his previous ones to be sure nothing serious was going on inside his brain. For now, he had more important things on his mind.

Once the conversion was complete, and he felt strong enough to move, he climbed out a side window. He walked past the camped-out reporters who had made a fire on the beach to keep warm.

He strolled about three-quarters of a mile south and hiked to the highway, where he called Uber from a gas station. He had arrived back in La Jolla at five-thirty. He dropped on his bed, exhausted. He was relieved that this diversion had been successful. He hoped it had worked, and the Angelica Rathburn, missing person case, would be closed. He was too tired to watch the news or plan his next move to bring Trish Morgan back to the living.

He had drifted deep into a dream about his wife, Molly, as he curled into a fetal position. His memories always wafted to the first time they met.

Molly Talbert had been a bartender at a small tavern in Palo Alto, California. He had become smitten with her the first time he had laid eyes on her. He was fascinated with her mannerisms and the graceful way she put her long hair in a ponytail. To him, she was a gorgeous woman.

With his chin resting on his hand, he watched, captivated as she moved behind the bar mixing drinks for customers. He tried to steal a glance without her noticing, but she always seemed to sense him staring and would turn around with a big smile.

Molly Talbert had been born and raised in San Francisco. She attended Stanford, majoring in Art History. Richards' shyness kept him from being able to talk to her. One night she surprised him and started a conversation.

She wiped her wet hands on her apron and formally introduced herself. "I'm Molly Talbert. You frequent my bar a lot. I can't understand why you're the only guy that doesn't talk to me. How come?" she pouted.

Todd blushed, not knowing what to say. "I…" he shrugged his shoulders, "I… guess I've been scared to talk to you, even though I've wanted to for weeks," his voice had a nervous edge.

She smiled, seeming to enjoy his bashfulness. "I like a man who's a little shy. I get tired of all the self-absorbed college types that think they're god's gift to women."

As she continued talking to him, he finally felt relaxed and returned her smile. "I wouldn't know how to be self-absorbed. I don't seem to have enough time to try to pick up women, even if I knew how to. Medical school keeps me very busy, with this being my last semester."

"Doctor? I'm impressed. You look more like a surfer," she said, as she gently touched his long flowing blonde hair with her left hand. Then, without warning, her right hand touched his muscular chest. She sucked in a nervous breath as she tried to get her thoughts back on track. "What's your field of interest going to be?" she asked, her elbows resting on the counter, letting her cupped hand cradle her head.

She looked so beautiful at that moment. Todd's heart would not stop racing, as he tried to reply. "I'm not sure. It's between research or cosmetic surgery."

"Which pays more?"

He smiled at her question. "It doesn't matter. Cosmetic surgery can be very lucrative, especially in La Jolla, where I plan on starting my practice."

A handsome man had entered the tavern and had called out Molly's name. He sat down at the far end of the long wooden bar and ordered a beer. Richards' heart sank as he listened to them talk in a warm, friendly banter. He was about to get up and leave when Molly returned and asked him to continue.

"You said you're going to settle in La Jolla? Can you do both? That is cosmetic surgery and your research?"

He had still been glancing at the college jock that she had left for him. He felt for the first time in his life like he had found the perfect woman. "It's possible. I'd have to develop my regular practice first. Research is time-consuming, slow, and expensive. I want to cure all illnesses. It's my dream."

They kept talking until the bar closed at two in the morning. They went to an all-night restaurant, had coffee, and an early breakfast.

During Richards' final semester, they had started seeing each other almost every night. Molly had captured his heart. She seemed to know what he was feeling and thinking and how she made him feel important. He had fallen head over heels in love with her.

A month after he graduated, they were married. They both moved to La Jolla, while he finished his internship and residency at UCSD Medical Hospital. What had started as a fairy tale romance, continued until the day she died in his arms in the hospital.

All his dreams about Molly ended with him soaked in sweat. He popped up in his bed and leaned back against the headboard breathing hard, his eyes filling with tears. He stood and took off the clothes he had fallen asleep in and headed for the shower. He looked at his muscular toned body and long blonde hair. He looked the same as he did the night he had first spoken to Molly.

"Oh, how I wish I had my serum completed before Molly died." he sniffled. Then his thoughts consumed him with what his wife would think of him now.

The Faces of Doctor Richards

Richards had turned on his TV while he dried off from his shower. He stood there, stunned. "How could this be?" he muttered.

The reporter was speaking into his microphone, uttering the words that sunk a dagger into his heart. *"The police are speculating that a fishing boat yesterday morning pulled up the body of Angelica Rathburn in their fishing net."* The reporter then said, *"A preliminary exam by the coroner says that the actress had been in the water for almost three weeks. Then, who was the woman posing as Angelica Rathburn at her Malibu home yesterday?"*

Richards dropped to the floor, perplexed, and in a panic. "Oh fuck, I'm screwed," he moaned.

55

Carolyn Hollister sat at her desk nervously, shuffling some patient files when she heard her boss coming down the stairs from his apartment. The office had two female patients. Richards attempted to greet them with one of his seductive smiles. However, today, it was not working. He was worried that the FBI would be back to see him now that Rathburn's body was recovered.

He picked up his schedule for the day and said, *good morning*. He immediately recognized one of the ladies in his waiting room. *Shit, it's that woman who waved at Meg and me a few weeks ago,* he told himself.

He had become flustered, remembering how that patient had been during and after her breast implants. She wanted to date him back then and kept calling his office after her procedure. He didn't need this today.

He bent down and asked Hollister, "Who's that woman?" he pretended not to recognize her.

"Carla Palmer. A few years back, you did a breast enlargement and some other facial work for her," she replied quietly, her voice had a nervous edge to it.

"What's she here for today?"

"She said she wanted to talk to you about something private."

"Okay. Send Ms. Palmer back to my office in thirty minutes."

He was ready to walk back to his office when he noticed his receptionist was looking sad. Carolyn was acting uncomfortable since he had come downstairs. "Is everything all right?" he whispered in her ear. I really need you to handle things today. I've got a lot on my mind."

She kept writing something on one of the charts on her desk, her head buried in her work. "Must have gotten up on the wrong side of the bed," she said unconvincingly.

"I know you better than that. Something's bothering you. Let's talk before you go home today," Richards said, giving her shoulder a firm squeeze.

Richards flopped down behind his desk, cradling his head. He did not have time for Carla Palmer but was curious about why she wanted to see him.

When it was time for Palmer to speak with Richards, it had turned out to be nothing more than her wanting to get a drink sometime, and maybe dinner.

"I am flattered," Richards said, feeling a relief blanket his body. "As I told you before, I can't date patients, either current ones or past ones," he said.

Carla furrowed her brow. "I saw you holding hands with Meg Cummings the other night. She was a patient, right?"

"We were friends. Nothing more. Now, if that's all you wanted to talk to me about, then I guess this appointment is over?"

Carla stood up, showing her hurt feelings. "Sorry to have bothered you," she said.

"If my office manager has your correct address, you should receive a bill for my time today," he said, smiling. "I don't want anyone to get the wrong impression about what might have gone on today."

After Carla stormed out of his office, he knew he needed to get back on track and figure out his next move. Now that the police had found Angelica, he knew the coroner would discover how she had died. Richards knew the San Diego coroner personally. He would discover Angelica had, postmortem, her fetus removed from her womb.

He cradled his head, thinking that in three weeks, his once perfect life was tumbling out of control. He was sure that the FBI with Angelica's body now at the morgue, with Lisa Beverly, and Meg Cummings bodies being autopsied, they would be close to figuring out what he has been doing with these female patients. How much time would he have before he'd be served with search warrants for his home and lab?

He knew he needed to dispose of Lea Strong and Beth Thomas, but how and when? The FBI was surely watching them, he guessed. He prayed he would have no more surprises before he could disappear.

56

Jill and Matt had found a large booth at the back of the Mesa Grill restaurant away from most of the patrons. They discussed how they would handle the two agents from SACU, so they would not lose their cases.

Emerson was acting edgy. "I've seen it before. What I've heard about these SACU agents is that they only need to believe Richards is doing abortions, and we can be kicked off our cases in a blink of an eye," Jill said. "Also, with Rathburn turning up dead, who was the gorgeous woman who planted a juicy one on your lips?"

Matt was about to say something sarcastic to Jill when he saw the two SACU agents enter the restaurant. He put his hand on her arm, squeezing it lightly, alerting her that they had company.

"They're here, and let's remind them we do have open cases that link Richards to everything we're investigating," he said, his hand masking his lips.

Jill nodded. "Let's hear them out. Maybe we can all work together?" She noticed Matt furrowing his bow. "What's with the face?"

"Are we that obvious when we're out in public?" Matt asked as he checked out their official FBI uniform of a dark suit, white oxford shirt, and black tie.

"I don't know how we look, but they look like a Men in Black commercial, except for the absence of their dark sunglasses," she said, amused, as her eyes focused on them.

Matt and Jill did not stand when they motioned for the agents to slip into their booth.

Agent Verduzco was first to speak. "Amy Verduzco," she said, extending her hand to Matt and then Jill. She pointed toward her partner. "This is agent Forrest Patch. Thanks for agreeing to meet with us. You do know that if it turns out Doctor Richards is involved with abortions, you'll have to turn over all the files you have on the doctor. SACU has confidentiality rules, you know, about protecting the privacy of our suspects, and we cannot coordinate with other FBI agents outside our unit. After our investigation concludes, and if our case is going nowhere, you'll be free to pursue your suspect," she said, her voice authoritative and cold.

Matt was about to lose it. Jill was sensing it by the rage she could see on his face. She responded. "I'm not interested in what you think or have as evidence. We have an ongoing murder and missing person's case that may involve Doctor Richards…"

Agent Patch interrupted. "I've looked into your cases, and none of them are even close to tying in Doctor Richards to them. Your first missing person, Angelica Rathburn, had turned up yesterday alive and well, and now could be resting in the morgue? I'll bet that your other lady will probably appear, one way or the other. So, let's not fight over something that hasn't panned out about the doctor at this time."

Jill and Matt sat there frozen in silence. What the two agents said was partly right. All Verduzco and Patch knew, Emerson thought, was that they were working three open cases, with a few pregnant women, whose pregnancies might be connected to Richards. The other detail that did not relate to the SACU unit was that Angelica Rathburn's body was recovered off the coast of San Diego, and their first case might now be a homicide. They did not want to tell the agents about what they had uncovered on Richards at this time.

Emerson tried to temper the meeting and her partner. She attempted to steer it back toward cooperation. "What have you two uncovered that makes you think Doctor Richards is doing abortions?" Jill asked, pinching Matt's arm hard.

Agent Verduzco brought them up to date on what Carolyn Hollister had told them, including her theory that the individual, Angelica Rathburn, was missing a new tattoo. Also, she believed the person the media had interviewed was not the real actress.

Emerson had a puzzled looked on her face. "This case is turning to shit every minute we sit here," she said.

"We're going to the morgue right after our meeting and check out the body for the tattoo Hollister said she had," agent Verduzco said.

Matt blushed, as he waited for the teasing to start up again. "If the person I had met was not the actress, then she was the best double I'd ever seen." He waited, but nothing happened.

Agent Patch spoke first. "I think we got off on the wrong foot. Here's how I see all this working out. We're not sure we have a SACU violation, and you're still working on a missing person and two possible murder cases. I think we can both work side-by-side for now, comparing evidence and hopefully wrap up both our cases sooner than later."

Emerson clapped her hands. "I think that can work for us."

Agent Patch was nodding. "It will only work if both of you agree to keep us in the loop with what you uncover about the Trish Morgan case, and your two murder cases. I'm still an FBI agent first and want justice to win out. I think we can do our jobs without stepping on anyone's toes."

Matt had calmed down, nodding his agreement. "I can live with that too," he said. He opened his files and pushed them over to Verduzco and Patch. "This is all we have so far. We're still waiting for other forensic results; however, as you can see, it all seems very strange, and bizarre."

Verduzco and Patch shook their heads in disbelief. They pushed over their files and watched St. Claire and Emerson's reaction.

Jill spoke first. "We might have a murderer that's doing abortions. Maybe Doctor Richards is eliminating the only people who know what he's been doing," she said. "Let us do what we do best, capturing murderers, and you find out if he's doing illegal abortions. We'll need your help, and you'll need ours. I'm glad we're not going to get into a pissing contest, marking our territories on our cases?"

Two hours later, the four agents stood and shook hands, agreeing to cooperate.

* * * * *

"Do you think they'll cooperate?" Matt asked as he pulled out of the restaurant's parking lot.

"I don't care. We're going to have to move a little faster and try to solve our cases before they do," Jill replied.

* * * * *

"I get the sense that they won't cooperate with us," Agent Patch said.

"We have access to their files via our computers. It's a little advantage SACU got when our new department was created. If they don't keep us in the loop, we'll know it. Then we'll cut them off and have them sitting around with their thumbs up their butts while we finish our investigation.

57

Carolyn Hollister sat across from Todd Richards, squeezing her hands nervously. She stared at her boss's serious face. She was convinced he knew what she'd had done. She tried her best to avoid eye contact, but couldn't, and before he even asked her a question, she had started to blather about her confession to the FBI.

Blotting her eyes with her yellow lace handkerchief, she started to sob. She could see that Richards had a puzzled expression.

Carolyn started talking fast. "I'm so sorry. I spoke with the FBI. I was upset at what I had heard a few weeks ago. You know what Angelica, Trish, and Lea were saying about abortions. You know how I feel about it, being the good Christian woman I am," she said, her torso rocking left and right. She sucked in a deep breath to control herself. It was not working. "I had to do the right thing. You do understand?"

Richards tried to stay unruffled and unemotional by her comments. However, his rage had begun to show. "Are you saying you reported me for doing illegal abortions?" He saw her head nod, as her uncontainable shaking consumed her body. "What was going on inside your head that you would not come to me with your concerns first? Haven't I been a good boss, no, a good friend to you?"

"If you were doing what I suspected, what would you have said?" she replied, sucking in a worried breath.

"The same thing I would say right now. I am not doing any illegal abortions or any abortions for any of my patients. Now you've stirred up a hornet's nest of trouble for me. Didn't it occur to you that once the

213

FBI's SACU unit opens an investigation for possible abortions, that it would make the news, and ruin my reputation, my business?" Richards was unable to control his fury. "Do you remember the names of the agents you spoke with?"

She told him their names. "I am so sorry. My priest, Molly's priest," she said, "told me to go with my conscience. I had no choice when it comes to protecting God's innocent children…"

Richards' facial muscles tensed as he thought of a response. He remembered Molly's priest very well and how he had made his wife feel guilty about aborting their son while she laid dying in her bed.

He looked at Hollister wanting to strangle her. What she had done had put the final nail in his decomposing life in La Jolla. He knew sooner than later that he had to disappear.

Richards was stone-cold sober, as he lashed out at his office manager. "My conscience has spoken to me also. Pack up all your personal belongings and get the fuck out of my office, now!" he screamed. "I'm so disappointed with you and your lack of loyalty to me after what I've done for you during the time you've worked here. You've made a bad mistake. Having to see you for another second makes my stomach want to retch. Get out of my office before I do something I'll regret."

As he watched Carolyn leave his office, he clicked on the SACU's website. After doing a quick search, he found the headshots of the two agents. He focused on Forrest Patch more than Amy Verduzco. An idea popped into his head. "It could work," he grinned.

58

After being fired, Hollister could not stop crying. She was sitting on her recliner curled up in her small two-bedroom Point Loma cottage. She was racking her brain about what she had done.

Having second thoughts, she placed a call to Agent Verduzco to recant her complaint. All she got was her voice message machine. When she heard the machine beep, she spoke into her mouthpiece. "*I think I made a big mistake about what I thought Doctor Richards was doing. He's a wonderful man. I was wrong in telling you he was performing abortions,*"

She felt a sense of relief. She hoped that the investigation would vanish. She leaned back, sinking deep into her soft recliner, and closed her eyes. She was praying everything would be all right for her in the eyes of God.

After her late husband had died, she had enough money to live a comfortable life. She wanted to work to keep her mind active and occupied from the painful thoughts of how her husband had suffered from his prostate cancer.

Eight years ago, during her interview with Doctor Richards, they had hit it off. They had so much in common, with their loss of their spouses to cancer. Being fifteen years older than Richards allowed her to act like a surrogate mother, using her organizational skills as office manager and nurse, something that the doctor so desperately needed at that time.

She understood how the Strategic Abortion Crime Unit worked. She had seen many TV reports about their power and how they must investigate all alleged perpetrators. Even with her recanting, she knew it was now out of her hands. With or without her testimony, the investigation would run its course.

There was a loud pounding on her front door. Carolyn had jumped, her body becoming rigid. She blotted her red eyes and dripping nose before opening the door. "Who's there?" she shouted, her voice hoarse.

"Agent Forrest Patch from the FBI," the male voice responded.

"Be right there," she shouted. "You got my message already?"

59

Jill had been on the phone with Doctor Steven Fleming, grilling him about why he had lent his helicopter to Doctor Richards, and why Richards allowed a Jeffrey Peters use it. The doctor had become defensive, as well as rude on the phone.

"I can't tell you why my friend lied to me. I've known him for a long time. Since referring Angelica Rathburn to him, we've become even closer, or so I thought."

Fleming had told Emerson he had never heard of a Jeffrey Peters. He acted genuinely upset that he had been deceived by his friend.

"So, what you're saying is that you did not know that this Jeffrey Peters character would be using your helicopter?"

"No. Definitely no!" Fleming replied.

Emerson's voice had become more serious. "You know that lying to an FBI agent, during an investigation, can put you behind bars. You'd lose your medical license."

Doctor Fleming's voice had started to tremble. "I've known Todd Richards for almost fifteen years," he said. "He had told me that he had to see a potential new patient in Bermuda, who was stranded there because of a tropical storm. He said he needed the Helicopter for one day. He returned it on schedule. I never thought to check up on who used it. My pilot knows Richards, and I think he would have told me about the change to the manifest. Have you spoken to my pilot? If Richards did not use it, and this Jeff Peters showed up, my pilot wouldn't have flown to Bermuda without calling me first."

Emerson was taking notes while thinking of her next question. "Where can your pilot be reached to answer a few questions? I'd like to know who was on your helicopter?"

"Me too," Doctor Fleming said, sounding annoyed.

I know you're unhappy with Doctor Richards, but if you can refrain from speaking to him until we have a chance to question him about this, it would be appreciated. We're conducting a murder investigation, and I wouldn't want you brought up on charges of obstruction," she threatened. "Am I making myself clear?" Emerson warned.

Doctor Fleming stammered as he tried to reply. "I…I…will not call him. Please don't speak to me as if I'm an idiot. If he's involved in a crime, I want to get this matter cleared up before my name becomes associated with his," Fleming said somberly.

"I have a few more questions." Emerson, her tone had warmed up now that she had made her point. "Are you familiar with fetal stem cell research?"

There was a dead silence, as Doctor Fleming tried to respond. "Yes. First, it's illegal to use a fetus for stem cell research or any research now," he responded puzzled. "Is Richards again involved with this type of experimentation?"

Emerson sounded surprised. "You say that as if you've known him to be capable of doing such a thing."

"Before it had become illegal, Todd back then was a gifted microbiologist and physician who had been experimenting with fetal stem cells. He believed that what he was doing would find a cure for his wife's cancer. I can't imagine why he'd be breaking the law now."

"I'm not saying he is, but the woman connected to Jeffrey Peters is dead, and was pregnant. With Richards using your helicopter, and giving it to Peters, who's now our prime suspect, has put your friend as a person of interest. We also have some extraordinary conditions regarding the decomposing of the victim's body. I've been reading some old theories about how fetal stem cells could have been the new frontier in helping the body heal itself…"

Fleming interrupted. "It had been thought that using fetal stem cells to enhance the brain receptors could one day allow us to use up to ninety-five percent of our brains. However, it is pure science fiction, even with today's technologies."

"What if this research had gone underground, and the future is with us today? Could the brain, with the right stimulant, be redesigned enough to control one's appearance?" Jill heard his sarcastic laugh. "I don't think what I've said is that funny," she said.

"It most certainly is," he said. "Just like H.G. Wells and Jules Verne had their theories about events in the future, what you are speculating about is impossible. Even if the brain could learn to heal injured parts of the body, humans don't have the ability today, or in the distant future to change their appearance. When it does happen, it would be from evolution, not some chemical that might stimulate the brain," Fleming said adamantly.

Jill had known she was out of her league asking questions about fetal stem cells, but needed answers to what she, too, believed were pure science fiction. "I've read that the brain is the master control center of the body. Doesn't it receive information from the senses about conditions both inside and outside the body? Then, why can't a drug or serum be designed to teach the brain to heal other parts of the body, even change the shape of a person's bones and skin?"

"It's true that some lower forms of animals can re-grow a severed part of their body. It is part of their genetic makeup. Humans don't have that ability. Back in 1994, a twelve-year-old boy had been born with a partial rib cage. Doctors used extracted cartilage cells and seeded them onto a porous mold of a designed polymer to create a new ribcage. It acted as a scaffold on which the cells could multiply. I'm not sure you need to know all of this, but it had been the first attempt in tissue engineering. Regenerating body parts, or as you are suggesting changing how one looks using the brain will not happen in our lifetime, or our children's lifetime."

"What if Richards had created a unique substance that...let's say was injected into the bloodstream. Could it modify or edit a person's DNA to help change one's body structure? The liver regrows. So why not other organs using fetal stem cells?"

Doctor Fleming sighed. "Even if that was possible, science is not even close to finding a serum, or hybrid stem cell or fetal stem mixture that could do what you are asking."

Emerson closed her notebook. "I hope that everything we've talked about will remain between us?"

Fleming snickered. "I'd be too embarrassed to speak of this crazy theory of yours," he mocked. "I do remember that Todd had once worked with a bioengineer, Thomas Franklin. He's still a professor at UCLA, where Todd worked years ago. I'm sure the professor would love to argue with you on your advanced brain concept. It's been a real pleasure talking to you agent Emerson," he said, with a loud chuckle.

Matt had been staring at his partner for the last ten minutes while she was on the phone with Doctor Fleming, wanting to tell her what had come back from the lab on Lisa Beverly. He knew not to interrupt her while she was interviewing someone.

He had been shuffling his papers on his desk, trying to get her attention. She had her head buried in her notepad as she listened to Doctor Fleming.

Matt snapped his fingers. "It's about time. I've never heard you talk so long on the phone," he said. "I've got some interesting news about the residue that our coroner found on Lisa Beverly's neck at her puncture site."

Jill closed her notebook and looked up. "You go first. What I've got to say might take me a while to sort out," she said, combing her fingers through hair.

"It is some unknown serum that appears to have fetal stem cells and the victim's DNA. There's a third DNA sample, but it's inconclusive at this point. We found no matches."

Jill kept nodding her head, lost somewhere with her thoughts. "It's Doctor Richards, I'm sure," she said with a grin. "If he's running experiments in his lab, and his office manager suspects something... We need to pay Ms. Hollister a visit."

"That's Patch's and Verduzco's case. They'll have our hides if they find out we talked to her without letting them know first."

"We're still investigating a homicide, and she's a material witness to our case. You coming with me?" Jill asked.

Matt stood and slipped his coat on. "I didn't say we shouldn't go," he grinned. "I thought you'd want to cooperate with the SACU agents."

"Yeah. Right, cooperate," Jill laughed. "We've got her address. Let's pay her a friendly visit."

60

Carolyn Hollister instantly recognized the rude Agent Patch from their earlier meeting at Doctor Richards's office. She felt uncomfortable that his partner agent Verduzco was not with him. At first, she refused to let him enter her home.

"Where's your partner agent Verduzco? I left her my message," Hollister said, defiantly, her arm crossed.

Agent Patch had been staring back at her with a scowl. "She told me about it and asked if I could talk to you. I have a few more questions for you. My partner's working on another part of this case. I only need a moment of your time, and then I'll be out of here."

Hollister bit her lower lip, digesting what he had said. "I hope you'll be more cordial this time," she said, standing aside to allow him in. "I want to recant what I told you about Doctor Richards," she said.

He appeared confused. "Yes, agent Verduzco told me. Tell me again what you said in your message?"

"Please have a seat," she said, pointing to an armchair near a bay window in her small living room. "I made a mistake. I think I was wrong in what I thought was going on. I spoke with Doctor Richards earlier. Now, he fired me for what I've told you. I regret ever saying anything."

"That doesn't matter now. What I need to know is who else have you told about your suspicions of Doctor Richards?" he said, his voice threatening.

Her eyebrows raised, trying to recognize the familiar voice. "Agent Patch, you should take care of yourself. Your voice sounds like you're coming down with a cold. I can fix you some hot tea with honey. It always helped my late husband."

Agent Patch laughed. "It didn't do that great of a job, right?" He died of cancer just like my Molly."

Her mouth dropped to her chest as she saw the revolver pointing at her head. "What's going on?" she screamed. "And, how did you know about my husband's cancer…" she said, puzzled, "Molly? That's Doctor Richards' wife's name." She gasped, her hands covering her mouth. "Who are you?" she cried. "You sound like Doctor Richards."

The man now standing in front of her answered in a low deep voice. "Good guess. You should not have meddled in my business. Everything is ruined because of you," Richards said.

Hollister, stuttered as she tried to speak. "You're not agent Patch? You look just like him, Todd."

He was now smiling. He was happy she would see who was about to kill her. He took out the photo of himself and held it in front of his face. Without any warning, he began transforming back to Doctor Richards.

Hollister almost fainted. She had begun sobbing, as she watched agent Patch disappear and become Doctor Richards. "What's going on? You're the devil," she cried.

"Not the devil, but a revengeful God that is about to take your life." Richards was now standing in front of Hollister, grinning at her shocked expression. Without saying another word, he pressed his index finger hard on the trigger. The bullet exploded inside her chest, knocking her back against her floral couch. Checking that she did not have a pulse, he then, with his left arm extended, concentrated on agent Patch's photo and waited for the change to happen again.

He started tossing things around her home, knocking things to the floor. He found her purse and emptied the contents on her coffee table. He opened her wallet and took out her credit cards and the little cash she had, slipping them into his pockets.

He had started wiping down everything he might have touched while in her home. He went back to her body, careful not to step in her blood that was pooling on her wooden floor. He lifted her dress and pulled her panties down to her ankles, making it appeared she had been sexually assaulted.

He was out the door, briskly walking toward his car. He had not noticed the two faces inside a Ford LTD that had been staring at him as he sped away.

"Was that Agent Patch?" Matt asked.

"Yeah. Guess we're lucky. How embarrassing if we would have run into him here?" Jill said, elbowing her partner. "Let's get our interview and get the hell out of here before the entire SACU squad finds us."

Matt had been knocking on the door for almost two minutes. He tried the doorknob, and it turned. "Miss Hollister, FBI. We're coming inside," he called out.

As they entered the living room, they found Hollister on her back lying in a pool of her blood. It was still warm, as steam floated above her body.

* * * * *

Doctor Richards had returned to the Art Gallery opening he had left earlier in La Jolla. His heart would not stop pounding inside his chest. He had changed shirts inside his car after the shooting. He hoped that no one at the art show had noticed his disappearance or the new shirt he was wearing.

He had started to mingle with friends and patients that crowded the tiny two-story gallery. Richards was surprised how easy it had been to kill his ex-manager. A strange sensation overtook him. He frowned, realizing he was enjoying the thrill of killing another human being.

A voice inside his head was whispering to him. *"Richards, you did well. Carolyn almost had a heart attack watching you transform. Sweet,"* the voice told him. A smug look appeared on his face. The voice returned. *"A few more people to deal with, and we'll be out from under all of this."*

61

The flashing police lights filled the night air as Carolyn Hollister's house got cordoned off with yellow police crime scene tape. Four news vans had gotten there almost at the precise moment the police had. Neighbors had flocked to the street, some in robes, others in shorts and t-shirts.

Jill and Matt had started to answer SDPD detective Bradley Connors questions when FBI agents Patch and Verduzco drove up. Jill, without warning, lunged toward Forrest Patch, and without saying a word, landed a left hook to his nose.

"You bastard," she shouted.

"What the fuck is wrong with you?" Patch said, holding his nose, the blood dripping through his fingers and onto his white shirt.

"We saw you leaving Hollister's house right before we arrived and found her dead body. You have some explaining to do," she said, taking out her cuffs.

Patch had gotten a gauze pad from the paramedics standing by their bus. He had a puzzled look on his face. "I've been with Verduzco all night at the coroner's office. You can check with my boss. He had both of us in a briefing most of the evening."

Jill's eyes echoed disbelief, dropping her arms to her side. "Do you have a twin?" she asked, blushing.

"No, I don't have a twin or even a brother. What the fuck is wrong with you?"

Jill and Matt took the agents back to their car and told them what they had seen. Jill brought them up to date on their end of the investigation, and her theory about Doctor Richards' possible experiments and shift-changing abilities.

Agent Emerson had gotten three queer looks from the agents as they listened to her theory about Richards. While she spoke, she didn't seem convinced herself, as her own words sounded rather bizarre.

"We know that some type of serum was injected into Lisa Beverly, our twilight zone chameleon, Trish Morgan. If Richards could change his appearance by only looking at a picture of a person, then Lisa Beverly could be Trish Morgan. Jeffrey Peters could be Doctor Richards," she said. At that moment, a bell went off in her head, remembering how Beth Thomas reacted when she heard Lisa Beverly's name. "Shit, I bet the Cosmetic CEO, knows more than she's saying."

Matt interrupted. "Then, what do you think about Angelica Rathburn turning up the other day?" he said.

Jill shrugged her shoulders. "I don't know. Maybe our nutty doctor, Todd Richards, murdered Rathburn, and had transformed into her to throw us off? If he's capable of doing what no one in the scientific community believes is possible, then he's more dangerous than we think," Jill fell back against the hood of the car. "What we need is a search warrant for this guy's office and home. We need to rip everything apart."

Agent Verduzco could not control her anger. "This sounds like a lot of smoke and mirrors. I find it hard to fathom that people can change their appearances with only their thoughts. I think your theory sucks," she lashed back.

Patch pulled on his partner's arm, as he removed the blood-soaked gauze. "Then, how do you explain my leaving this crime scene when I was with you and our boss downtown? Also, how do you explain the body of Rathburn having the tattoo Hollister told us about?"

"Shit, I don't know," Verduzco moaned. "Possibly someone who looked like you…it's fucking dark out. They could have made a mistake. Maybe Rathburn had a movie double at her house?"

Matt slipped his hands inside his pants pocket. "If your partner's identical twin hadn't walked under that," he pointed behind them to a streetlight that stood directly in front of Hollister's front walkway, "it was bright enough for us to make a positive ID. Perhaps, we should look at Agent Patch for this murder, if you still don't believe what my partner is saying. I find it hard to believe, but after seeing Angelica Rathburn..." he saw Verduzco ready to say something... "Don't go there," he gave her a stern look. "Oh shit. What if Rathburn was Richards?" he said, wiping his lips, recalling the wetness from the kiss he had gotten at the actress's house. "I'm feeling sick," he scowled.

Emerson took over the conversation. "You can believe me or not. We now have a bloated corpse at the coroner's office, who, by all indications, is Rathburn. If our doctor can do what I'm saying, then we better get our ducks lined up, or we're going to all look like fools."

Agent Patch removed the gauze from his nose. "This is too much X-Files for my liking," he said, shaking his head.

Emerson stopped him and spoke. "To prove to you that our brains are capable of more than what we're using them for, I spoke to a guy in Arizona who believes he can talk to his cells and make them repair his body. The guy is over eighty and looks and acts like he's fifty. He has a pretty big following," she said.

"But, can his thoughts change his appearance?" Agent Verduzco lashed back.

"I don't want to get into a spitting contest with you. If you have a better theory, let me know. We have too many strange coincidences that all point to Doctor Richards. I, for one, want to arrest the mother-fucker, and then search his entire office," Jill said. "If you won't get the warrant, I'll do it myself. You should have the collar."

Verduzco could not find the right words to say. She had thrown her arms in the air surrendering to Emerson. "By the way, what the hell were you two doing out here in the first place?"

Matt stepped in front of his partner. He knew her all too well and didn't want to have to explain why two FBI agents had battered noses.

"Our job," St. Claire responded. "We're still investigating two murders, and Richards is our only suspect now. We thought Hollister might have some important information for our case," Matt said, gently pushing Emerson away. "If we hadn't gotten here when we did, we might be spinning our wheels on both our cases. At least we have a lead on who might have killed her," he said, looking at agent Patch and shaking his head in disbelief. "Believe me. That guy was the spitting image of you."

"I can get an arrest warrant tonight, but a search warrant will be a little harder until we can convince a judge that Richards is a prime suspect in two murder cases, and doing abortions," said Verduzco. She was not a happy camper as she walked over to her car. "Shit, we have to be pretty specific on the warrant. No judge will give us the warrant to search a house or office based on this science fiction theory."

Jill put her arm around Patch's shoulder. "Sorry. I get a little overzealous at times. Let's go arrest the bastard."

Forrest mumbled something, as he held the bloody gauze tight against his throbbing nose. "Sorry, my ass." He was listening to his phone messages. He was unable to control his temper. "Mother fucker," he screamed.

St. Claire looked at his partner. She had her hands up, feigning innocence that she did not attack agent Patch again. Matt looked at Forrest. "What's happening?"

"Six hours ago, Hollister left Amy a message recanting everything she had accused Doctor Richards of doing. Shit, no judge will give us a warrant now."

"I bet Richards is eliminating everyone connected to his house of horrors, and Beth Thomas and Lea Strong are the only two people left who can implicate him doing abortions and his shape-shifting abilities," Emerson said.

"If you're right about him, we are running out of time before he permanently disappears with a new identity," said St. Claire.

62

Richards strolled back to his office after the Art Gallery fundraiser. He was pleased with what he had accomplished at Hollister's apartment.

Richards, with all of his reading, understood the law. He was confident with his office manager dead, and her recanting of her complaint, it would be difficult for the SACU agents or any law enforcement agency convincing a judge to sign off to search his premises.

Richards stopped abruptly, frozen in his tracks, his eyes wide with disbelief, seeing four FBI agents banging on his front door. Angled by the curb in front of his walkway to his office were four patrol cars, their multicolored lights flashing.

"How did they get here so fast? No way they'd suspect it was me at Hollister's home?" he moaned.

His first impulse was to turn and run. Being at the gallery's open house might give him an alibi. It wasn't worth the risk to walk right up to his office at that moment.

Richards knew he could not afford to be locked up or detained at this time. He needed access to his serum and to keep to his regular schedule.

He was panicking. His brain sorted out all of his prepared getaways if cornered. He made an abrupt turn and headed back toward the cove. He started running. He had a second garage there, at an apartment building, where he kept a second car.

He kept scolding himself for his reckless behavior as he jogged toward the ocean. He kept going over all his options, and nothing was surfacing. He knew if he gave himself enough time to think, he'd figure out a plan and disappear off the face of the earth. First, he had to get back to his lab one more time and pick up his new hybrid vials. He didn't know how he would do that.

He kept shaking his head as he sprinted down a steep grade. He was talking incoherently out loud, trying to inject a positive outlook on a dismal situation. He passed a few late-night strollers that walked hand in hand on the winding pathway that bordered the famous La Jolla Cove. He kept muttering out loud, unaware of the turning heads, and puzzled faces, staring at him as he rushed by.

He had to change identities without being noticed. He found a public restroom and darted into a vacant stall. He turned his reversible sweatshirt inside out and unzipped his travel pant legs, making them into a pair of shorts. Before he left the restroom, he checked himself out in the cracked mirror to verify his driver's license was for Chad Green. He swiped a tear from his cheek. He was all alone again. His stomach was in knots; his head was spinning out of control with hopelessness, reminiscent of the evening Molly had died.

He had made it to the underground garage and jumped into his SUV. Within seconds he was heading out of La Jolla and north toward Interstate 5. *Think*, he kept telling himself as he slammed his palm against the steering wheel. *Don't panic. The secret is still safe. Damn, what about Beth and Lea. They'll need their shots. H*e hit the steering wheel again. This time harder. *They only have three days left. What if I'm on the news, they might call the authorities. No, they'll go to jail too. Shit, if they don't get their shots, they'll begin to deteriorate.*

He had not noticed he had been going over ninety, as he headed toward his apartment in Santa Monica. *Slow down, idiot. A ticket is not what you need right now. The police are looking for you.* Then he remembered he had changed his identity in the restroom before leaving La Jolla. It had finally hit him as he passed through the closed immigration checkpoint outside of Camp Pendleton.

63

Agent Verduzco looked at Agents Emerson and St. Claire, frustration on her face. "How much longer should we keep banging? It's obvious that he's not home or coming home any time soon." She looked around at the parade of police, and nosey neighbors and tourists who had gathered behind the half dozen police cars on the street.

A few local news vans had already pulled up and started recording the commotion. One reporter, near Emerson, was talking into her microphone.

"We're outside doctor Todd Richards medical building. There are four FBI agents, all tight-lipped as to why they are here. The SDPD is here too and can only say that they are backing up the FBI on an open case," the reporter said. She walked a little closer to Amy Verduzco and extended her arm that was holding her microphone.

"Can I get your name, please?" she asked.

Special Agent Verduzco unsmiling pushed the microphone away from her face. "You need to step back. You're interfering with our crime scene," she said, realizing that was the wrong thing to say.

"Crime scene? Did someone die?" the reporter inquired.

"Look, we need to do our jobs right now. I will address the press when we are done."

The reporter was handed a piece of paper from one of her crew from her news van. She read it and was back in Verduzco's face.

"Special agent Amy Verduzco? From the FBI's SACU unit? You're here investigating someone doing abortions?" the reporter asked.

Her questions caught Amy off-guard. "No. We are following up on an anonymous tip, nothing more than that. We get them all the time, and most turn out to be nothing at all," Verduzco responded, walking toward Richards's front door.

The reporter spoke into her microphone. "It appears that the FBI's SACU unit has a tip that Doctor Todd Richards is allegedly performing abortions at his La Jolla Cosmetic Surgery clinic."

Verduzco briskly walked to her partner, noticeably upset. "I think I blew it. My big mouth will be plastered all over the news tonight," she said.

Emerson asked. "What did you say?"

"The reporter somehow knew who I was and that I was with SACU. She asked me who we were here for, and that's when she made a horrible assumption that we are here checking out if Doctor Richards was doing abortions. Shit, I'm not sure what I fucking said," she cursed, before storming off to her car. "She might have mentioned Doctor Richards in her question."

Agent Patch looked frustrated and followed his partner back to their vehicle. He threw his arms in the air. "Shit, if Richards was coming home, and saw all of us; this fucking circus...well, I know what I'd do if I were guilty," he said, his anger showing.

Patch walked over to the police officer in charge. "Please get a couple of unmarked vehicles here, and stake out Richards' office," he ordered.

The officer seemed confused. "Is this an SDPD case, or a SACU case?" he asked.

Agent Emerson tapped the officer on the shoulder. With a big smile said. "We're not sure about this case. It might be ours or yours. Now until we do, can you help us out? Please, a little professional courtesy? We're dealing with a couple of murders and numerous violations of Federal laws." she said, looking deep into his eyes.

"Fine. Don't keep us dangling too long. We're short-staffed right now," the officer said, as the agents walked past him.

"We need to get the hell out of here and regroup," Agent Patch said. "I can try to convince a judge tomorrow to allow us to search Richards' office."

Jill met up with everyone. "I don't know about you guys, but I'm starving. Anyone know a decent place to get some food around here?"

Agent Verduzco nodded. "Follow us. I know a place that's opened all night. They have edible cuisine. Last time I was there…" she grinned, "It had a 'B,' or a 'C' rating posted on the window. A hospital's close by."

Matt smiled and elbowed Jill. "See, she does have a sense of humor, unlike you."

* * * * *

The coffee shop was off La Jolla Village Drive. The four agents tried to relax and act friendly. Agent Patch kept touching his sore nose, Agent St. Claire read the menu, and Agents Verduzco and Emerson had gotten locked into a staring contest. Matt had started to make small talk with Forrest, ignoring his obstinate partner.

"Married?" St. Claire asked.

"Been. Divorced five years," Patch said with a sad shrug.

Matt acknowledged with a shrug. "Never been, and at the rate, my love life has been lately, it doesn't seem I'll ever get married in this lifetime. It's the typical cliché: we're all married to our jobs. Who would want to be part of all of this crap?"

Agent Patch had perked up from Matt's remarks. "In the beginning, it seemed okay. My wife worked—we saw each other mostly at night. Then, when I got assigned to SACU, everything changed. I changed mostly. My ex was for a woman's right to choose, and when the Supreme Court threw out Roe V. Wade, our fights started. It seemed to go downhill from there," he said, a painful sadness in his voice.

"I don't know your whole situation, but she had to understand it was your job, not your belief?"

"I never did believe in a woman's right to choose to murder an innocent baby. I volunteered for this assignment. I guess it took SACU to bring out the honesty in the two of us we kept locked away during the honeymoon years. It's no big deal. I date when I want to; it seems to fit in better with my moods and schedule," Patch said somberly.

St. Claire sat up straight, desperate to find out how another single male FBI agent got dates. "What's your secret? I can't seem to find anyone to go out with, even for coffee," he said, letting his sadness percolate in his voice, as he struggled with his words.

Patch smiled. "I didn't mean to brag. I can get a date whenever I want to. I have dry spells. I have no moves I make. Sometimes it happens, and other times, well, I strikeout."

Verduzco had been listening to her partner and blurted out some knifing words. "His moves go back to the sixties. What's a nice girl like you doing in a place like this," she said in a deep baritone voice. "What's your sign," she kept going, laughing hard. "Looks like you work out?"

Matt felt terrible for Patch. He tried to duck for cover as Jill jumped in with Amy.

"Matt has so many problems getting a woman to go out with him that even escorts won't shave their legs if you get my drift," she laughed, raising her hand to high-five with Verduzco. "It's been how long?" she asked her partner.

While the women acted despicably, Matt stood, his face on fire. "I need some fresh air. Tap on the window when the food's here." He stormed out, not before lip-syncing *fuck you*, to his partner.

"Hey St. Claire, wait up. The frost queens are getting on my nerves too." Patch had thrown his napkin in Verduzco's face, as he followed Matt outside. He looked back and yelled, "Can't wait to hear your interview on tonight's news."

The two women looked at each other, their eyebrows raised in surprise at what just happened.

Jill had a bewildered look on her face. "I've never seen him that sensitive before. He must be horny, or it's his time of the month?" she said, shrugging her shoulders.

Verduzco didn't seem too interested in her partner's mood, either. "He's dished it out worse to me at some of our morning briefings. They're both acting like little girls."

For the first time, it seemed both women had found some common ground and had begun to talk about their cases. Jill had told Amy about her concern for the last two women on their list, as well as finding Trish Morgan, or determining if Lisa Beverly was her. She had gotten no argument from Verduzco. They both had come to the same conclusion. They agreed they had too many loose ends and working together might be their best alternative.

Agent Verduzco opened her notebook and thumbed through a few pages. "We need to find Richards and get into his office. We need to look around. On the way over here, I had put out an APB for him. Hopefully, he'll turn up."

Amy could sense Jill was about to remind her about the possibility he could be in a new identity. "Don't say it," Verduzco put her hands in a 'T.' "I'm still not convinced about your theory. For the time being, place those thoughts on hold. We can talk more about it later."

"I've got to find Lea Strong and Beth Thomas before Richards does. If they're due for one of their treatments, and he's not at his office to help them, we can bring them in to tell us what's been going on," Emerson said.

"If Richards still has this serum at his office, we might have a perfect bargaining chip for them to turn on him," Amy said.

"So, you believe me about this magic potion," said Emerson.

"Hold your horses. If these women need a shot for some medical reason, that's one thing. I'm not giving in to your theory just yet."

The food had arrived, and Jill tapped her keys on the restaurant window. She signaled for Matt and Forrest to come in. The two men had a cold silence between them, as they started eating.

Jill and Amy brought them up to date on how they all would be working together, and what they'll do next. The two men nodded as they chewed on their food. They listened to the plan of action, and after thirty minutes, the four of them paid their bills and went their separate ways.

Inside the car, Matt had been fuming, his hands squeezing the steering wheel tightly. He was now speeding north back to Los Angeles.

"You're an ass," he said. "I can take your putdowns privately… shit, I've never been so embarrassed. Your constant *'busting my chops'* sense of humor has finally gotten to me." He had the accelerator floored as they headed north.

Jill struggled to find the right words to say, but nothing coherent came to her. She was always uncomfortable expressing her feelings. So, in her normal defensive mode, blurted out a response. "Shit St. Clare, if I had a dollar for the times you and the boys have embarrassed me since we'd become partners, I'd be rich and retired." Her words had released her bottled up sadness.

Since losing Alex years ago, Matt had become her surrogate boyfriend. Not in the romantic sense, only in the verbal banter that a man and woman have. Losing the only man she had ever loved made it hard for her to be with other men. Her relationship with her fiancée was complicated, but she never questioned his love for her.

She was stubborn and bull-headed, and Alex easy going always giving in to her moods with his arms open wide.

Alex Martin, when on the job, was a hard nose DEA agent. When he was with Jill, he was a romantic, thoughtful, and compassionate friend, as well as a gentle lover.

After Alex died, Jill fell into the darkest pits of despair and guilt. Everything she had done, not done, for him or toward him, had sprung up like a jack-in-the-box, every waking hour of her day. Her moods and verbal abuse had lost her many partners until Matt St. Claire decided to give her a chance.

Her eyes welled as she tried to forget about Alex and concentrate on the problem at hand. She had been looking over at her partner for the longest time before she spoke.

"I'm so sorry, Matt. I don't know what gets into me sometimes. This toilet of a mouth I have needs a plumber to unstop the shit I've kept bottled up inside for so long. I know my baggage is not your problem. I know you don't deserve the crap I dole out to you," she said sniffling. "I don't want to lose you. You're more than my partner; you're my best friend."

St. Claire's foot eased up on the accelerator, he turned his head, smiling. "You can't lose me. We're friends first, partner's second. It really hurts when you remind me of the pathetic love life I have. You know my deepest secrets like a priest during confession. But I forgive you. Just don't do it again. I don't know how much more I can take."

Jill reached over and squeezed his arm. "I'm buying Velcro tomorrow, and taping it to my lips," she said with a forced smile. This emotional talking was in territory that was unfamiliar to her. She had started squirming in her seat, uneasy about letting her feelings escape.

The long drive to Los Angeles kept them both in their dreamlike state. She had started thinking about the guy she had met at the dance club, Chad Green. *Maybe it's time to start thinking about dating, and getting on with my life*, she told herself.

Matt had been thinking about agent Verduzco. She was not a looker like Jill. Nevertheless, he fantasized about going out to dinner with her some time.

64

Richards, weary and exhausted from his escape from La Jolla, flopped down on the couch in his Santa Monica apartment. He laid his head back, squeezing his eyes tight, and admonished himself for another horrible misstep. Recapping what had transpired these last four weeks put his mind in a tailspin. He knew he was a genius, even calling himself a God at times. At this moment, his confidence was fading.

He opened his eyes, gazing at the stark apartment he would be calling home for a while. It was a far cry from his La Jolla home he had enjoyed with his wife. For the first time since discovering his fountain of youth serum, he was not feeling confident about the path he had put himself on. He felt his personality changing, and he did not like it. Again, he reminded himself to get a Cat-Scan and compare his brain receptors to the first scan he took eight years ago.

Richards had multiple medical insurance policies under two other aliases he used. One for Chad Green and one for Jeff Peters. He knew Peters' identity could not be used again for obvious reasons.

He had begun to shake from nerves and uncertainty. He blamed his missteps on his current serum hybrid. Richards knew he had to find a safe location with new subjects to perfect a hybrid solution that would allow him to extend the interval between his injections.

Murdering his office manager, and posing as agent Patch, had been his biggest blunder for far. For the first time, his cocky attitude to change appearances might expose him. If that happened, then the CIA would want to capture him and lock him up in a secret laboratory. He felt he could stay one step ahead of the FBI, but the CIA was another problem he didn't think he could hide from.

He had a pounding headache. He had started to make a list of his symptoms. He now believed his worst nightmare was coming true. He had predicted these side-effects were possible. He had not anticipated them happening so soon.

He was happy he had moved some of his equipment to his Santa Monica storage facility. It would allow him the opportunity to begin creating the changes he needed. His other problem was that he had to figure out how he would get back into his La Jolla lab, undetected, and confiscate enough serum vials, fetuses, and extra laboratory equipment.

With his headache subsiding, he drove to his storage locker to begin his work. He drew some of his blood and then distributed a small amount onto four Petri dishes. He then added serum samples from four different hybrid vials with his blood DNA.

After two hours, he observed how his blood samples had changed. He then mixed portions of the four new samples to create a fifth hybrid. He placed the new sample under his microscope. He smiled as he noticed the changes within his blood.

"Shit, this hybrid is mutating my blood. Could this be what I've been looking for?" Richards said. He then mixed the new serum with the other hybrid vials. His final combination had gotten his attention.

"This is it," he clapped. "Now, to prove my theory."

He stared at his shaking hands. His headache had returned, but this time stronger. He filled a syringe with his new formula. He glanced around his storage container, looking for his neck mold.

"Shit, it's at my La Jolla lab," he cussed.

He had not injected himself for years without the neck guide. Today he had no choice. He slid his index finger on the side of his neck until he located the exact spot on his carotid artery to inject his new formula. Looking in a mirror, he pressed on the syringe slowly, releasing the fluid into his bloodstream. He felt the warm liquid flow into his brain. He waited thirty minutes, allowing his body to adjust. Next, he picked up a scalpel. He slowly traced a line on the palm of his hand, forcing the blade to go very deep. Blood had begun gushing from his hand. The pain was unbearable.

He took a deep breath to calm himself down. He focused on the pain he was feeling on his throbbing hand. As he would do when he looked at his photos, within seconds, the blood had stopped, and the wound started closing. A minute later, his hand had stopped hurting. Where he had sliced his skin open, it had disappeared. He poured disinfectant over his hand, wiped the blood off, and noticed the wound was gone.

Richards smiled with pride. Now more than ever, he needed to get back to his office and lab. "I need to use a few more aliases," he told himself.

After four more hours of painful testing on his body, he was pleased with what he had created. He knew what had to come next.

He needed the serum vials for his other female patients. If he could not get them, then he would have to start over with new women and new fetuses. He did not have the luxury of waiting for that to happen. He was now a hunted man.

He had to get his duplicate laboratory equipment at his La Jolla office, still boxed, never opened, to his Santa Monica storage facility. He figured the police and FBI most likely were staking out his office. Getting inside might prove to be impossible.

For now, he needed to rest. He was tired and depleted from the experiments he had been doing on his body for the last four hours.

Back at this Santa Monica apartment, his head hit his pillow, and the room began to spin. He again was feeling like he was out of control, unable to stop the runaway train he was on. He extended his arm and found the folder on his nightstand that contained some of the aliases he could use. "This alias will work just fine," he said. "No way the police or FBI will be able to stop me from getting into my office as this person," he muttered, as he kept staring at the photo.

He closed his eyes and smiled broadly. While he did not know how he was going to solve the Beth Thomas and Lea Strong problem, he was confident a solution would show itself soon enough.

With his eyes squeezed tight, a thousand thoughts began swirling inside his mind. He wondered if he'd kill again. He prayed he had learned his lesson. Something deep inside him was telling him there would be more to come.

Richards had finally understood how a drug addict felt when the desire for a fix controlled the brain. Richards' fix now, to create the perfect serum, had become his obsession, with murder as his vehicle. His last thought before he drifted off to sleep could he become a new person, someone he'd respect in a new identity.

65

Agents Verduzco and Patch had an early morning appointment with Professor Franklin, Richards ex-boss, at his UCLA laboratory. They had called him right after their meeting last night with Emerson and St. Claire.

Verduzco and Patch decided that since they were with SACU, the professor would be within their authority. They got word that the search warrant they needed would be ready late afternoon to search Richards' office.

Before they met with Franklin, Patch and Verduzco decided to listen to one of his lectures. *"Stem cells, the future of medical science,"* a futuristic title, they thought.

"This should be noteworthy," Amy said.

"Maybe the title should be *'Shift-Changers, the Future is Now,'"* he mocked.

Professor Franklin had over a hundred eager students captivated by his theory on how the human brain had the potential to cure diseases in the body. The professor hinted that one day it would be possible for the mind, with one's thoughts, to transform a person to go back to a younger, more youthful age.

"Do you think this guy knows what Richards has created?" Patch asked.

"Richards worked with him here. It's possible," Verduzco responded. "I don't want to speculate. This entire case is one step away from the

Twilight Zone and bordering on X-Files shit. Let's talk with Franklin first, before we make too many assumptions."

All Franklin knew was that they wanted to ask him some questions about his ex-employee Todd Richards, and the fetal stem cell work he had been doing during his tenure at UCLA.

After introducing themselves to Franklin, he ushered them into a small conference room, where two men, in black suits and dark sunglasses, were sitting.

Amy was the first to react. "We asked specifically to meet with you privately," she said, her tone testy. "We're working on an open case that involves Todd Richards. We do not want to share what we have with other people."

Franklin responded. "I had to mention this meeting and its subject matter to the government agencies I work with here at UCLA. My work has a classified, top-secret, long-term contract with the CIA, Defense Department, and Homeland Security, which was in effect when Doctor Richards had worked here. There is little I can say about what we were doing back then, or what role Todd Richards played in it," he said.

Agent Patch interrupted. "Aren't you going to introduce us to these spooks first?" he asked, sarcastically.

"Excuse my rudeness. "This is CIA special agent Ralph Bingham, and from Homeland Security Leroy Todd."

Bingham took over the meeting. "Professor Franklin will not be answering any questions today. I have a few for you." He had put his feet on the conference table, his hands linked behind his head, arrogance spewing out of every pore on his body.

Verduzco slammed her fist on the table, not liking Bingham's attitude, and disrespect he was showing them. "This is bull-shit. We're investigating two murders, as well as a handful of illegal abortions. What the fuck does the CIA have to do with Doctor Richards? What were you two goons creating here?" she asked, pointing her middle finger at Bingham's face.

The CIA agent was unmoved by her antics. "I've read your file. You're a real ballbuster since moving over to SACU. Get this straight. I will be asking the questions today," he said.

Patch looked at Professor Franklin, ignoring Bingham. "Have you ever, or are you presently working with fetal stem cells? We listened to your lecture today, and it sounds like you are," he said, firing off a second question. "Did Doctor Richards ever work with fetal stem cells while here at UCLA?" he was cut off by Bingham.

"That work was and still is classified and above your paygrade. If those are your questions, then I guess this meeting is over," Bingham said. "I assume you believe Richards is using fetal stem cells now and creating some type of serum with it?"

"We didn't say anything about a serum, but thanks for the heads up," agent Patch said. "Any other clues you'd like to share with us today?"

They headed to the door. Amy turned and said. "Thanks for your cooperation. You tipped your hand. We now have a new direction to pursue...something that the government doesn't want anyone to know about, right?" Verduzco said, slamming the door.

Bingham looked at his partner. "I think we're going to have a problem with those two. We need to find Richards and get him back with us before they lock him up. We can't watch him from afar anymore."

Leroy swallowed hard, afraid to tell Bingham about Richards. "We've lost the doctor. When the SDPD and FBI were at his clinic yesterday, he never returned. I'm not sure where he's at," he said. "He could now be in an identity we don't have in his file."

Bingham jumped up and tossed his chair across the room. His rage exploded. "I want that fucking Richards found and brought in. Check all of his goddamn aliases and other apartments he has rented," he cursed. "We know what he's capable of doing. I don't want the FBI figuring it out until we have him back here, locked up so we can throw away the key."

Professor Franklin stayed seated, shaken by Bingham's outburst. "Ralph, before we bring Richards in, we need to secure all of his research, and serum he had produced at his La Jolla laboratory. I'm sure the FBI is trying to get a warrant to search his property. I cannot begin to tell you what it will do to our research if they find his serum and fetuses before we do. We need samples of what he's created, as well as any notes he has, or our program will go nowhere," he said.

"Are you telling me that the billions of dollars we've invested in you, and your program, can't move forward without Richards?" Bingham asked.

"I'm closer to what you...the CIA wants, but having Richards serum, his notes...even him cooperating, would make it easier for me to complete the military's project. I'm concerned that if we bring him in too soon, you know before he's perfected his hybrid formula, we might not have what we need for your covert operators," Franklin said. "I know him too well. He won't cooperate if he realizes you're militarizing his serum."

Bingham combed his fingers through his scalp. He was pacing around the conference room. "I have ways to get Richards to cooperate," he said. "I want him in our lab within a month. I cannot delay the president's project any longer."

66

A crisp, drizzly marine layer had engulfed La Jolla at eight-thirty in the morning. Visibility was less than ten yards. It was perfect for what Richards needed to accomplish.

He had parked his car a block south of his office. Richards was now Chuck Feldman, his attorney dressed in a black pinned striped suit. His dress shirt was pale blue, with a bright red silk tie. He walked past two officers who sat in their patrol car, drinking their hot cups of coffee. He stopped, leaned in, and asked them a question.

"I was out late last night and noticed all the commotion. Is Doctor Richards all right?" Feldman asked with curiosity.

The officer, by the passenger door, looked up, eyed the nicely dressed gentleman. He folded his newspaper and replied with a pleasant tone. "It's police business, sir. We can't discuss it right now. You should keep walking."

The attorney handed the officer his business card. "Sorry for being so nosy. I'm Doctor Richards' attorney, Chuck Feldman. Was there a murder at Doctor Richards' office? If not, why is it still cordoned off like it's an active crime scene?" he said in a steady voice. "This is affecting his business," Feldman said, pointing at the ten patients waiting across the street for their infusion treatments.

The officer had a surprised look on his face after reading the card. "You're Doctor Richards attorney? What are you doing here? The doctor's not inside?" he said. "It's best you leave the area until the FBI gets back. Our orders are not to let anyone in his office," the officer said, pointing toward the front door.

Doctor Richards smiled, thinking what his real attorney would say at that moment. "Can I see your warrant?"

"We do not have a warrant," the officer responded awkwardly.

"Then, remove this god-damn yellow shit from my client's property, before you scare off all of his patients. I have to get inside and pick up something for my client," he told them.

The officer looked at the business card, and then up at the man in the expensive suit. "I can't let you inside. It's a crime scene," he said.

"What crime?"

Now the officer was tongue-tied. "All I know is that the FBI asked us to cordon off the property and not let anyone in or out until they got back here."

"Unless you can show me a warrant or provide probable cause to call this property a crime scene, you had better let me go in on behalf of my client," *Feldman* said, his tone aggressive. "Your police department cannot afford another defamation of character lawsuit from one of San Diego's most respected doctors. Now, get your two asses up and remove this crap in front of my client's office."

The young officer's partner was already on his phone to his Sargent. "Yes, sir. I understand, sir. Copy that," he said, opening his side door. He walked over to the attorney.

"Well, can I go in?" *Feldman* asked.

"Sir, it would be better if you can wait for the FBI to arrive, the SDPD would appreciate it. They should be here in fifteen minutes."

"Thanks, but no thanks. Now remove this fucking crime scene tape. Please let the FBI know mister Richards' attorney is inside and to knock on the front door. I will talk to them then," *Feldman* said, smiling that his disguise was working as planned.

Inside, Richards began putting all the vials he needed in a metal suitcase that contained foam rubber cutouts. He had two metal cases that would hold forty-eight bottles.

Next, he went downstairs to his laboratory and began removing his frozen fetuses. He knew this would be more difficult to carry out of his office. He placed them in three large temperature control metal containers.

At the back of the sub-zero refrigerator, he found his escape hatch. It led to his backyard, where he had a metal door by the back-brick wall. He placed the sealed fetuses outside the metal gate in a garbage bin. He hoped his plan would work.

When he finished gathering what he needed for his new lab, he ran upstairs to his bedroom. He found another suitcase and began stuffing the items he wanted to save, his most cherished photos, his wedding album with Molly.

Now he was ready for the FBI and whatever they wanted to do to him.

67

Twenty minutes after Richards' attorney entered his office, Agent Forrest Patch banged his hand on the roof of the squad car, causing the two officers to jump. "I'm impressed. No donuts. Any activity?" he asked

"Yeah. Richards' attorney, a Chuck Feldman, came by and demanded to go into the building," the officer said, handing Agent Patch the attorney's business card. "Our Sargent told us we could not stop him without a warrant," the young officer said, uneasily.

"Fuck. The warrant's coming. You're relieved. Get some breakfast and be back in an hour. I'm waiting for Agent Verduzco. She's got the warrant, and she should be here in an hour." He noticed the two policemen seemed relieved. Without another word, they had pulled out from the curb, made a sharp U-turn, and headed down Prospect toward their favorite breakfast spot.

"Lazy bastards," he muttered softly. He had started to walk toward the front door when one of Doctor Richards' patients, Beth Thomas, had come running up behind him, all frantic. Agent Patch noticed that the woman looked desperate.

"Has something happened to Doctor Richards?" Thomas asked. She could not stop fidgeting with her hands. "I have to see him now. I've noticed the police have been here all night. Are you with the police?" she asked.

"I'm FBI agent Forrest Patch. I'm sorry to say that the doctor is missing. We're looking for him too. We have some questions for him.

Beth Thomas had become more animated, as she paced the walkway in front of Richards' office. "Carolyn Hollister…Murdered? Oh my, that's horrible," she said. "I need to get inside and pick up a prescription the doctor left for me. I'm in a real rush and need it now," she pleaded.

"His attorney's inside. Perhaps when we're done talking with him, he could help you find Doctor Richards?" said Patch, wishing his partner would arrive. "So please step back and let us do our jobs."

Beth Thomas had one thing in mind and rushed toward the front door ducking under the crime scene tape. Standing on the porch was a man she did not recognize. He was waving her to come toward him.

"Who are you? And, where's Doctor Richards?" she asked.

"First, come inside, and I will explain everything," Franklin said.

Beth was used to getting her way, and as the door closed behind her, she blurted out the one thing that was on her mind. "Could you see if you can find a vial that has my name on it. It should be in a refrigerator in the doctor's laboratory. You would be doing me a big favor. I'm leaving for New Orleans on business and need that medicine."

"I'll see what I can do, Beth," he said, in his Doctor Richards voice.

Beth had a puzzled look on her face. "Todd, is that you? What's going on here? I heard on the news that Carolyn Hollister is dead?"

"Yes. Everything is unraveling, and I needed to get into my office to get our vials. I needed to disguise myself. They think I'm a suspect in Hollister's murder. I'm only here to clear out all the evidence of my research and relocate our serum. If they find them, well, I can only imagine what the headlines would say. We'd be all locked up."

"Shit, what the hell are we supposed to do about our shots?"

"I've got a plan. It would take some cooperation on your part to make it work for all of us," Richards said.

"Anything. Whatever you need, I'm ready to help. I need my shot before I go away," Thomas pleaded.

"I have it ready for you. I heard you talking to agent Patch. Come with me. I can have you on your way in five minutes.

He had Beth lie down on a recliner. He tilted her head so that the left side of her neck was exposed. Richards gently inserted the syringe and slowly pushed the cold fluid into her artery. He doubled checked that it was the correct dosage. He did not need another body to dispose of with the FBI standing outside. It took only ten minutes, and she was good to go for another two weeks.

"That should do it for now. When do you get back from your trip?" Richards asked.

"Six days. Why?" Beth asked, puzzled.

Richards could see she had doubts about everything that has happened. "We need to figure out how to work out a new schedule, as well as a new location to meet. It's almost time for you to abort." He handed her his attorney's business card. "My new cell number is written on the back of the card. Call me as soon as you return."

As he opened the front door to let Thomas out, he saw Agent Verduzco and Agent Patch coming up his walkway. His heart started pounding; his knees began to buckle as he closed the door. He observed the two agents lead Beth toward their car. To his surprise, the two agents pulled out their guns, rushing toward the front door.

He almost panicked. Then realized he was Chuck Feldman. The loud banging on the front door startled him. One of the metal suitcases opened, spilling all the vials onto the carpeted hallway. He called out, "Just a minute." He did not want them busting down the door and seeing all the serum. He grabbed a handful of vials and started to place them carefully back in the case.

The constant banging was driving him crazy. "Just one fucking minute," he called out. As he closed the case, the front door burst open. Standing over him were two FBI agents, their guns were drawn and pointing at his head.

"Hands in the air," Agent Verduzco shouted. "Put those cases on the floor and back away. Keep your hands where I can see them," she ordered.

With his hands stretched high above his head, Feldman spoke. "What the fuck are you two doing entering this property without cause?" he barked.

"Who the fuck are you?" Agent Verduzco asked.

The Faces of Doctor Richards

"*Chuck Feldman*, attorney-at-law. I'm Doctor Richards lawyer. Now I will ask you again, what the fuck are you two doing busting in my client's front door?"

Agent Verduzco handed him her warrant. "A judge issued this warrant to search these premises for evidence that Doctor Richards is performing abortions, and using fetal stem cells, which I am sure you know is against federal law," she said.

Richards studied the warrant and laughed. "You do know that this building is a multi-use property. It's got a separate office and residence with two distinct addresses. Your warrant is only for Doctor Richards's residence. That entrance," he pointed to the adjacent door, "is the address on your warrant. So please leave and don't come back until you have the correct paperwork to search my client's medical facility."

Patch grabbed the warrant from *Feldman*. His face drained of color. "Fuck! We'll be back. Be sure to have Doctor Richards with you when we return," he said.

"Amy. Did you not read the warrant the judge signed?"

"I told him we needed to search Richards home. How was I supposed to know this building was multi-use? Shit, our laws are chicken-shit," she moaned.

"No, you fucked up. Warrants have to be very specific on what you want to search for, and where," said Patch, shaking his head.

Doctor Richards enjoyed watching both agents fight. He went back into his office and grabbed all five of his patient's files.

Fifteen minutes after the two FBI agents left with their tails between their legs, Franklin was out the front door. He gave both agents a friendly wave as he headed toward his car.

He shouted at the agents. "Doctor Richards is upstairs, I think. He won't be seeing any patients anymore," Feldman said as he walked to his car.

He drove to the back of the property and scooped up the frozen fetuses from the trash bin. He put the two metal cases with the vials and the file folders inside the trunk.

Richards` looked back at his office and home, a sharp pain gripping his heart. He realized that he'd never again step into the house he had made for himself and Molly.

He drove the car around to the front of his clinic, listening to the two agents banging on the front door and calling out Richards' name.

"Doctor Richards," he heard. *"We don't want to hurt you. We only want to talk to you."* They were loudly pounding on his residence door.

He found Beth standing beside a traffic light pole, tapping her foot, unable to speak. She glanced at Feldman, waving him over to her.

"I didn't want to leave in case you needed my help," she said.

Richards raised his finger to his lips, signally her to be quiet. "Get in. I'll take you to your car. I need to see what those agents are going to do. Then, we need to talk," he said. The crazy voices inside his head were getting louder again. He was afraid he was about to make the wrong decision.

68

Two hours later, Verduzco and Patch were handed the correct warrant and were inside Richards's office. The doctor had not left the building, so they believed that he was still at home. Agent Patch, his gun pointing down, slowly walked up the stairs. Agent Verduzco's gun was in her hand as she walked sideways, hugging the wall, backing up her partner ready to fire her weapon if necessary.

In less than five minutes, the agents cleared the house. Richards was nowhere to be found.

Amy heard a car pulling away from the curb. "Patch, he's getting away," she shouted, as she headed out the front door.

Right behind her came agent Patch looking up and down the street to see which way the car had headed. "Did you get a license number?" he asked her.

She had begun to curse. "No, I didn't get the fucking license number. Where the hell are the two officers we placed here last night?" she shouted, waving her gun. She looked at the two tires on their car. They were flat. "Richards must have punctured them," she growled.

A moment later, the two police officers drove up and got out of their patrol car. "You guys look fit to be tied," one officer said with a smile.

"Wipe that goddamn grin off your faces. Why'd you leave your post?" Verduzco grilled them.

One of the nervous officers spoke. "Your partner relieved us. He said to go get some breakfast, and be back here after we eat," he seemed confused.

255

Agent Patch's face drained of color. "Did I say to take a two-hour break? Did you check the attorney's ID?"

"We… his business card looked legit…we thought," the young officer stammered.

"Shit, how could you make such a stupid mistake?" Forrest shook his head, scowling at the two men.

"How the hell would we know a fake attorney from a real one. The guy was Chuck Feldman, the lawyer," the officer barked back. "I googled him. His photos on his website," he held up his smartphone and shoved it in the agent's face. "See, this is the guy we spoke with," he said.

"Fuck this," Verduzco grumbled. She looked at her partner, noticing his concern.

Forest frowned. "If Agent Emerson's correct… damn, this guy can become whoever he wants to, and we wouldn't know it until it was too late."

Amy had given him a nasty gaze. "Don't you start believing this 'Shift-Changers' crap. It only happens in science fiction movies," she said. "Now that we have the correct search warrants, it's officially a crime scene, and we can get forensics down here to look for clues of abortions. Also, get Richards fucking attorney on the phone. I want to know where he's been all evening?"

Patch smiled. "What are you going to do if he has an alibi? Will you become a believer?"

69

Beth would not stop crying. Richards was speeding out of La Jolla toward Pacific Beach. "Stop your crying. I need your full cooperation," Richards said. "We have our supply of serum, so relax and let me get us the hell out of here."

Thomas calmed down and looked at the man who had been yelling at her. "Todd, what's going on here?"

"Things have changed. It's you, Lea, and me. I never wanted to harm anyone. It just happened. I was protecting our secret."

She gasped. "You killed Meg? Morgan? And Hollister? Don't tell me you killed Angelica too?"

He nodded. "Angelica was first, but that was an accident. The others, well, I had no choice. I couldn't let us get exposed," he said. What could I do? I can't go to jail. Can you?"

Beth lashed back. "Was killing them the only solution? They could have taken on new identities and, with their money, started new careers or whatever."

Richards turned sharply onto a side street off Garnet and pulled into a vacant parking lot. He felt an emotional rush flow through his veins, like the one he felt before he killed Hollister. He did not like being scolded.

"It was necessary. Just leave it alone. Everyone had turned on me. Are you turning on me too?" Richards said menacingly.

Beth acted as if she had not heard a word he had said. "You killed all of them to keep our secret," she screamed. "They trusted you, shit, I trusted you," she sobbed, swatting the cascading tears off her cheeks.

Richards's nostrils flared as he faced her. "Are you saying you don't trust me anymore?" he asked, his voice becoming raspy and harsh. "I am close to making the perfect serum. Nothing will stop me," he screamed.

Beth sat there, mesmerized by his words. "No more shots," she said, her voice trembling. "How long can I go without the serum booster?"

Richards was holding a photo in his hand. He kept staring at the picture while Thomas spoke. Before she could finish talking, Chad Green appeared. He raised his hand, signaling Beth to stop talking.

"A few more tests, a few more fetuses, a few more cooperative women, and I will be able to become whoever I want, whenever I want, healing my body too, all without having to do these fucking shots every two weeks." He was gasping for air as he spoke. "I just need a little more time. I don't need you to be questioning me," he whispered, his voice calm as he pointed a gun at her head.

Beth gasped. She put her hands up, trying to protect herself from what was about to happen. "Please, don't do this. I don't want to die," she cried.

Without saying a word or hesitating, Chad Green pulled the trigger. He was emotionless, as the explosion of cartilage and brain matter splattered the inside of the car. He leaned across her motionless body and opened her door. With a hard shove, she fell out like a sack of potatoes onto the black asphalt. He pressed on the accelerator, the tires squealed, slamming the passenger door shut. He sped out of the parking lot and back onto Garnet.

The voices inside his head were getting louder and more oppressive. *That was easy, wasn't it?* "You're damn right it was," he said to the empty passenger seat. His eyebrows rose, wrinkling his brow, as he spoke to himself. *We need more serum to survive. What are you going to do? You only have one patient left.* "Shut the fuck up," he screamed at Chad Green. "I'll think of something. I always do. So, don't you worry…okay?"

He was on interstate five heading North toward Santa Monica, mumbling the entire way.

70

Agent Patch answered his cellphone. He could not believe his ears. "Is she alive?" he shouted. Amy had been pulling on his sleeve.

"What's going on?" she asked.

"Beth Thomas was just shot in the head. They don't expect her to make it. Shit, we just spoke with her a few minutes ago."

They ordered the two police officers to park their butts at Richards office until forensics got to the scene. They jumped into their car and sped toward Scripps Memorial Hospital.

Forrest saw it on his partner's face before. She liked cases that were neat and tidy, and this one wasn't. "We need to call Emerson and St. Claire. They need to be part of this," he said.

"We should have taken Beth Thomas into protective custody the moment we saw her at Richards's office. That's what Emerson wanted to do. Shit, we were too pissed off about not finding the doctor," she said, pounding her fist on the dashboard.

Forrest knew he had screwed up. He should have called St. Claire and Emerson as soon as they got to Richards's office and met Thomas. "When we get to the hospital, we can size up the situation. Then we can call them," he said.

Amy was already on her cell. "I want them meeting us at Scripps. They need to be involved. Even if they were here, who's to say Thomas would have let us put her in protective custody? We aren't sure about anything, notably about Richards. The Thomas woman was very anxious to get the heck out of there."

Patch looked at his partner. He knew she was right. "I don't want to hear her lame theory of the many faces of Doctor Richards. However, I'm beginning to become a believer."

"We're going to have our hands full collecting evidence at the doctor's office, and his laboratory. We need them to be involved in all of this before we screw this up anymore," Amy said.

Patch's cell pinged. He looked at the screen. "It's St. Claire," he said, as he took the call. "Boy, do we have a lot to talk about," he said.

"We sure do. I'll go first. We've been at the coroner's office waiting for the results on Rathburn's body. You know the one snagged in a fisherman's net?" St. Claire said, out of breath.

"You might want to hear what we have first," Patch said. "This case is getting stranger and creepier by the minute."

"Fine, go."

"Beth Thomas was just shot. She's on her way to Scripps in La Jolla," Patch said.

Agent Verduzco yanked the phone from her partner. "Shit, we spoke with her, as well as Richards attorney, Chuck Feldman, just thirty minutes ago. His attorney lied to us about Richards being upstairs in his residence. "Fuck, Feldman might have been Richards," Amy said.

"Damn it. Why didn't you put Thomas into protective custody? We told you and Forest that we believe a serial murderer is killing off all of Richards female patients?"

"We know, we screwed up. Sorry," Amy said.

"Any suspects?" St. Claire asked.

"Richards, I'd stake my reputation on it. I'm beginning to believe that the doctor can transform himself into whoever he wishes to be. We have a call into his attorney right now to see if he has an alibi so that we can rule him out as a suspect."

Agent St. Claire wanted to smash his cellphone. "We'll meet you at Scripps. Oh, for your information, the body at the morgue has been positively identified as Angelica Rathburn," Matt said. "You'll not believe how her body is decomposing. Same as Cummings and Beverly.

She did have a chain tattoo around her waist, just like Hollister said. Let's finish this at the hospital. And, you're right, this case is very eerie and disturbing."

71

Jill and Matt had gotten to Scripps two hours after the shooting. She had been in surgery all that time. They found Verduzco and Patch sitting in the waiting room, flipping through old magazines.

Forrest stood and greeted them, while Amy sat there uninterested. She had become further pissed, forensics at Richards office, and his home had not gone the way she had wanted.

Forensics confirmed that Doctor Richards had what appeared to be a stem cell laboratory. They had found five frozen fetuses, with dates going back eight years. They are running DNA analysis to determine if the fetuses matched up with any of the dead women. There was an empty freezer that might have housed vials of serum. It was beginning to look like Richards's office manager was right.

"What's the word on Thomas?" Jill asked Patch.

"Been in surgery for almost two hours. She's lost a lot of blood. They don't give her much hope of recovering."

Emerson turned and saw a nurse walking out of the operating room. "I'm FBI agent Jill Emerson," she said, flashing her badge. "How's Miss Thomas doing?"

The nurse appeared uninterested in her question. "I cannot say at this time," she said in a tired voice. "What I had seen when the woman came in… it looked pretty bad, even if she comes out of surgery alive, she'll be in recovery for hours before you can talk to her," she said, removing her bloodied scrubs as she rushed way. The nurse turned back and yelled.

"Before going into surgery, they ran her bloodwork and discovered she was six weeks pregnant."

Jill turned to the others. "I'm going over to Richards office. I hear forensics is having a grand old time over there. I want to check things out. Sitting around here isn't doing me any good."

Amy looked up and forced a smile. "I'm staying. I want to talk to her the moment she's out of surgery," she said

"Great. I'll keep you posted on what I find," said Emerson coldly. "Matt, you coming?"

"I'll stay here and interview our victim too," he said, sitting down across from agent Verduzco.

"I'll tag along with you," Forrest said. "We can both work on our cases while…" he pointed at his partner, "She interrogates a dying woman."

* * * * *

During the drive back to Richards' office, they both made small talk. Patch wanted to know more about her theory on the doctor's ability to change his appearance. The ride was too short to open any meaningful dialogue. He let her know that he was beginning to believe her.

"Richards got past us twice and was able to murder another of his patient's right under our noses. He even transformed into me. I've got to figure out how he's doing it," Forrest said sorrowfully. "If he's able to change his appearance… shit, he could become anyone he wants to like he did with me. What if he's chosen a new identity now, and never goes back to being Richards?"

Jill turned her head and smiled. She had not noticed before how nice looking he was. She felt flattered he was interested in her assessment of her case and liked the way his voice sounded.

"I know I sound like a loony bird. I can't explain the facts I have right in front of me. Thanks for believing me anyway."

"I would have appreciated you giving me the benefit of the doubt at Hollister's the other day before jumping to conclusions," Patch said, patting his bruised nose.

Before she could reply, they were at Richards' clinic. She had made a mental note to find the right moment to talk with him further.

The forensics team had started to wrap up their sweep of the house and laboratory when Agent Emerson asked what they had found.

Jill had been talking to Fredrick Mullen, the lead forensic investigator at the San Diego FBI field office. Forrest had stepped outside, wandering around the backyard when he had come upon a mulching machine used to make compost.

The foul smell had almost knocked him off his feet. "Shit. Who the hell died?" He gagged on his words, as he scurried back toward the back porch. "Hey, Emerson," he shouted, tasting the bile that had pasted itself on the lining of his throat. "You need to see this… bring Mullen…" he coughed.

He walked them to the mulching machine, pointing at the razor-sharp shark teeth. "Mullen, I want your guys taking this thing apart," he said, covering his mouth and nose with his hand. "That smell is not rotting compost. It smells like death."

Jill's eyes had almost popped out of her head, hearing his words. Mullen, without a second thought, stuck his head inside the mouth of the machine.

"I think you might be right," he said, holding what looked like a decaying twig as he rolled it around on his latex-gloved hand. "My guess it's a bone, a small one. I'll need to run some tests to see if it's human or animal."

"How soon can you dismantle that machine, and see if there are more bones lodged inside?" Emerson asked. She could see Mullen look at agent Patch for his directions.

"She's okay, Frederick. If the bones are human, it's part of her case too. Give her the same courtesy you'd give me," he said with a wink.

Emerson looked at Mullen. "You like him?" she teased.

"Yeah, he's one of my favorite agents," he replied before he dove back into the jaws of the machine. "He's one of the good guys at the Bureau."

Jill had not noticed she had touched Forrest's arm as they walked back into Richards laboratory to check on what the others had found in the freezers. She blushed as he flexed his bicep. *Shit, he works out as well as being handsome.*

Jill dropped her hand, acting nonchalant about the awkward moment. "Doctor Richards might be my first mad scientist," she said uneasily.

"I… have a hunch…we're dealing with something more than meets the eye right now," he said, touching her arm and giving it a gentle squeeze. "When Amy and I were attempting to interview Professor Franklin, you remember, Richards' supervisor at UCLA?" he said. "Well, he was being protected by two CIA agents and couldn't talk about anything Richards was doing for them when he worked there. I believe we have some spooks getting their hands dirty here," he said.

"Let talk about this when we are all together. CIA shit? What's going on here?" Emerson mumbled.

72

Richards rocked back and forth on a chair at his kitchen table. He was feeling overwhelmed by the recurrent thoughts swirling inside his head. "How did it get to this?" he lamented. "I loved those women. They trusted me as I trusted them." Agonizingly, a familiar voice inside his head was arguing with him.

"I know I had no choice," he said. "But, why revert to murder?"

The words inside his mind got louder. *"You have a lot to contribute to the world. You cannot allow anyone to stop you. You are all that matters now."*

He absorbed what he had heard, shaking his head. He had laid out all the remaining aliases he had, looking over all of the full-body photos he had on each of them. They all had the proper Id's he'd need to travel inside or outside of the United States. His only problem right now was Lea Strong. He expected that she'd be in protective custody, making it difficult for him to dispose of her.

He knew Lea had only four days left before she'd need her serum injection and would be desperate to see him. Richards knew she was not the smartest of his patients and would be in a panic if she could not find him.

Being rushed the other day at his office, he had not been able to pack all the vials for Thomas and Strong, or the remaining fetuses he had frozen. Once the FBI thoroughly searched his office, they'd find the refrigerated storage locker with the leftover serum and fetus that had Lea's name on it. Whether they would give her what she needed, and at

267

the right dosage was another story. They could have another Angelica Rathburn reaction on their hands.

"Too little or too much, you'd kill her," he whispered. He thought of sending them a message, instructing them on what to do. She was his loose end that needed to be severed, one way or the other.

Richards had to keep his Chad Green identity, at least for now. What he needed was a new laboratory far away from Santa Monica.

Richards remembered he was owed a favor from a man, a criminal, who trafficked in young girls. He had helped him with one of his girls who had been beaten badly by one of his pimps. He had never thought he'd have to call in his chip, but he was desperate.

"Salvador, it's Todd. I need your help," he asked.

"Doctor Todd, my friend. I've been waiting for you to call. You're all over the news. Have you fallen into my world now? Is it true you are doing abortions?" he asked.

"I'll tell you all about it when we meet."

"Okay, my friend. Whatever you need. I'm here for you," said Salvador Conte.

Richards let out a long sigh. "Thank you. Can we meet as soon as possible?"

Salvador did not answer him right away. "Tell me where you are, and I will have my men pick you up," he said.

"No. I'll come to you. Let's meet at the northwest park bench in Echo Park tomorrow at ten in the morning. You won't recognize me. I will find you and explain everything to you. Please come alone so that we can talk first," Richards said.

"Fine, my friend. You can trust me. I owe you for fixing my best girl."

"I'm glad you understand," Richards replied, ending the call.

Emerson and St. Claire waited for Patch and Verduzco to arrive. Jill was fidgety. The restaurant in Hillcrest had two customers, giving them the privacy they'd need.

"We don't work well with others," she said. "I know you've got the hots for Amy, but we need to stay focused."

Her partner, his eyes had become little slits. "Knock it off. I saw you fawning over her partner, too. So, give me a break. We have no choice but to team up with them," St. Claire said, his tone biting. "They're good agents, like us. We should all get along fine."

"Oh, keep it in your pants. Miller wants us to work with them too. I don't have to be happy about it," she said.

Matt ignored her and tapped on the window. "They're here. Now put on your big girl panties, and deal with them. We all want to find Richards, right? We need their help, as much as they need ours."

Jill rolled her eyes as the two agents slid inside the booth across from them. "Sorry, we're late. Our boss got us up-to-speed on what the Director wants the four of us to do about Richards."

Agent Emerson was first to comment. "You're telling us that our case has moved up the food chain?"

"Yup. It seems that the Director wants Richards, captured and turned over to Langley. It's POTUS's orders. It seems they believe our crazy doctor has discovered something our government wants," said Verduzco.

Agent Patch could see that both women were going to keep the back and forth going for a while and interrupted them. "Look, we have our orders, and cannot do anything about it. Now, let's formulate a strategy with what we already know about Richards," he said.

"What we do know is that he's off the grid right now. I imagine he's transformed into another identity and hiding out somewhere. What I do know is that his fifth woman patient, Lea Strong, is being picked up at Lindbergh Field by the head of your SACU security team, as we speak. She's returning from a photoshoot in Europe," Matt said.

"What are they going to do with her, and the serum we found at Richards office?" Emerson asked.

Amy responded. "First, they'll interrogate her. We need to know what this serum does exactly. She might know how the doctor transforms himself. Also, because her aborted fetus, was found at Richards lab, she's going to be accused of breaking the Federal Law and then arrested. If she helps us capture Richards, then she'll avoid being in a jail cell. Then, and only then, if she cooperates, they plan to give her shot to her."

Jill leaned forward, her hands flat on top of the table. "We," she pointed at her partner, "need to talk to her. She's part of our original case," she said

Agent Patch patted her two hands. "Calm down. We came to get the two of you. Once we get texted that she's in custody, we'll head over to the San Diego Field Office. She's all ours, but for only a few hours. Then, the CIA takes over."

Emerson pulled her hands back. "Okay. Let's make a plan," she said.

Matt had something he wanted to get off his chest. "I don't want to bring this up; it makes me sick. We know that Angelica Rathburn is the victim in the morgue. She had her fetus removed minutes after she died." Matt waved off Verduzco from speaking. "I don't want to hear any of your wisecracks. I'm certain Richards has created a magic potion that gives him and his ladies the ability to change their appearance," he said.

Amy spoke first. "There is nothing to joke about now. I think our biggest problem is the CIA. That Special Agent Bingham is hiding something. I've been thinking about Richards' serum and how it would be a formidable weapon for them. Could you imagine how invincible our special forces would be if they could transform into any terrorist, any diplomat, or whoever they'd needed to be to infiltrate a country?"

"Then we have to find Richards first," Emerson said. "But how?"

Agent Patch was scratching his head. "If Lea Strong is the last of Richards patients, we need to find out if she knows any of his aliases he uses. We can't let Richards get to her first, or we'll never close this case."

Emerson was shaking her head. "How would we know if Richards hasn't already become one of the agents assigned to pick her up? He fooled us once posing as Forrest."

Her statement silenced everyone.

The four agents kept talking, devising a strategy to capture Richards. They had a lot of common ground with both of their investigations and divided up their jobs. What they all agreed on was that Richards would be trying to eliminate the last person who could implicate him. They all knew what they were saying sounded crazy, but there was no other explanation at this time.

"What kind of heartless monster can transition from lover to murderer with women by all appearances he loved in some twisted fashion," Emerson said.

"Maybe his serum is changing his behavior? I'd bet he's going mad," said St. Claire.

Verduzco was not entirely on board with this shift-changing theory. However, she was confused as to why all the bodies were decomposing at an accelerated rate that defied logic. They were still waiting for DNA results from the unborn fetuses, as well as the fetuses they found in Richards sub-zero freezer.

They suspected it would turn up that Richards was the father. They knew that the CIA was moving at a fast pace and wanted to take over their two cases. They understood that once that happened, the murders, the serum, and what Doctor Richards had been doing would be buried away in some far-off basement. The four of them agreed that they would not let that happen.

271

The Faces of Doctor Richards

When they got the text that Lea Strong was going to be at the San Diego Field Office later that afternoon, they felt they had a good plan that might draw out Doctor Richards.

74

Lea Strong was met at her boarding gate by two FBI agents. They flashed their badges and introduced themselves.

"Ms. Strong, I'm Agent Keith Morrison, and this is my partner Agent Paul Goodman. We need you to come with us."

Lea stepped back, bumping into a young mother pushing a stroller. "What's this all about?" she asked playfully. When she realized that the two FBI agents were unmoved by her antics, her smile evaporated. Fear blanketed her body; she was trembling as they ushered her out of the airport terminal.

"Everything will be explained in our field office. The agents in charge will be there to brief on everything."

"Am I under arrest? I have a doctor's appointment. I can't miss it," she pleaded. "I promise after I see my doctor, I'll come down to your headquarters."

"We know about your appointment and can assure you that what you were going to do at Doctor Richards office will be handled at our field office by one of our onsite nurses," Agent Goodman said. "Now, we need you to cooperate and come with us.

"Has something happened to Doctor Richards?" she asked, her voice trembling. "He's the only one who knows what I need," she pleaded.

Both agents did not respond and guided her toward the baggage area.

* * * * *

Chad Green had been watching one of the FBI agents picking up Lea's luggage. He was troubled that the other agent was in a heated conversation with her about her shot. *Shit.* He rushed through the terminal and hailed a taxi.

"10385 Vista Sorrento Parkway."

"FBI field office?" the Pakistani taxi driver asked.

"Yes."

"FBI agent man?" the driver questioned.

"Shut up and drive, or I'll ask you for your papers," Richards said, raising his voice.

"Me, citizen. You no worry. FBI field office right now, boss, sir."

* * * * *

The black Ford LTD pulled up to the side entrance of the field office. Waiting for them were Verduzco and Patch. It was four-thirty in the afternoon, and the marine layer was thick and moist.

"Ms. Strong, please come with us," Agent Patch said.

"Where am I going?" Lea asked.

Agent Patch did not respond. He guided her inside and allowed the four-inch steel doors to slam shut.

She was guided to a small eight by ten interrogation room, which had a six-foot by four-foot one-way mirror. Standing by the far-left side corner, was a male nurse, his hands resting on a metal medical cart with a syringe, and one small vial with Lea's name on it.

Lea stumbled a bit. She was feeling lightheaded when she saw her serum. *"I'm not supposed to talk about any of this,"* she reminded herself. *"Doctor Richards made me promise."*

"Please sit down," Agent Patch asked politely, pointing to the chair that was facing the one-way mirror. Agent Verduzco was standing by his left side.

"I'm sure you have lots of questions. I hope to answer most of them if you cooperate with us," Agent Verduzco told her.

Lea looked at both agents, then at the one-way mirror. "Do I need a lawyer?" she asked.

You can have your attorney at any time," Agent Patch replied. "We'd have to stop right now. You know if you wait for your lawyer, and going through all that back and forth crap about your rights, however," said Agent Patch, pointing at the single serum bottle on the medical tray, "if we get your lawyer in here now, then I will have to remove this nurse, and what's on this tray. I imagine that you need this in the next few days?" he told her, holding up the bottle and pretending almost to drop it. "Oops. I nearly had a little accident here. I'm all thumbs sometimes."

Lea almost passed out. "Okay, okay. How can I help you?" she replied.

For the next four hours, Agent's Patch and Verduzco questioned her. At times having to calm her down, as she told them of her sinful vanity and all the abortions, she allowed Doctor Richards to perform on her and her friends.

Lea was now sniveling. "I was …have always been a supporter of a woman's right to choose when it comes to her health and pregnancy. I never realized that my agreeing to keep me young and viable as a model, I would have to sell my soul to the devil. Doctor Richards is the devil, you know?" she said, blowing her nose.

The *male nurse* by Lea's vial wanted to smash it and run away. *"You little bitch,"* Richards thought. *"First time you're in trouble, and you fold like a tent."* He wanted to leave, but the door was locked.

Agent Verduzco was not buying her story. "You say Doctor Richards is the devil. Did he, when you came to him at the beginning, force you in any way to become part of his Frankenstein plan?"

Lea bowed her head in shame. "No. I wanted to stay young and beautiful, like my friends.

"Friends? You mean, Rathburn, Cummings, Thomas, and Morgan? The friends that are now dead murdered by Doctor Richards. Did you get them involved with his crazy scheme?" barked Verduzco.

Lea had a puzzled expression on her face. "How do you know about these women. I thought…" she paused, deep in thought.

Agent Verduzco lashed into her. "You thought what?"

She began violently shaking her head. "I don't know anything. I need my shot," she pleaded. "I did not know I'd have to continue to receive my shots every two weeks." Strong was now getting hysterical. "Missing a serum dosage, the correct dosage, would accelerate my aging process Doctor Richards had told us," she was unable to control her crying.

Agent Patch could sense she was telling the truth. She was not ready to confess about what was going on at Doctor Richards's office. He did not know if what she was saying was accurate, but she was genuinely frightened.

"Our lab technicians are testing the serum to see if what you say is correct."

"I'm wasting my time talking to you. I need my shot today or, I don't know what will happen to me," she whined. "If something terrible happens to me, how are you going to find out everything Todd was doing?

Agent Patch pulled his partner out of the room. "We need to address this issue," he said. "We can't have her dying on us. She's our only link to Doctor Richards.

In the hallway, Agent's Emerson and St. Claire were waiting for them. Jill was the first to speak.

"I'm not buying her bull-shit, but what if she's right? We can't lose her," said Emerson.

Patch had the lab results from all the serum they had. "This is bad. Our people have never seen a chemical compound like this. They can't even advise us what dosage to give Ms. Strong," he said, his face furrowed with confusion.

Verduzco had her doubts and interjected. "Maybe we watch what happens to her. If she's having a problem, then we give her the serum?"

"What if she's right that the reversal is quick, and nothing can stop it." St. Claire said

"Let's move her to the infirmary, and they can monitor her. I am uncomfortable giving her this serum we know nothing about," said Emerson. "Shit, we don't know shit. We could kill her?"

Agent Verduzco was nodding her head. "What's wrong with waiting to see if her fear is justified. Then, we might know what we're dealing with," she said. "She's a criminal. She did confess to having multiple abortions. So why not let her rot, so to speak," she said coldly.

* * * * *

The *male nurse* who handed Lea's serum results to the agents was almost knocked down by Agent St. Claire. He heard everything the agents had said.

Let them watch Lea age. They'll panic, inject her with her serum, and maybe give her the wrong dosage? Without the antidote, they will not be able to stop what will happen to poor innocent Lea, Richards said to himself.

He turned and followed Agent St. Claire and Agent Emerson outside, where his taxi had been waiting for him. "My job is done. I have to meet Salvador. It will be a new and better beginning," he muttered. "This time, I will not get involved with my patients."

The taxi driver turned to his new passenger. "I'm waiting for my client. You need to find another ride, sir," he said.

"Your ride said I could have you take me to Echo Park." Richards threw a hundred-dollar bill at the driver. "Now drive."

The Pakistani taxi driver looked at the money and smiled. "You, the boss man now. Echo park we go to."

* * * * *

A nurse had started screaming by an open door at a utility closet. "Come quickly," she was waving her arms at Agent Patch.

Inside the closet was the male nurse that collided with agent St. Claire. "Shit, Richards was the nurse, and he was in the same room with us," Matt said to his partner. "He's toying with us."

"I'll call Emerson and St. Claire and warn them," Verduzco said.

75

Doctor Richards sat on a wooden park bench in his *Chuck Feldman* identity. Since injecting his new hybrid serum last night, he was able to transform quickly and with less pain. He also tested his new healing abilities, pleased his ability to heal himself was working. He knew that the man he was meeting with at the Park was a brutal man, known to torture associates as a negotiation tool. He hoped he would not have to test his new powers.

He stretched his arms, resting them on the back of the bench. He was smiling, as he watched all the happy couples on Echo Park Lake, laughing as they enjoyed navigating their paddle boats while the sun's warm rays beamed down on their heads.

He swiped a tear off his cheek, wishing he was out there with Molly. He knew that his wife would be very disappointed with him for what he had become.

"I'm so sorry," he mumbled. *"I risked everything to save you and failed,"* he apologized. *"Now, I'm a mad scientist running for my life."*

Richards was oblivious to the people walking by him, as he spoke to himself. He lifted his head, staring blankly, thinking about the new life he had created for himself.

After setting up the meeting with Salvador Conte, he had figured out how long he'd need to perfect his final hybrid serum. He realized that no one, even Conte, could know what he was trying to develop.

Salvador Conte, he understood, would take his pound of flesh from him, for what he was going ask him to do for him. The risk he calculated was worth it.

A wayward soccer ball smacked him on his legs, snapping him back to the present. "Sorry, mister," the young boy said timidly.

Richards forced a smile as he handed the ball back to the young man. "No problem," Richards's attorney said.

He looked off to his left and saw Conte walking toward him. He wanted to wave to get his attention, then thought better of it.

Salvador kept panning the area searching for the man he was going to meet. Richards knew Conte did not know his new identity, which was what he wanted.

It would be tricky approaching him. He knew he carried a gun and was trigger happy when meeting strangers. This gangster had survived numerous attempts on his life, all successfully. He was not a man you tried to surprise.

When Conte was in front of him, Richards spoke to his friend. "Salvador, please sit down here. We have a lot to discuss," the doctor said, his voice non-threatening.

"Who the fuck are you?" Salvador cursed. His hand slipped inside his opened jacket.

Richards could see two of his bodyguards marching toward them. He knew what he was doing was dangerous.

"It's me. Doctor Todd Richards." He watched Salvador remove his pistol with his right hand. "Please stay calm. I can explain what's going on." Richards held up both his hands, revealing he was not a threat.

"Where's Doctor Richards?" Salvador asked.

Richards stood and pointed at the restroom building behind them. "Follow me," he said. "All will be revealed in a moment." He took out the photo of himself, showed it to Conte, as they entered the men's room. It smelled from urine and littered with used syringes.

"Now, please watch closely," Richards said. "It will all come clear in a few minutes."

Salvador stood there, amazed. "What's going on here?" he bellowed.

The Faces of Doctor Richards

Richards held up one finger, as the transformation was about to be completed. Salvador watched the stranger he just met, begin to shudder and twist. His hair changed colors and grew long. His facial bone structure had begun remolding itself as if he was a sculpture of molding clay.

"There. Can we now talk?" Richards said, leading them outside and back to the bench.

"What just happened?"

It took Richards about forty-five minutes to explain to Conte the serum he had created. He told his friend what had transpired with his patients, the FBI hunting for him, and the drastic actions he had to take to stay out of Federal prison.

"You see why I need your help," he told Conte.

Salvador, his brain on overdrive, spoke. "You need my girls, yes?"

"Correct. I need more time to perfect my formula. I need cooperative female subjects to get them pregnant."

"All my girls do what I say," said Conte, rubbing his chin, deep in thought. "Then, I will need something from you if you want my help."

Richards had already anticipated his request. "Anything you want."

"Can this work for my men? And, me? We can change into whoever we want, I want?"

"Yes. If you and your men can get a woman pregnant, then I can create a serum for them. I mean for you to use. Understand, you'll have to have patience. The process is not fast."

"Perfect. We go now. I have the perfect place for you to do your experiments, and fucking. I mean baby-making," Salvador said, clapping his hands. "You now a criminal like me," he grinned.

Richards handed Conte a business card with his cell on it. "I need a day or two to gather all of my vials and equipment. Text me where to meet and when?"

* * * * *

Two men in an unmarked car were shocked at what they had just witnessed. They were from the FBI's division on human trafficking. They had been working a three-year investigation into Salvador Conte's crime syndicate.

"What happened?" Agent Hernandez said. He was handing his digital camera to his partner. "Conte went into that restroom with the guy from the bench. Then, in under five minutes, he comes out with another guy. You think they killed someone in there?"

"It's possible, but Conte would never be that reckless, especially in broad daylight," Agent Small said. "He came back to the bench with the new guy and sat there for almost forty-five minutes."

The two agents continued video recording Conte and the stranger, as they left the park. They rushed to the restroom, pushed the door open, holding their noses from the putrid smell. Agent Small slowly opened the only stall in the room.

"Shit, where's the other guy?" Small asked, a puzzled look on his face.

Agent Lucas Hernandez shrugged his shoulders. "We need to get these photos and video back to the lab. We need to ID the two guys."

76

Lea's body was experiencing rapid changes. She had begun to sweat, as well as exhibit overall body weakness, not getting her serum injection.

"Help me," she begged. "Doctor Richards has the photo I use," she pleaded. "I need that one and that one only."

Agent's Verduzco and Patch rushed into the infirmary. "What picture? Don't you have your own we can use?"

"No. I don't carry photos of me fully naked. Are you nuts?"

Forest looked at Amy. "What the fuck do we do. We didn't find Lea's files at Richards' office," he said. "None of his five patient files were there."

Verduzco looked at the panicked woman. "Can we retake a photo of you, now?"

Lea had a puzzled look on her face. She smiled and started to remove all her clothing, including her undergarments. "I sure hope so," she said, standing in front of the two agents in her birthday suit.

Agent Patch turned around, embarrassed. Agent Verduzco smiled at her partner. "When was the last time you saw a naked woman in the flesh. One of your porno magazines?" she whispered in his ear.

"Shut the fuck up, and snap the damn photo of her," he barked. Forrest heard Lea saying something directed at him.

"Agent Patch. You can act real tough with me with all my clothes on; however, seeing me nude turns you into a bowl of Jell-O?" she teased. "You can look at me. I am used to being stared at by all the photographers when they photograph my beautiful body. So, it's okay to turn around, unless you don't like what you see?"

Agent Verduzco grabbed her partner's shoulders and twisted him around to face Lea. "Shit, Amy, I'm not comfortable with this. She could accuse us of …me of sexual harassment." He turned around and barged out of the room.

Waiting outside was his boss, Brian Miller, and three men.

"Agent Patch was introduced to CIA agent, Ralph Bingham, Stuart Lewin from Homeland Security, and Mark Murphy from the US Attorney General's office."

Forest had a puzzled look on his face. "I've already met agent Bingham. Why are they here?" he asked.

"They're here to take Ms. Strong into custody. She's no longer our problem. She's violated federal laws, and the justice department will now be dealing with her crimes."

"That's a load of crap. We need Ms. Strong to help us find Richards. You do know that there's a killer out there that she can help lead us to," he said, his frustration showing.

"I'm sorry," he shrugged his shoulders. It's out of our hands now. Orders from the president," Miller replied.

"Look, this woman needs her serum, and I won't let her leave without it. If what she says is correct, she'll be dead before they get her back to Langley," agent Patch said.

Bingham nodded at Agent Patch. "Okay. Do what you can with her, but she comes with us right after she gets her injection," he said.

Forest rushed back into the infirmary room. He noticed that Lea was lying on a hospital bed, her body under a white sheet. Her left arm was resting by her side. A doctor, in a white lab coat, had a syringe in his hand and was filling it with Lea's serum.

"Amy," he whispered in her ear. "We've just been screwed."

"What are you talking about?" she replied, not taking her eyes off the syringe inserted into Lea's neck. "Shit, I hope the doctor knows what dosage to give her."

"Is he guessing?

"Yup. Lea didn't know. She had told him that the injection has to go into her neck. Richards's method was through her carotid artery. Shit, while you were gone, she started changing right before our eyes. She's aging rather quickly. We're guessing right now about her dosage."

They both stepped back, giving the doctor and nurse some room. Holding their breath, they watched the doctor slowly push the syringe, letting the serum flow into Lea's neck.

The room had become silent as everyone watched. Within thirty seconds, the beautiful young woman began twisting in agony, her body arched, it looked like it would snap in two. She cried out in pain; tears flowed down her cheeks. She was holding the cellphone tightly, staring at her photo. She began transforming to the surprise of everyone.

The doctor started checking vitals. The nurse stood frozen as she watched the beautiful woman's face begin to reshape itself.

Agent Verduzco rushed over and leaned in. "Are you alright?" her question had a panicked tone to it.

Lea extended one finger in the air, still gripping the cellphone. "Just a minute," she muttered. "Just a few more seconds," the model said, her beautiful smile once again appearing on her face. She handed agent Verduzco her phone.

"There," Lea said, sitting up on the gurney. "Now, I feel so much better."

The men from the CIA and Homeland Security, who had been watching the entire procedure, stood frozen, unable to move. They were amazed at what they had witnessed. "I would not have believed it if I did not see it with my own two eyes," Agent Bingham said. "I guess Richards created the formula we've needed. Now, we just have to figure out his formula so we can replicate it for our program."

As Agent Verduzco entered the hallway. Agent Bingham handed her an authorization form from the CIA director. She slowly read it and slapped it against his chest.

"What the fuck is this?" she growled. "This is our case. We need her to help us find Doctor Richards."

"With what we've found at Richards office, and the federal laws she's broken, the president feels Miss Strong is a threat to National Security," Bingham said, his tone unfazed by Amy's antics.

"That's bull-shit, and you know it," she said.

"It doesn't matter what you think right now. Ms. Strong is coming with us. You and your partner can find Doctor Richards and turn him over to us when you do. That's an order from your director and the president," he said.

Amy was ready to break his nose, but thought better of it, and stormed off. She stopped and turned, her right hand flipping him the bird. "This is not over."

* * * * *

"Mister President, you would not have believed what just happened. Lea Strong changed right in front of everyone," Stuart Lewin from Homeland Security said.

President Floyd Christopher sucked in a deep wheezing breath. "How are we going to replicate this serum and have it ready for our military?"

"Sir, we only have a small amount of serum for Ms. Strong that she needs to stay alive. Professor Franklin is not sure it will be enough for him to break it down and determine the right combination of DNA editing and fetal stem cells Richards uses to create the liquid," Lewin said. "He says that it's not just combining fetal stem cells and the donor's blood. It's an intricate process only known by Richards."

"Then, do everything in your power to capture Doctor Richards, bring him to our Black Ops facility and lock him in the lab until he gives us what we want," the president ordered.

"We have every law enforcement agency looking for him. He's gone underground with a new identity. Unless we catch a break, he's gone from the picture," the Homeland Security Secretary said.

"Find a fucking way. Our country needs this weapon. I need this weapon to wipe terrorism from our planet," President Christopher said, ending the call.

77

When Emerson and St. Claire stopped their car in front of Richards office, they noticed that their forensic team had cordoned off the entire block on Prospect. The crowds had gathered, as well as news crews from all the major networks.

"It looks likes the circus has come to town," Emerson said, shaking her head.

"Behave yourself," St. Claire told her. "We need their help. No need to piss them off, like Verduzco, did with the CIA."

Jill had a mischievous smirk on her face. "Me? I'm miss congeniality," she smiled. "Bingham stole our only lead to Richards. There's no telling what they'll do to that poor girl. I'd bet they are on their way to block us from doing our job here too."

"Then, we need to work this part of our case quickly and see where it takes us. Okay?"

"Fine," she said.

They bent under the yellow tape and walked toward the front door. Jill flashed her credentials in the face of the agent standing guard, and without incident, he waved them in.

Richards' office looked like the doctor was moving out. Every file had been organized in *Banker Boxes* and labeled. Inside a thick journal, each record accurately categorized so the data could be inputted into the FBI's forensic computers.

Emerson and St. Claire were greeted by their boss, Brian Miller. His mood was somber. Matt spoke first.

"Anything you can give us?" asked Matt.

Miller shook his head. He looked tired and frustrated. "This place was an abortion factory. So many fetuses frozen. Shit, we even found bone fragments inside a wood chipping machine in the backyard," he said, looking like he was about to throw up his guts. "Forensics thinks the bone fragments are from the species of chimpanzee."

"Get a grip, boss. Any leads on Richards?"

"Nothing so far," he said. "Lots of evidence, but nothing that would lead us to find this bastard. How did it go with Lea Strong?"

St. Claire had a puzzled look on his face. "You don't know?

He shook his head. "Know what?"

"She's now the property of the CIA. Per the president, and your boss. We're on our own with what we have here," St. Claire said, his voice cracking from all the stress he was feeling.

"That's not the directive I have. Something's going on. It smells fishy," Miller said. "You guys do your job here and let me dig into this a bit more."

Jill headed upstairs while Matt went to the backyard to see where forensics found the bone fragments. They had not noticed that Agent's Verduzco and Patch had pulled up to the property.

They found St. Claire, his head inside the woodchipper, cursing. "Hey, Matt, poor choice for a haircut," said Verduzco.

St. Claire tried to pull himself out, snagging the top of his collar on one of the sharp blades. "Shit," he screamed. "Please unhook me," he shouted.

Agent Verduzco was now laughing hard. "Not until I get a photo of this," she said.

Her partner was a bit more compassionate, pushing her arm down, stopping her from snapping a photo. He stepped over, lifting the collar of Matt's jacket off the blade. St. Claire stood, straighten out his collar, his expression livid, as he stared at agent Verduzco.

"Give me your damn phone. You need to delete all the photos you took," he said, walking over toward Amy, who was holding her phone high above her head.

"A little insurance for down the road when you don't feel like sharing," she said, grinning. She was thumbing what seemed like a dozen photos across her screen.

"Give me that," St. Claire said, grabbing her phone from her hand. He kept searching for the photos on her phone. He was frustrated he could not find them. "Where are the damn photos?" he shouted.

Amy could see that he was unable to take a joke. "Calm down. I was just having some fun with you. There are no photos. I would never do that to a fellow agent, especially you," she said. "This shit is so depressing, and I thought…"

Jill from the upstairs window, stuck her head out. "Stop the horsing around and get up here. I think I've found something we can use," she said.

Agent Emerson was holding a thick photo album. "I've got a pretty good history of who Richards is. He looks like he was a great husband. Very much in love with his wife, Molly," she paused to catch her breath as she stared at a photo of Richards' wife.

Her partner came over and took the album from her. "You look like you've seen a ghost?" Matt said. Then he noticed it too. "Damn. Richards' wife looks like your twin sister."

"I know. It's a little bit scary," Jill remarked.

"It could be useful," Verduzco said. "It might lure him out if you remind him of his wife."

"Or it might put her in danger," said Agent Patch. "Let's review the rest of these photos and see if there is a place that they frequented, as husband and wife. He might go back to a familiar spot while he tries to stay under the radar."

Agent Verduzco was thumbing through the photos when she came across one that had Richards and his wife Molly on some tropical beach. "He was…I mean, he still is a hunk. Nice muscle tone. His smile, well, it doesn't look like the smile of a killer," she said.

Jill could not get over the striking resemblance she had with Molly. "Maybe he cracked after his wife died. He may believe he's responsible for her death. I bet he believed he could have cured her."

"Let's not start feeling sorry for this guy. He's killed five women that we know of and broken at least a hundred Federal laws with his abortion clinic, and experiments," said agent Patch. "We've found at least ten fetuses. There's no telling what had gone on here until forensics gets back to us."

Jill could not let go of the photo of Molly and Doctor Richards. "I'm going to keep this photo book for a while. Something about all the doctor's photos are bothering me. I need a little more time to study them," she said.

"Just don't get all soft and mushy on us," Matt teased. "He's about the best-looking guy you've been in a photo with lately. I mean, your exact twin has been with." He got a hard punch to his shoulder for his remark. "Ouch," he cried. "Emerson, you can dish out the jokes, but you can't take them."

Standing by their cars, discussing their next move, Agent St. Claire got a call. "Yes, sir. We'll all be there in an hour. Depending on traffic."

"Who was that?" Agent Emerson asked.

"Miller. He says he needs all of us at the LA field office ASAP. He has two agents with a video of Chuck Feldman. You remember, Richards attorney. The video shows him disappearing inside a restroom, and reappearing as Richards."

78

FBI agents Lucas Hernandez and Leo Small introduced themselves. They briefed the five FBI agents on their case against Salvador Conte, and his international human trafficking syndicate of young women in Mexico.

Agent Hernandez said. "We've been trying to gather enough evidence to lock this son-of-a-bitch up for the rest of his life, but he's smart. He keeps his distance with any of his associates or with the kidnapped women. We want to cut off the head of the snake, but until now, we haven't been able to connect him to anything illegal."

Agent Verduzco was losing her patience. "I thought we were going to see a video of our murderer…" Agent Hernandez stopped her.

"I'm getting to that. I thought you needed to know how your suspect intersects with our case. We received approval from the director to join your team. Now, perhaps, we can all close some big cases for the FBI."

Verduzco gave a puzzled look at the Regional Director Miller. "What's up with this. We don't need two more agents tripping over us," she said.

"You do now if you want to capture Doctor Richards. Look at the video they took. Then you decide what direction you want to go," Miller said.

Agent Patch signaled his partner to shut up. "Agent Hernandez, please show us the video," he asked.

The video lasted almost fifty minutes. They were all mystified at what they saw.

Agent Patch said. "We are assuming he transformed inside the restroom. Right? I watched Lea Strong react to her serum. It appears from this video that Richards' ability to switch identities is more natural for him.

"I'm sure he's been doing this longer than his patients, and his serum might work easier and better on him," said Emerson. Or maybe he has a different formula for himself?"

Agent Miller said. "The six of you take all your files and lock yourselves in the conference room. Don't come out until you have a plan to find and capture Doctor Richards. You're a team now. The director wants Conte and Richards captured and brought to justice."

* * * * *

Seventy-five miles away from the Los Angeles FBI field office, Doctor Richards was settling in at his new employer's pharmaceutical company, about twenty miles East of Ventura,
California. It was a fully equipped laboratory with every piece of equipment he would need to create more serum.

The building was over fifty-thousand square feet. Ten-thousand square feet of the building designated for Doctor Richards living quarters so he could have privacy to impregnate the women surrogates Conte allocated to him. The facility was secluded. The closest building was over five miles away. Salvador had gotten him ten of his most beautiful ladies that would rather work at the laboratory than as a Call-Girl for his abusive pimps.

"Todd, my friend. While you create your new serum, I want you to create one for two of my most trusted men and me."

Richards had anticipated this was coming. He did not want to have more men roaming the world, able to change their identities, especially the kind of men associated with Salvador.

"Okay, but they cannot use the ten women you gave me. I need their fetuses so my DNA will not get contaminated."

"How many of my girls will my men and me need?"

292

"Give yourself and your men two-women each, and if they can get them pregnant, I can create their serum too."

While Richards was at the facility, he was not a prisoner. He was free to come and go as he pleased. Conte's deal was for him to keep his current supply of vials in the facility's walk-in refrigerated safe. Salvador needed an insurance policy so the doctor would not run away from him and his plans. He gave the doctor a Mercedes E-Class Convertible, better IDs for his three aliases, with one condition: He could never be away from the laboratory for more than seven consecutive days.

79

Four months had gone by in a flash for Richards. He was adjusting to his living arrangements at Conte's pharmaceutical facility. The residence he occupied had five bedrooms, each with a full bath so each of his surrogates could maintain a regular hygiene schedule.

Richards apartment was very spacious, with a living room with large panoramic windows welcoming in the grassy hillside that bordered Conte's property. He had a dining room that could seat twelve people. He enjoyed, at the end of each day, sitting down for a massive dinner for himself and his new ladies.

The women doted on Richards, massaging his shoulders, caressing his entire body at all hours of the day. Some days his surrogates would walk around the house naked, trying to get him excited. They knew that their only job was to get pregnant or go back into the dark world where they were working.

At times Richards was exhausted from the constant lovemaking he had to do, but he realized things could be worse for him. He could be in federal prison or working for the CIA.

Currently, six of the ten women Conte had provided him had become pregnant. They were all in different stages of their pregnancies. In one week, the first fetus extraction would happen. Salvador did not know that these fetuses had an edited DNA from his new Hybrid serum.

Since four women could not get pregnant, they were replaced and put back to their other job. Richards had four new women to break into his routine.

The Faces of Doctor Richards

Salvador and two of his men finally got their women pregnant. It had taken over twenty-four women. They were behind schedule. Their women were four weeks away from aborting their fetuses.

Richards had a plan for Conte and his men but knew he'd have to find the right time to execute it.

While Richards felt like a prisoner, he had been able to perfect his new formula without Conte's knowledge. Late at night, he'd run more experiments on himself, testing how much pain he could endure, as well as how fast he would recover from any physical injury.

Also, he had been working with advanced gene therapy and stem cells on mice. He hoped to find the place in the brain where he could paste the right edited gene, along with the correct dosage of stem cells. His idea was to be able to visualize only, no photo needed, the person he would want to change into, and it would happen within seconds. That ability would allow him to become whoever he wished, making capture next to impossible for the authorities or Conte.

Doctor Richards, after a long day of work in his lab, needed some R &R as Chad Green. During his free time away from the complex, he would hang out at some of Emerson's favorite bars in Westwood. Sadly, he kept striking out, as she was nowhere to be found.

He missed her. He told Conte he needed some time off to clear his head. He chose a route down Coast Highway toward Los Angeles. The top was down, his head caught the sun's rays, as he thought of his FBI friend.

He glanced at the newspaper, resting on the passenger seat. He had it opened to the third page where an article about himself, with his photo and a picture of FBI agent Jill Emerson. The article was about the progress her team was having on finding him. He had seen her on TV two nights ago, and she did not look happy. She wanted him as much as he wanted her now, but not for the same reasons.

"I hope you're at your tavern tonight. I hope you still remember me," Chad Green said. "Oh, how I would like to get you pregnant. Molly would be so happy," he mumbled.

80

After four months of dead ends, Richards was nowhere to be found. In a meeting with FBI regional director, Miller, it had not gone well for the six FBI agents assigned to find Doctor Richards. Their investigation had been deemed a failure by the CIA and the FBI directors.

"President Christopher wants to shut down your cases and move on to more important crimes plaguing our country. He's giving you one more month to come up with concrete leads on Richards whereabouts, or all four of you will be re-assigned," Miller told them.

"That's a load of crap. We've been busting our asses looking for Richards and feel we're getting close," Emerson responded. She knew it was a lie. She just wasn't ready to give up.

Miller was shaking his head. "You've been to Mexico, Europe, and South America, and all of you have not produced any viable leads. The CIA is pressuring the president to let them handle the entire case."

Agent Hernandez, the agent in charge of the Conte human trafficking criminal case, interrupted. "Maybe we need to expand our search parameters. We've been looking at Conte's illegal businesses, not his legitimate ones. Maybe that's where Richards is hiding. If you can get us FISA warrants to monitor Conte's other companies, we might get those new clues you want," he said.

"I'll see what I can do. FISA warrants need some justification to be issued. Send me a list of your reasons why you believe Richards in being harbored by Conte. Also, be specific on what businesses you want to monitor," Miller told Hernandez.

Just as Miller had finished talking, his cellphone rang. He glanced at the screen and groaned. "Shit, it's the Director. I've got to take this," he said, signaling everyone to leave the conference room.

Outside in the hallway, agent Patch was speaking with Hernandez. "You think Conte would be that stupid to hide Richards at one of his legitimate businesses?" Emerson, St. Claire, and Verduzco had heard Patch's question and huddled with them to listen to the answer.

Hernandez was looking around to be sure no one else was listening. "The more I think about it, the more it makes perfect sense. Conte's a smart man and knows we cannot monitor his businesses without the proper warrants. We've struck out everywhere else. What do we have to lose at this point?"

Emerson, in a low whisper, responded. "Let's meet tonight at Sully's and formulate a plan. Hernandez, can you bring a complete list of all of Conte's businesses that are legit and their location?

"Sure can. Let's meet at eight this evening," Hernandez said.

* * * * *

Five hours later, the six FBI agents were all drinking at Sully's, a hangout for most of the West Los Angeles field office. They had been there for over two hours. They had reviewed all of Conte's businesses and could see a faint light at the end of the tunnel on their cases. What they already knew was that Salvador Conte was not near any of his known trafficking businesses, or prostitution outlets.

"If we don't get a break soon, we won't get our FISA warrants, our little team will be over," Emerson said. "I can't believe we've hit a brick wall."

"Like I told all of you earlier, we're looking at this case all wrong. Conte has a pharmaceutical company East of Ventura," Hernandez said, jabbing his finger on the file he had in front of him. "It's very legit. We've checked it out before, and it's clean. I'll bet Conte relocated a handful of whores to that location for the crazy doctor to fuck around with?"

Agent Emerson was nodding in agreement. She got distracted when a man she recognized walked into the bar. "I think your idea has merit," she said, staring off in the distance.

The other agents noticed her mind was somewhere else and swiveled on their barstools. St. Claire said. "Is that *'Hanging Chad'*?

Emerson blushed, pretending to ignore Matt's comment.

Chad Green had entered the low-lighted bar and noticed that Jill had spotted him immediately. It had been over six months since he had first spoken to her. His heart was racing. His adrenaline was pumping through his veins like a rushing river.

She smiled at him, tossing him a friendly wave. He waved back and found a seat at the backend of the lounge.

Matt was first to see Jill's face turn bright red. He looked toward where she was staring. "Oh my. Do you want him?"

Verduzco and Patch turned around. "Wow. He's a looker," Amy said. "Are you seeing this guy or what?" she asked.

"No. Well, not yet," Emerson said, still flustered.

"If not you, then I'll take him," said Amy.

"Keep your panties on, girl," Jill barked back. "Let's see what tonight brings. She turned and faced Hernandez. "I like your idea. Let's present it to Miller in the morning and see what he thinks? Maybe by then, he's got the FISA warrant we need?"

St. Claire kissed the top of his partner's head. "Don't stay out too late little sister. I need you at your best to convince Miller about our plan," he said. The five agents said goodbye.

They left Jill sitting all alone at the bar. Jill cussed when she saw they had stuck her with the bill. She was taking out her credit card when she felt a hand touch her shoulder.

"Let me get that," Chad said. "Can I buy you another one?"

Jill turned her head. She was struck by how he reminded her of Alex. "Chad? Right?" Jill said with a sweet smile. She was feeling her memories of Alex kicking in. She sucked in a deep breath and forced a friendly smile. "That would be nice."

"You remembered me after all these months?" Chad said.

"You're too good looking to forget," Jill said. "You're right. It's been six months. Where have you been?"

Her question took him by surprise. "I travel a lot. Pharmaceutical rep. First time I had some free time and thought of you. I was hoping to catch you here."

"Then it's your lucky night. I seem to be here almost every day anyway."

They chit-chatted for the next hour and a half. Jill talked about Alex way too much, as she kept downing one drink after the other. She needed something to eat before she passed out. They went inside the restaurant to continue their conversation.

Jill turned the banter around to him. For the next hour, she could tell that he was lying about who he was or what he did for a living, but she was mostly lying too. It did not matter that much. After dessert, she began touching his thigh. She could tell he was excited.

Jill had a good buzz. When that happened, her inhibitions go right out the window. "Your place or mine. I'm about forty minutes from here."

Chad waved his hotel room key at her. "Around the corner at the Marriott."

They barely made it to the room with any clothes on, as the elevator doors opened on the thirty-fifth floor. They kept mauling at each other's garments. It took all the skill Doctor Richards had to slide the key in the door slot. They both fell inside. He was strong and lifted her in his arms. Like a gymnast, she straddled his waist with her naked legs.

He tossed her on the bed. He kicked off his loafers, undid his belt, and allowed his pants to drop to the carpet. He noticed her staring at him. He was standing, breathing hard, naked, his manly part ready for action.

Jill stood on the bed, unsnapped her bra, and then removed her panties. She was happy she had a few days earlier, had her waxing done, and shaved her legs. She fell back on the bed, pulling him toward her, and guided him inside her. It took almost twenty minutes before they both climaxed. They were both drenched in sweat, her head resting on his shoulder.

"Wow," she said. "I haven't felt that good…well, I can't remember when."

"Me too," Chad said, smiling. He knew his beautiful patients had been great instructors to him after Molly died, but he did not want to tell Jill that.

She sat up and looked at the digital clock. "Shit, I've got to get back to my place. I have a meeting in three hours, and I haven't slept yet."

"When can we meet again?" Chad asked as he got out of bed and headed toward the shower. He looked back, signaling her to join him. "You can clean up here and then go to your meeting."

"If I show up with the same clothes I had on yesterday…well, I'll never hear the end of it from those agents you saw me with last night. Thanks, but no thanks. I'll be back at Sully's in three days. I have a business trip to go on. Come by then if you're in town," she said.

"I'll try," he replied. When he turned around, he did not notice Jill staring at his firm butt, and his lower back.

Emerson was racking her brain about the odd birthmark Chad had. She had seen it before. It looked familiar, but she was in a rush and shrugged it off. She was out the door heading to Sully's parking for her car.

81

Professor Thomas Franklin had been working late at his new lab at Langley. He had orders from the CIA and Homeland Security to figure out Richards' formula, or they'll find someone who can. Bingham knew he was running out of time and needed his liquid weapon for five Special Operation soldiers.

During the first few months, Franklin worked with Lea Strong. She had been a willing participant. As her pregnancy progressed, her demands to abort her baby had escalated. "I don't want a baby. I want you to create more serum for me as you promised," she protested.

Franklin, too, was becoming exasperated with his progress and began acting out his frustration on his patient.

"I've told you a million times; I can't abort your child. First, it's against the law, and second, you're past your fifteen weeks. I will not kill a healthy baby."

"Against the law? What do you think you're doing with me here at this secret facility? Does the CIA and Homeland Security have different rules than other people?"

"Look, the Attorney General has signed off on my research. If you have a beef with what we're doing, take it up with him," Franklin shouted back. "I'm positive once you give birth, we will be able to harvest better stem cells from your umbilical cord," Franklin said. "Possibly, your baby's blood will be the key to a better mixture."

Ralph Bingham had been listening to the two of them go through their daily ritual. He decided today was an excellent day to interrogate Strong about Doctor Richards.

The door to the lab flew open. CIA agent Bingham marched in with two guards. "You two are done for today. Ms. Strong, I have some more questions for you. Please follow us," he said, grabbing her arm roughly.

What type of questions? I've answered everything you've asked a million times now. I do not know any more than I knew a week ago," she said.

"I have some new questions that I hope you'll be able to shed some light on about Doctor Richards."

"Fine," she said, crossing her arms as she marched out of the lab.

Bingham had decided that today's line of questioning needed to be in a setting that was more hospitable than the cold, sterile interrogation rooms Lea experienced the last four months. Instead of a hard metal chair and gray metal table, the room had a soft leather couch, with floral throw pillows, and two padded armchairs. There were original oil paintings by Picasso on the wall, as well as a one-way mirror, giving them enough privacy that would allow her to feel more relaxed.

"Ms. Strong, I want to apologize for the way Professor Franklin has been acting toward you. I know we've been keeping you here against your will. Our priority is to keep you and your child safe from doctor Richards," Bingham said. "Also, the attorney general has given you immunity for your crimes, as long as you keep cooperating with us."

"I'm not so sure you care about my safety. All you want is my baby as your lab pet," she said cynically. "You said you have more questions for me? Fire away."

"We've never asked you about all the aliases Doctor Richards used during the time he was your doctor. Do you know any of them by name?"

Lea closed her eyes tight, deep in thought, like she was thinking hard. "Well, Doctor Richards did have other aliases…Chuck Feldman and Jeff Peters," she said, watching the confused look on Bingham's face.

"Are you saying he only had two aliases?"

Lea was giggling, her hand cupping her mouth. "The doctor had many more aliases," she said, unable to control her laughing. "I'm thinking of others," her index finger pressing against her temple. Well, after Angelica turned up off the Pacific, I'm sure he was once Rathburn," she kept giggling.

"Ms. Strong, these questions are important to the security of our country. Why are you laughing?"

"Well, Doctor Richards has an odd birthmark on his lower back. It doesn't disappear when he transforms. I saw it on TV when he posed as Angelica."

"Really?"

"Yes. Richards had, on numerous occasions, tried to get us pregnant while he was in one of his other identities. At first, he told us he wanted to create a serum for a friend, so we agreed to have, you know, sex with this friend of his. We girls all noticed his birthmark, so we were not fooled."

"So, did all of you confront the doctor about this?" Bingham asked, leaning forward in his chair. She had gotten his undivided attention.

"Not at first. You know that all of Richards's lady patients…we were all close friends. We'd talk about Richards, and these so-called friends, you know his aliases. When we all discovered these men had the same birthmark, we knew Richards was experimenting with us," she said, smiling.

"Please make your point," Bingham said.

"Okay. As I said, Richards has this unusual birthmark on his lower back. It looks like Italy. When all of this had started with Doctor Richards, you know," she made quote signs with her hands, "us ladies doing the wild thing with his friends, we all started talking about the wild sex we were having with these guys."

Bingham was getting annoyed. "Do these men have names?"

"Let me finish. I'm getting to the best part," Lea said. "We girls like to brag about how it was…you know the sex. We'd compare his cock size. Was he rough or gentle? You know, what everyone talks about after sex," she said seductively.

Lea's answers triggered other questions. "Do you have any suspicions as to which alias might have gotten you pregnant? I mean, did it happen as Richards or one of his so-called aliases?" Bingham asked, mimicking Lea's hand gesture.

"My sexual activities for this pregnancy was always with Jeff Peters, but I knew it was Richards," she said. "Oh, I do remember once that Richards asked me to do it with one of his doctor friends. But, again, the weird birthmark gave it away."

Bingham was shaking his head. "I never knew that women talked so openly about their sex partners. Thank you, this information is beneficial," he said, standing up. "Do you remember the other doctor's name you mentioned?"

Lea looked up at him, noticing a slight bulge in his pants, realizing he had gotten excited by the way she was talking. "No, I can't remember the doctor's name. It was some middle-eastern name, I think?" she said, still staring at him.

Bingham could see where her eyes were focusing. He put his hands in his pockets. He couldn't stop blushing. "What shape is the birthmark again. The description is an important piece of evidence so we can capture Richards if he's in one of his other identities."

Lea stopped her giggling. "I said, like Italy."

"Thank you," Bingham spoke into his lapel, requesting the guards to take Lea back to her room. The interview was over.

He was on his phone to Homeland Security Director Stuart Lewin. "I think Lea Strong's baby was conceived by one of Richards other identities, Jeff Peters. You know the one that killed Lisa Beverly and Meg Cummings. Richards's experiments seem to be evolving. Ms. Strong might be having a baby with unique DNA properties," he said.

82

Deputy Director Miller had his agents on speaker. He was over the top impressed with their plan. "That's brilliant. It makes sense that Conte would hide Richards there. I believe I can get that FISA warrant you need to search the facility?" he asked.

Agent Hernandez responded. "Not yet. Let us get you the necessary details you'll need to present to the FISA court. It has to be detailed and unambiguous. Right now, we do not know what's going on there. We'd need to convince a judge that Conte's business is doing an illegal act. If we're wrong, we've violated his fourth amendment rights, like we've done a few times before. We don't need a judge coming down on us." Before anyone else could comment, the agent ended the call.

Matt's eyes stayed focus on agent Hernandez, acting shocked he had finished the call. St. Claire always had a way with words. Not this time. "Fuck his constitutional rights. If Conte's hiding a murderer, and someone who's violated multiple federal laws," St. Claire said. "We need to move on Richards first."

Agent Hernandez sucked in a deep breath. "You want Richards. I want Conte. I've known for years what he's been doing. He's slippery, and we've never been able to catch him in the act. If we tip Conte off, he could disappear again, possibly in Mexico. If that happens, we would be fucked. Richards would vanish. He'd be out of our jurisdiction, and we'd all be screwed. I suggest we stake out his company and see what materializes."

St. Claire reluctantly agreed with Hernandez. He noticed Jill was nodding off. He jabbed his elbow into her ribcage. "Did you get any sleep last night? You look like shit," he whispered.

"We'll talk about it later. I'm trying to listen," Jill said as her eyes fluttered closed.

Verduzco looked at St. Claire. "I think she scored last night. Way to go, girl," she said.

Agent Small opened a manila folder and spread out five sheets of paper. "Here's what I was able to dig up on Conte's Pharmaceutical company. First, this company has numerous silent partners. The pharmaceutical business is part of a shell company out of Mexico," he said, biting his lower lip. "I have a thin trail of breadcrumbs that points to ties with a small group of crime bosses, drug lords, and weapons traffickers. What I find strange is that Conte's company does not manufacture any drugs. It imports and exports products from legitimate manufacturers around the world."

Agent Verduzco was first to speak. "Are you saying we have inside the United States a legitimate company that is being used by criminals? Maybe for money laundering? Drugs? What does the attorney general say about all of this?"

Agent Small looked at Verduzco. "We've gone to justice before and have been shot down on all of our investigations into Conte. I am not sure what to make of any of this.

All I can see is that Conte's company is acting as an import/export business and makes sizable donations to influential senators and congressmen."

"Has your surveillance come up with anything since we started looking at this location?" Verduzco asked.

"Our satellite imaging the other day did detect a laboratory, and a lot of lab equipment on property. There are living quarters for at least twenty people. Our infra-red camera from one of our drones detected thirty people living inside the building, fourteen of them women."

Agent Patch interrupted. "Do we have a name for this company?"

"Revitalization Pharmaceuticals. The company filed a new DBA about the same time Doctor Richards disappeared with Conte," he said.

"Perfect name," said Emerson. "A little too overconfident. Could Richards be creating new fetuses; you know fucking all fourteen women?"

Agent Hernandez shrugged his shoulders. "If what you know about Richards is correct, I'd bet he is. Why else would the women be there?"

Emerson stood and stretched. She looked tired. "It wouldn't surprise me if Conte is having him create a serum for him and maybe some of his men. If that happens, we could be looking at a whole new world of crime within our borders."

Agent Patch jumped in. "I, for one, don't want that to happen. We need to get out there and get the proof we need to raid the facility."

"St. Claire and I will take the first shift tonight. I want to see this place, firsthand," Jill said.

Miller agreed. "Good idea. Be sure to take the portable infra-red camera. I need pictures and videos to show the FISA court."

Agent St. Claire stood and started walking around the room. He was deep in thought. "I think we need to dig into Conte's partners. If Richards starts creating a serum for Conte and his men, what will stop him from doing it for his other crime bosses? Shit, I don't want to think about what criminals could do with his *shape-shifting* drug," Matt took his frustration out on the wall with his foot.

83

Richards had Jill Emerson on his mind as he worked in his laboratory. His feelings had become irrational. He was fantasizing about how to re-create his happiest years with Molly when she was healthy. Then, he realized for that to happen, he'd have to be Todd Richards, not Chad Green.

He knew Agent Emerson would never accept his true identity after all the crimes his Richards persona had committed. She'd lock him up and throw away the key. Then, his thoughts began running different scenarios, as Chad Green and Emerson as his pregnant wife. He knew it was a longshot and decided to be patient. *"Let's see how things progress over the next few months,"* he told himself.

Richards chose to bury his head in his work. He was reviewing his notes he took about the remarkable breakthrough he had a few weeks earlier.

It happened after he had completed his last experiment on his lab chimpanzee. The unique mixture he injected into the animal was potent. He had modified the new formula mixture he had created at his temporary Santa Monica lab. He liked what he was witnessing. A once wild and uncontrollable animal, was now calm, exhibiting no aggression. When he cut the chimp, when he stabbed her with a scalpel, she was not frightened. She displayed an eerie, unusual calm as she was able to within minutes, heal those parts of her body that were injured, leaving no trace of the slice or puncture marks from the scalpel.

Richards needed to experiment on himself to be sure it would work on humans. A week later, Richards had his new hybrid serum, identical to the one his chimp had gotten except with his edited DNA and fetal stem cells from his new surrogate's recent abortion. He knew he had to keep this secret from Conte. He felt it was time for him to try it out and see how well it worked.

Richards wished he had someone to share in his recent accomplishment. He thought of Professor Franklin, but he was the enemy now. He now had a serum he believed that could heal a damaged body, which included cancer. Once he completed this test, he planned on testing his formulary on cancer cells he had stored in his freezer. "Molly, I'm sorry this is coming so late," he muttered.

After Richards injected himself, he did not feel any change at first. It was not until he became Chad Green and was thinking of a new happy life with Jill Emerson, that he felt an eerie calm blanket his mind. His crazy, irrational thoughts subsided. He needed to see if he could control his body, not by transforming himself, but with a different form of power.

Later that day, back as Richards, he was completing his last test on his chimp. Salvador Conte interrupted his work to introduce him to three men.

"Doctor Richards, I want you to meet three of my colleagues who I hope you'll help?"

Richards understood what was coming next. "As I promised, whatever you need, I will do."

Conte smiled. "I want you to meet Boris Vasiliev. He is a weapons exporter and will need his serum so he can travel freely from Russia to his business contacts around the world." Boris extended his hand toward Richards. I also want to introduce you to Sayid Bishara. He'll need a new permanent identity. He had to get out of Syria before Assad, and his generals brought him up on war crimes." Salvador noticed the disgust on the doctor's face.

"I don't expect you to like these men. Just do your job," Conte said in a threatening tone.

The Faces of Doctor Richards

Richards did not mask his displeasure with Salvador. "You know each serum, and each process requires these men to be here for the allotted time it takes to get their surrogate pregnant. Then, we must wait at least six weeks for the fetus to grow to the correct stage. Are they willing to cooperate and live here for the time it takes to create their serum?" he asked grudgingly.

The third man, who had kept quiet, finally spoke. "I'm Alejandro Munoz, a major smuggler of drugs into the United States. Maybe you've heard of me," he said, stabbing his index finger into the doctor's chest. "I don't like you telling us what we must do. First, I need to see proof you are this magician Conte say you are," he said, stabbing his finger harder into Richards' chest.

Salvador could see that the other men were also appearing a little doubtful about Doctor Richards. "Todd, please show them how your serum works," he said.

Richards was angry, except he felt rational. A plan materialized he liked. "Right now? I'm in the middle of my work. Stopping now will only delay what you and your men need, Salvador," he said.

"I don't care. Just do it," Conte ordered. "Ten minutes won't set you back."

Richards asked Munoz to step over toward the area where his camera rested on a tripod. "I'll need to take an image of you," he said to the Columbian drug lord.

Munoz seemed shocked at the request. "No fucking photos of me," he complained.

"If you want proof of how my serum will work for you, this is the best proof I can give you. I will delete the photo once I prove to you and your friends what I can do," Richards said.

"It's all right," Conte said assuredly. "I'll make sure he deletes it."

Richards took four photos of the drug lord. One full frontal with him in his boxer shorts. Then, from the left and right angles. And, finally, a shot of his back. Then he projected all the images on a seventy-inch digital screen. He told Munoz to repeat four sentences in Spanish and then in English. "Now, get dressed and watch."

Todd stepped in front of the four images on the monitor, turned on the voice recording, and began his transformation. He did not need a serum injection, as he had his new mixture in his bloodstream.

As Richards' face began to reshape first, his arms and torso followed. His height shrunk by four inches. His hair changed from his long blonde color to a short curly black mop.

He could see the startled expressions on everyone's face. He was pleased his new formula was working and without any pain.

Richards walked over to a shocked Munoz and stood shoulder to shoulder with him. "Gentlemen, let me introduce myself. I am Alejandro Munoz, the biggest drug trafficker to the United States," he said, his voice identical to the drug lord.

Munoz jumped away from Richards like he was some disease he did not want to catch. "What the fuck just happened?"

"I've been trying to tell you guys, Richards is the real deal," Conte said. "Think of all the possibilities we all could do with the right serum? It's been a fast six weeks, and our fetuses are almost ready to be extracted. While you're here, you'll have your pick of some of the most beautiful women that will help you get them pregnant, as well as anything else you'd like them to do for you while you stay on campus," Conte said, smiling. "A dream come true, my friends."

The three men asked Salvador to step out of the lab so they could talk privately. As soon as they left, Richards pulled out his photo of his younger self with Molly without any clothes on. He swiped a tear from his cheek and began the familiar transformation. He knew that Doctor Richards would be gone forever after the new hybrid formula was fully functional.

He needed a little more time, which Conte would not allow, as his impatience was growing thin for his serum. Nevertheless, Richards knew he had to keep delaying Conte so he would be free of Salvador and his brutal life.

The three men returned, big smiles on their faces, except for Munoz. "Well, gentlemen, do we have a deal?" Conte asked.

Boris Vasiliev, grinned, nodding his head. "Impressive. Maybe I can buy this Doctor Richards from you. I pay a high price for him," he said.

Conte laughed. "He's not for sale. For the price we've discussed, you can use his services, but our terms and rules are non-negotiable," he said.

Sayid Bishara was shaking his head. "Everything has its price. Name it, and I will pay you whatever you want."

Salvador could see that Alejandro was about to speak. He raised his hand like a traffic cop.

"Gentlemen, what part of no don't you understand. I have a service I am providing. You only have to say yes. The price per completed serum vials is ten million dollars. For that price, you get a beautiful woman for all your fantasies. Time will go by very quickly, and then your serum will be yours. It's an excellent deal."

"This is very impressive," Munoz said. "But, how do you control the doctor. Can't he transform and disappear?"

"Yes. However, I have all the vials he needs. Richards needs them every two weeks. He lost his laboratory to the FBI. I am the only one who can provide him with what he needs right now."

Sayid and Boris agreed to the program. They needed a few weeks to put their affairs in order. Alejandro was not ready to commit.

"I need a little more time," Munoz said. "I can't abandon my drug business right now. Too many DEA agents following my men and me."

"Then, that is why you should come on board. You'll be able to move your product with all new identities. You can have one of your trusted men to transform to you, and let the DEA watch him," said Conte.

"I still need time to think about it," Alejandro said and stormed out of the building.

Boris leaned into Conte and whispered in his ear. "Watch your back with that one. He's a selfish son-of-a-bitch. If he got the chance, he'd kidnap your doctor. He has some of the finest laboratories in South America."

The Faces of Doctor Richards

Conte was upset at Boris's remarks. "Thank you. I will be careful. With you and Sayid here, Munoz would be very foolish to try something like that."

* * * * *

Richards was listening to what the men said, especially Munoz. He checked his camera and verified that the memory card had uploaded the drug lords' images to the cloud.

Richards went back to what he was doing when Conte interrupted him. He picked up the syringe and inserted his blood into a mutated virus he had created. If this worked, he knew he'd have a new serum for himself that would allow him to go twelve months or maybe more, between injections. His hope that he could extend it to five years between doses. His objective was to have enough vials to last him the rest of his life.

He knew his time was running out, especially if Munoz got his way. He heard the door to his lab opening. Salvador was moving toward him.

"We have two more guests that will be staying with us, beginning on Monday. You're making me a nice income," he said. "Now, when will my serum, and my men's serum be ready?"

"Tomorrow, I will be aborting the fetuses I need. It will then take about three weeks or four to create them. Then, I will have to train you on how to transform your body. In four weeks, you and your men will be able to go about your business without a care in the world," Richards said. "Oh, I almost forgot. You'll need to find aliases with full-body photos. It's best to find men that have no family and have been dead a while."

Todd sat down, his hands shaking from what just happened. He knew he didn't have much time left to rid himself of Conte and his business associates.

84

"They've been in there four hours. A lot of movement and talking," Emerson said.

St. Claire looked down at his infra-red video screen. "See here. I'll bet that's Doctor Richards. If I did not know better, he had just shapeshifted to show those guys proof of what he's capable of doing?"

Emerson was nodding her head, holding back a laugh. "You are fully onboard about this X-Files shit now," she joked.

"Can we call what he does something else? I feel like we're part of a Night of the Living Dead episode."

"If you have a better name for this shit, then be my guest. I'm all ears." Jill replied.

St. Claire shook his head. "I don't know what to call what he's created. What I do know is we have to stop him before he creates his magic potion for those criminals," he said, stabbing his index finger at the camera screen.

Emerson was first to see Alejandro Munoz storming out the front door. He was on his cellphone, shouting into the mouthpiece. Jill's heart was pounding as she looked at the man who had killed her Alex.

St. Claire pointed his parabolic microphone and video camera toward the drug lord. Munoz's words were in Spanish and garbled. "Not sure what we've got," Matt said.

Jill listened closely. "I think he said something about buying something. Maybe kidnap? I think I heard: *I will take Richards* and the word *'kidnap,'* Emerson looked confused. "My Spanish sucks. Let's get this back to the field office for analysis."

Matt was elbowing his partner's arm. "Shit. I can't believe these guys got into our country undetected. Look, that's Boris Vasilev and Sayid Bishara. They have at least fifty separate charges pending. We should arrest them now," said Matt.

"Right. The two of us against at least a dozen armed men. I don't think so. Even if we did, how would that help us with Doctor Richards and Conte? We need to know for sure it's the doctor. It's an all or nothing deal if we want to get the FISA warrants we need," said Emerson.

"Look, if we take what we have to Miller, I think he has enough to get us the search warrants to search Conte's facility for Richards and his experiments," Matt said.

Before Jill could comment, Amy Verduzco was tapping on her window with the barrel of her gun. "Open the back door," she said.

Emerson looked at her watch. "Fuck. It's been eight hours already?"

As their two replacements got in and closed the back doors, Agent Patch spoke. "We've been watching you guys for the last fifteen minutes. Who were those guys leaving Conte's business?"

St. Claire passed the video back to them and brought them up to date on what they knew so far. "Any clue what they've been up to?" Patch asked.

"Nothing concrete. We are not a hundred percent sure that Doctor Richards is even there. We think we noticed someone, maybe him, shapeshifting, and shrinking into someone around the same height as Alejandro Munoz. Rewind the video about twenty minutes or so and see for yourself," said Matt.

"Holy shit. If that's not Richards, then who is it?" Agent Verduzco asked.

"Do you two think this is enough to get us a FISA warrant?" Emerson asked the other two agents.

"If it were me, I'd have already been inside handcuffing everyone and asking questions later," Verduzco said.

Patch looked at this partner, scowling. "Yeah, and if you're wrong? You could kiss our case goodbye. We'd be out of a job too. We will do this by the book. You two are relieved." He ejected the tape and inserted a new one. "Take this stuff back to Miller and try to convince Miller to get us our warrants."

* * * * *

Richards tried to mask the terror he was feeling from his encounter with Munoz. What he overheard had sealed the decision for him. He sprinted back to his laboratory and downloaded the images of the drug lord from the cloud onto his laptop. He printed up five color photos he would need to complete his plan.

Thirty minutes later, he had transformed into Chad Green. He found Salvador inside his office. "Sal, I need some free time to think about what just happened. Munoz scares me. He can't be trusted." Richards said, his voice cracking from nerves.

Conte did not seem surprised that Richards was Chad Green. "Off for a little foreplay with your new girlfriend? You should bring her by to the house soon for me and Isabella to meet your friend who is making you so happy," he said, ignoring Richards' concerns about the drug lord.

"Did you not hear me?"

"I heard you. Let me worry about Munoz. You relax tonight. Enjoy yourself and come back fully rested so we can begin the next process with my three associates. Alejandro is more talk than action," Conte waved his hand dismissively.

Before Richards got on the freeway going south to Los Angeles, he pulled off highway 101 at a rest stop. He remained in his car and opened his laptop. He clicked on the file that had the images he wanted and transformed into Alejandro Munoz.

Richards knew the drug lord was staying at a hotel in Burbank. He had a surprise in store for him and Agent Emerson.

After listening to Jill open up her heart to him the other night, Richards believed what he had planned might let her move from the loss of her fiancée, and get on with her life with Chad Green.

85

Richards got to the Hotel Amarano in Burbank around eleven-thirty in the evening. He did not know the room number of the drug dealer. The four-story, one-hundred-thirty-two room hotel would make his plan easy to accomplish. It only had one main exit by the front lobby and a service exit at the rear of the building.

He had parked his Mercedes four blocks away. He walked briskly toward the front entrance of the hotel, mindful that every traffic camera and security camera in the area had vivid images of Munoz's face.

When he was satisfied the cameras had captured him, he walked toward the front lobby of the hotel. He made sure that every surveillance camera on Pass Avenue, and at the hotel entrance, took more images of his face.

The two bellmen had surprised looks on their faces. "Mister Munoz, we did not see you leave the hotel. Where are your guards?" the bellman asked, puzzled.

"I snuck out the rear service entrance. I needed some fresh air so I could relax before my long flight home tomorrow," he replied. He handed both men a one-hundred-dollar bill. He put his index finger to his lips. "Don't tell anyone I slipped out. My head of security would kill my guards if he knew they were not by my side," Richards said, his voice identical to Munoz.

"No problem, mister Munoz. Whatever we can do to help you," the bellman said, as he slipped the hundred-dollar bill into his pocket.

Richards looked around one last time, his eyes catching the security camera above his head. "Perhaps I go for one last stroll...maybe out the back?" he said, heading inside.

He was walking rapidly toward the elevators, waving back to the two bellmen. He got in and pressed the basement button. When the elevator door opened, he saw the service exit sign and slipped out unnoticed.

He walked briskly to his car and once inside phoned 911. He quickly transformed back to Chad Green. He told the operator that he saw Alejandro Munoz, the drug dealer, walking on Pass Avenue and heading into the Hotel Amarano.

"I've seen his face on the news. The FBI is looking for him, right?" Richards asked nervously. "I don't want to get involved. I just wanted to be a good citizen and thought you'd need to know. Goodbye, and good luck," he said, hanging up before the operator could ask for his name.

He waited inside his car for twenty minutes. He smiled when he saw the parade of flashing police cars speeding down toward the hotel.

"Good. Now one thorn in my ass is gone," he whispered. Then his heart skipped a beat when he saw Agent Emerson jump out of her unmarked car, her gun in her right hand. "Oh, wow," he said. "I'd like to tell her I did this for her, but that would not be very smart. Let's see where she goes later."

"What room is this man staying in," Agent Emerson shouted, shoving a photo into the bellman's face.

"Room four-zero-two. But..." he could not finish telling her that he had left the property before she and the other officers ran to the stairwell. *"He's not inside, you, dumb bitch,"* the bellman said under his breath.

Ten minutes later, Alejandro Munoz, his hands handcuffed behind his back, was escorted out of the hotel and placed into a police van. The two bellmen had shocked looks on their faces. "I thought he was out walking?"

The other bellman reached inside his pants pocket and pulled out the one-hundred-dollar bill. "Me too," he said. "Who do you think gave us this," he said, waving the C-note in the air.

"I don't care or want to know. We've got our money," the other bellman said, high-fiving his buddy.

* * * * *

St. Claire had a broad smile on his face as he watched the police van speed away. "Are we lucky or what? We should get our FISA warrants ASAP. Having Munoz on tape at Conte's business and here will have us breaking down the doors at the pharmaceutical company very soon. I'll get this scumbag booked, and hand Miller the necessary videos and paperwork to release him into our custody and hopefully get our warrants. It should take about a day," said Matt.

"A day. Shit, I'm exhausted," she moaned.

"Go home and get your beauty sleep. I can handle the paperwork. See you tomorrow around Noon," Matt said.

"Thanks. I think I'll get a quick one at Sully's first, and then home," Emerson replied.

86

Chad had followed Jill to Sully's. He was happy she did not go home first. Seeing her in action had gotten him aroused.

He entered Sully's at around twelve-forty-five. The bar was thinning out. He noticed that there was one seat open next to Jill. He walked over and tapped her on the shoulder.

"I was hoping you'd be here tonight," he said.

Jill did not turn around. She lifted her purse off the barstool and said. "I was hoping the same thing," she said, touching his hand.

"You look tired. Rough day?" Chad said

"You don't want to know. It comes with the job. Now I need to relax," Jill replied, smiling at Chad. "Tomorrow's a big day. Hope to solve a big case I've been working on."

Richards' heart started pounding loud inside this chest. It was making so much noise that he thought Jill could hear it. "Want to talk about it," he said. Taken it to mean she was talking about her Doctor Richards case. He started to wonder if, during their last encounter, he had mentioned where he was living.

"I can't discuss anything with you, or I'll have to kill you," she said, grinning while tapping on her revolver. She noticed the scared look on Chad's face. "I'm joking. Have a drink. Let's see what this morning brings us."

Ninety minutes later, they were both inside her apartment, tearing off their clothes. She kissed his neck, then his lips, undulating her lower body slowly, thrusting her hips back and forth until Chad had started to moan. She loved being in control and regulated her movements so he would not explode inside her too fast.

"What are you doing?" he cried out.

"You don't like it?" she teased.

"Like it? I love it," he moaned.

"I can stop if you don't like it," she tormented him. Jill was pausing her movements, which was getting her more excited.

Chad shook his head. He bit his index finger. "Don't stop what you're doing...oh shit," he screamed.

She felt herself climax at the precise moment Chad did. It was amazing. She rolled off him and put her head on his chest.

"You're the best stress release I've ever had," Jill said, kissing his cheek. "Better than drinking or medication."

"I serve at the pleasure of the FBI," he replied.

"I don't know what it is about you. I'm beginning to enjoy the connection we seem to have." Once she had said those words, she shut down. Richards noticed it.

"It's obvious something is bothering you. Do you want to talk? I'm a good listener. You look like you need to vent," Chad said, combing his fingers through her hair.

Jill sat up and turned toward him. She lifted the bedsheet, covering her exposed breasts. For the first time since Alex, she felt vulnerable.

"I lost someone I loved very much about eight years ago, my husband Alex. He was everything to me. Since then, I've buried myself in my work and stayed a million miles away from any emotional relationships," she said, swiping a solo tear from her cheek.

"I understand. I lost someone I loved very much too. About ten years ago. It's hard trying to find someone new, which only triggers thinking about my wife. I keep comparing every woman to my wife..." he stopped himself from saying her name. He knew it would expose him. "Denise," he said, staring at the woman who looked like his Molly.

Jill noticed it and put her arms around him. They kept talking about their loss for the next hour and a half. They both, without any effort, made love again. This time with intimacy, they both had not experienced in a long time.

They both fell into a deep sleep. Both of them were exhausted for two different reasons. They were startled awake when Jill's cell rang. She reached over to her nightstand and answered. "Emerson here." It was from Matt. "I'll be there in forty-five minutes," she said.

"It's noon. I'm waiting outside with some hot coffee and a warm croissant," St. Claire said.

"Shit," she said. "Wait in the car. I've got company."

"Hanging Chad?"

"Shut the fuck up and drink your damn coffee."

Jill looked over at Chad. He was smiling at her. "You're beautiful in the morning," he said.

"This?" she said, ruffling her long hair. "I need a shower, and you need to get going."

"When can I see you again? I'm…well, enjoying our time together," Chad said, kissing her on the lips.

"Me too. I can't commit to anything right now. This case is too big to mess up," Jill replied.

"I'd like to know more about what you do?" Richards asked. He was hoping for some indication if he needed to stay away from his new laboratory.

"Maybe after today. Our case is about to break open. Now get your cute little ass out of here so I can get to work."

Richards felt his new identity taking over. He believed he was Chad Green and had a future with her. "Promise me that we'll find more time to talk? I loved what we did last night. I want more. I want to get to know you." He was now seeing Molly more and more in Jill's face. He held back his tears as he jumped out of bed.

She saw his sad face. She decided to ignore it. She watched him bounce out of bed and slip on his boxer briefs. Again, she noticed the birthmark on his back that had an odd shape to it. She wanted to say something, but she was out of time for any more chit-chat. She quickly grabbed her phone and snapped a photo of his back.

Matt, with the windows in his car fogging up, watched Chad leave Jill's apartment. He noticed his car and jotted down the license number. "Better check this guy out," he muttered. "She's seeing him a lot. It would be great if she could forget about Alex."

87

Richards instincts told him he was not safe. He believed the FBI would be raiding Conte's facility either today or tomorrow. Before he drove off from Jill's apartment, he called Salvador.

"You need to get the girls away from the laboratory. It's not safe today. Clean up the lab, and remove any trace I was there, or that the girls are living there," he said, sounding anxious.

"Todd, what's going on?"

"I'll bring you up-to-date later. Just have everything spotless. I'll have my attorney there later,"

"You're not making sense."

"Look. The FBI has warrants to raid your facility. They are looking for my new laboratory and me. You'll understand more when we meet. I am staying as Chad Green for the day. Doctor Richards needs to hide for a while."

While on the phone, Salvador walked over to his security screen on one of his laptops. "There's nobody outside watching us," he said, confused.

Richards pounded his fist on his steering wheel. "Get the fuck out of there. If I'm wrong, then you can come back in a day or so. I know you've built an escape tunnel for this reason. Use it now!" Richards shouted. With that, he ended the phone call.

* * * * *

Jill jumped into the passenger seat, smelling like a pine forest.

Matt said. "You smell good. Even look happy for a change."

"Are you saying I stink most of the time?" she shot back. "But, thanks. I am feeling good today."

Matt gave her a thumbs up. "I've got our warrants, but there's a catch. The judge was skeptical about everything we were requesting. We can look inside Salvador Conte's business for Doctor Richards and any traces of his work, or look for a lab that proves the doctor is working with fetuses. If there's no lab, we cannot search for anything else that is owned by Conte. We cannot even interview the women we think are Richards' surrogates for his research."

"Shit, the women are needed to collaborate what we suspect," Jill argued. "What about searching Conte's files?"

"No. We cannot do anything to Conte. When we have evidence on Conte that he's doing illegal business there, then and only then can we go back to the judge for another specific warrant," said St. Claire.

"Didn't the judge see the video of the drug lord, weapons trafficker…" Matt cut her off.

"The judge was an asshole. He didn't care about our video. He said we didn't have a FISA warrant even to conduct our investigation," Matt let out an exhausted breath.

"Well, Richards better be there. Or we don't have Jack," she said, pounding her fist on the dashboard, as they drove to Conte's facility.

Waiting outside the eight-foot metal gate were Agents Verduzco and Patch. Still sitting inside their car were Agents Lucas Hernandez and Leo Small. Speeding up the driveway to Conte's facility were five SWAT vans.

St. Claire extended his arm out the driver's side window and waved his warrant. He signaled Patch to press the intercom button on the pillar by the front gate.

A gruff voice answered. "Go away, we're not open to the public," the voice said.

Patch looked at Verduzco, shaking his head. "FBI, we have a warrant to search the premises," he shouted back into the speaker.

"Flash your ID and the warrant at the security camera," the gravelly voice demanded.

Before everyone could pull out their badges, the gate had begun to swing open. "Fuckers," Verduzco moaned. "Conte's messing with us.

All the agents got back into their cars and proceeded toward what appeared to be the main building. The massive structure where they expected to find Conte and Richards was almost a half-mile from the gate. Security guards patrolled the grounds, their automatic rifles in a non-threatening position.

"Impressive for a pharmaceutical company that only does import and export. Wonder what they're afraid of," Emerson said.

Before they could knock on the front metal door, it swung open. Standing under the tall archway was Salvador Conte. He had a big grin on his face.

"FBI agents, um," he said. "What does the FBI want with a pharmaceutical company?" he asked.

St. Claire handed him the warrant. "Read it," he said, slapping it on his chest. "Step out of our way. We have work to do."

Standing in the background, Emerson recognized the man in a Blue Pinstriped suit. "Is that Chuck Feldman? Doctor Richards' attorney?" Emerson asked. "Is Doctor Richards here"?

Conte had a puzzled look on his face. "Doctor Richards? Who's that?" he replied with a chuckle.

"Wipe that smart-ass grin off your face," Emerson said, pushing Conte off to the side. She stormed toward Feldman.

"Agent Emerson. So nice to see you again," the attorney said, his eyes riveted on her face. He wondered if she could see some Chad Green in his eyes. He wanted to take her in his arms. Then thought about it and held himself back — b*ad idea.*

"Don't tell me you're the attorney for Conte too?"

"I have many clients. Why do you find that strange?"

"What connection does Doctor Richards have with Conte?"

"While I can't tell you much, you understand there's attorney-client privilege involved. I can tell you that Doctor Richards did do business with Salvador Conte, like the thousands of cosmetic surgeons around the world. Is that a crime?" Feldman asked.

Emerson turned toward Conte. "Our warrant specifies searching a laboratory, and all things related to it. Direct us to your laboratory," she demanded.

"Lab? I have no laboratory here," Conte said with a smirk.

"Is Richards on these premises?" Emerson barked at Feldman.

"I haven't seen my client since your people destroyed his office and home. Just so you know, I will be filing papers to sue the FBI for damages and emotional distress my client had from you ruining his business," Feldman threatened.

Emerson pivoted, trying to control her temper. She was pissed. She walked back toward Feldman, almost knocking foreheads. "I should arrest you right now. Do you know how Beth Thomas was killed? She was last seen in our car the day she was shot."

Feldman smiled; he was enjoying Emerson's musky scent. "It's such a shame what happened to her. I drove her back to Prospect, where she said her car was parked. Then, I left," he grinned.

"If you know where Richards is, you have a legal obligation to tell us. He's wanted for murder, and performing abortions," she said.

"If I knew where he was, I'd be obligated to tell you. I respect the law," he said, backing away from Emerson.

After four hours of searching every corner of Conte's property, they came up empty. Nothing that resembled what they had video recorded the last few days was there. No laboratory. No beds, or evidence that the women they had on tape had ever been on the premises. The place had been wiped clean. The only thing remaining was Conte's warehouse of his products, and a laboratory that did not seem like anyone had been inside it for months.

Emerson was the first to speak. "There is no way Conte could have known we were coming," she said, storming outside.

"That's impossible. This operation was known only by the six of us, our boss, and his boss," said St. Claire.

"Let's get back to the field office and re-think this," Agent Verduzco said. "I can't believe Richards or Conte is that smart. We have a mole and need to find out who's screwing with our case."

Emerson's face had turned fire red. "Let me see the recent infra-ray video you guys had taken during your shift," she said, extending her hand toward agent Patch.

Patch looked at his partner, shrugging his shoulders. "We stopped. We thought we had enough evidence. It's been the same stuff for the last five shifts," he said.

"Shit, I bet this bastard has a tunnel under this building. We need to find it," said Emerson.

Feldman overheard the agent. He quickly scanned the warrant and pasted it to agent St. Claire's chest. "Your warrant is only for Doctor Richards or any laboratory equipment he might have here. Nothing in the warrant mentions Salvador Conte or his company. Now get the fuck out of here," Richards' attorney shouted.

88

Richards went back to his apartment at Conte's pharmaceutical company. Staring at his photo of himself and Molly, he attempted to transform back to himself.

Without warning, the transformation that had started on his body had become very painful, causing a burning pain he had never experienced before. He tried to sit up; his muscles were cramping, putting him into a fetal position. He had thought he had improved the process so there wouldn't be any pain while shifting from identities to identities. As his body re-molded itself, the fire inside his joints escalated. He closed his eyes, clenching his jaw, and prayed the pain would stop.

He tried to catch his breath, hyperventilating out of control, trying to take command of his thoughts. A tornado of images exploded in his brain. He was looking at Angelica's motionless body sink to the bottom of the Pacific Ocean. Then it was Trish Morgan, aka, Lisa Beverly dead on her bed in Bermuda. He was begging for forgiveness, when Meg Cummings and Carolyn Hollister looked down on him, asking why he had to kill them.

He was woken by heavy banging on his bedroom door. "Todd, are you alright?" Conte screamed. "Let me in."

He sat upright, trying to get his bearings. Like most of his dreams, he remembered what had happened. Conte would not stop banging on his door.

"I'm good," he called out. "Must be a bad reaction to my serum. I'll talk to you later about it," he said.

He had always suspected that with frequent makeovers, it would begin to disrupt his molecular system, possibly leading to permanent damage. He was baffled, wondering if he had made a drastic mistake with his new hybrid solution.

Right now, it did not make sense. Todd had tested this new batch numerous times, and it had allowed him to heal without any side effects. He had to get into his lab and look at his blood to make sure his DNA was not beginning to mutate. Survival was all that mattered now. He needed a new endgame, a new safe house, away from Conte, and he needed it fast.

Richards was charting new territory, and for the first time since he created his fountain of youth serum, he was scared.

Being on the run from the FBI had him stressed, especially after their recent raid. He was aware that his obsessiveness about a life with Jill Emerson might be causing him to make mistakes and be distracted.

"I need Todd Richards to disappear forever. Pick a new identity," he told himself. "Chad Green would be my first choice," he muttered, pulling back on the syringe in his arm.

He wrote down some ideas he needed to test first. He had to make time to reformulate this new serum. He had begun to worry that if he didn't, he could get stuck with an identity he could not live with, or worse, go mad.

Two hours later, he met up with Salvador Conte in his office. "You were perfect," Richards said.

Conte did not seem happy. "What was going on in your room earlier? How the fuck did the FBI know to come here? How the hell did they know that you and my girls were here?"

"First, I'm okay for now. Just a few glitches that need straightening out. As for the FBI, I'm on their most wanted list now. I'm their number one suspect who they believe murdered my four women and my office manager.

"Okay, but how did they know you were here?"

"I can only speculate that we got made at Echo Park, and it was reported, probably by someone watching you? It's the least of our worries."

"What the fuck are you talking about?" Conte asked, his tone caustic.

"I heard it on the news this morning. The FBI has Munoz in custody. If he tells them what he witnessed here, I can assure you they'll be back with a more specific warrant."

"Any suggestions?" Conte asked, his arms in the air surrendering to his frustration.

"Yes. Do you have a laboratory outside this country? I need more time to perfect my work. I cannot keep having these interruptions. I'm rushing too much and making mistakes," Richards said. "You need to have Bishara and Vasiliev lying low for a while. I found a small anomaly in my formula. I need more time to work out the kinks," he said.

Conte had both hands combing his hair. "I have the perfect place, but my two colleagues are not the type of men who you can tell to wait. How much time will you need?"

"Six months. I'll still need your women, and a few lab monkeys for my experiments," he replied, focusing on Conte's expression to see if he was buying his little white lie."

"I can give you three months. Then, you'll have to deal with Boris and Sayid. They have paid me a healthy sum of money for your serum. I'm not inclined to return it," Salvador said. "I, too, need my potion. You have my fetus. You must create my serum for me immediately."

"It's too soon. I need at least three weeks for optimum results," said Richards "You don't want any problem with the formula. Right?"

"Fine. Three weeks for me, and no more than three months for my associates," Conte said.

Richards nodded. "Fine. If I need more time, you'll have to give it to me. What I am doing is a delicate process that takes time, or someone might die," he replied.

"Pack your things. We leave tomorrow morning," said Conte.

"I'll be ready. I have a few loose ends to deal with," Richards said, his thoughts focusing on Jill Emerson.

89

Munoz had been sitting on a metal chair in the FBI's interrogation room for over six hours. He was getting antsy, rocking back and forth. His butt was stiff, and he was irritable.

When agent's Emerson and Verduzco entered the room, his angry expression had vanished, replaced with a smile. "Now, this was worth waiting for," he said, gawking at both agents. "Who wants to blow me first?" Munoz grinned.

"If I had my gun," Emerson said. "I would blow your fucking head off. You're a piece of worthless scum." She held back her rage, unable to look at the man she suspected murdered her fiancée.

"Now, now, play nice with our guest," Verduzco told Emerson.

"Okay, little ladies, what the fuck am I doing here?" he cursed.

"Because you're stupid and arrogant. You were walking on the streets of Burbank, looking up at every security camera on your walk. Even your hotel has you on their security videos. Shit, didn't you think we'd be watching?"

Munoz was fuming. "I was not walking outside my hotel. Who tipped you off?

"No one, you moron. You did this all by yourself," Verduzco said.

"Someone's going to pay. I can promise you that," Munoz threatened.

Verduzco set her laptop on the interrogation table and slid the screen in front of their suspect. "Here, let me refresh your memory," she said, pressing the arrow button for the video to start.

Alejandro had spittle crusting at the corners of his mouth. He was furious, as he slammed the laptop closed. "That can't be me," he shouted.

"It looks like you," Verduzco said. "If not you? Who then? You have a twin brother in the swamp of a family you come from?"

Munoz was deep in thought. Then, he slapped his forehead. "Doctor Richards, that asshole," he grumbled. "He promised to erase the images and the voice imprint he took. It was him who was walking the streets. He set me up. When I see him, I will kill him," Munoz shouted, slamming his fist on the interrogation table.

"Doctor Richards?" Emerson blurted out. "You know where he's hiding?"

"Yes. We had a demonstration at that asshole Conte's company the other night. Richards proved to me how his miracle liquid worked. I offered to buy him from Conte, but Salvador refused," Alejandro said, his mood boiling over. He squeezed his eyes tight as he realized he was talking too much.

"Who else was at the demonstration?" Verduzco asked.

"I'm not talking anymore without my lawyer."

"You will not get a lawyer today. You're on our terrorist watch list, as well as a murderous drug trafficker. There are at least a dozen countries that would like to get their hands on you. So, right now, you better talk to us, or you'll be locked away in one of our Federal Super Max prisons, where men like you disappear," Emerson threatened, looking straight into his eyes. "Now wipe that smug grin off your face and tell us what we want to know."

"What kind of deal can I get if I tell you everything that went on at Conte's business?"

"You tell us Richards' whereabouts, and what Conte has going on at his company, and what they are planning, then I'll try to make sure you do not get housed with some of your competition we have locked up," Emerson's face was stone-cold serious. "I'd shoot you right now if I could. I won't let my personal feelings toward you get in the way."

"Okay, okay. Conte's selling Richards serum for ten million dollars to criminals who want it. If we want a new serum for our men, then it's an additional ten million each. Your country is screwed if Richards can give Boris and Sayid what he promised. You'll never be able to recognize, as you say, the good guys from the bad guys," he laughed. "Imagine not being able to screen for terrorists on your watch list. They will be able to travel from any part of the world to your country, and…" he paused, his hands pressed together, then shouted, "Boom," as his hand exploded apart. Oh, you are so screwed," he said clapping.

Verduzco looked at Emerson. Her face drained of color. "Follow me," she said. They both were out the door standing with their partners.

Agent Patch said. "What the hell just happened?

"We need to refocus our strategy," Emerson said. "If Richards slips out of the country and finds a new location where we have no jurisdiction to extradite him, and he creates vials of his shift-changer shit for the bad guys we're screwed, our country is screwed."

St. Claire did not seem as worried as his partner. "Let's all take a deep breath. We need to rethink how we approach our Doctor Richards case. Right now, he's able to slip through our security, but Salvador Conte can't. I'll bet if we keep an eye on Salvador, we'll find Richards, or what version of Richards he changed into."

90

Inside a conference room at the West Los Angeles FBI field office, every piece of paper they had on Doctor Richards was either spread out on the walnut rectangle conference table or pasted on a whiteboard. Agents Small and Hernandez were there to help with the Conte aspect of this case.

Emerson and St. Claire were reviewing all their documents and checking photos, videos, and lab notes. Something about the videos of Conte's facility had Jill frustrated. She kept pointing something out to her partner.

"See that," she said, pointing at Angelica Rathburn's video at her home. "Now look at the guy in Echo park before he went into the bathroom. You see it?"

St. Claire leaned in, trying to see what Emerson was seeing. "No. Help me out here."

"Watch it again. See how the guy in the video tugs at his crotch in the park? Now, look at how Angelica did the same thing when she was talking to the reporters on her driveway. That's his tell," she said, smiling.

Verduzco and Patch had slid over to the computer screen to understand what was rattling Emerson's feathers.

"Damn, you're right. That is Richards' fucking tell," Verduzco said. "What's with you guy always yanking at your junk?" she laughed.

Both St. Claire and Patch pretended to zip their lips. They were interrupted by a lab tech from forensics.

He was a young freckled-faced redhead, who didn't look over eighteen. He said. "I've got some more bad news. The coroner confirmed that Lisa Beverly was, in fact, Trish Morgan. Dental and DNA don't lie. Not her sister, as we first thought."

"Emerson looked at her partner. "Shit, just as we suspected. Richards has been eliminating everyone that knows about his secret program."

"We need to talk to Lea Strong. She's our only link right now to Richards," Verduzco said.

Patch patted her on the back. "It's never going to happen. Homeland and the CIA have her hidden away, doing, I don't know what to her. I've tried calling up some favors, but she's essential to some people high on the food chain. My contacts do not know where she is or if she's alive."

St. Claire was waving a photo in the air. "Guys look at this," he said, pointing at Richards' wife in the picture.

Patch leaned in." Damn, Emerson. She's the spitting image of you," he said. "I think it's time to use you as bait," he said.

"Don't remind me," she said. "But it's not a bad idea. Anything to draw Richards out."

St. Claire did not like putting his partner at risk. "I know you look like Richards's wife; there just has to be a better plan."

"I've been running some scenarios, and nothing is making any sense." She grabbed the photo and stared at it again. "Shit, if I had a missing twin, I'd bet his Molly would be my sister." She gave the photo back to her partner and began sifting through all the albums they had of Richards and his wife with the life they had before she died.

"Is there a magnifying glass in this room?" she asked. She had in her hand a photo of Richards in his bathing suit.

"Here," St. Claire said. He saw his partner still staring at the photo. "You see something?" he asked.

Jill was rubbing her chin, deep in thought. "That birthmark," she said, her index finger tapping the photo. What does it look like to you?"

All three agents grabbed the magnifying glass, focusing on what Emerson was seeing. They all gave the photo back to her, with puzzled looks on their faces.

Emerson was deep in thought. "Shit, I know it's a little blurry. I've seen it before," she said.

They were all interrupted when their boss stormed into the conference room. "You all have to leave immediately. Conte is on the move. He's leaving the country," Miller said. "We can't lose him."

Emerson stuffed the photo of Richards into her front pants pocket and followed her partner.

91

Later that evening, agents Hernandez and Small got word that Conte had snuck out of the country on his private jet. The Coast Guard could not intercept the plane once Salvador was over Mexican airspace by the time they caught up with him.

They alerted the American Embassy in Mexico City about Conte. They asked the CIA if they could spare a security detail and keep tabs on him.

"I'm exhausted," agent Verduzco said. "I need a good night's sleep before we trek to Mexico City."

Agents Patch and St. Claire agreed. Their stress tattooed on their faces.

"If we get a good fix on Conte, we can all be in Mexico City late tomorrow," Emerson said. "Right now, I need a stiff drink, and then some shut-eye. Anyone care to join me?"

Matt had not mentioned to his partner that he was running a search on her new boyfriend. He had gotten back the registration info on Chad Green's car. He could not believe who was the registered owner. He decided to bring it up tomorrow after he got a good night's sleep.

"Sully's?" Matt asked. "I could use a drink too," He said.

"Sure, I'd love some company." Then, she thought about Chad. *Shit, I don't have time for that tonight*, she told herself. *I hope he doesn't show up unexpectedly.*

The Faces of Doctor Richards

* * * * *

The lounge at Sully's was packed. Emerson decided she was more hungry than thirsty. She convinced Matt to eat something too.

Jill smiled. She enjoyed her time with her partner, especially when they were not thinking about work. "Let's eat at the back of the restaurant. It's quieter back there."

"Good idea. I need to talk to you about a personal thing," Matt said.

The restaurant was about to close. Jill chose a curved booth in the dimly lit portion of the dining room. She signaled Matt to speak.

"What personal thing do you need to talk to me about?" she asked.

Matt had hoped he'd have time to prepare his words, perhaps after a few gulps from his whiskey and soda, but Jill had always been an impatient person. "I don't know how to begin. Here it is. About a week ago, I noticed your boy-toy, Chad Green, leaving your place while I waited for you in the car..." she interrupted him.

"You're not going to give me that big brother advice you always do about who I see, are you?" she teased.

Matt raised his hand like a traffic cop. "Don't interrupt. Let me finish what I have to say. Okay?" he said, his tone serious.

"Fine. Continue," Jill replied. She saw her waitress and grabbed her drink. "Now, go ahead and talk."

"Shit, Emerson, you don't make anything easy, do you?" he protested. "What I did, as your partner and friend, was run a vehicle ID on Chad's car. I found out a little bit about the man you seem so fond of," he said, taking a long sip of his drink.

Jill frowned; her expression had become somber. "I appreciate that you wanted to protect me; however, my personal life is my business. You need to learn to trust my judgment," she said.

Matt raised his eyebrows and ignored her remarks. "I think you're going to be interested in what I found out."

"No, not really," she said, showing her annoyance with her partner. "But, by the way, you look, you're going to tell me anyway, right?"

"His car is registered to Salvador Conte. Nothing on the registration reflects Chad Green has any joint ownership to it," he said, noticing he had her attention now.

Jill let out a long sigh. "Interesting, however, not so strange. He's a drug rep. Maybe it's a company car," she said unconvincingly.

"Do you believe that?" St. Claire asked. "It's too much of a coincidence. You're screwing around with a guy that drives one of his cars. Especially the night before our raid."

"What the fuck are you trying to say? Do you think I talked about our case and tipped off Conte through Chad? I'm sure there's a logical reason for all of this."

"I don't believe you'd slip up or be careless. Can you think of anything you might have said in front of Chad that might have given him the impression, Conte, his boss, was going to have a warrant served on him?"

Jill's eyes grew wide as she barked back at Matt. "I never talk about any of my cases with anyone outside of the FBI," she paused, deep in thought. "Shit," she slammed her hand hard on the table. "Fuck, I could have tipped him off. I did mention I was going to be wrapping up a big case. If he thought it was about his boss, he could have mentioned it to Conte that we see each other…shit…shit, he could have told him about me, and my case," she said, her anger boiling over.

"Look, don't get upset. I am also running a background check. It has not come back yet. I should have something while we're in Mexico."

Before Matt could finish talking, she was dialing Chad's cell he had given her. "Hey Chad, Jill here. Can we meet tonight at my place?" she asked. "I 'm going out of town and would like to see you before I go," she said, trying to keep a calm and even tone. There was a long silence at the other end of her line. "Chad, you there?"

"Yes. You caught me off-guard. I can be there in an hour and a half if that works for you?"

"Yeah, that works. I am just wrapping up dinner. See you at eleven-thirty."

"You're going to meet him now? Shouldn't you wait to confront him until we have more information?" Matt asked.

"Doing my due diligence. If we need more info on this guy, I'm going to get it," she said.

They ordered their food. The rest of the time at Sully's, they both kept silent. Matt knew his partner was thinking things through about how to handle her boyfriend. They finished their dinner in forty minutes.

"See you at LAX tomorrow at twelve. Get a good night's sleep and stop worrying about me. I can take care of myself," she said, giving him a big hug and a wet kiss on the cheek.

"Be safe," he said. Matt cared for his partner and wasn't going to tell her that he'd be watching her place tonight.

92

Chad was punctual. He had brought a bottle of red wine, and one red rose.

He entered Jill's apartment, leaned in, and gave her a light kiss on the lips. "I'm so glad you called. I am going out of town too, and did not know how to reach you," he said, hoping he was hiding his lie. "I have so much I want to tell you…but…well, I'm nervous."

She was taken aback by the rose and bottle of wine. It was the same thing Alex had done the first time he had picked her up for their first date. Jill closed the door and followed Chad into her living room.

"Can I pour you a drink?" she asked, her voice edgy. She had gotten distracted by what Chad had said.

He had the bottle of wine in his hand. "Let me open the wine. You'll love it. It's from a great vineyard in Napa, 'Crooked Vine,' one of my favorite places to go." As he started to walk to the kitchen to find a corkscrew, he reached between his legs and adjusted his pants.

Jill, saw what he had done and laughed. "Why do all guys do that?"

Richards looked back at her, a puzzled look on his face. "Do what?"

Jill did not reply. "Oh nothing," she said, trying to digest that he had picked a wine from the vineyard she and Alex had gone to on their first overnight trip together. "I know of that winery," she said, holding back her surprise.

They sat for over an hour talking about their past lives, and what they wanted down the road. Chad continued to remind her of Alex in so many ways. She was feeling emotions she had not had in many years. She chose not to question him on his car at that moment.

They spent the next two hours in bed. This time it was not the wild sex that they had previously. Their intimacy felt very natural to Jill. Chad was charming and loving to her, something again that reminded her of Alex.

About two in the morning, she asked him to leave. He did not object, as he too had to get ready for his trip out of the country.

She again noticed his birthmark. This time she decided to comment and see where it led. "Cute little birthmark you have on your back. It looks like Italy," she said. She noticed his face turn bedsheet white. She remembered the photo of Richards she had in her case file, sending off alarms in her head. She remembered she had already taken a picture of his back the last time they were together. She decided to compare them after he had left.

Chad was looking deep into her eyes, trying to figure out why she brought it up. "I hoped you'd not notice. Something I wish I would have had surgically removed when I was a kid," he replied.

"What's the big deal?"

"Boy, it was. Getting teased constantly was no fun growing up," he said, hiding the anger he was feeling toward himself. *How stupid, Todd. If she's as good an FBI agent as you think, she'll figure things out very quickly.*

Jill noticed she made him uncomfortable, but that was what she wanted. "Sorry for even mentioning it. It's a non-issue with me. I like it. It goes well with your cute firm butt," she said, giving him a little slap.

Chad had gotten very quiet. He kissed her on the forehead rushed out the front door. After she locked the front door, she swooped up his wine glass and placed it in an evidence bag.

She went over to her case file on Richards and found the photos of the doctor and his wife. She then clicked on the picture she had of Chad's back. Her body had begun to shiver. It was as if a cold bucket of water had been poured on her when she saw Richards identical birthmark on the man who had just left her apartment.

"Shit, shit, shit," she cursed. "How could I be so stupid? That bastard is using me as a substitute for his wife."

She needed to go to her field office to drop off the wine glass before heading to the airport. She wasn't so sure how she would explain this to Matt.

She texted a friend at TSA to check on when, and where Chad Green was going. She also needed to talk to someone on her forensic team and determine if Chad's birthmark was a common phenomenon in men. As she tried to rationalize what she had just discovered, she prayed it was just an unfortunate coincidence. Something like the red blotch marks kids have when they are born.

Jill tried not to think about it, but her thoughts would not go away that she had been sleeping with the enemy, and it was making her sick to her stomach.

93

Richards had boarded his Aero Mexico flight to Mexico City. He smoothly went through customs as a Doctor Mark Baldwin. He was confident that the FBI did not know about this identity.

He had all his paperwork in his carryon for three other aliases he planned on using while out of the country. He prayed that he'd not have to do too many transformations until he fixed the anomalies that had popped up during his change at Conte's property outside of Ventura.

Jill Emerson had shaken him to his core after she noticed his birthmark. Her joke about it had thrown him off-balance. His preference for permanently being Chad Green was slowly evaporating. He believed he'd get back on track while in Mexico.

Spending those last few hours with Jill, listening to her talk about her life and what she wanted down the road, had him believing he could share his life with her.

What upset him the most was his carelessness. He was falling in love, realizing it would not matter after she discovered that Chad Green was Todd Richards. He didn't like the thought of her becoming his enemy.

Richards inserted his earbuds, turned up the music on his phone, and leaned back in his soft leather seat in first class. He closed his eyes, drifting off like always to his fleeting memories of Molly and their once perfect life together.

* * * * *

For the first time in his recurring dream, Molly was angry with him. He shuddered in his seat, feeling the ache in his heart. He hated to see his wife upset.

"I'm sorry," he said, his head bowed, embarrassed at what he had become. "I'm so, so sorry. I know you're watching me, but I cannot stop myself," he whimpered.

"Todd, look at what you've become," Molly said, crying. *"You had so many positive dreams and aspirations for your work,"* she paused, exhaling. *"You've created a monster you need to destroy,"* she scolded. *"You cannot play God."*

Still locked deep inside his dream, he began to cry softly. "I can't stop. I need more time with my research. I'm close to achieving what I tried to do for you," he said.

"Would you have become this man, this crazed man, if I were still alive?" Molly asked, shaking her finger at him.

The question jolted him awake. He looked around, the man next to him was sound asleep, as were the other passengers across the aisle. He blotted his forehead with his napkin. With his hand still shaking, he gulped down the rest of his bourbon and water and pressed the call button for another.

After Molly's death, his dreams had only been about her and the relationship they had. He was getting terrified after his numerous transformations, that something inside his brain was changing. Knowing right from wrong was no longer something he could control. Now, his dreams about Molly had become confrontational and stressful. She was beginning to disappear, and her attitude toward him was judgmental. He wished he had gotten the Cat-Scan to confirm his worst nightmare about what was happening to him.

Richards took the new drink from the flight attendant, sipping it slowly. He was now contemplating his next move as Doctor Richards. He knew he had to figure out how to prevent his DNA from mutating before he took on his new and permanent identity.

The announcement startled him. They were landing in Mexico City in fifteen minutes. Since the recent problem with his new serum, he was back on his old protocol. He needed to take another shot before they landed. He snapped open his seat belt and stood up, stretching his arms above his head. He rushed toward the front of the plane for one last restroom break.

The flight attendant signaled him to return to his seat, against his plea to use the restroom. "I'm sorry, Doctor Baldwin, but we are in our descent. You will have to hold it until we're on the ground.

Richards was feeling his blood pressure rising. He needed his shot within two hours. With all the rushing around, seeing Jill the night before had thrown off his schedule. "I'll be quick," he pleaded, crossing his legs.

She signaled him to go. "Please be quick."

Inside the restroom, he put his hand in his front pants pocket. "Shit, the syringe is in my bag," he cursed. He also needed the serum, and photo of Mark Baldwin for this to work.

He realized he'd have to wait until they landed. He prayed that he'd disembark on time, but he knew in Mexico City, there were always delays.

94

Doctor Baldwin rushed off the plane, running down the gangway in search of a restroom. The plane had sat on the tarmac for over an hour waiting for a gate to open. In his panic to take his shot, he almost knocked down two Aero Mexico employees who were greeting every deplaning passenger. He apologized, skidding to an abrupt halt.

"Donde Esta El Bano?" he asked in his horrible Spanish accent.

The pretty airline employee understood his question. "It's over there," she pointed, answering in perfect English. "Thank you for speaking our language," she said.

He waved at her as he rushed off. "Thanks a bunch. Oops, I mean, Gracias.

Inside the restroom, he found an empty stall. He removed the syringe from his pants pocket, checking that the dosage was correct. He let out a little fluid to remove any air bubbles. His fingers searched for his artery in his neck and inserted the needle. Within seconds he could feel the warm liquid flowing through his bloodstream. He sat down on the toilet seat, holding the photo of Baldwin in front of his face, waiting for his body to refresh in his temporary identity.

Like it did two days ago, the process took longer and was more painful. Richards had become apprehensive about all of this.

Fifteen minutes later, he was out of the restroom heading toward baggage claim and immigration. He was relieved to see a man holding a cardboard sign with his name on it.

The Faces of Doctor Richards

The nicely dressed man, in a chauffeur's uniform, looked at a photo in his hand. He confirmed that the man he watched walking toward him was his pickup. "Senor Dr. Baldwin," Senor Conte sent me to drive you to his home. We go now. No immigration required. I take baggage tags. My men find them, and bring you bags later," he said.

"How long a drive will it be?" Richards asked.

"Tres Horas, mas or menos. Excuse me, please. I mean three hours or less to Senor Conte's home."

"I need something to drink and eat," Richards said.

"Everything thing you'll need, in the car. All of your favorites," he said proudly, puffing out his chest.

* * * * *

Richards could not relax as they sped toward Santa Maria Atarasquillo, a remote town outside of Mexico City. They passed an old church, with a massive hand-carved wooden door, the walls were painted white with beige trim. The steeple's bell chimed three times. Nevertheless, modern times had caught up with the town, as there was an oversized clock right below the bell sounds, so those who were not paying attention to the signals would know what time it was.

The few people walking in the streets looked away as Conte's limo speed through their town. Some bowed their heads, and others scurried inside an open business. There was a fair amount of graffiti on the walls in the village. Richards was unable to read the tagged words or understand the symbols. It didn't matter. He could care less. He wanted to get to his new lab and solve his immediate problem.

When he passed the Universidad Tecnologica, he wondered if that was where his new laboratory would be. As they drove further outside of town, he realized that the car was heading into the hills, hidden away from what little civilization he had seen so far.

* * * * *

The two agents from the CIA kept their distance from Conte's car. They had taken a photo of the man who had gotten off the plane. Once they confirmed it was a Doctor Baldwin, they forwarded the picture to their CIA office in Virginia. When they saw where the car was heading, they pulled off the road and called agent Bingham.

"Sir, Doctor Baldwin...I mean Doctor Richards, will be staying at Conte's hacienda outside of town. We'll observe and keep you posted."

"Good. Keep your distance. I don't want Richards getting spooked," Bingham said. He was happy that Lea had cooperated and told him about his Doctor Baldwin alias.

95

Two days after Richards and Conte returned to Mexico, six FBI agents in a Hawker 1000 landed at Mexico City's International Airport. The plane taxied to a private hanger facility away from the central terminal. The six FBI agents had permission to arrest Richards and Conte.

Waiting for them were three armored vehicles, led by the chief of the AFI, Hector Flores, who had come with six of his men, all carrying AK-47's.

"What a wonderful reception," Verduzco said. "You know I don't trust any of these guys," she whispered to her partner.

Patch scowled. "Don't start any trouble here. We're here as their guests. Please behave," he scolded.

"You do know that they are still investigating almost forty-percent of their old police force that worked for the Sinaloa Cartel?"

"I do. These guys are new, and from what I know are all straight shooters. They want to stop the illegal activities in their country," Patch said.

Emerson heard them arguing. "You guys are too loud. I know this guy. He is one of the good ones," she said.

Hector Flores approached the six agents, unsmiling. He walked directly toward Agent Emerson, acting like he was going to arrest her.

"Agent Emerson," he said grim-faced. Then, a smile exploded on his face, and he gave her a big hug. "So nice to see you, Jill," he said, in perfect English.

"Hector, it's great to see you too. How's Isabel, and your two boys?" she asked, kissing him on both cheeks.

"Isabel is as beautiful as ever, and hounding me to lose some weight," he said, pinching his belly. "Diego and Raul are not boys anymore. They are young men in college in the United States."

Agent St. Claire interrupted the two of them. "Are you going to introduce us?"

Emerson looked over her shoulder. "These are my assistants," she smiled. Agent's Patch, Verduzco, and my partner St. Claire. I know you know Agents Hernandez and Small."

"Yes. We've been coordinating on the Conte case for about three years," Hector said. "Let's get all of you to headquarters so I can bring you up-to-date on Salvador and his activities since he returned from California."

"Any sightings of Richards?" Emerson asked.

"No. We have a lead on someone who's being watched by your CIA. The suspect got to Conte's hacienda three hours outside of Mexico City. We'll keep monitoring."

Before they could leave the tarmac, four military Humvees, and one black S-Class Mercedes, with two Mexico Flags on the front two bumpers, skidded to a halt, blocking their exit. Twenty soldiers, all dressed in SWAT gear, pointed their automatic rifles at the six FBI agents.

Emerson looked at Hector with a puzzled expression. "What the fuck's going on here?" she said, whispering in his ear.

"I'm not sure. You can bet I will be finding out," Hector said, walking over to the General who had stepped out of the Mercedes.

"Hector, stay calm," the general said in Spanish. "By orders from our president, your friends have to leave our country right now," the General said.

"General Sanchez, I have permission to work with the FBI on the Salvador Conte human trafficking case. We need their help," Hector said.

"I have my orders. Our president and their president have agreed to back off Conte for a while. Something to do with Doctor Richards?" the general said. He handed Hernandez a piece of paper signed by their President. He read it. He folded it up and walked back to the six FBI agents standing by the ladder to their plane.

He looked at Emerson, shaking his head. "You will have to leave my country," he said, his voice cracking. "My president and your president have agreed to hold off on breaking up Salvador Conte's human trafficking ring."

Agent Verduzco stepped in front of Emerson. "Fuck this," she said, her voice loud enough for the General to hear. Amy read the orders from the Mexican president. She was fuming. "Here," she said, pasting the paper hard against Hector's chest.

Emerson said. "What's going on, Hector?"

"My case, your case has been buried, while your government figures out what they want to do about Doctor Richards. It seems that your CIA has a lot of pull with our military and government. There's nothing I can do right now."

St. Claire seemed to understand what had occurred. "Let's get out of here. I'll bet that our friend, agent Bingham, needs Richards more than we do. The CIA must be working on their serum with Professor Franklin and getting nowhere. They want to capture Richards, and get him to perfect it for them." Matt said, turning and walking up the ladder to their plane.

Inside the plane, all six agents looked dumbfounded at what had just transpired. Agent Patch spoke first. "I have a sick feeling our country believes it has a new weapon with Richards serum," he said.

Emerson felt her cell buzzing. She saw she had a text from Hector. *Sorry for what just happened. My orders have not removed me from my case against Conte. I will keep you up to date over the next few months,* he wrote. *Maybe Richards will turn up soon?*

Jill looked at her team. We need a new plan. Any ideas?" Before she could wait for an answer, she bounced up from her chair and rushed to the bathroom. She felt like she was about to throw up.

Verduzco asked. "You all right?"

"Must be something I ate?" she said, her hand covering her mouth.

St. Claire spoke. He didn't seem to notice his partner. "I need to call a friend at the CIA and find out what's going on. We have five unsolved murders that need explaining. It will be interesting how everyone justifies blocking our work?"

Verduzco didn't seem interested in what Matt had to say. "If the president and his CIA don't want us involved, we'll probably get reassigned and be kept far enough away and in the dark. Our case is over."

* * * * *

Conte was pleased with what General Sanchez had told him. "Perfecto. We need, let's say, six months to finish our work. I hope you can protect me a little bit longer. It will be worth it for you, my friend."

"You better be right. Forging the president's signature is a dangerous thing in our country. I will need my new identity, and money very soon."

"Don't you worry. Doctor Richards is a wizard. You only have to figure out who you want to become?"

96

Six Weeks Later

Richards had his lab up and running. To everyone in the small town near Conte's hacienda, he was Doctor Baldwin. While working at the compound, Richards had to be his old self. It was a necessary stipulation he had to adhere to so Salvador could keep a watchful eye on him.

The women he had impregnated at the Ventura site had remained with him, enjoying their new life away from their pimps. Richards was a gentle lover. He never raised his voice or hand toward them or had angry words spoken to them. It was a relationship that was a unique experience for these ladies of the night.

For every healthy fetus, Richards' harem produced it was worth five thousand dollars to them. It was their retirement plan if they survived long enough to collect it.

Richards's favorite surrogate was a beautiful young woman named Margarita. She was stunning, as well as intelligent. She had turned out to be more than just an incubation vessel for him. He enjoyed their quiet time together, talking, and eating their meals by themselves.

Richards learned that Margarita was kidnapped when she was fifteen and thrown into the harsh life Conte created for them. She was now twenty-two, still in remarkable physical and mental condition and a survivor. She had never fallen into the depression trap like the other prostitutes getting on heroin like all the others.

She was petite, with long black silky hair. She liked talking to Richards about her old life, and the future she was beginning to imagine she might have with him.

Just as Richards had been with Angelica Rathburn, he was becoming attached to her. He had become melancholy these last few weeks in Mexico. He, too, started enjoying the intimacy they shared. He tried to keep Emerson out of his head, convinced she was off-limits since she most likely knew that Chad Green was his alias.

Margarita lived with him in a small cottage at the backend of the hacienda. When they were not having sex, Margarita was taking care of his other needs. She had become vital in his life.

He had made a promise to himself that this time, he would figure out an escape plan for the two of them.

His new gene/stem cell combo, he created in Santa Monica, was finally showing remarkable results with his chimpanzees after some critical modifications. The first test fetus from his lab animal had produced a more potent and powerful serum. He had experimented with numerous physical pain tests on his lab animal, each time it passed with flying colors.

In two days, he would conduct a trial experiment again on himself using the new formula he made with Margarita's fetus.

He was unsure if it would work. He believed the risk was worth it, even if he might die. If he did die, then no one would have his serum. If it worked, he would be unstoppable. Then, he'd be able to eliminate all his threats and move on to his new life as Doctor Baldwin.

Todd heard the loud voices getting closer. It was Salvador screaming at his men like he did every day. Without even a knock, the laboratory door swung open.

"Todd, my friend. I have good news. My Maria is pregnant again. When can we start my serum again?" Conte asked, slurring his words, drunk as usual. "This time no screw ups with my fetus," he said, waving his pistol. He almost shot Todd when this first batch of serum failed to work for him.

Richards arched his eyebrows, frustrated with Conte. "I've told you we have to wait until the embryo is six weeks or older. You forced me to abort your first fetus too early before we got here, and your serum was unworkable if you recall. It failed. Patience, my friend, your time will come very quickly." Richards was getting tired of having to reason with the drunk lunatic.

Flushed with anger, Salvador started screaming. "I want my fucking serum now. What am I paying you for?" he shrieked as he walked over to a chair.

"Sal, calm down. You'll get what you've paid for, but only at the right time, so please have patience," Richards begged.

"Don't fuck with me. I want to be first," Conte demanded.   He turned away and stormed out of the laboratory.

"What an asshole," Richards muttered. "He'll be the first, but he might not like the results," he said, an evil grin on his face.

97

Agent Emerson had taken some vacation time she had accumulated after getting back from Mexico. Doctor Richards had gone off the FBI's most-wanted list and was not a top priority anymore for Regional Director Miller.

Jill was frustrated their case against the doctor was going nowhere, even though they all knew he was in Mexico. Salvador Conte was not the only one protecting Richards. Ralph Bingham of the CIA was keeping a watchful eye on the doctor and his progress with his serum.

The bug Emerson had gotten after leaving Mexico had not cleared up. She had been throwing up every morning for the last six weeks. She did not want to think about the apparent reason and decided to put the question to rest. She had bought a pregnancy test and finally took the test.

"Shit. It can't be?" Jill cursed. She racked her brain, thinking about how this could have happened. She hadn't had intercourse since that night with, *"oh damn, Chad,"* she said.

"Damn it…damn it," Jill screamed. "It can't be Chad? I thought he used protection? I am on the pill," she questioned herself. Then, she remembered. Her emotions that last night had gotten in the way of common sense. "Fuck, fuck, fuck," she cried. She took a second test, only confirming the first test.

She knew she had been taking risks with the men she went home with from the bars. She even took the morning after pill, just to be safe. That night no precautions had been considered.

Retracing her footsteps kept leading her back to Chad Green, or Todd Richards. He'd been the only man she had allowed herself to let her guard down. She knew Richards' case was stressful. She prided herself on the steps she usually took to be careful and safe. Obviously, that's not what happened that night.

St. Claire was coming to pick her up. They were meeting with Miller in two hours. She let her bathrobe slip off her body. She gazed at her toned body, focusing on her stomach. It was firm and tight. Not an ounce of fat showing.

She turned on her shower, putting the knob on extra hot. While waiting for the cold water to turn to the right temperature, she looked in her medicine cabinet. She grabbed her dial of birth control pills. She was stunned to see that the empty days were out of sync. "Damn, I missed four days back then," she said, combing her fingers through her hair. "I can't have this baby now," she said, holding back her tears. Especially if it's Richards?"

She grabbed her morning-after prescription and read the instructions. *Shit, it's too late to take this,"* she told herself.

Before she jumped into the shower, her cellphone rang. She looked at the screen. It was St. Claire. She thought of letting it go to her message machine, but she knew he wouldn't call if it weren't necessary.

"Good morning, Matt," she said, trying to hold in her sadness.

"Well, good morning to you too," St. Claire said. "You sound like shit. Up late last night drinking?"

"No. I'll talk to you about it when I see you," she replied.

"Well, I have exciting news about your friend Chad Green," he said, his voice serious.

"Can it wait? I was about to jump in a shower. You can brief me over coffee," she said rudely, ending the call.

Inside the shower, St. Claire's words spun inside her head. "He must have gotten the background on Chad. More bad news, I bet," she muttered, tapping her stomach.

* * * * *

At the coffee shop with St. Claire, Jill's head was down, her eyes staring at the dark, steaming cup of coffee in front of her. She waited for Matt to speak. "You go first," she said.

Matt knew his partner very well. Something serious was on her mind. "You have me worried. I've not seen you like this since Alex died," he said.

"No one died. Just get on with what you want to tell me about Chad?"

Matt opened a manila folder. He pulled out a report. "Chad Green or the real Chad Green died in nineteen seventy-seven at age forty-one. Here look at this picture of him when he was forty-one. Look familiar?"

"Could this be his father?" she asked.

"No. These records show this Chad Green died single. I need you to see this next photo of him in the morgue; then you'll understand what I am about to tell you." He slipped the nude photo of Chad Green lying on an autopsy table before he was about to be examined.

Jill stared, lost in thought, not saying a word. She looked up at Matt, her eyes glassy. "I'm ready for the final blow to your little investigation."

Matt passed another lab report in front of Jill. "The fingerprint analysis you got from Chad's wine glass. It came back as a perfect match for Doctor Richards. That asshole was truly fucking with you," St. Claire said, not realizing his words were right on point.

Jill's face drained of color. Tears cascaded down her cheeks as she said, "I'm pregnant. I have this motherfucker's baby," she said, unable to control her sobs.

St. Claire was speechless. "Are you sure?"

"One thing a woman knows is who got her pregnant. It was Chad or that fucker Richards," she said.

"What are you going to do?"

"Do? What can I do? It's illegal to get an abortion, right?"

"Not in Mexico. Maybe your friend could help?"

Jill took in a deep breath. "I'm going to wait and let this all sink in. I still have time. I've made a few rushed decisions lately. I don't want to make one that I might regret," she said. "This baby should not be punished for my mistake."

St. Claire bit his lower lip and said. "Well, if you decide to go ahead, and abort, which I am not encouraging you to do, maybe we can use it to lure Richards out of hiding. He might be desperate and want this fetus for his research?"

"You're talking about using my baby and me as bait?" she asked.

"Not bait. That was a poor choice of words. Let me rephrase it. It can be a well-coordinated sting operation. You'll be safe, and so will your baby, unless you want to go through with the abortion in Mexico?"

Jill, with a painful expression, said. "You've got an excellent idea. I have to capture this bastard. I want to blow his brains out and save the taxpayers the cost of a long and lengthy trial."

"I have accumulated vacation time. It's almost six weeks," Matt said. "I know you've not used all of your vacation time. If we put our plan together, we could be in Mexico in three weeks. It shouldn't take more than six weeks to capture Richards."

Jill scratched her scalp. "What do we do about Miller? He's not going to let both of us leave together."

"He's already on board with me taking some time off, and I am sure he would approve you taking more time. Unless he asks, let him believe we're going in opposite directions."

Jill had a strange look on her face. "I'll be right back," she said, holding her mouth with her hand, rushing off toward the restroom.

98

Richards had woken up from another disturbing dream. Molly's screams from her this time were more intense. She was distraught, admonishing him. *"Todd, God disapproves of what you're doing,"* she said, grieving. *"Remember how you were when you first started your practice? It's not too late to repent and ask for forgiveness. You can do some good with your serum. Save lives now with your gift."*

Richards attempted to respond. He was frozen, unable to speak. When he tried, his words had come out garbled. Reasoning with Molly was not working. *"I know I've done horrible things,"* he said, unable to look at Molly. *"I will repent when I've perfected my new hybrid serum, and then you'll be proud of me."* Nothing he was telling her was changing her disapproval of him.

He kept trying to explain to her that he was close to not having to use fetuses anymore. That in Mexico, he would be able to replicate his formula using in-vitro fertilization. No more aborting fetuses. He looked at Molly, checking for any indication she approved of his new method. His dream evaporated when Margarita had begun shaking his shoulder.

"Senor Mark, you're having a nightmare again," she told him. Margarita was pleased she remembered to call him by his new name. "You need me to calm you," she said, sliding her gentle hand between his legs.

He looked over at her, taking in a deep breath. "I'm fine. Just a bad dream," he said, kissing her on her lips.

She kept her grip on his manly part, her nails from her other hand gently combing his chest. "I disagree. I can feel you want me right now."

Richards did not seem to argue as he put his arms over his head, unable to resist her naked body as she straddled his waist. She was right, they made love for fifteen minutes, and he had calmed down. He looked at her and smiled.

"I've got to get to my lab. I expect the breakthrough I mentioned to you a few weeks ago. If this works, and you become pregnant again, you can go full term and have our baby—no more abortions. Our child will be extraordinary, with skills no one can imagine. We can start our lives over again, away from Salvador, and his people."

She looked at him with loving eyes. "Mark, me like that? Would we marry too?"

He was caught off-guard by her comment. A chill had come over him, as Angelica's identical words, before he accidentally gave her an overdose, filled his head.

He looked at Margarita, her eyes welling up as she waited for his response. He was still unsure if he would welcome a baby into his twisted life. He had never imagined being a father without Molly. Now, a young woman he had become very close to wanted to start a family. "Let's discuss that after I test my new serum," he said, kissing her on the forehead. "If it works, then a new life might be possible."

Inside his lab, Margarita's question repeated itself in his thoughts. *"What would it be like to have a child, perhaps two?"* he whispered. *"All with special abilities."*

He knew it would be risky conceiving a baby with his modified DNA. He suspected the child would be born with powers similar to his. However, those answers were unknown.

He worked through the day, his mind dreaming of being a father and what he had heard Molly say to him in his dream.

The idea of changing his approach and living a life doing good in the world was making him feel happy. The possibility of that happening would require him first to eliminate some terrible people, so he would no longer have to look over his shoulder. "I need a plan," he whispered.

99

Professor Franklin threw a vial at his laboratory wall. He had failed again to replicate Doctor Richards formula. He had analyzed Lea Strong's blood dozens of time, broke down the solution in her vials, and he still did not have answers for Bingham. He knew something was missing, but what?

In fifteen minutes he was going to attempt his first human experiment. He created a fetus with eggs from two of his female combat veterans and the sperm from two active SEAL Team Six members. Today, everyone was excited, especially agent Bingham.

"Franklin, do not disappoint me," he said, his tone threatening. "I don't want to have to replace you." What the professor did not tell everyone was that his serum was not even close to what Richards had created. He had no choice except to do his first trial test. He had another idea he believed would work but needed the president's approval.

The CIA Director had become impatient with Bingham, putting him under a lot of pressure to get their program up and running. Bingham transferred that pressure onto Franklin.

The professor wanted to use stem cells from Lea Strong's baby. That was a non-starter. He kept hearing from Bingham, "*it was against the law and God's will.*"

Earlier that morning, hours before his first test, his frustration had exploded. He was talking to his lab assistant. "I'm hitting a brick wall with Richards work. Nothing in any of his notes or analysis of his serum we took from his office is giving me an idea of the right combination of edited DNA, or fetal stem cells he used."

His assistant just listened, afraid to speak. Franklin saw it on his face. "Sorry for my attitude," he apologized, right before Bingham barged into the lab.

Ralph Bingham was noticeably unhappy with Franklin's progress. "Are you ready for my first test on a human subject?" he asked. "You guaranteed you'd be able to have the fucking serum perfected without Richards help," he said, his anger showing. I hope you won't embarrass me today?"

Franklin sucked in a deep breath. "You do know what we're about to do today is risky? Once I inject my solution into your test subject's arms, we'll need to keep our fingers crossed that we won't kill him. Finding the right mixture is like looking for a needle in a haystack," he said. "Possibly, the solution to our problem lies within Strong's baby's blood?"

"Are you suggesting we abort her baby and harvest its fetal stem cells to discover Richards formula?" asked Bingham.

"Never," Franklin shouted. "I will not be part of murdering a baby or breaking the law. I'm pro-life," he said. "I am only suggesting we wait for the baby to be born so that we can test its blood."

Bingham's face looked like it was ready to burst. "You've already broken at least fifty laws with what you've been doing in your lab. Maybe it's time to pick Richards up in Mexico and bring him here to finish this fucking project. We are running out of time. The president wants this completed and his new special force team ready for action."

Franklin had never seen CIA agent Bingham so angry before. He knew something had to give, and he was afraid it would have to come with Todd Richards once again working with him.

* * * * *

The theater in the lab was full. Sitting in the audience was the Attorney General, the CIA director, the president's Chief of Staff, the Joint Chiefs, the Homeland Security Secretary, and CIA agent Ralph Bingham.

"You confident this will work, Bingham?" the CIA director asked.

Bingham did not reply as the curtain opened, displaying the professor, his lab assistant, and one soldier on a tilted gurney. There were IV's in each of his arms. Franklin was holding up a vial with his test serum, making sure everyone saw what he was about to use.

"Gentlemen today will be our first experiment on a human subject. I would have preferred more time to run more tests on our lab animals, but as you know, we are on a short timetable to get this project up and running."

The room had become quiet as if someone was going to be executed. All eyes were on Franklin inserting the syringe into the IV port in the soldier's left arm, and slowly releasing the liquid into the IV.

Everyone in the room, including Franklin, held their breath. At first, nothing was happening. Then without warning, the soldier arched his back. His body shook violently.

Franklin started to panic, believing he had just killed the soldier. As fast as it had started, his test subject calmed down. He sat up straight, waving to his audience.

"I feel fine," the Navy SEAL shouted. "I'm ready for the next test."

Franklin stepped in front of the soldier and addressed his audience. "I will now test to see if the serum works. Lea Strong told us that at the beginning for her, it was difficult, and did not happen at first."

Professor Franklin opened a manila folder and grabbed an eight by ten photo of a wanted Iranian terrorist. He attached the picture into a metal frame. He asked the soldier to lie down again.

Franklin turned toward his audience to explain the next step in the transformation process. "Our subject needs to be prone, on his back for this process to work. Next, I will be aligning the picture of Rashid Hussain in such a manner that our subject can see his full body details."

Franklin's hands were shaking as he affixed the photo and moved the tripod frame holding the picture directly over the SEAL's face. "Master

Sergeant Hutch, please concentrate on the photo you see and ask your mind to transform you," the professor said.

After fifteen minutes, nothing had happened. Franklin didn't know what to say about his failure.

Gentlemen, as I mentioned at the start of this first test, it doesn't happen at first try. I need to run blood panels to be sure the serum is mutating with this soldier's DNA. Give me a few days to report back to you on my progress," Franklin said and marched off the stage.

Bingham was biting his lower lip, his face beet red, while he was being chewed out by the CIA director. "Bingham, we've put a lot of taxpayer's dollars into this project, and I am beginning to feel it's been a waste of time without having Doctor Richards in our custody. I am not impressed with Professor Franklin. I do not believe he has the smarts to manage this project."

Bingham took in a deep breath before he replied. He hated the Director and had to endure his abuse. "Sir, I've been ready for weeks to raid Conte's compound and capture Doctor Richards. Are you ordering me to make that happen?"

CIA Director Roger Kramer craned his neck, making sure no one was listening. "I want Richards in our custody before the end of the month. That gives you two and a half weeks to get the job done."

100

Later that afternoon, Bingham was on a secured conference call with the Attorney General and the Homeland Security Secretary. "Kramer wants us to pick up Richards before the end of the month. Franklin's experiments are useless. He called the president and told him he wants to wait for Strong's baby to be born. It's speculative, but he believes the child will have unique abilities. Then he wants to harvest the child's blood and build his serum using its properties."

The Attorney General sounded upset. "Are you saying that what we saw today will not work?"

"I don't know. What I am concerned about is what we are doing with Lea Strong and her pregnancy. We might be slowly killing her, and her baby with all the experiments Franklin continues to do," he said. "If that happens, all we've been doing would be for nothing."

"What's your solution?" Murphy asked.

"Pick up Richards first. We know he's still with Conte in Mexico."

Murphy was getting frustrated with the CIA agent. "How do you propose doing this?"

"We've been monitoring Richards in Mexico for months. My sources inside Conte's compound have told me he's on the verge of completing his new formula. My CI working at Conte's hacienda will let me know when it's time for us to strike," Bingham said.

The Homeland Security Secretary jumped into the conversation. "First, it's too risky to grab up Richards at Conte's lab. We could lose everything, including the doctor. Second, the president has been convinced by his military advisors that Strong's baby might be born with its transformation powers that we could then harvest. So maybe Professor Franklin is on the right track?"

Bingham controlled his laugh. "She's most likely having a normal baby, by all indications," he said.

"You know the president, and the first lady are religious fanatics. They believe God conceived this baby. They want it alive so they can reproduce more like him, or her, for their new religious army," the attorney general said.

Stuart Lewin, Homeland Security Secretary, interrupted them. "We've got another problem. I just got word that two of Conte's associates are going to be making a move to kidnap Richards in the next three weeks. We need to move up our plans, ASAP," he said, "or we might lose Richards forever."

"If your intel is accurate, then I can have a team ready in forty-eight hours. My Director gave me orders to make this all happen." Bingham said.

Lewin said. "Please wait. I'm meeting with the president this afternoon. I will let everyone know his wishes."

101

Mexico's AFI chief sheriff, Hector Flores, six weeks ago, was ordered to back away from his case against Salvador Conte. Then, today, without warning or any logical reason, was re-authorized by his president to arrest Salvador Conte and Doctor Richards. His orders were to work with the CIA and the United States Homeland Security agency.

Flores had always believed his president was easily swayed by his chief of staff, who had a close relationship with the CIA Director. He was suspicious that the FBI was left out of this operation. Something was happening, and now his team was going to be right in the middle of it.

He knew how crucial arresting Doctor Richards was to his FBI friend Jill Emerson. He could not understand the CIA's interest in him. Flores knew from talking with Emerson that Richards was wanted for four murders back in the United States. He had to find a way to alert Emerson about this joint task force operation and stay under his department's radar.

Using a secure line that evening, he was able to connect with Emerson. "If you want to capture Richards, you need to find a way to get down here. If you don't, I believe your CIA will make him disappear," Flores told her.

"What's going on?" she asked. "You know where Richards is?"

"I'm not sure. All I know is that there is a doctor Marc Baldwin living at Conte's hacienda. When you were kicked out of my country, strange things have been happening inside my government," said Flores. "They're secretly working with your CIA."

"Why does your government want to arrest Doctor Richards and Conte now?"

"We're not arresting him. We're turning them over to your CIA. I've received specific orders to turn everything over to your government of what we find inside Conte's lab, including this Doctor Baldwin and the women."

Jill was unable to think clearly. "Who's this doctor, Baldwin?"

"He entered our country about the same time Conte did. He's been at his compound over six weeks now. All I know is that the CIA has been watching this man."

Emerson did not believe in coincidences. "Richards must be Doctor Baldwin," she said.

"No. I've seen his picture. It's not Richards," Flores said.

Jill realized she had said too much. "You're probably right."

She wanted Richards behind bars. She wasn't ready to let her friend in on what Richards had created.

"I need you to find a way for me to contact Doctor Baldwin without Conte knowing about it." Jill was worried about her baby and needed to know if it would be born with defects from Richards's mutated DNA.

"I can be down there with my partner in five days. I will need some help getting across the border without creating waves," she said. "I need a way to contact Baldwin when I get there. Then, I need to talk with him one-on-one."

"I can handle that. I will send you instructions by tomorrow."

102

Richards overheard Salvador arguing with his associates. What he could make out did not sound right.

"My men will defend this place to their death," he shouted. "When are they planning this raid?"

"The Americans want Doctor Richards, and everything thing he's been doing there, including your girls," he said. "I can hide the doctor deep in Russia, where nobody will find him. I have a perfect place for him to complete our serum."

What Richards heard next frightened him. He recognized Boris Vasilev's voice.

Salvador slammed his fist on his desk. "You're not taking Richards, or my girls anywhere. I will find a new location in Mexico. Here, money buys me whatever I want," he boasted. "Your girl and Sayid's girls are almost ready to abort their fetuses. Soon we'll all have our serum. Then, we can vanish in our new identities. Relax, I will handle my government and the Americans," he said, disconnecting the call.

Margarita had nuzzled up to Todd's back, trying to pull him away from the door. "Senor Conte, no like when people listen to his conversations. You move away now before he hurts you and me. Come away now, senior Todd."

Richards turned toward Margarita, anger filling his face. "You NEVER call me by my real name. Never!" he said, tone harsh. "I am

Doctor Mark Baldwin now. Doctor Richards is dead," he said, twisting her arm hard enough that it made her wince.

"I so sorry, Mister Mark. I scared for you. Maybe we run away now. Before FBI captures us," she said, tears on her cheeks.

"So, you heard everything? Well, we do need to go, but not until I make one quick run into town. I have some unfinished business to attend to," he told her.

That evening he snuck out of the compound. His identity was now Chad Green. He needed to call Emerson and tell her he was sorry for deceiving her.

* * * * *

Outside a small cantina, he dialed Jill's cell. She picked up immediately. "Jill, it's Chad," he said.

Jill had put her phone on speaker so everyone inside her apartment could hear the conversation. St. Claire, Verduzco, and Patch all perked up. She put her finger to her lips, signaling them to stay silent. She was stunned he was calling.

"Chad? Now, this is a surprise. You calling to turn yourself in?" she said, her tone serious. "We were just talking about you. Your ears must have been ringing." Jill was wondering if her friend in Mexico had contacted Richards.

There was a momentary silence, then Chad spoke. "No, hello? Or how are you? Maybe I've missed you?" he said, overamplifying his hurt feelings.

"I know all about you, Doctor Todd Richards. When I find you, I have a bullet waiting for you," she said.

St. Claire could not believe what his partner was doing. He wanted to put a gag in her mouth. Verduzco and Patch were puzzled at Emerson's tactic also.

"I'm so glad the truth is out there. I never wanted us to have any secrets. I did care for you. The way you confided in me, I think you cared for me too," he said.

"I know about your Molly, and how much I look like her. You're a sick fuck, fantasying that I was your dead wife. You killed her, and your son with your stinking experiments."

Richards felt his blood pressure rise with her hurtful words. "You leave Molly and my son out of this. You have no right to talk about her that way," he said, his voice taking on a sad tone. "I tried my best to save them."

Emerson knew she had him right where she wanted him. "I'm the FBI. I can do whatever I want. How are you going to feel when I abort the demon seed you put inside my body?" she said coldly.

Richards fell back against the wall in the alleyway. "You're having a baby? My baby?" he said. "Your FBI. You can't abort a baby. It's illegal in the United States."

"Not if I do it in Mexico," she said.

"Mexico? Can I see you before you do it? I want to hear its heartbeat. Please?" he pleaded.

I'll be in Ensenada in three days. Give me your cell number. I'll text you my location when I get there," she said. Without hesitation, Richards gave her his burner phone number. Then, the phone call went dead.

Jill looked at her team. "Was I convincing? Do you think he'll show up?"

St. Claire shook his head. "He'd be an idiot to show up. He knows you won't be alone," said Matt.

Verduzco interrupted. "I think he'll show up. He's got a big ego. He'll be in a new identity. If he sees trouble, he'll split. I still believe he thinks you'll be coming by yourself."

"Why?" asked Patch.

"Because Richards knows getting an abortion is illegal for any American, even if it happens outside of the USA. Richards realizes that Emerson would never get her partner or us involved in an illegal act. Right?"

St. Claire was grinning. "Emerson, you're a genius," he said.

Jill was not smiling. She was thinking about aborting her baby. She could not tell her partner her real plans. "I hope he takes the bait.

"We'll know in three days," agent Patch said.

103

Driving on a dirt road back to the compound, Richards stopped his car. He noticed off to his right high on a plateau, were a dozen military vehicles. The men were all dressed in SWAT gear. What made the scene even more frightening were the two-dozen black Suburbans off to his left. They were a half-mile away from where Conte was hiding.

Richards was now panicking. He knew that one day he'd be captured or kidnapped, but he had not imagined it would happen so soon. Margarita was trapped inside, along with the new serum supply he had created for the two of them. It was essential for him to get to his cottage before all hell broke loose. He bolted toward the tunnel system Conte had built precisely for this situation.

Richards parked his car under a thick bush. He sprinted as fast as he could to the tunnel's entrance. Within seconds he heard the gunfire and explosions shaking the ground around him. He had gotten to the cottage's front door as the blasts from the bullets erupted in the main building.

He found Margarita huddled in the bathroom, shaking. She was terrified. He pulled her up and said. "We need to stay calm. I need you to pack some clothing, and your passport with the new identity I gave you last week," he ordered.

"I already pack my things, after I hear senior Conte earlier. When I hear the gunfire, I knew we must go. I was scared you not come back for me," she said, hugging him tightly.

Richards pushed her away, cupping her face with his hands. "I'd never leave you here," he said. "Now listen to me. I want you to go into the tunnel and wait for me at its back door. Look at the photo of your new identity and concentrate on changing. I wanted to teach you how to do this, but right now, you will have to figure it out by yourself," he said, kissing her on the forehead.

She looked at him, a puzzled expression on her face. "You not coming with me now?"

"I will be with you shortly. I must get into the lab to get our vials and your frozen fetus. If I am not there in twenty minutes, leave, and never come back," Richards said. He knew that if Margarita were on her own, in her new transformed state, she would be dead within a year unless she got another shot.

Richards changed back to his Mark Baldwin alias, as he rushed toward his laboratory. The gunfire and shouting had become more intense. He stopped right before entering the lab, to peek outside. No more than a hundred yards from the medical clinic were Conte's men behind their trucks, defending themselves from the convoy he had seen on the road.

Conte was firing his automatic weapon while shouting out orders to his men. Richards noticed that three of Salvador's men were on the ground, not moving. Without warning, a massive explosion destroyed four of the convoy's cars, causing the men attacking the compound to retreat. Within seconds, the other military vehicles he had seen on the plateau had surrounded Salvador and his men.

Richards knew he'd be next. He rushed inside the lab and found his two metal cases of serum for himself and Margarita and the metal tube containing his fetus. He heard the front door to the laboratory get kicked in.

"Doctor Richards, this is the CIA. Come out with your hands up," Agent Bingham shouted. "We are not here to hurt you," he said. The agent realized he was talking to an empty room.

Richards did not wait around to see if the agent was telling the truth. He was inside the tunnel, standing next to Margarita, who had transformed herself without any problem.

"Sweetheart, you did good," he said. He opened the back door to the tunnel. He did not see any of the military vehicles or men in SWAT gear. Then he and Margarita ran toward his car. They were back on the dirt road, heading to town to a hotel room he kept pre-paid just for this situation.

"Margarita, we have to go to Ensenada for a few days. I must do some business before we cross the border into the United States. You'll love the home I have for us," he said.

Margarita's identification had her as a US-born citizen with the name of Luisa Hunt. She was twenty-nine and was born in Escondido, California. She had taken the identity of a young woman who had died in nineteen-hundred fourteen.

Margarita squeezed Todd's hand. "Will I ever see my family again?" she asked, sadly.

Richard shook his head. "That would be impossible. Everyone from now on will be looking for us. We cannot risk it. I promise you the life I have planned for us will be much better than what Salvador Conte had planned for you, or what the United States government would do to you," he said.

It was fourteen hours driving time to Ensenada and his meeting with Jill Emerson. He knew he needed to get there faster. His mind was thinking of different scenarios on how to get Emerson's fetus, his fetus. He had many ideas he was considering, playing each of them out in his brain, trying to determine the one that would prevent him from being captured.

104

Chief Sheriff Hector Flores, from the AFI, was shouting orders to his men. They had killed five of Conte's bodyguards.
They had twelve more of his men on the ground with their hands cuffed behind their back.

Flores was frantic. Salvador Conte appeared to have escaped. Inside the compound, he found a dozen beautiful young women, all huddled together, petrified.

The Chief Sheriff walked over to them, holstering his weapon. "We are here to rescue you," he said, with a reassuring voice.

One of the women began ranting. "We need señor Baldwin. He our doctor now. We need him now to remove our babies," she cried. Her panic had triggered the other women to wail at the top of their lungs. They were all harmonizing the same pleas. The cacophony of cries had blended into one loud chant.

"Ladies, please calm down. I don't understand what you want?" Flores said. "Please, one of you speak at a time."

One of the women, who seemed surer of herself, stood and spoke. "We work for señor Salvador. We no more have sex for money. We make babies with other men here," she said. "Doctor Baldwin promise us a miracle shot that will keep us forever young," she said, nodding her head.

"Doctor Baldwin?" Flores said, a puzzled look on his face. "Is there a Doctor Richards here too?"

The woman furrowed her brow, shaking her head. "No Doctor Richards. Doctor Baldwin is our doctor. We need to have babies taken out so he can make our magic shot. We don't want to be mothers.

"Where is this Doctor, Baldwin?"

"He lives in the cottage back of hacienda with Margarita. They in love. They maybe start a family. She already has her magic shot," the woman said.

Flores sucked in a deep breath. His frustration had begun to show. He pointed at two of his men. "Go find this cottage. Find this Doctor Baldwin and Margarita and bring them to me," he ordered.

Fifteen minutes later, his men returned empty-handed. "The residence was emptied. We found the escape tunnel at the far end of the property," the Mexican police officer said.

Flores called his office to get a forensics team out to the compound to look for any DNA evidence that would give him some clues about who lived on Conte's property. After his call, Ralph Bingham from the CIA had entered the crime scene.

With his ID pushed in Flores's face, he started ordering his men to secure the property. "I have permission from your president," he said, waving a signed order in the air. "This is now under the jurisdiction of the United States. Please remove your men from my crime scene and leave any evidence you have bagged.

Flores tried to argue, but Bingham stopped him. "There's no discussion or explanation needed. Get your damn Mexican ass out of here," the CIA agent ordered.

* * * * *

Flores was on the highway driving back to his office. He had finished talking with his superior. He was furious. His case against Conte was in the CIA's hands now. Finding Doctor Richards was not his responsibility anymore.

He needed to give a heads up to his friend Emerson. She picked up on the first ring. "Jill, there's a problem here. Your CIA and my president have taken over the Richards and Conte case once again," he said.

"Slow down. Tell me what happened?" Emerson asked.

It took him fifteen minutes to recap everything that had transpired. He told Jill about a Doctor Baldwin, and a woman named Margarita and the escape tunnel.

"Richards is Baldwin. Were there any photos left behind? Anything with Baldwin's face on it, or photos of this Margarita woman?" she asked.

"I'm confused. How is Richards this Doctor Baldwin? How can that be?" Hector asked.

"Shit, I didn't want to tell you, but maybe it's time you know. Richards is a fucking mad scientist. He's created a mutated serum from the stem cells of aborted fetuses and his modified DNA. He can transform his appearance into anyone he wants and when he wants," she said.

"Really? So that's why Conte's ladies were crying that Doctor Baldwin needed to abort their babies. They said Baldwin promised a magical liquid to keep them young. Conte's gone too. What's going on here?"

"I'll explain more when I see you. Is everything in place for me to enter Mexico?"

"Yes. No one will know you're here. If Doctor Richards is this Doctor Baldwin, how will you find him?"

"I have a way to draw out Doctor Richards. I'm on my way to Ensenada. I should be there tomorrow. Can you meet me there? We might be able to solve this case on our own and make you a hero," she said.

105

Assistant Deputy Brian Miller acted surprised about what Bingham had told him. "Are you sure they're heading to Ensenada?" he asked.

Bingham kept pressing Miller. "Any idea why?"

"She needed some time off. Since you took her case away from her and her partner, she's been unable to work. I ordered her to take some time off and use her banked vacation time to chill out on some exotic beach.

"Really? Ensenada? Their beaches suck. Why not Cancun?" Bingham asked.

"What's the difference? She's going on vacation. I never try to figure that woman out anyway. She's a real ball-buster. If she likes Ensenada, so be it."

"Don't say anything to her about our talk," he said. "I'll handle it from here," he said.

Bingham was on the phone talking to Attorney General Murphy, and Homeland Security Secretary, Lewin. "Any ideas why Emerson would be going to Ensenada?" he asked.

Murphy replied. "Not sure about that, but her partner is going to Rosarita Beach for his vacation. Do you think they're a couple? The two places are a stone's throw from each other," he said.

Bingham sucked in a deep breath. "Is it possible she's still working her case?"

The attorney general replied. "Not logical. She's been told by her director to stay away from Richards. Emerson's always been one step

385

away from being fired. She's on shaky ground as an FBI agent. So no, I don't think so." said Murphy.

Bingham wasn't so confident. "I'm going to dispatch a few of my men to monitor her. It might be nothing. Better safe than sorry. The president wants us to find Richards fast, and bring him into custody," he said. "It's now a matter of National Security." He ended the call.

106

Emerson and St. Claire had met up at her hotel in Ensenada. It had been five days since she had spoken to Richards. She was now worried that Bingham was after Richards too and might interfere with what she had planned for the crazy doctor.

"It's time to go fishing," she said. She sent a text to the burner phone Richards had given her.

I'm in Ensenada. I am having the procedure in three days. Don't be late. Text me when you arrive. You will receive my location then.

"Do you think he'll come?" Jill asked, seeing Matt's disapproval etched on his face.

"I think you're crazy for even being here under these circumstances. Are you going to have an abortion?" St. Claire asked.

"I'm thinking about it. It scares me to bring a child into this world, especially one with a monster for a father, and with DNA, God only knows what it will do to the baby. I don't know what crazy poison was inside his sperm…shit, what will my baby be like?" She swiped a tear from her cheek.

"You're FBI. You cannot break US laws in any country. Even though it's legal here, you're subject to our laws," St. Claire reminded her.

Jill looked at her partner; her eyes had narrowed. "Are you saying you'd arrest me if I decide to do this?"

Matt's chin rested on his chest and was unable to look at his partner. "You know I care about you more like a friend than my partner. I'll have your back whatever you decide," he said, leaning forward and kissing the top of her head.

"Thanks. I appreciate that. You're a good friend. It's very worrisome, this baby shit," she said. "Right now, I want to arrest Richards. He's a fucking murderer. Once we apprehend him and I see him behind bars, I'll feel better. My pregnancy right now is secondary."

St. Claire's cell pinged. He looked at her, puzzled. He turned his cell screen toward her to show her it was agent Forrest Patch calling.

"Hey, Forrest, haven't heard from you or Verduzco in a few weeks. You guys mad at me?" Matt said. There was an uncomfortable silence before Patch responded.

"Are you and Emerson in Ensenada? I got a call from the director that the two of you are there checking out abortion clinics?"

Matt was speechless. "I…we needed some time off, after the Mexico City fiasco. I'm staying in Rosarita Beach and Emerson's in Ensenada. I came down today to have lunch with her," he responded, avoiding answering the question about abortion clinics.

"You didn't answer my question," Patch persisted.

"Where did you hear that?"

"That doesn't matter. Answer my question," Patch snapped at him.

Jill could see how uncomfortable Matt was becoming and yanked his phone from his hand. "Forest, Emerson here. What the fuck is it your business where we are or what we're doing? We're on vacation, so bug off," she said. She could hear Verduzco in the background, asking for Patch's phone.

Agent Verduzco was on the phone, shouting out profanities. "You don't talk to my partner that way. Now answer our god-damn question," she shouted. "Jill, tell us why you're down there, and why all the interest in an abortion clinic? The director knows what you're doing and wants answers."

Jill knew that Amy was like a pit-bull. Once she bit into a piece of flesh, she would not let go until she got what she wanted. "I had heard from my friend at the AFI, that Richards might be hiding out here in

Ensenada. That he might be using abortion clinics to get his goddamn fetuses," she said, holding her breath, as the lie flowed out of her mouth.

"Why would you not call us? We're a team, right?" Verduzco questioned her.

"If it had proven to be true, then we would have called you guys. I wanted to enjoy my vacation, too," she said. "So, drop this grilling, and let me relax," she said, handing the phone back to her partner.

St. Claire was nodding his head in approval, with a thumbs up. "Amy, Matt here. I'll call you if something pans out about Richards. Trust me," he said. "Are we all good here?"

Amy allowed an uncomfortable silence float before responding. "I don't know what you two are up to, but my suggestion is to be careful, especially at these abortion clinics. They are run by the local cartels, and they do not like the FBI in Mexico, especially when they are, snooping around," she said. "Take care, my friend."

* * * * *

Amy looked at her partner. "You buying their bull-shit?"

Forest was shaking his head. "No way."

"We need to get our asses down there and see for ourselves what they are up to," Amy said.

"I agree. I think Emerson's obsessed with this Richards case and him being the father of her baby. She's taking it too personally. I can be ready to leave early tomorrow," he said.

"Great. I'll drive," Amy said.

107

Richards had barely made it out of the hacienda to one of Conte's small airfields with Margarita. He had packed up all his working files, including everything he had completed for Conte, as well as the data on his associates who wanted to kidnap him. This time he did not want to leave any of his research for Professor Franklin to find.

His escape from Mexico City to Ensenada required him to commandeer Salvador's plane. He had all of Conte's photos, which he needed to execute his plan.

About a mile from the airfield, he stopped his car. He took out Conte's full body photo and began his transformation. This time it happened quickly and with little discomfort. He was anticipating Emerson wanted to capture him, by any means possible. If his new formula worked, he'd be too powerful against anything Emerson threw at him.

He asked Margarita to step out of the car. He handed her a photo of Salvador's mistress, who was pregnant.

"I need you to become Silvia. Do you remember how you did the transformation when we were escaping?" he asked.

She took the photo without saying a word and began changing before his eyes. "See, I do this well," she said, smiling. Maybe we now partners?"

Richards was pleased. He now had a competent cohort to help him with the rest of his plans. He wanted Emerson's fetus, and Margarita was proving to be ready to help him.

He drove up to the hanger panning the area for Conte or any of his men. All he saw was his pilot sitting on a folding chair, earbuds in his ears, listening to some music. When the man saw Conte exit the car, he jumped to his feet. He had a puzzled look on his face.

Señor Conte, you said you'd be here in one hour. The plane is not ready," he said.

Richards began to mimic Salvador's voice and temper, which he surprisingly did very well. The pilot turned around and started putting fuel in the plane. "Sir, the plane will be ready for liftoff in fifteen minutes. Where do you want to go?" he said, his voice cracking from nerves.

Richards tossed him a piece of paper with the location on it. "I need to be in Ensenada today. Can you do that, or do I need to get another pilot?"

"No, sir. I will be ready and have you there in less than three hours."

Richards and Margarita carried their luggage on board with the cases of serum and her frozen fetus. The hatch to the cabin closed, and the pilot took his seat. He began clicking on switches, checking his instruments, as the plane started backing out of the hanger. When the aircraft turned toward the end of the runway, Todd could see three black Mercedes speeding toward them.

He shouted to the pilot. "You need to get this plane in the air right now. The Police are coming," he said.

Without hesitation, the pilot had the plane speeding down the smooth asphalt, and airborne. Richards looked out his window and could see Conte firing his gun at the aircraft.

"Shit, he's pissed." Richards leaned his head back against the beige leather seat and closed his eyes, a big smile on his face.

He opened his folder and found the photo of another identity, Doctor Theo Bashir. He was confident that no one knew about this identity.

* * * * *

Conte was screaming into his cell. "Who took my fucking plane?" he cursed. "I need another one immediately."

"Sir, you took your plane. You were with Silvia," the man in the control tower said with a confused expression.

"Look at me, you idiot. That wasn't Silvia or me," he said, raising her arm in the air. "What was the plane's flight plan?"

"The pilot did not say, but I did get a confirmation from the Ensenada airport, giving you permission to land there."

"Why, Ensenada? Shit, never mind. Get me a plane, and get it cleared to land there too," Conte ordered.

108

FBI agents Lucas Hernandez and Leo Small met with Regional Director Miller, and CIA agent, Ralph Bingham for a confidential meeting about Richards, Emerson, and St. Claire.

Bingham led the meeting, with facts about what happened at Conte's hacienda and not very flattering words about their partners Emerson and St. Claire. He came close to accusing them of working their old case on Doctor Richards and violating a direct order from the FBI Director.

Bingham let them know that Emerson and St. Claire were in Ensenada interviewing abortion clinics under the disguise of catching Richards buying fetuses. The CIA agent told the two agents that Salvador Conte was on his way to Ensenada too.

Bingham handed Hernandez and Small orders from the attorney general to arrest Conte and deport him to the United States. The CIA agent told the two FBI agents that they would have the full cooperation of the Mexican authorities.

Agent Hernandez was uneasy. "I have a few questions, sir," he said. "First, what is agent Emerson and agent St. Claire really doing there?"

Bingham pretended to be annoyed by his question. "Agents Verduzco and Patch are handling that part of this task force. Your only assignment is to arrest Conte and bring him back to the United States."

"Why, after all this time, are we now able to go into Mexico and arrest Conte? You do remember when we had our best opportunity to get him, as well as Doctor Richards, you and the Mexican president kicked us out of that country?" Hernandez said, showing his frustration.

"That was then, and this is now. Can you follow orders and do your god-damn job?" Bingham shouted. "You have one objective, and one objective only: end Conte's human trafficking ring. You cannot alert St. Claire and Emerson you're coming to Ensenada. I'll be dealing with them."

With that last order, both agents Hernandez and Small had one last question. Small interjected. "Are we having an FBI convention in Ensenada? Or are we getting set up for a cluster fuck of major proportions?" his sarcastic tone did not go over well with Bingham.

"Get the fuck down there, do your job, and bring back Conte," he replied.

"What about Emerson and St. Claire? What are they doing there? We don't want to step on their toes," said Hernandez.

Bingham had become frustrated with the two agents. "Just follow my orders. Stop asking so many fucking questions. Copy that?" he asked, gesturing them to leave the conference room.

* * * * *

Hernandez and Small sat in their car, baffled about their orders.

"What do you think is going on in Ensenada?" asked Small.

"I don't know. I do know who might have those answers," Hernandez said as he dialed a number at the Los Angeles Field Office.

"Peggy Lynn, this is Agent Lucas Hernandez. We met a while back. We're working with Emerson and St. Claire on the Richards and Conte case."

"I remember. How are you and your partner?" she asked.

"Just fine. Do you know how we can get a hold of Jill and Matt? We have some questions for them on the Conte matter," he said cautiously.

Peggy had been with the FBI for over twenty-five years. She had a good sense when an agent was blowing smoke up her ass. "I do know, but they made me promise not to let anyone disturb them on their vacation," she said, without any hesitation. "If you can give me your questions, I might be able to call them and let them know you want to talk, that is if it's official FBI business. Anything social in nature will have to wait until they return in two weeks."

Hernandez was shaking his head at his partner. "Only tell them we have questions about Conte and Richards. Let them know we're heading to Ensenada on a lead that Conte will be there. We wanted to give them a heads up, you know since they are on vacation," he said, hearing a big sigh from Peggy.

"Is there something more they need to know about your assignment before I interrupt their vacation?"

"No, nothing more. You've been very helpful," agent Small said.

* * * * *

Peggy was on her phone, calling Emerson. Jill did not pick up and let it go to voice messaging.

"Call me ASAP!" Peggy said, her tone was serious. "I heard that a major operation is going to happen in Ensenada that involves Conte and Richards. Just a heads up. All your buddies will be down there too. Agents Hernandez and Small called me wanting to know your whereabouts. They said they were going to Ensenada regarding the Salvador Conte case. I heard yesterday that Verduzco and Patch were heading down there too, regarding abortion clinics," she said, breathing heavily. "Sorry for such a long message, but I thought you and St. Claire needed a heads up. You do know how I feel about surprises? Watch your back. CIA agent Bingham will be there too, with his spooks. Please be careful," she begged.

109

Emerson listened to Peggy's message. She was pissed.

"I think we need to go to plan B," she told Matt.

He had a blank stare. "What did Peggy tell you?"

"I am not sure how everyone found out, but Verduzco and Patch are on their way here, even after my conversation with them. Hernandez and Small are coming here too so they can arrest Conte. Everyone knows we're in Ensenada. Shit, Bingham, and his small CIA team will be in Ensenada too. Our plan to arrest Richards is going sideways on us very fast," Jill said.

"This is a big deal. I hope everyone doesn't know about your meeting with Richards, or what you're thinking of doing?" He said, scratching his head.

"This might end up being a big cluster fuck," she said.

"Verduzco and Patch know you're pregnant. They might put two and two together. There aren't too many abortion clinics in this small town," he said, "and money can get them a lot of information."

"Look, we need to proceed with our plan to bring Richards out in the open. I'm going to text him for our meet, and see where it leads," she said. "I have an idea that might throw them all off."

St. Claire did not seem so confident. "With everyone heading to ground zero, we could be caught right in the middle of a take-down operation that could put us in everyone's crosshairs. Need I remind you we had orders to back off, Richards?" said Matt. "Shit, we're supposed to be on vacation. Me in Rosarita Beach, you in Ensenada. Nothing right now seems okay with what you want to do."

Emerson did not respond immediately. "You might be right. You should leave and let me handle this on my own. I'm a big girl. I've been taking care of myself all my life," she said.

"I'm not going anywhere, you little twit. I'm your partner. If the shit hits the fan, then I'm going to get some of it too. So, contact Richards and get this shit-show started," he said, giving her a light punch to her shoulder.

110

The CIA had intercepted the text message Emerson had sent to Doctor Richards. Special Agent Bingham had set up his command post in an abandoned warehouse ten blocks from the abortion clinic where he believed Emerson would meet Richards.

FBI agents Verduzco, Patch, Small, and Hernandez, waited with Bingham's team. They were uncomfortable working with the CIA agent. Miller did not give them a choice.

Bingham had gotten the Governor of Baja, Agustin Barrera, to authorize Hector Flores from the AFI to be part of this joint mission to capture Conte and Richards.

"We have two jobs to accomplish here," Bingham said, pacing back and forth in front of his whiteboard. He had a laser pointer focusing more on Emerson, than Richards or Conte. "My team had intercepted a text which I believe mentioned a baby Emerson was carrying. I am certain it's Richards." His words shocked everyone in the room.

"You're making a bizarre statement," Verduzco said. "What's that based on?"

"I'm not sure what Emerson is up to, but I believe she has gone off the rails on her Richards case. If she's truthful in her text, then she's pregnant. Why tell the Richards unless he's the father. And why meet at an abortion clinic in Mexico?" Bingham said. "I'm just saying," he threw his arm in the air.

Verduzco was not going to let it go. "You're crazy. First, what makes you believe she's carrying Richards baby?" she said, raising her voice.

Bingham was beaming. He was delighted to answer her question. "I'm glad you asked. You and your partner know she was seeing a man going by the name Chad Green, right?"

Verduzco sucked in a deep breath, nodding. "Yes, we do."

"My team has photos of Emerson, and Chad Green at her favorite bar, Sully's. And he spent the night on three separate occasions at her apartment. I don't think they were playing cards, based on the loud moaning and grunts we were able to record," he said.

"Now the CIA and FBI are invading my private life? I know Emerson had met other men at that bar and had taken them home with her. I've seen it," Verduzco argued. "Since you've been conducting a surveillance of an FBI agent's sex life, do you have all the videos of her other boyfriends too?" she asked, looking like she was ready to break some noses.

Bingham was taken aback by her accusation. "We were not surveilling Emerson. She got caught up in our investigation of Richards. Chad Green was or is one of his current aliases."

Agent Patch jumped into the conversation. "Let me ask you something. How long have you known that Richards could transform himself into anyone he wants?"

The question had caught Bingham off-guard. "That's a national security issue and above your paygrade. We're here to catch a known human trafficker and a murderer," he replied. "Emerson might be collateral damage here, as a US citizen breaking our laws."

Verduzco was furious. "Emerson is a great agent, just a little rough around the edges. What makes you believe she's pregnant, and the baby's father is this Chad Green guy or Doctor Richards?"

"I don't. It's too much of a coincidence that Emerson's on vacation in Ensenada where abortions are free, with no questions asked. Richards received a text giving him instructions to meet her at this abortion clinic, threatening him that she is going to abort his fetus if he doesn't come and meet with her," Bingham said. "What do you think she's up to?"

Patch did not seem comfortable talking about another agent's personal life, but he felt he had to defend her. "Could she be here to lure him into a trap so she could capture him, and put her case to bed? We've all lied before to suspects to get them to confess or to turn themselves in. Have you thought about that scenario?" he asked.

"That could well be the case here. My orders are to capture Richards alive and capture Conte dead or alive. If Emerson is not doing anything illegal, then I will apologize to her," Bingham said.

Verduzco laughed. "Once she finds out you have videos of her, you'll be lucky if she only breaks your jaw and does not kick your balls up into your throat."

Bingham's face drained of color. "Let's refocus on our mission here. Chief Sheriff Flores, you and agents Small and Hernandez will engage Salvador Conte. I'd prefer him alive, but if you have no choice, you have permission to use deadly force to stop him. We already have his girls in custody."

Hector Flores did not like his orders. "What if Emerson is in the middle of our attempt to capture Conte? Her life could be in danger," he said.

"You have your orders. Emerson is a big girl. She knows how dangerous her job is, and what she's gotten herself into," Bingham responded coldly.

Verduzco shook her head. "I don't like this plan at all," she said.

"The president has authorized this joint mission with Mexico. He wants to stop human trafficking by Conte and bring the murderer, Todd Richards, back to the United States. If Emerson gets in our way, so be it," he said. His cell pinged. He read the text message.

"We go in ten minutes," he said.

111

Doctor Richards stared at the text from Emerson. It had come from an unknown number, raising some red flags. It pleased him that she had used specific keywords, convincing him it was her. He had the address and time to be at the abortion clinic. He needed to scan the doctor and nurse directory at the clinic to determine who he and Margarita would have to impersonate.

"Margarita, I will need you to become this nurse while we are at the abortion clinic," he said, holding up her photo in the directory.

She had a bewildered look on her face. "I know nothing about being a nurse," she said. "What do I do if asked a question?"

"You will not have to do anything. You will have your nurse's scrubs on. Just act like you know what you are doing," Richards said.

"Why we have to go to this abortion clinic?" she asked.

"It's personal. We will only be there for a little while. I need to complete my business with this pregnant woman," Richards said, holding up a photo of Emerson. It won't take long, and then we can leave Mexico and live a beautiful life with our child," he said, raising the two metal cases with their vials of serum.

Margarita knew when it was the right time to stop asking questions, and she could see it in Richards' eyes, the time was now.

Richards had a photo of the doctor he had to become. He glanced at his watch and told Margarita it was time to transform. He did not notice that she had also just taken a snapshot with her phone camera of the doctor.

The Faces of Doctor Richards

* * * * *

Conte had gotten the return call from his contact at the AFI. He had also gotten his text from Margarita and knew where Richards would be with his serum, and who he would be impersonating.

He had paid twelve of his men extra money to distract the FBI and CIA. He wanted no distractions while he faced Richards and got back his serum.

Salvador had been feeling nervous about killing Richards. He could not forgive him for deceiving him. Conte realized after Richards took his plane, the man he was keeping safe had been manipulating him since the day they met in Echo Park.

"I saved this bastard, gave him a good life in Mexico," he ranted to his men. You need to engage the AFI and American law enforcement. Kill as many as you can, and then return to the airfield," he ordered.

His man in charge asked. "Won't you need a few men to help you with Richards?

Conte pondered his question. "Si, maybe two men. I don't want Richards dead before I get my serum," he said. "Kill the female FBI agent, Jill Emerson, if you must, but the doctor," he said, showing the photo of the clinic physician, "this man cannot be hurt until I say so. Understand?"

His man nodded. "Si, senor Conte."

112

"Are you ready to do this," St. Claire asked. "You do know that Richards will not look like himself, or Chad Green. I bet he's transforming into one of the doctors inside this directory," he said, holding up a white booklet.

"I have considered that. Today, there are only two doctors and two nurses at this clinic," she said, pointing at the two faces inside the directory. "I've paid one of the doctors, and his nurse to take a long lunch while we are here. You'll have to keep an eye on the other doctor. If this works, we'll know who Richards transformed into," she said.

St. Claire noticed the fear on his partner's face. "You're not one hundred percent sure your plan's going to work, are you?" he asked.

"Possibly seventy-five percent sure. I'm going to be vulnerable inside the exam room, without my gun under my gown," Jill said.

Matt was shaking his head. "Maybe we need to rethink this crazy plan of yours?" he said. "Richards could be coming to kill you and take your baby?"

"That's one theory. Remember, Richards thinks of me as his deceased wife, Molly. I must make him believe I am willing to abort this baby. While he prepares the procedure, you'll come to my rescue with your gun drawn, and handcuff him," she said.

St. Claire was shaking his head. "This is one of your dumbest ideas. It's very risky," he said.

"I've trusted you with my life before. What's so different now?" she asked, with a wink.

"One, we are not in the United States. We're in Mexico where trust is not in their vocabulary unless we back it up with bundles of money.

Emerson rolled her eyes. "My appointment is in one hour. Richards should show up in fifty minutes if he follows directions. Let's get inside so you can get into position," she said. "Remember, you need to stay hidden since Richards knows what you look like."

Matt was showing his displeasure with her scheme. "Maybe I shoot him and rid our world of this madman," he said, patting his gun.

Jill gave her partner a sharp look. "Please follow my directions, and everything will work out just fine," she begged.

* * * * *

Richards had seen the doctor and nurse they were going to impersonate, leave the clinic. They appeared to be heading toward a restaurant for an early lunch. What surprised him was that Emerson and her partner were entering the clinic at the same time as the doctor he was going to transform into was leaving. He saw Jill hand the doctor a thick envelope.

"Not very smart," he mumbled, out of earshot of Margarita. He looked inside the directory and found another doctor's photo. He had to make sure that one was on-call.

113

Agent Verduzco had been acting antsy all day, working with the joint task force, especially with Bingham in charge. She knew something did not seem right. "Do you believe we've been told everything about what's going down today?" she asked Forest.

"I haven't been comfortable with that spook since the day I first met him— typical CIA. I think Emerson and St. Claire will be nothing more than collateral damage to him. He only wants Richards alive. Everyone else is expendable, including us," Patch said.

"Knowing Emerson as we do, do you believe she would make it this easy to find her, especially at an abortion clinic?" Verduzco said.

"You've read my mind. What if we sneak away, and figure out where Emerson and St. Claire might be?"

"I'll tell Bingham we need a lunch break. He's got enough men from the AFI, and his CIA team to handle this small clinic," she said, walking over to the front of the warehouse.

She saw Bingham on his STAT phone. He was in a heated exchange with someone at the other end of the line. "Sir, yes, sir. Will do, sir. Copy that sir," he said, slamming the phone on the table. He looked up and saw agent Verduzco and Patch coming toward him.

"I've got no time for you two."

Verduzco smiled. "We don't either. Just letting you know that we're taking an extended lunch break. You've got enough men here. You won't need us for a while," she said, taking Patch's arm and yanking him toward the warehouse door.

"Verduzco, get your ass back here. You'll leave when I tell you to leave," he barked. His eyes grew wide when she gave him a single finger salute as they walked out the door.

Bingham looked at agents Small and Hernandez, his face beet red. "Go and arrest those two assholes," he screamed.

Small and Hernandez shrugged their shoulders. "Arrest them for what. Perhaps we too should go on a long lunch," Hernandez said. "What we're doing here is bullshit. It's not about Conte, but your fixation on Richards," he said.

Bingham was about to read them the riot act when he got a call. "He's where? Okay, position your men, Richards should be close by." He snapped his fingers at Small and Diag, still talking into his phone. "Do you see Emerson and St. Claire?" he asked.

Bingham pointed to Hernandez and Small and mouthed for them to sit down. He ended his call. "Conte has been sighted. We will be moving in fifteen minutes. Take your position."

114

Richards transformed into a doctor from another abortion clinic not listed in the clinic's directory. He told Margarita to wait for his signal for her to enter.

He walked through the front door of the clinic, nodding to the security guard, who was sitting on a folding chair, looking at his cellphone. "Nice day today," Richards said to the guard in Spanish.

The guard looked up and signaled the doctor to pass. He did not question the man in a white medical coat. Richards went to the nurse's station and found an appointment book. He located a room Emerson might be waiting in and texted Margarita to come inside.

Richards read the logbook and discovered that the schedule only had two women for that day. There were no names in the appointment book for privacy reasons, he guessed. One client was in for a checkup, and another for an abortion consultation. Room fourteen had the patient for the check-up, and room sixteen had the abortion consultation.

Richards stopped walking when he saw Emerson's partner sitting in a waiting area down from the two rooms. He watched St. Claire glance up at him as he walked toward the exam rooms. He could see that the FBI agent was checking out photos in the directory. Richards smiled, realizing he'd be unable to find him.

Richards pretended to be looking at some charts, as he made his way toward the exam rooms. He knew which exam room housed Emerson. He decided to see the patient who was there for a checkup first, hoping it would remove any suspicions St. Claire might have about him.

He glanced over at St. Claire to check if the FBI agent was acting alarmed or concerned about him entering room fourteen. When Matt went back to looking at his directory, he knew his deception was working.

Inside the room was a petite woman who looked like she was ready to give birth today. She was lying on her back, her legs bent, and in discomfort.

When she saw Richards come in, she started to wail very loud. She began speaking in Spanish to Richards, who she thought was her doctor.

"Doctor, my water broke," she cried. "Baby coming now!" She started screaming, as a painful contraction happened.

Richards looked at her. He had not imagined he'd bring a child into the world today. His only mission was to get Emerson's fetus. He stuck his head out of the exam room, looking to see if any nurse had heard the screams. No one was in the immediate vicinity. He ducked back into the room and texted Margarita to come inside.

The woman would not stop screaming as each contraction ravaged her body. Richards could not think. He was in panic mode. He wanted to smother the pregnant woman so she would shut up, but decided he needed to act as a doctor, and deliver this baby. Emerson, he felt, would wait for him.

He once again stuck his head out of the room and called for a nurse. He saw two nurses stick their heads out of two exam rooms. In perfect Spanish, he ordered them to help him deliver a baby. He saw Margarita running toward him, in her nurse's uniform. She was noticeably scared and nervous with all the commotion happening.

"Doctor, how can I be of help?" Margarita said, trying to act professionally. Before she could speak to Richards, two heavyset nurses pushed her aside.

She was relieved that Doctor Richards would have real nurses to help him. When she saw all the blood on the floor, she almost fainted. She tried to leave the room, but one of the nurses grabbed her arm and ordered her to get behind the pregnant woman and elevate her to a forty-five-degree angle.

Richards wanted to leave the room and be with Emerson. The lead nurse started examining the pregnant woman's birth canal, her face showing alarm. "The baby's breached, doctor."

The nurse looked at Richards for his approval, "Should I try to shift the baby now?" the nurse said, "We cannot do Caesarean sections here. I don't think she can wait for an ambulance to take her to the hospital."

Richards did not reply. He pushed the lead nurse out of the way. He placed one hand on the pregnant woman's stomach, and his other inside her birth canal. Panic exploded on his face as he felt the umbilical cords wrapped around the baby's neck.

He looked at Margarita, terror on his face. He had not envisioned this for today. While he wanted to leave the exam room and run away, he knew it would alarm everyone, especially agent St. Claire. He began barking out orders to everyone in the room. At that moment, he was the doctor he was trained to be when he first left medical school. He had to save the baby and the mother.

"I need a surgery kit, now," he shouted. "Everyone put gloves on. We're going to get this baby out right now," he commanded.

Margarita's eyes met his. She was petrified. She saw him look at her, his eyes little slits. She understood he wanted her to leave the room and be with Emerson. She had the syringe with the sedative he had given her.

Richards ordered one of the nurses to replace Margarita at the head of the exam table.

Outside in the hallway, everyone, including agent St. Claire, was wondering what was happening. He grabbed Margarita by the arm. "What's going on?" he shouted in English.

Margarita pretended not to understand. "Yo, no habla ingles, senor," she said, yanking her arm free. She walked toward the other exam room.

Matt had become distracted by all the commotion coming from room fourteen that he did not notice the nurse he had stopped was going into exam room sixteen.

The Faces of Doctor Richards

Margarita was very nervous and sweaty. When she entered the room where Emerson was waiting, she noticed that she was already wearing a hospital gown.

Emerson saw the fear on the nurse's face. "What's going on? Where's my doctor?"

Margarita cupped the syringe in her left hand and said. "Doctor, very busy. Baby coming right now," she said, walking toward Emerson. "Relax, please, and lie down. It won't be long," she said, trying to help Emerson get on her back. When she resisted, Margarita, with her right hand on Emerson's shoulder, squeezed her tightly, raising her left hand that had the syringe. With a swift downward motion, she aimed the needle for Jill's shoulder.

Emerson watched as the nurse's arm rise. Then, she noticed the nurse was holding a shiny object. Her first instinct was to block the syringe that was coming down fast toward her left shoulder. Jill's defensive move caught the needle in her left forearm. She felt the warm fluid enter her body. She swung her right fist hard, striking the nurse across the bridge of her nose, causing her to scream.

Emerson was already beginning to feel dizzy. Instinct took over, and with what little energy she had left, jumped off the table, pivoted, and aimed her fist for the nurse's jaw. She caught it solidly, causing her to fall backward, and then everything went dark.

115

Agent's Verduzco and Patch were surprised to see agent St. Claire when they entered the abortion clinic. He seemed out of sorts outside one of the exam rooms. He had a frightened expression when two nurses ran out of their exam room, full of blood, holding a crying baby.

A moment later, a Mexican doctor followed, he too was covered in blood. He was trying to get his bearings. He ran over to exam room sixteen, slamming the door behind him.

St. Claire, fear engulfing his body, ran toward Emerson's room. He saw Verduzco and Patch and waved them to follow him. "Emerson's inside, she might need help," he shouted.

Both agents were now sprinting toward St. Claire. The door was locked. St. Claire was banging on it, shouting demands to open it up.

Verduzco could see the panic in his eyes. "What's going on? She said, grabbing his shoulder.

St. Claire's eyes teared up. "Emerson's in there. I believe the doctor that just went in is Doctor Richards. We have to get inside now," he pleaded.

* * * * *

Richards was concerned to see Margarita with a deep gash on the side of her forehead and blood gushing from her nose. She had a stunned look on her face. Next to her was Emerson, unconscious. He heard the banging on the door and knew he did not have a lot of time before St. Claire broke into the room.

Richards shook Margarita by the shoulders. "Snap out of it. We need to get my child from this woman," he said. "I need your help," he told her.

Margarita acted confused. "Your child? I have your baby," she said. "Who is this lady you wanted me to give a sedative?"

"It's a complicated story. It happened long before you came into my life," he said.

Margarita had started to cry. "Why you say you love me? Maybe, I just one of your experiment girls?" she said, her voice rising.

Richards heard the banging on the door get more violent. "We will be the perfect couple, with perfect children," he whispered. "Now help me, and keep quiet," he said, his finger on her lips.

He lifted Emerson's hospital gown and spread her legs. He inserted his hand inside her vagina and felt the canal that contained his baby.

The banging had become violent. Richards knew time was running out to extract the fetus and not kill Emerson. He so wished he was back at his La Jolla office with the proper tools and equipment to perform this procedure safely. At that moment, keeping Emerson alive and getting his fetus was an impossible choice. He drew in a deep breath and made his decision.

"Sorry, Jill, but my baby comes first," he said, pressing with his finger where he needed to make the incision on her abdomen. He told Margarita to go out of the bathroom window and wait for him in their car. He'd be along shortly.

The banging on the exam room door had stopped. Then, a woman shouted, *Stand back.* He lowered the scalpel, cutting a straight line on Emerson's belly.

* * * * *

Verduzco pushed both men aside and drew her gun. "Out of my way," she ordered. Without any hesitation, she blew the lock handle off the door and kicked it in.

Lying on the floor was Emerson, her hospital gown covering her face, exposing her to the world. They all noticed the blood flowing from her abdomen.

St. Claire fell to his knees. He had started to cry. "I killed my partner," he wailed. "I knew this wouldn't work."

Agent Patch and Verduzco kept their composure. Like competent law enforcement professionals, they surveyed the room.

Amy knelt and felt for a pulse. "She's breathing. She found a towel and began compressing the wound. "St. Claire, get a grip. Your partner's alive and needs you to stop this bleeding. Press your palms here and be a hero. I'll go get help," she said, getting up and leaving the room.

Agent Patch had heard a noise inside the bathroom. He tried the door, but it too was locked. With one swift kick, it opened. He heard someone drop to the ground outside. He looked out the window and saw a doctor running across the parking lot.

He jumped out the window, running as fast as he could. He had drawn his gun, ready to shoot the man who had hurt his friend. He saw the man heading toward some stores in town.

After thirty minutes, Patch had given up. The doctor had disappeared. He did find a bloodied lab coat and bloodied towels. He brought them back to the clinic so he could bag them. They were the only evidence he had.

Sitting in the waiting room was Amy and Matt. They both looked like they had lost their best friends. St. Claire had his head in his hands. Verduzco was staring blankly at the wall.

"How's Emerson doing?" he asked, dropping the bloodied lab coat and towels on the floor.

Walking toward them was Emerson's new doctor. They all looked at him, noticing the sad expression on his face.

116

Richards and Margarita sped out of town, heading north. He wanted to get back into the United States before nightfall.

"Margarita, you did well today. I'm sorry you got hurt," he said, gently touching her cheek. "When we get to our apartment in Santa Monica, I will teach you how to heal yourself. Now, transform to this person," he said, handing her a photo of a pretty woman that matched up to the passport he laid on her lap.

Richards saw her confusion as she stared at the picture of his wife, Molly.

"I thought I was supposed to be Luisa, from Escondido California, not this woman," she asked.

Richards did not have time to explain his reasons for the change. "Just make the change, and you'll understand later," he said.

Margarita looked at the photo, and two minutes later, she checked herself in the visor mirror. She was surprised her nose did not look broken. The gash on the side of her head had disappeared, but not the pain. "I don't know how you do this with your serum. I like it. Can I be Luisa later?" she asked. "I no want to look like that woman you cut open at the clinic. She not nice to me," she said, touching her nose that still hurt.

"When we get settled into our new home, you can look like whoever you want. I have new identities for us that you will love. Right now, you must look like Molly," he said.

Ten kilometers north of Ensenada, Richards went inside a gas station restroom and transformed back into Doctor Theo Bashore. He had the FBI agent's photo and ID that he had used when he murdered Carolyn Hollister that he'd use later if needed.

The line of cars entering the United States at the Tijuana border moved at a snail's pace. The congestion did not worry Richards; it was passing through customs was his biggest concern.

"You need to know about the woman that struck you," Richards said. "She's an FBI agent I dated while I was Chad Green."

"Si, Chad Green. I remember," she nodded.

"I was seeing her for only one reason, to get clues on how the FBI's investigation was progressing. I had to date her and get her to trust me. During one of our late evenings together, she must have gotten pregnant," he said. "We were meeting with her so I could take her fetus for my research. Nothing more. You are the person I want to spend my life with now, Molly," he said, instantly realizing he had made a mistake. "I meant Margarita."

Margarita had a puzzled expression on her face. "I don't care about this FBI person. Why do you forget and call me Molly? Who this Molly?" she asked.

Richards shook his head. "Maybe another time, I will tell you." He put his fingers to his lips as they reached the border patrol agent.

117

Conte's men shot an RPG. Bingham and his team were the targets. Salvador clapped his hands as the rocket-propelled grenade hit its mark. The warehouse where they had been monitoring the abortion clinic had become a ball of fire.

Now it was his turn to confront his traitor and take back his serum that cost him millions of dollars. As the gun battle going on between his men, the CIA, and AFI, Conte ran toward the abortion clinic.

He had his AK-47 Russian made rifle strapped across his chest, sprinting as he had to dodge over fifty locals that were running in all directions away from the explosions and gunfire, screaming and clutching their children.

Inside Salvadore kicked in every door that had a placard: exam room. He looked at the photo Margarita had sent him of the Doctor Richards's new identity, searching for the man he wanted to kill. He found three doctors: none of them fit the description.

Conte grabbed one nurse and shoved the photo in her face. "Where's this doctor," he screamed, his weapon pressed into her chest.

She seemed confused and frightened. "This doctor does not work at this clinic. He works at the clinic at the other end of town. He may be there today," she said, shaking from fear.

"Is there a central computer system that logs in all appointments for your clinics?" he asked.

The nurse nodded. "Si, señor," she pointed at the nurse's station. "We are all connected. If a patient makes a mistake, we can send them to the right clinic," she said, taking in deep nervous breaths.

Conte again showed her the photo. "Today, which clinic can I find him?"

The nurse pressed a few keys on the computer's keyboard. She found the doctor's schedule. "He is working today at the clinic at the corner of 18 de Marzo and Avenida Mexico."

"Show me the appointments at that clinic." Salvador scanned the computer screen and was out the door, jumping into his car, heading toward the abortion clinic where he hoped to find Richards. "That bastard better have my serum, or he's a dead man," he muttered, texting his men for an update on their assault.

* * * * *

The explosion had caught Bingham by surprise. He saw that two of his men were down, struggling to remove the debris from their bodies.

AFI agent, Hector Flores, and his men signaled that they were okay as they engaged in a gunfire battle with a group of men high on a hillside behind where the warehouse once stood.

Hector was on his stat phone, calling for more men to back them up. He looked at Bingham. "I think you fucked up. We were sitting ducks here," he said, his voice resonating disgust for the man.

Bingham shrugged his shoulders. "How was I to know Conte knew we were here. You must have a traitor in your organization." he lashed back.

Flores did not respond. He thought about those remarks, realizing the man might be right. The AFI agent walked away from Bingham and started demanding to see all his men's cellphones. He found two with text messages right before the attack.

He was shocked to see that one of his men, a most trusted one, had been communicating with Conte. The texts were incriminating. His man had given out their position and operational details.

417

Hector walked over to that agent and pressed the barrel of his gun to the back of his head.

"Felipe, drop your weapon, get on your knees. Lock your hands behind your head. You're under arrest for treason," Flores said, angrily. He roughly slapped his handcuffs on his agent.

Once Hector was done securing his traitor, he began reading the other texts Salvador Conte had sent on his phone. He learned that Conte had identified which doctor Richards was impersonating.

Flores had the entire work schedule of every doctor and nurse at all three abortion clinics. This doctor was not at the clinic they wanted to secure. He was at another clinic three miles from their location.

He looked over at Bingham, disgusted with his stupidity and arrogance. His desire to capture Doctor Richards at all costs had risked his men's lives and maybe that of his friend, agent Emerson. He decided to go to the other clinic with his men and get the job done on his own.

He walked over to Bingham, his cellphone in his hand. "I got word that my men have captured two of Conte's men and killed eight others." Hector did not want to tell Bingham the correct abortion clinic to enter. He wanted him far enough away so he could get his job done without any loss of life.

"You can storm this clinic," Hector said, pointing to the building a hundred yards from their position. "You can capture Richards, and your two FBI agents can arrest Conte," he said.

Bingham began shouting out orders. "Everyone get your butts out of here and head to the clinic. Remember, I want Richards alive. Do what you want with Conte."

118

Hector Flores and his men were at the correct clinic within five minutes. He was surprised to see the entire building encircled with yellow crime scenes tape.

He flashed his badge, raised the tape, and passed under it. He stormed into the clinic to find agent's St. Claire, Verduzco, and Patch all sitting in a waiting area, all looking sad.

He walked over to St. Claire. "What happened here? Where's agent Emerson?" he asked. St. Claire's eyes moist. He thought the worst.

"She's being attended to by a doctor and a team of paramedics. Richards drugged her, then attempted to cut her open and remove her baby. She's lost a lot of blood. They are getting her stable for a medivac helicopter to transport her to Scripps hospital in San Diego," he said, trying to catch his breath.

"What happened?" Flores asked.

"Richards, a nurse, shit, I left her unprotected," he stammered. He sucked in a deep breath and continued. "Richards was impersonating this doctor," he held up the doctor's picture in the clinic directory. "He had a nurse. She was an impersonator too, who gave Jill a strong sedative. He tried to cut her baby out," he said, realizing he had said too much. "You need to forget what I just said. You're her friend, right?"

Flores, his jaw dropped to his chest. "Baby? When? Why would Richards…" he paused, "His baby?" he asked.

St. Claire stood up and put his arm around Hector. "Let's walk," he said.

For the next fifteen minutes, St. Claire told Flores all about Richards, Chad Green, the shift-changing he'd witnessed, and Jill's pregnancy. Matt told him she wasn't a hundred percent sure it was Richards. He said that she had not had a DNA test yet to confirm. He told him about their plan to draw Richards out.

"Everything was going according to plan until that bastard transformed into another doctor from another clinic. I did not see the nurse go into Emerson's room until it was too late. Richards and the nurse both disappeared in town. He could be someone else right now if he keeps to his same MO," St. Claire said.

Hector was on his cellphone, dishing out orders. "I need a report on all persons going through immigration at the San Ysidro, Otay Mesa, Tecate, Calexico, and Andrade," he said. "No, don't worry. There will be no problem," he told his secretary. "US Customs and Mexico have an agreement to help each other catch criminals leaving or entering our countries. Yes, as soon as you have the report, email it to me immediately," he said.

St. Claire looked at Emerson's friend. For the first time that day, Matt was smiling. "I can see why you two are friends. She's always liked people who are not afraid of taking swift action," he said. "Do you think this will work?"

"I will be alerted if a man and woman try to cross our borders at any of those entry ports. Then we'll have to screen all of them. It might take a while to figure it out, you know, to figure out who he is now. We'll do our best to find him," said Flores.

St. Claire felt a tap on his shoulder. It was the doctor treating Emerson. He turned, noticing the tiredness on the doctor's face. "Is she alright?" he asked.

The clinic doctor was silent deep in thought. "Yes. The baby and mother are okay. We were able to stop the bleeding and stitch her up. The sedative has started to wear off. We wanted to give her some pain medication for the deep cut she sustained. She refused," he said. "Perhaps you can talk some sense into her?"

St. Claire laughed. "She's one tough woman. She won't even take aspirin for a hangover. Talking sense into her won't work either. Can I see her now?" he asked.

Matt was at Jill's side, as the paramedics rolled her out to the ambulance that would be taking her to the heliport. "Shit, Emerson, you scared the holy shit out of me," he said, grabbing her hand and pressing it firmly to his lips.

She looked at him, her eyes still glassy. "You worry too much, St. Claire. I told you I could take care of myself. I think I broke that nurses' nose and jaw," she bragged. "I don't want to go to no goddamn hospital," she complained.

Matt squeezed her hand tight. "You'll listen to the doctor and get checked out. You do want to know if the baby's alright?

"Fine," she said, her eyes fluttering from the effects of the sedative. "I want to go home. This vacation didn't work out as I planned," she frowned.

119

Bingham was rushing through the front doors, while agents Small and Hernandez were coming through the back entrance. They saw Salvador Conte yelling and threatening every nurse. He was shoving in their faces his cellphone display that had the photo he believed was Doctor Richards. He was screaming for them to tell him where the doctor was hiding.

"Don't you fucking tell me he's not here," Conte cursed. "I know he's here." He was getting angrier with every denial. He raised his rifle, threatening one of the nurses. "Tell me, or you'll be the first to die."

Just then, the doctor who had gone on an extended lunch break returned. He stopped frozen in his tracks when he saw a man pointing a gun at him.

Conte noticed the doctor he thought was Richards. He swung his arm around, aiming his rifle at the center of the doctor's chest. "Richards, you mother-fucker. Where's my serum?" he screamed.

The doctor, a puzzled look on his face, shouted back. My name is Doctor Gomez. I am not a Doctor Richards."

Agent Small noticed Conte was pointing it at a doctor. He rushed him, grabbing his hand that contained the rifle, and with one swift move, foot swept him to the ground, his face slamming to the floor hard.

Agent Hernandez stepped firmly on Conte's wrist, bending down to grab the weapon. "Salvador Conte, you're under arrest for Human Trafficking and murder. You have the right to remain silent or allow me to put a bullet in your fucking head and save our taxpayers a lot of money," Hernandez said, his knee pressing hard against Conte's spine.

"Get the fuck off of me," Conte screamed. "You broke my nose. Do you know who I am? We're in Mexico. The FBI does not have jurisdiction here," he seethed.

Agent Hernandez let out a bellowing laugh. "It's either you get locked up here, or in the United States. Your government has wanted to put you behind bars for a long time. I'm sure you do not have many friends in your Mexican Federal prison. Trafficking of women, especially young girls, is as bad as a pedophile in United States Federal prisons," said Hernandez, pressing a little harder on his spine with his knee.

Agent Small waved a warrant in front of Conte's face. "Your president is giving you to us first. When your sentence is over with us, and if you are still alive, Mexico will have their time with you," he said. "You'll never be free again."

Once Conte was handcuffed and dragged outside, Bingham took both agents aside. "I hate to break the news to you; President Christopher wants Conte in CIA custody for a while. We need to find out what Richards had been doing at his laboratory. It's a National Security issue. We have eight women, all pregnant, and we believe they were part of Richards' experiment."

"That's bull-shit," agent Small said.

Bingham threw his hands in the air. "Take it up with your director. He's under orders from the president to turn this bastard over to us," the CIA agent said, grinning.

120

Hector Flores was showing the spreadsheet he had received from US Customs. "Here," he pointed. "A Molly Talbert and a Doctor Theo Bashore crossed into San Diego at six-twenty-two this evening, at the Otay Mesa border crossing. They were in a green Toyota Camry, license 8TMA567," Flores said.

St. Claire stood up, unable to comprehend what he had heard. "Molly Talbert? She's Richards dead wife. Doctor Bashore wasn't on any of our lists."

Flores was nodding his head. "I don't know why Richards was so careless?"

Verduzco said. "Maybe he wasn't prepared to come across the border today, and only had those photos, and passports of his dead wife for the woman traveling with him. He's desperate and not thinking clearly. He's been like this for a while now."

"We all know what he's like when he's reckless, and can't think clearly," Agent Patch said. "Like he's done with his patients when he feels threatened, there is no telling what he'll do next. I fear for the passenger in his car."

"We need to get video on all traffic cams from the border and to Los Angeles," St. Claire said. "I want to find this bastard and put a bullet in his head. He should not be allowed to walk the earth."

"If we want to get this guy, we need to move fast. If we've figured this out, I bet Bingham has too. There's no telling what the CIA will do with Richards if they get him first. I'll bet it won't be a bullet in the head," Verduzco said. "They want him for what he can do for their sick experiments."

121

Driving at the speed limit, Richards and Margarita were making good time to his safe house in Santa Monica. The apartment's rental agreement with Chad Green posed a severe problem since the FBI and CIA knew of this identity.

"We will be home safe in a couple of hours. We will take our serum and change into our new identities. We won't be able to stay there and will need to find another location waiting for our baby to be born," he said.

"Where will we go?" Margarita said, looking at Richards.

He turned his head, staring blankly, his heart pounded in his chest. "Molly, everything will be perfect. Our baby will be born, your cancer will be gone," he said, wiping a tear from his cheek. He realized his mistake. "Sorry, I meant Margarita. Just had a bad flashback."

Before he could react, the San Diego freeway was all lit up by a police helicopter. Loose dirt swirled on the road, impairing his visibility. Right then, he knew that he was not going to Santa Monica. Six green and white immigration and customs vehicles surrounded his car. They were slowing his car down. He heard the command from one of the blow horns.

"Stop your car now, Doctor Richards! Don't force us to stop you. Doctor Richards, it's over," the voice repeated.

He looked at Margarita, panic on her face. She still looked like his wife, Molly. He spoke above a whisper. "I'm so sorry. It looks like we're not going home right now," he said, an empty sadness in his voice.

The Faces of Doctor Richards

The Helicopter landed on interstate five. Richards's face had turned bedsheet white as CIA agent Bingham jumped out, his revolver pointing at him.

"Doctor Richards, don't make me shoot you," he shouted over the swirling dust on the freeway. "I've got a new home for you."

122

The sedative Emerson had in her system had begun to wear off. She was lying on a medical gurney. St. Claire had been briefing her about what had happened at the abortion clinic. A medivac helicopter would be airlifting her to Scripps Green Hospital in La Jolla, for further tests.

"What's the status on Richards?" she asked, her voice raspy.

"The nurse who attacked you is working with him. We believe she's one of Conte's girls. She took on the appearance of a nurse we found unconscious at the clinic. Richards is brilliant. He fooled us by transforming into a doctor from another abortion clinic," he paused, sucking in a nervous breath. "I fucked up. I should have seen this coming," he said.

Emerson gripped his hand, giving a reassuring squeeze. "The bastard fooled all of us. I never thought I'd have to watch out for two people," she said, pressing on the thick bandage under her hospital gown, trying to hide the pain she was feeling. Jill wanted to ask another question. She was interrupted by agent Patch.

He was holding his cellphone, anger exploding on his face. "Richards was captured by Immigration and Customs. They cornered him on interstate five between Camp Pendleton and San Clemente," he said, showing them the Breaking News Alert.

St. Claire turned the screen toward him. "Shit. We need to get there and arrest him," he said.

Agent Patch shook his head. "The report says Homeland Security had taken him into custody. See here," he pointed. "There's Bingham, Mark

428

Murphy the attorney general, and Stuart Lewin from Homeland Security. Richards is going to be put somewhere deep in the cellars of the CIA," he said, frustrated. "He'll become a ghost now."

Agent Verduzco jumped in. "Our investigation is over. I received an email from Miller that Patch and myself need to be back in DC by tomorrow morning. They've closed our fucking case," she cursed.

St. Claire was now reading an email on his phone. "Shit, I'm being reassigned. It says, until Jill is fit for duty, I will have a new partner. I have to be back in DC tomorrow too."

Emerson looked confused. "What's going on? A new partner for a little cut on my belly? I'm unfit for duty?" she said, her voice cracking. "Something's not right. I feel it has something to do with," she tapped her stomach, "my baby," she said, sadly

St. Claire was typing on his phone's keypad. "Can't make it back tomorrow. I'm staying with my partner until she's safe to leave the hospital. Not changing partners at this time," he wrote, signing his name, and adding an angry emoji for effect.

Verduzco whispered in her partner's ear. "You with me on this," she said. Forest nodded.

Amy punched Matt's shoulder. "We're staying here with the two of you. Something does not smell right, and Jill needs our protection."

Matt was nodding his head in agreement. "If the CIA has Richards, they must have his serum too. They have all of Conte's girls. They must want Emerson too," St. Claire said. "I'll quit if necessary, to protect you." He squeezed her hand.

Patch spoke up. "We need to be careful. We don't want anyone at the CIA or Homeland suspecting we know what they're doing," he said.

"Do we know what they are doing?" St. Claire asked.

Emerson was listening to all of their concerns. With her voice low, she said. "I've been throwing this theory around for a while since we began investigating Richards's shape-shifting abilities. The CIA and Homeland have, for a long time, wanted to create a covert military unit that would be able to infiltrate our enemies and methodically wipe them out. The crazy doctor has the formula that could accomplish that goal.

Richards serum is the key to all of this," she said, as her gurney rolled toward the medivac helicopter. "Just think about that," she shouted.

St. Claire ran after the medics. He was not going to leave Jill alone. He looked back at his two friends. "Meet you at Scripps. Let's figure out how to protect Emerson and her baby, as well as ourselves. It's going to get hairy very fast," he shouted as he jumped inside the helicopter.

123

Regional Director, Brian Miller, was stumbling through his answers to the deputy director of the FBI. He was finding it hard to explain why St. Claire and Emerson had been at an abortion clinic in Ensenada

"Sir, they both had taken some well-deserved vacation time. Why they were both in Ensenada at the same time, beats me. I have not been able to talk to either one of them since Emerson's attack," Miller said, fumbling with some papers he had in his hands.

Deputy Director Kipher was getting frustrated with Miller. "Do you have a handle on your agents?" he questioned. "Why has St. Claire refused to come back to DC, and brief all of us? You did tell him it was an order from the Director?"

Miller had begun perspiring. "I most certainly did relay the Director's orders. Sir, agent St. Claire did not want to abandon his partner while she was in the hospital. He did not think she was safe, as you have called back all the agents that were in Ensenada. Richards almost killed her." he said.

"I fully understand your agent's concern. I approved a team from Homeland and the CIA to protect Emerson. I want St. Claire on a plane ASAP."

Miller had gotten defensive. "Why Homeland and the CIA to protect one of our own? The FBI should be the only one looking after our agent. I don't trust the CIA. They have their agenda, and from what I've heard from agents Verduzco and Patch, Emerson's life during their operation, per Bingham, was expendable," he lashed back.

"I don't know anything about that," Kipfer said. "Bingham oversees a top-secret program for the CIA and Homeland. Your agents almost screwed up capturing Richards. You're lucky Immigration and Customs got him and his serum," the deputy director said.

Kipher dismissed Miller. He had a knot in his stomach. While he knew St. Claire and Emerson did not like him, he felt he had to warn them about the CIA and Homeland agents coming to the hospital.

Miller left a message for St. Claire to call him. For the first time since this operation had taken place, he realized that Emerson was not safe from her own country that she had sworn to protect and defend.

124

Professor Thomas Franklin, Richards mentor, and supervisor at UCLA got an earful from CIA agent Bingham and attorney general Mark Murphy.

Bingham had a nervous edge, as he spoke. "Franklin, it's good news for you that we now have Richards in custody, right?"

Franklin shrugged his shoulders. "Possibly. I first have to try to convince him to cooperate with us," he said. "We need his full support. My serum formula is not working."

"Shit. Well, you've told us you need Richards to get you over the hump on your serum formula, so now you have him. The president is on my ass. We are so fucking behind on his project."

"I know. I don't have any clue what Richards is like now. I haven't spoken to him in over eight years. He left UCLA under bad circumstances if you remember. He held us all responsible," Franklin said.

"Responsible? What for?" Bingham asked.

Franklin took a deep breath. He knew that Bingham wore blinders when it came to his secret project. Richards dislikes you. He knows that the CIA, you, in particular, have had the ear of the last two presidents. He blames you for convincing the president to ban abortions and for his wife dying.

"Ask me if I care? Shit, his wife would have died anyway based on where he was with his cure. So give me a break," Bingham lashed back, his frustration escalating.

"Ralph, Richards has never forgotten how you supported your friend, President Christopher, for abolishing Roe v. Wade. If you remember, you did not want any council from me or the Justice Department on the long-range implications for that decision."

Bingham's face turned fiery red. "Don't lecture me. We've had the president's support for our secret project all this time. That's all that matters to me right now. I have one goal, and one goal only, build an elite military force that can wipe out all of the enemies of the United States…period."

Franklin shook his head in frustration. "Sadly, Richards doesn't see it that way. I believe he's still an idealist. He's not going to help you use his serum to create an army of killers."

Bingham got up from his chair, looking like he wanted to murder someone. "Idealist? That's bull-shit. Richards a murderer now? Just do your fucking job. The President needs Lea Strong healthy ASAP. Her baby's vitals were strong for a while. We don't know for how long. We need more of her serum to give her. Our religious fanatic president wants her baby to come full-term," he said. "President Christopher believes this baby will have some magical powers that have come from God."

"This is a delicate situation. Richards might allow the pregnancy to miscarry so he can use the fetus to make more serum," said Franklin.

Bingham did not seem so concerned. "I don't care. Anyway, what's so different about this woman? She's from Richards's first group of women. We now have eight pregnant women we captured at Conte's Mexico lab. We have Richards and his mistress, who, by the way, is pregnant too. So, I don't give a rats ass if Lea Strong dies, along with her baby?" he said. "Maybe it's a good thing that Richards gets another fetus?"

Franklin had not adjusted to the heartlessness he had been experiencing inside the government, as it pertained to Richards serum, and the coldhearted attitude everyone had toward all the fetuses. "All life matters. I'm not working with all of you to risk this woman's life or her baby's," he replied.

The attorney general jumped into the conversation. "What you're doing here is for our National Security. What Richards has created will provide our military with a distinct set of skills that can help us win the war of terrorism and the war on drugs. You signed up to help us. It's too late to back out now," Attorney General Murphy said.

Bingham interrupted. "We're flying you, and Lea Strong back to California. Speak with Richards and get him to cooperate with us. Have him help Ms. Strong to get strong if he can? If not, she's expendable as far as I am concerned," he said. "We have all of his serum. Most of it is for him and his mistress. Some for Salvador Conte. We have a good bargaining chip for him to cooperate with us."

"I do remember you promising us that you'd be able to figure out Richards' formula if you got more of his samples, as well as his test subjects. I'm holding you to that promise," the attorney general said.

* * * * *

Bingham and Murphy stayed back after Franklin left the conference room. "I just found out that my wife is pregnant with my fifth child," the CIA agent told Murphy. "I just look at her, and she seems to get pregnant," he said jokingly. "I want Richards to create a serum for me, and I don't want any more children."

"What are you saying," Murphy said, surprised. "You can't knowingly abort your child. You'd be breaking the law. I'd have to arrest you," the attorney general said.

"You know you won't do that. I have too much on you, and the president. Do you think what we've been doing with Lea Strong and what we're planning on doing with Conte's ladies will be supported by the American people or even the world?"

Murphy started shaking. "You wouldn't do that. You're knee-deep into this program too," he said.

"I'm CIA. My fingerprints are nowhere on this program. I've been following your orders and that of the president. I'm a good soldier," he laughed. "I'm going back with Franklin and bringing my wife. If I must beat the shit out of Richards, I'm going to get my serum from him."

"You're one crazy son-of-a-bitch. What about Emerson and her baby? We still need her?" Murphy asked.

"As I said in Ensenada, she's expendable. We're not even sure Richards, or his alias, Chad Green, got her pregnant. We believe she was fucking two other guys during that period time. She might not be so unusual," he said, looking at his watch. "I've got a plane to catch. I'll keep you posted on my progress."

125

St. Claire didn't seem surprised when Miller told him about the CIA and Homeland sending a team to protect Emerson. He knew it was total bullshit. Matt was skeptical that his boss was showing some support for them. Nevertheless, he thanked him for it.

"When do you think they'll be here?" St. Claire asked.

"All I know is that the wheels were put in motion two days ago. For all I know, they're there now," Miller said. "Can you move Jill to a safe location?"

St. Claire did not respond immediately. He was thinking. "I think the doctor is going to release her today. If so, then I have a place where she'll be safe," he said. "I've gotta go and talk to her doctor."

Matt had told Verduzco and Patch about Miller's concerns. He asked them to help his partner get dressed and ready to leave the hospital ten minutes ago.

After fifteen minutes of searching for her doctor, he skidded to a halt when he saw three government types talking to Emerson's doctor.

"Shit, it's too late," he muttered. He turned and staggered back to Emerson's room. He was on his cell talking to agent Patch.

"Yes, move her now. I'll distract them. You get her the hell out of the hospital undetected, pronto. Let's meet in Pacific Beach, at Hennessey's. The safe house I have in mind is nearby," he said, short of breath.

He carried a chair outside of his partner's hospital room, pretending to be reading something on his cellphone. He heard the heavy footsteps getting closer and looked up.

They all had their badges out, a confused expression on all their faces. Matt had his FBI badge in his hand. He flashed it above his head. "Gentlemen, this is a secure area. You'll have to move on," he said, mustering up as much authority as he could.

"We're here to put agent Jill Emerson in protective custody," the six-foot-five, two hundred- and fifty-pound CIA agent said.

St. Claire was not impressed. "FBI agent Jill Emerson is my partner, and she will be perfectly safe with me watching over her," he said.

The tall agent raised his voice, his anger showing. His facial muscles were flexing as he spoke. "We're under specific orders from the CIA director, and the Homeland Security Secretary to bring Jill, I mean agent Emerson back with us to DC," he said, sounding irritated.

"My partner's FBI, and we take care of our own. Do you have any orders from my Director? Any written orders?" St. Claire asked.

The CIA agent was becoming exasperated. He bent down, his face nose to nose with Matt, shouting out his demands, spittle shooting out of his mouth, and onto St. Claire's face. "I need you to get out of our fucking way, or we'll physically remove you and put you in cuffs," he threatened. "I don't need any written orders, asshole."

Matt was looking at his cellphone while the agent kept shouting at him. A big smile appeared on his face as he stood up.

St. Claire remained standing, a big grin on his face. "Get out of my way, you big goon," Matt said, pushing the husky agent off to the side. "Oh, I forgot to mention, agent Emerson checked out of the hospital thirty minutes ago."

"Where did she go?" the flustered agent asked.

"Not sure. You'll have to ask agent Emerson yourself," Matt replied, turning and walking away.

* * * * *

"Yes, sir, she's gone. Vanished," the CIA agent said. "I've got my men checking all security cameras and traffic cams. We should have a fix on how she had gotten out of the hospital.

Agent Bingham was furious. "I need Emerson in custody, and back here ASAP. She's vital to this program," he shouted.

126

Professor Franklin, at first, was nervous sitting across from his protégé he once considered a son. Observing him transform himself back to his Todd Richards identity made what he had to say easier.

Franklin could see that Richards did not appear happy. He struggled with his handcuffs, turning his wrist raw.

"You can look at me," Franklin said to Richards. "I'm here to help you."

Richards raised his head, letting his bloodshot eyes meet Franklin's. "Help me? You call this helping me?" he shouted, yanking on his cuffs.

"Todd, you've killed a lot of women. They were patients that trusted you. You've proven that restraints are our only choice. I'm here to offer you a deal if you can convince CIA agent Bingham and me, we can trust you," Franklin said.

Richards perked up. "What kind of a deal?"

"We've been monitoring you ever since you left UCLA. We know what you've accomplished with your serum. I have witnessed what you can do. I've been attempting to re-create your formula. Unfortunately, I've failed due to our restrictive abortion laws, and the ban on using fetal stem cells for research."

Richards had a puzzled expression on his face. "Monitoring me? Who has been watching me?" he asked.

"The CIA and Homeland Security. They had authorization from President Christopher," Franklin said. "I've come close to replicating your serum. Without fetuses, my serum has too many life-threatening side effects," Franklin said.

Richards did not say a word for almost a minute. He kept staring at the man he too once called a friend. "Let me guess. You want me to help our government build a military force that can transform when necessary, and destroy all of our enemies around the world," he mocked.

"Something like that. Terrorists are killing men, women, and children at a record pace. The war on drugs is failing. You have a formula that can turn the tide, and rid our world of these barbarians," Franklin said, gasping for air.

"Really. If I help you and our radical religious president, I can use fetuses, do abortions, and break federal law?"

"Yes. President Christopher believes that God approves of him protecting our country any way he can."

Richards, for the first time, smiled. "And, if I do agree to help, what's in it for me?" Richards asked, his wheels turning, as he visualized a new plan.

"You get to continue doing your research, having the supply of your serum for your use. And to stay out of prison and keep access to your injections," Franklin said.

"By the sound of things, it seems that the president needs my help more than I need his help. I've sometimes wondered what it would be like to join Molly. What I've done recently has changed me into a man I never imagined I would ever become," he said. "If I decide to help you create this new weapon, then I will need to be back at my laboratory in La Jolla. I want to be back at my home, sleep in my bed with all the good memories I once had there," he said.

Franklin appeared puzzled. "Your La Jolla office? We have a facility ten times the size of that laboratory," he argued. "I'm not sure the CIA will go along with that."

"Accept my offer or put me in prison. Also, if you agree to these terms, I want Margarita with me. She's having my baby, and I want my child growing up in the home Molly and I had created," He watched Franklin digest what he had proposed. What the professor did not know is that his new serum in his blood, allows him to go a year or more before he needs another injection.

Franklin had a befuddled expression on his face. "I'll ask. Just don't get your hopes up."

* * * * *

Thirty minutes later, Franklin was sitting down across from Richards again. He was smiling. "It appears you won. You've got your wish. Your laboratory, Margarita, and your new baby can be living with you in La Jolla."

"Thank you. When can I get started? I need all the serum vials you took from me. Then, I will need to examine the soldiers and their surrogates. I suspect you are not going to use women from Conte's trafficking business. So, where will they be coming from? I will have to examine them, too," Richards told him.

"The president has authorized us to use IVF equipment..." Richards interrupted him.

"You will let me use invitro-fertilization equipment? How hypocritical of our president. It's okay to do this if it will make a weapon, not a baby? When I wanted to try to save Molly, it was against the law," Richards said, his voice rising.

"I know. It's politics. You'll be growing your fetuses with their eggs and sperm," Franklin said. "The women donating their eggs are also part of the military. You will be creating a serum for both donors.

"Very interesting. You do realize that this special army might have the potential of creating off-springs, progenies, who could have greater powers than their parents," he said.

"You've always been very astute, Todd. Then, I assume you'll have what you need to create a serum for each of the subjects. Right?"

"That's been my theory all along. When can I get started?"

"The equipment is being delivered tomorrow. Your subjects will be at your office in two days," Franklin said.

Franklin watched Richards get escorted back to his cell. Something about his mannerisms had put him on edge. If he didn't know better, he thought his friend was acting unusually happy. Why? His cell pinged; it was Bingham.

The CIA agent had some doubts about Richards agreeing to help them. "What's your opinion about your friend. Do you think he'll work with us?"

"He's not the same man I knew at UCLA. He's changed. It might be the murders, or his serum has caused drastic side-effects. I suggest you watch him closely. I wouldn't trust him," Franklin said.

"No problem. Richards will be monitored twenty-four-seven. We're installing security cameras in every corner of his office, laboratory, and home. It will be tighter than federal prison," Bingham bragged.

127

Emerson slipped off the blonde wig and medical scrubs, in the restroom at Hennessey's. Verduzco folded the doctor's white coat she was wearing and took off her red wig.

"I think we pulled it off in our hairpieces," Verduzco said, high-fiving Jill.

Emerson did not smile. She looked exhausted from her near-death experience. "I want to thank you guys for helping me," she said, squeezing Amy's hand.

Verduzco nodded. "I know it didn't seem like it when we first met," she smiled. "I now consider our friendship first, and the FBI second. I'm concerned about leaving you while I go back to DC for my briefing," she said.

Jill shook her head. "I've got St. Claire. He's a little rough around the edges. There is no one I'd want watching my back than him," she smiled. "Go back, don't fight it, and figure out what our government's next move might be? It's all politics now with our religious fanatic president."

Amy frowned. "Something's going on with this Richards serum thing. I believe they want your baby. Rest assured, it won't happen on my watch," she said.

"I want my baby too. Nobody's going to take my child from me," she said. "I'll be getting a DNA test to see if it's Richards, or," she felt a shiver radiate over her entire body, "Chad Green's. What an idiot I was," she said.

"Not an idiot. Just letting off a little steam with a handsome man," Verduzco said

St. Claire was banging hard on the restroom door. "Girls, we've got to go. We're too exposed here."

The four agents said their goodbyes. Amy gave Jill a big hug and kiss on the cheek. St. Claire and Patch did some guy hugs with slaps on the back. Forest and Matt were self-conscious about showing their own emotions toward Amy and Jill and gave them awkward waves.

Emerson was the first to speak up. "Look, you inept morons, give us both a hug and kiss. We're all friends here," she said, winking at Amy.

Patch leaned in and whispered in St. Claire's ear. "Where's the safe house?"

"It's not too far from here. When it's secure, I'll get a message to you," Matt said.

* * * * *

Matt was driving south toward Coronado. He had a retired military buddy who was not using his vacation home on the island. St. Claire told Emerson they could have it for a year. It would be enough time for the baby to be born, and with some time to adjust to being a mother.

"It's a small two-bedroom cottage, on a secluded street. It's walking distance to the beach. Perfect for morning strolls, especially with a baby in tow," Matt said.

"Have you figured out what we are going to do about our jobs?" she asked.

"I still have enough unused vacation days to last almost fourteen months. I'm not abandoning you. You're not safe from Richards or Bingham," Matt said.

"We're both not going to be able to avoid talking with our boss or the CIA. I think it's time for me to retire. Alex left me enough life insurance and pension. I'll be comfortable as a single mom," she said. "You can't quit. You need the FBI, and the Bureau needs you," she said.

Matt turned his head, his eyes glassy. "I've got enough time to figure that out. Let's be cautious and let me protect you and my niece or nephew.

128

Four months after his capture, Richards had been hard at work creating embryos for the CIA. His serum for the military proceeded along on schedule. Four soldiers were in the first test program. He worked with two men and two women from a SEAL team, preparing themselves for their upcoming transformation test.

There were still some glitches with the serum Richards was creating for them. He discovered that invitro-fertilization made a weaker DNA strain. When the soldier transformed into a known terrorist, staying as that person only lasted, at the most, two days. That was unacceptable for the military.

Richards was surprised about that problem. Combined within the serum solution, were the correct proportions of the subject's edited DNA and the embryo's stem cells. All he could surmise was that a fully formed fetus had more mature stem cells, and that problem degraded his serum.

As an alternative, he had gotten Professor Franklin to approve growing an embryo outside the woman's womb and extracting the fetal stem cells at six weeks. He understood he was pushing the limits of the law. Since the president had already broken so many of them, his necessary approval came quickly.

Richards was going to be ready to abort his first test fetus in a week. It had to work, or his usefulness would be over. He had been formulating a survival plan for himself and Margarita if his current batch did not work. He needed three more months before his child was born.

Then, he could once again disappear with his family and be rid of the government forever.

129

Franklin was back in Virginia. He was briefing the Homeland Security Secretary, the Joint Chiefs, the CIA director, and agent Bingham, on the status of their entire project. The meeting took place in a secret conference room at the Pentagon.

"Gentlemen, let me first bring you up-to-date on the six women from Salvador Conte's Mexico laboratory. All their pregnancies are progressing well. All the babies are healthy. I have run extensive blood labs on all the fetuses and have discovered their red and white cells have innate immunity. I believe these babies will have stronger immune powers. Each of these babies received a hybrid serum from previous fetuses that came from their mothers," Franklin noticed he had confused his audience.

Bingham was first to question the professor. "Are you saying these children will be born with built-in natural abilities to transform without any of the serum we're asking Richards to create?"

"I'm not one-hundred percent sure," he shrugged his shoulders, "I believe so. I won't know until each of these children are born. If I am right, it would be possible that these infants' blood might be a natural supply for us to make a more potent serum, Franklin said with confidence. "What I am telling you is just speculation. It looks promising that we could be harvesting an elite military that could become our greatest weapon since the hydrogen bomb. I cannot give you a definitive timetable?"

Bingham had become agitated with Franklin's remarks. "The military won't wait too much longer. What about Richards serum he's creating for us?" he asked. "Can't it do that now?"

Franklin acted surprised by the question. "This serum hybrid Richard made from the in-vitro fertilization process isn't as potent as his original formula that came from aborted fetuses. Our existing laws, as you know, prohibit Richards from going in that direction. We'd then need to let our test subjects engage in intercourse, then abort their babies. What you're asking is immoral to most Americans," he said.

Bingham smiled. "Thank you for your moral high ground. Since Richards's invitro-fertilization experiment is not producing a powerful serum, the president has approved us to move ahead with Richards proven method," he said. "You can begin to abort the fetuses in Conte's women. Then, we have six subjects, all in the military, who have volunteered their bodies for their country."

Franklin shook his head in disbelief. *"Idiots. Everyone's going mad," he said to himself.* "Are you crazy? Those fetuses won't work with our soldiers. Their DNA is not a match." He walked out of the room without saying another word.

130

Two Months Later

Eight weeks after Franklin's meeting at the Pentagon, CIA agent Bingham was caught on the lab's security cameras threatening Richards. He had ordered him to create a serum for him and his wife's fetus he wanted to use. His harassing threats had gone on for the last four weeks.

Franklin, like Richards, hated Bingham. The CIA agent was a ruthless man with no moral compass. The professor was building a solid file on the CIA agent to present to the Attorney General.

Franklin was reviewing security footage of Richards in a loose-fitting white medical coat looking through the lens of his microscope, examining a blood sample. Bingham snuck up behind Richards and grabbed him by the collar and threw him backward, slamming him to the cement floor in his laboratory.

Richards bounced up and faced Bingham, a big grin on his face. "Is that the best you've got?" he said.

Bingham did not notice that the gash on Richards' forehead had started to heal and disappear. The recording from this point on was sketchy. The video showed that Bingham had pulled out his revolver and shoved the barrel of the gun inside the doctor's mouth.

The five security cameras had sound and recorded the CIA agent's threats and demands. "You will remove my wife's fetus now. I cannot wait any longer. You need to create my fucking serum today," Bingham shouted.

The Faces of Doctor Richards

The next thing that came across on the video was a shiny spear-like object penetrating Bingham's back, exiting through his heart, and out the front of his chest. The agent was unable to twist his body because the second person holding the spear was strong.

Within seconds, Bingham was on the floor, lying in his pool of blood. His eyes were frozen with disbelief, as his last breath escaped from his lungs.

The next thing the security camera picked up was Doctor Richards stepping in front of the camera and waving. He smiled, putting his arm around another Doctor Richards.

The person who Bingham had first assaulted started transforming in front of the camera. Within fifteen seconds, the first Doctor Richards in a loose-fitting lab coat had turned back to a pregnant Margarita.

It seems that Richards had been patiently preparing for his escape. Three cases of his vials and lab equipment were on a dolly ready to be placed inside a laboratory van.

He then, in front of the camera, opened a manila folder, and took out two photos. To everyone's shock, he and Margarita transformed into Bingham and his pregnant wife.

When they opened the door to the lab, Richards asked Bingham's two guards to help them take the equipment to the van.

Once Bingham's men were out of the building, Richards moved the CIA agent's body to a freezer inside the lab and stuck a post-it note to his chest. *Bingham is where he belongs. Don't waste your time trying to find me. You won't know who to look for from this day forward."*

Since Bingham's murder, neither Richards or any of his previous aliases had turned up on any law enforcement's radar. When Emerson and St. Claire were told about Bingham's murder, what concerned them the most was that Richards was on the loose. Matt seemed more worried than Jill.

131

Seven months had passed since Richards attacked Emerson in Ensenada. Her safe house on Coronado Island kept her sheltered from Professor Franklin and the CIA, and they prayed they remained hidden from Richards.

Jill took a temporary leave of absence without pay so that she could heal and take care of herself. Her baby was due in six weeks.

Miller did not want to know her location. Knowing she and her baby were safe was enough for him. He kept up on her status through St. Claire.

Her OB-GYN was a friend she had met in college. He was practicing in San Diego and agreed to honor her privacy.

St. Claire had moved into another small cottage on Coronado Island, near Emerson's house. He was more a bodyguard/friend than her partner. Their friendship had gotten even closer these last few months. He treated Jill like his little sister, which she hated.

"I don't need a big brother watching or worrying about me," she'd yell at him, as her hormones kicked into gear. "You should hang out with some of your friends, and give me some space," she'd complain.

Matt would ignore her like he did when they were on a case. He was used to her and knew she did not mean any of the foul words she yelled at him. "You know I won't leave now since Richards broke out of custody. He's still too dangerous. He still believes you're having his baby."

His words brought a chill to her body. Her mouth went dry, making it difficult to respond. She lifted a cold glass of water to help calm her down. She walked over to her desk and picked up the case file on Richards. She was amazed at how he had fooled everyone and escaped.

No matter how many times she had read the timeline since this case had started, she could not believe how smart and ruthless he had become.

Over the last seven months, Jill had begun to show signs that becoming a mother was going to be good for her.

Matt was enjoying the new Jill. He discovered that she was an excellent cook, enjoying many new recipes she would try out on him.

Being on extended leave allowed him to lose some weight and workout at the gym with a regular schedule. Jill would tag along with him, wearing her wig and dark sunglasses, always alert for anyone watching them.

Emerson did not enjoy exercising in her condition. She relished the time when she could go the gun range with Matt and keep her shooting skills up to her FBI standards. The best part was challenging her partner and comparing targets to see who was better.

She still had not gotten a paternity test done. She did not want to know. She loved the baby that was growing inside her and did not want to let Richards influence how she would love her child.

Going back to the FBI was the furthest thing from her mind. She was toying with the idea of retiring and when her baby was old enough, starting her own PI business.

Matt noticed her daydreaming while she was using the treadmill. "Hey, Emerson, a penny for your thoughts."

Jill slowly turned her head at the sweaty hunk her partner was becoming. "Oh, nothing. Only thinking about my baby and what I want to do after I give birth."

Matt smiled. "It's so wonderful seeing you embrace motherhood. It suits you."

She stopped the treadmill and hopped off. Then she did something that surprised Matt. "You've been wonderful these last few months. I don't know how I could have done all of this without you. You'll be a great Uncle to my baby," she said, giving him a big hug.

"Back at you," he said, holding back a tear. "I will never leave you or go away. You're stuck with me, now as the kid's uncle."

Standing near one of the weight machines was a tall attractive man, staring at Emerson and St. Claire. He had his phone to his ear, and his camera lens pointed at the two FBI agents.

"You keep at your routine. Soon I will have my child," the man whispered into the phone.

132

Professor Franklin had been working on another *Richards Protocol* for the last four months. After the doctor had escaped, he had found notes that were left behind that proved to be the key he needed to unlock the formula for their military project.

Professor Franklin had been threatened to cooperate or go to prison as a traitor. One way or the other, the CIA was going to have their serum, which would be like no other weapon America's enemies imagined.

He had six test subjects. Four out of the six female volunteers, all Special Forces, were pregnant. Their fetuses were a week away from being removed. Next, Franklin would harvest fetal stem cells. And, finally, if his calculations were correct, he would begin the first testing of America's new weapon against terrorism.

* * * * *

At another facility at Langley, they tested another protocol using Salvador Conte's women. Each mother had given birth to their babies that had unique DNA properties. The CIA doctors, with some help from Professor Franklin, replicated a version of Richards's serum from the infants' blood. Since Conte's men were dead, they used their stem cell serum on the mothers threatening them to cooperate or shipped back to Mexico and the life they had there. Each mother was able to transform themselves into whoever the CIA wanted. They were scared, not knowing what they would be asked to do for the United States military.

The Faces of Doctor Richards

Lea Strong was another project. She had not been doing well since she was not receiving her shots every two weeks. Her baby was still healthy, which is the only thing the president cared about. Strong's child was due any day now. The famous model's appearance had faded from what it once was, and her health had become frail and weak.

So many what-ifs had been floating around Langley about what powers this baby might have. Its blood markers were off the charts. Franklin was out of the loop on the progress of Lea Strong's baby. The day he had been removed as her doctor, he had heard the CIA and Homeland Security Secretary talking about the way the baby was growing inside the mother's womb.

The professor tried to get answers. All he knew was that the mother and unborn child were at a more secure facility. All Franklin knew was that the anticipated birth of this baby had become everyone's top priority.

Now that he was off the case, he could only guess what was happening. Knowing what Richards had created with his serum and knowing that Lea Strong's baby had his mutated DNA, gave way to a lot of speculation. It was the baby's DNA that had everyone believing it would be an extraordinary human being.

133

Richards had located Emerson's house weeks ago. After one of St. Claire's briefings with Miller, he followed him back to Coronado to his house.

After a week of monitoring where St. Claire lived, the agent slipped up and walked from his home to Emerson's.

Each day, Richards would transform into someone else. Mostly utility workers that frequented the old community that was in constant need of repair.

Margarita tried to help. It was difficult for her to transform, being so close to having her baby. She'd pretend to live in the area, walking each day by Emerson's cottage, wearing her maternity outfit.

One day, Emerson was picking up her morning newspaper when the two pregnant women crossed paths. Margarita was afraid to make eye contact. Jill was not so shy.

"I see you walking here every day. When are you due?" Jill asked.

Margarita had become nervous, beads of sweat forming on her brow. "Two weeks. Perhaps three. I want it out now," she said, shaking her belly lightly.

Emerson turned sideways. "Me too," she replied, jiggling her belly.

Both ladies started to laugh. "Would you like to come in for some hot tea?" Jill asked.

Richards, a water and power repairman that day, could hear them laughing. *"Don't be stupid, Margarita,"* he whispered. *"Don't go inside."*

Margarita smiled. "Not today. I have to finish my walk, and then go shopping for dinner," she said.

"Then, maybe tomorrow when you walk by?" Emerson asked.

Margarita was caught off-guard. "Tomorrow, not good. I see my doctor tomorrow. Maybe another day?" she said, walking away without saying goodbye.

Agent St. Claire had opened the screen door. "What was that all about?"

"Just two very pregnant women talking. She's been circling the block for the last week. She always tries to glance over at my house. I thought she'd like to come in for some tea."

Matt looked worried. "A week? Only checking out this house?" he said, a puzzled look on his face.

Emerson laughed. "Now you want to protect me from a pregnant woman ready to give birth any day?" she giggled so hard she peed in her pants. "Shit, how embarrassing. You made me wet myself." Before she could say another word, the contraction hit her hard. "Oh my god," she moaned. "My water just broke."

"The baby's coming now?" Matt stuttered as he realized what was happening.

"Yes, you moron. Get my go-bag, my wallet, and the car keys. We're having a baby," she said, her face twisted, as another contraction hit her.

Richards heard the screams coming from Emerson's house. "Shit, she is having my baby now," he said, humming the song that was playing in his head. Margarita had finished circling the block and opened the passenger door to their car.

"What's happening," she asked.

"Emerson's having her baby now. We have to beat her to the hospital if my plan's going to work," he said, as he took out the photo of her OB-GYN.

He was happy that after killing CIA agent Bingham, he had found all the files about Emerson and her baby. He was fortunate to have located her. Once he discovered who her doctor was, his plan was back on track.

His ideas for the baby were different than what the CIA had planned. With Bingham out of the way, what he was about to do would be more comfortable.

He and Margarita watched from a secluded spot near Jill's house as St. Claire carefully eased Emerson into his car. Richards smiled. He imagined that he'd finally have the family he had always wanted.

He started his car, made a U-turn, and sped toward the Coronado Bay bridge. The last time he rushed off the island, it was for another reason. He pressed on the accelerator, feeling the car pick up speed.

* * * * *

Emerson struggled to be composed sitting next to Matt in the car. The frequent contractions had her losing control of her emotions. "Can't you drive faster?" she screamed. "You drive like a little old man. Do you want to deliver this baby in the car? Right here? Right now?" she cried out.

Matt pressed his foot down on the accelerator and had the car speeding over the Coronado bridge toward La Jolla with his portable flashing lights affixed on top of his car. He tried to stay calm. It was the panic in his eyes that told a different story.

Jill stayed focused, doing her breathing before and after a contraction, unlike Matt, who appeared to be hyperventilating, as they drove to the hospital. She had called her doctor, and all she had gotten was his answering service. She prayed he'd be waiting for her.

134

Three thousand miles East of La Jolla, were six military women in a makeshift maternity ward, deep in the basement at Langley. The only government officials that knew of this project were the director of the CIA, Homeland Security Secretary, the Attorney General, the Joint Chiefs, and the President.

Professor Franklin, along with his team of scientists, medical doctors, and nurses, were in total lockdown. No communication with the outside world, including the internet, TV, or Radio, would be permitted. Doctor Richards serum was ready to be created. These six women were anxious to get started with their mission.

Lea Strong had given birth to a baby boy. The first *Progeny of Doctor Richards*. It was too soon to tell, but Franklin was optimistic that this baby would have unique qualities. What qualities, it was anyone's guess. Unfortunately for Lea's child, her son had deformities, which did not sit well with the President and the First Lady.

The professor had heard that the CIA was monitoring Emerson's pregnancy and working with the Justice Department on how to remove the child from its mother legally. The President wanted a healthy baby born from God's will.

At the White House, President Floyd Christopher, with help from his Evangelical leaders and his Chief of Staff, were formulating his re-election committee and focusing on God's new race of Americans. He believed that what he was doing would enhance humanity. The progeny venture was currently using a slush fund the CIA had at its disposal. The president had his new weapon and would soon deploy his invisible army of killers before his re-election campaign kicked off.

135

Richards had gotten to Scripps Memorial fifteen minutes before Emerson. He parked his car in the visitor's parking lot and handed Margarita a photo of a maternity ward nurse who would be assisting Emerson's doctor in the delivery room.

"Here's the picture of the nurse you need to impersonate," he told her. "Do it after we have found the nurse and Emerson's doctor."

Margarita looked concerned. So many changes lately. Won't this hurt our baby?" she asked.

Richards paused before responding. He was thinking about her question. "Maybe you're right. You were okay transforming four months ago, but in your eighth month, I just don't know." He started nodding his head. "I have a better idea. I'll find Emerson's doctor, Russell Bradshaw, and his nurse, Elsie McDonald. Once I get them secured and out of the way, then you can stay as you are and help deliver the baby," he told her.

"How are we going to get the baby out of the hospital?"

"Let me worry about that. I've been planning this for a few weeks. "Here's a hospital ID badge with your photo on it. I had made it up for you in case we needed it. Find some scrubs in the nurse's locker room. I'll meet you at the delivery room," he said, breathing heavily. He was getting very anxious about seeing his baby.

"I hope you know what you're doing. Everything seems risky," Margarita said. "We have everything we could ever want now: new identities, new home. What more do we need?" she said.

Richards ignored her. "Everything hopefully will be quick and easy. Emerson should have her contractions coming in short intervals," he said, pressing his hands together in prayer.

Richards left Margarita and began his search for Emerson's doctor. He was sure he had gotten a phone call that his patient was on her way to the hospital and decided to check the doctor's locker room.

Richards pushed the locker room door open. He heard a few loud voices and some laughter. His plan did not call for dealing with more than one doctor. He peeked one more time at the photo he had palmed in his hand. As he walked around a row of lockers, Doctor Bradshaw talking with two other doctors and a nurse he thought was the maternity ward nurse, but he wasn't sure.   Richards was now panicking.

His plan was beginning to unravel. He was trying to figure out a way to break up the conversation and get Bradshaw alone.

"Doctor Bradshaw," he said, sounding urgent. "Do you have a minute to talk with me about my patient who's on her way here to deliver her first child?" Richards asked.

Bradshaw smiled and waved off his colleagues. He was staring at this phone. "Elsie, I got texted that Jill Emerson is in the delivery room. Her contractions are a minute apart. I'll be there in less than five minutes," he said, turning his attention to Richards. "As you can see, I don't have much time to talk.   Tell me your concerns while I get into my scrubs," he said, a pleasant smile on his face.

When Richards heard the locker room door close, he turned, walked away from the doctor, and locked the door. He heard Bradshaw shouting at him.

"Are you going to ask me a question? I've got to get to my patient," he said, never seeing the butt of the revolver coming toward the back of his head. Like a hammer hitting a coconut, the doctor's skull cracked. He fell to the floor like a rag doll.

Richards' heart was pounding so loud that he did not hear the banging on the locker room door. He took Doctor Bradshaw by his ankles and dragged him to a storage closest. He stuffed him inside and shut the door. He was running out of time, as the constant banging kept getting louder. He slipped the doctor's ID badge over his neck and then took out the photo he had, and within fifteen seconds, his face had transformed into Emerson's OB-GYN.

Banging on the door was Elsie McDonald. She was red-faced and breathing heavy. "Emerson is having her baby now. She's in a lot of pain. The fetal monitor shows the baby's in distress."

They both ran the fifty yards to the delivery room, where Emerson, her knees bent, was screaming on a gurney. Agent St. Claire was about to pass out.

Richards met Margarita by the door and grabbed her arm as he followed nurse McDonald into the room. "What's all the screaming going on here? You don't want to scare your baby and have it crawl back into your womb, do you?" he joked.

Emerson had been screaming so loud that she did not hear the doctor come into the room. When he touched her arm, she grabbed it hard; her eyes were dark pools of hot oil.

"Where the hell have you been? You said, when I got here, you'd take only five minutes to change. What took you so long," she gasped as another contraction engulfed her body.

St. Claire lifted his head, happy to see the doctor by Jill's side. He could not stop shaking. "Glad you're here," Matt said. "She's driving me nuts with her screams," he jested as Emerson pounded her fist on top of his head.

"Matt shut the fuck up. If you don't, then you're switching places with me and having his baby."

Richards did not like having St. Claire in his delivery room. He allowed it so he would not raise any suspicions about him. "I need you two to behave, or I'm going to have to ask one of you to leave," he said, pointing at Emerson.

Jill lifted her head. "I can leave. She shouted as another contraction hit.

Richards sat down in front of Emerson's bent legs. He could see the baby's body. "Don't push yet," he said, his tone unsure. "Elsie, give me a reading on the fetal monitor."

McDonald tapped Richards' shoulder hard. "Baby's heart rate is dropping. We'll need to go to the OR STAT, and cut the baby out," the nurse said.

"No. We're having this baby here and now," pressing on her stomach. "The baby's breached. I have to try to turn the baby," he said, concentrating. He was watching the monitor, seeing how fast the baby's heart rate was dropping. It was now at dangerous levels.

Another contraction had come. Jill was now screaming at the top of her lungs. "Get this demon out of me now," she shouted, with a vise grip on Matt's hand.

Richards tried to act confident. With his hands on her abdomen, trying to reposition the baby, he felt something strange happening. The baby was moving on its own, putting itself in the correct position, without any help from him.

"Jill noticed his concern. "What's going on?" she asked, breathing very hard.

"It appears you will be getting your wish," he replied. Richards was focusing on his child's head, excited he was about to become a father. Only he knew that Emerson's wish was not going to be what she had imagined. "There, the baby's in the correct position. Jill, I need you to, on the next contraction, push as you've never pushed before. This baby's coming out now," he said.

St. Claire took Emerson's hand, holding it tight. "I don't care if you squeeze my hand as hard as you'd like," he said, noticing the shoes on Richards's feet. "Doctor Bradshaw, I thought you only wore your multi-color tennis shoes when you deliver?" he said.

Elsie walked to the front of the hospital bed. "Russell, you had your lucky shoes on when I left you in the locker room. What happened?"

Richards started to sweat." I'll tell you about it later. Now, I have a baby to deliver," he barked. "One more push Jill, one more," he shouted.

With one final scream, Emerson gave birth to a beautiful baby boy. Nurse McDonald took the baby from Richards and cut the umbilical cord. She cleaned off some blood and mucus from the baby's face and hands and placed the little boy on Emerson's chest.

St. Claire let go of Jill's hand and shook off the pain she had caused. He was now more focused on Doctor Bradshaw, and the way he was talking to the other nurse. Matt racked his brain as he looked at the other nurse. She looked vaguely familiar. He then glanced at the doctor's shoes again and then back up at his face. Something was bothering him. He couldn't put his finger on it.

"Isn't he beautiful," she said, waving for Matt to come near her and her baby.

"He's got your beauty and your lungs," he said, remaining distracted with Doctor Bradshaw. He was still talking to the pregnant nurse who he was sure he'd seen before.

Emerson noticed that her partner's attention was not with her and her son. "You want to be somewhere else?" she said, slapping his arm.

Her hit got his attention. "I'm here. I can't figure out where I've seen that nurse before," he said, pointing toward the door.

Jill lifted her head, her finger pointing at the other nurse, her words a little slurred as the color drained from her face. "That's the women from my house," she said, before passing out.

Nurse McDonald left the baby in Jill's arms. She signaled Margarita over to watch the baby. St. Claire's attention had now moved to his partner's.

"What's happening?" he asked. "Is Jill okay?"

Nurse McDonald was nodding. "Her blood pressure dropped. It frequently happens with difficult births. See, it's coming back up, and now our new mother is opening her eyes."

Matt wanted to give his attention to his partner. Then his attention turned to the other nurse carrying Jill's son out of the room. Doctor Bradshaw was following right behind her.

"Where's that nurse taking the baby?" Matt asked.

Elsie craned her neck. "I'm sure she's taking the boy to the baby warmer to get him checked out and cleaned up," she said, with some doubt in her voice.

"You don't sound too confident?" he asked.

"It's…" she frowned. Doctor Bradshaw has always had me take the baby out and give it a complete exam."

St. Claire recalled Jill's last words before she passed out. *"Woman from the house."* Then, it hit him. "Shit! Without telling his partner, he was out the door, running toward the nursery. He saw the pregnant nurse walking side-by-side with Doctor Bradshaw.

"Doctor Bradshaw can I have a word with you," St. Claire shouted. "I have a few questions for you and your nurse friend," he said.

It happened so fast for him to react. Doctor Bradshaw grabbed the baby from the nurse's arms and held the little boy up above his head. "Stop where you are. I will hurt this baby if you come closer," he said, his face distorted. Something unexpected was happening to Richards. He was in a panic.

St. Claire had reached for his gun under his surgical robe. He stared at the doctor who had begun to transform into Doctor Richards. "Doctor Richards, it over. You're not getting out of here," he said. "Put the baby down. Don't force me to shoot you," he ordered. He had the sight of his revolver pointed at Richards' forehead.

Richards turned to his left side and gazed at his reflection in a mirror that was by the nurse's station. *Shit, this has never happened,"* he mumbled. *"Somethings wrong,"* he muttered.

He was unable to think clearly as his entire body kept changing itself to Doctor Richards. *"How could this be happening,"* he muttered. *"I am not* looking at a photo of myself. He was wondering if his DNA was mutating to where he could imagine the transformation image he wanted, and then it would happen.

He did not see Matt lunging toward him. St. Claire grabbed the baby, and at the same time, landed a side-thrust kick to Richards' gut. He watched the doctor tumble to the floor, hitting his head hard.

Two nurses from behind the desk, came to his aid, while two others came to Matt's rescue. One wanted to take the baby. Matt was not having any of that and waved his gun. "I'm FBI. No one is taking this baby," he said, backing away from Richards, who was now on his feet.

Richards started running toward St. Claire. Before he could get off a shot, a bullet flew by him. Emerson, in her bloodied hospital gown, her back exposing her naked body, fired two shots. The first shot hit Richards in the shoulder, the second in his thigh.

"You'll never get close to my son again, you motherfucker," she shouted, collapsing to the cold floor.

St. Claire turned to see his partner holding her gun in her lap, her arms shaking. He handed off the baby to her, took her gun, and turned to handcuff Richards.

The pregnant nurse was helping Richards out of the hospital. As Matt reached the front door of the maternity ward, he saw Richards's car speeding down a circular driveway.

St. Claire knew that Richards would disappear again. He ran back to Emerson's room. Inside the room were two unarmed security guards. Emerson was in bed, swaddling her son while she nursed him.

"Well, Annie Oakley, you're were having a baby, and in your go bag, you felt it was necessary to bring your gun to the hospital," he laughed.

"Well, someone's got to protect you. You do know I can multitask?" Jill attempted to laugh, but her stomach hurt too much. "Thanks for saving my son," she said, as tears started cascading down her cheeks.

"All in a day's work. He's my nephew, you know. Nothing's ever going to happen to him on my watch," he said, bending down and giving Jill and her son a kiss on their foreheads.

Emerson grabbed his hand. "You're my only family." She said, lifting her son, exposing her nipple and said, "Alex, meet your uncle, Matt."

St. Claire was blushing, trying not to stare at his partner's exposed breast. "Thanks. Could you cover yourself, please? It's distracting," he said.

The baby's eyes were open and alert. Neither Matt nor Jill noticed the facial changes happening on the baby's face. It was quick and only lasted for a second or two.

136

Lewin, in one stressful breath, briefed Attorney General Murphy on the events at Scripps Memorial Hospital. "Emerson had her baby. Richards impersonated her OB-GYN and almost kidnapped her new son. There was a shootout in the hospital. Richards was shot. He slipped away. We're hunting for him as we speak,"

"No problem," replied Murphy. "We've been monitoring Emerson for months now, and will continue to do so, as her child gets older. As far as Richards is concerned, we'll get him back with us again. He'll get caught when he tries to snatch Emerson's son again," the attorney general said. "He's obsessed with her and that baby."

Lewin shrugged his shoulders, shaking his head. "Do you think he'll try again?

"I think he has some anomalies with his serum. Did you see him without warning change back into Richards? That might be his downfall," Murphy said. "I'm sure he'll have that problem fixed before he tried to snatch Emerson's son."

"He must know we'll be watching her."

"He's fixated with her, and I don't believe he'll stop until he gets her baby. Now with his ability to transform, he's becoming careless and arrogant. He believes he's smarter than us. That will be his downfall, Murphy said."

I'm not so sure. Jill's the spitting image of his dead wife Molly, and now with his son being born, he's crazy enough to try again. Trust me, we have not heard the last from that stupid son-of-a-bitch," said Lewin.

"We've got this handled."

Lewin did not seem so confident. "I hope you're right. Richards is irrational and could kill all of us, and we would not see it coming."

"We don't need him anymore. Our doctors, with Franklin's help, are doing an excellent job interpreting the notes we found. Our first serum batch, using Lea Strong's baby's blood, has allowed our Special Ops team to infiltrate two ISIS cells in Syria. They got in and out, undetected, killing all of their targets."

"How long can we continue to take blood samples without harming her baby?" Lewin asked.

"Not much longer. Our other test babies have some remarkable abilities too. We'll have enough vials for our military. Besides, Franklin believes that with our next batch of fetuses, he feels he can create a more robust serum."

"I hope you and the president know what you're getting us into?"

"We do. These first test babies, Franklin believes, will produce an unlimited supply of serum from their blood alone," Murphy said.

"When did we lose our moral compass? Are we going to create human guinea pigs and keep them locked up forever? If we're discovered, we're all going to prison," Lewin said.

"We'll never be found out. The only witnesses are their mothers. They will soon be out of the way," he said indifferently. "We're at war. We need every possible weapon to rid the world of the worst scum on earth. The president believes God has permitted him to do this."

"I'm not so sure it's God that is talking to our president," Lewin said, jumping up, knocking his chair backward. He slammed the door on his way out.

Murphy was on the phone to the president. "Sir, I think we have a problem with the Homeland Security Secretary. He's letting his moral beliefs get in the way of his job to you, and this country."

137

Richards barked out instructions to Margarita on how to remove the bullets in his shoulder and thigh. Her hand was shaking as he told her to insert the forceps into the wound.

"Don't worry about hurting me," he said, as he took a big gulp from the whiskey bottle in his hand. "Slowly spread the forceps open, feel for the bullet. When you touch the lead slug, close your grip, and guide it out in one slow pull." His calm directions were not making it any easier on her.

"I can't do this," she moaned. "I'm going to faint," she whimpered. "You think it out of your body," she suggested.

Richards tried to fight off the pain he was feeling and think at the same time. He recalled how he could make a knife wound heal.

He nodded. "Perhaps it will work on a bullet," he said, closing his eyes tight. "Give me a moment and let me concentrate. If not, you're yanking these lead bullets out of my body."

Richards looked at Margarita and raised his index finger, pressing his eyes tight. "Don't talk to me. Let me concentrate," he told her. He kept his eyes closed and began focusing first on the bullet in his shoulder. He clenched his jaw tightly, letting his mind target the location and pain that was coming from the bleeding wound.

"There, I got it," he smiled. "I feel it moving." Fifteen seconds later, the slug slipped out of his bloodied skin, and onto the white bedsheet. Then, he closed the hole in his shoulder without using stitches. He then turned his focus on his thigh. This time the lead shrapnel slipped out quickly.

Margarita, her mouth agape, clapped. "That was a miracle," she said.

Richards was breathing heavily. In a low whisper said. "No miracle. My mind's evolving from my new serum," he said before he blacked out.

* * * * *

He woke up two hours later, soaking wet from the fever that had broken. "What happened?" he asked.

Margarita was upset. "You were dreaming…horrible dreams, I think," she said. "You transformed four times. First, into Chad Green, then agent Emerson. Then, you were weeping and became many beautiful women I do not know. You finally changed into Molly, who was crying out of control. You were delirious. You kept mumbling something about it came too late. Your dream calmed down, and you transformed back to yourself," she told him.

Richards was trying to remember his dream. Then, it came back like a rushing river. He remembered all the women in his life he murdered. Then, he remembered watching Molly drain her cancer from her pores. He knew why he was crying as Molly. He had found his miracle cure too late.

He sat up, leaning against the headboard. "I have more testing I need to do. My new serum has more potential than I ever imagined. Our baby might be the key to a disease-free future for people.

"Do I have those powers?" Margarita asked.

"I don't know yet. Our baby might. We won't know until he or she's born. We need to pack up our things and leave this area for a while. I have another home in a small mountain town in Nevada. It's very secluded. We'll be safe there so I can continue my work."

"How will I have our baby?" she asked, confused.

"You watched me deliver Emerson's son. I can do ours. Don't you worry," he said, realizing that he only wanted his baby to be safe. Margarita was expendable.

473

138

Two weeks after Emerson had her son, she and St. Claire flew back to the Hoover building to brief Deputy Director Ron Kipfer and their boss, Brian Miller, about the Richards case. Emerson reminded them that she was retired. I will cooperate with you on my terms only," she told them unsmiling.

Agent's Verduzco and Patch had come out of the conference room first. They both seemed pissed. Emerson's eyes met Amy's; they didn't have to say a word. Forest acted differently.

"Fuck them. If I want to speak to you guys, I'm going to do it no matter what my orders are. Jill, sorry we could not be there for you," Patch said, his voice filled with regret.

"I know," Emerson replied. "Thanks for the nice stuffed animals you sent. Little Alex loves them."

Amy was acting uncomfortable. "Shit. Fuck them too," she cursed. "The bureau has its head up its ass about this Richards serum shit. How are you doing as a mother," she asked.

"I love the lack of sleep, lack of energy, and St. Claire acting like a mother hen over both of us. Other than that, I am loving being a mother," she smiled.

Patch sat down on the bench and slid next to Jill. He leaned in and whispered in her ear. "They are obsessed with your baby. They kept pounding on us to reveal who the daddy is. They are hoping it's Richards or Chad Green," he said.

"What did you tell them?"

"Nothing. How am I supposed to know what you do in your personal life? Amy was more direct. She told them to go fuck themselves," he smiled.

Emerson started to giggle. "Thanks, guys. You need to swing by and say hello to your new nephew. I've been telling Alex all about you guys." Before she could finish, she and St. Claire were being called into the meeting.

"We've been reassigned to the cyber division. We're on their shit list for now," Verduzco said.

"Well, stop by when you can," Emerson called back as the conference room door slammed shut.

* * * * *

The conference room had more people than Jill and Matt had expected. Attorney General Murphy and Homeland Security Secretary, Stuart Lewin were sitting at the far end of the long conference table. Off to their right, was their ex-boss, Brian Miller, and next to him, Deputy Director Kipfer. They were directed to the only two empty seats and told to sit down.

Kipfer was first to speak. "Agent Emerson, you've been through a lot these last few months. I hope you're healing okay?" he said awkwardly.

Emerson touched St. Claire's arm, signaling him to let her respond. "No concern for my son? Or, how am I doing after a shootout minutes after giving birth?" she said, not hiding her contempt.

"Agent Emerson, watch your tone with me," the Deputy Director said. "You still work for the FBI, and need to show some degree of respect," he said, angrily.

Emerson was shaking her head. "Don't you guys communicate with each other? I'm retired and am here as a favor to my ex-boss. So, if I want to tell all of you to go fuck yourselves, I can," she said with a smirk.

St. Claire could not control himself either. "Respect. You don't deserve any. You left us vulnerable in Mexico…no you thought we were

475

expendable because you wanted Richards. So, go fuck yourselves too," he said, his arms folded across his chest.

Brian Miller did all he could not to laugh. "Agent St. Claire calm down. We asked you and Emerson here to see if you can shed some light on Richards's case."

Attorney General Murphy stood and began pacing around the room. "I'm not interested in Richards or what you might know about him. I'm interested in who's the father of your boy," he said, scrutinizing Emerson.

Emerson pushed her chair back with such force; it slammed hard against the wall, leaving a sizable dent. "That's none of your business. My son is my business and my business only," she said. "If you asked me here to discuss my personal sex life, then I am out of here."

Deputy Director Kipfer jumped in. "Jill, please sit down. We need some questions answered about you, and your relationship with Chad Green. We know for a fact that Green was Doctor Richards. We had a video of you and Green when you spent the night together at your apartment on more than one occasion. So, stop stonewalling, and tell us who the father of your son is?" he demanded.

Emerson was fuming. She was ready to kick his ass. Something deep inside her brain told her to control herself. "I'm not interested in what you think you know. You can take those videos, and put them where the sun don't shine, you asshole." She was boiling mad. "What about the pregnant women you held like prisoners, while you waited for their babies to be born. You know, Conte's human trafficking girls?" she said, enjoying watching all of them squirm.

"I don't know what you're talking about? We are not holding any pregnant women prisoners," Attorney General Murphy said. "Where were these so-call women being held?"

"I'll bet somewhere at Langley, in one of your secret laboratories in the basement," St. Claire blurted out.

Kipfer wanted to get the meeting back on track. "Are you going to tell us who the father of your baby is?" he demanded, waving her son's birth certificate in the air.

"What's it say on that paper?" she asked.

"Father unknown."

"Then, there's your answer." She threw an envelope at her boss. "You can take this as my official letter of resignation," she said, turning and storming out of the room.

Everyone was stunned by her actions. "St. Claire, you need to get control of your partner," Kipfer ordered.

Matt stood, glared at everyone in the room, and tossed an envelope in the face of the deputy director. "I quit, too," he said.

Do I need to remind both of you that Richards's case is a top-secret issue," Murphy said, "Am I making myself clear?"

Jill stopped in her tracks—her fist clenched. "You leave me alone, and I will not interfere in your cover-up and anything else you are going to do with your version of Richards serum." She turned and walked out of the room, St. Claire, right behind.

The men seated looked at each other. "I guess that went well," Miller said.

* * * * *

Later that day, another meeting was held at Langley. Kipfer, Murphy, Stuart Lewin, and CIA director Roger Kramer were discussing what to do about Emerson's son.

"I think we should leave her alone for now. We can't afford to have her leaking to the press what we're doing. We'll have enough babies that fit the same criteria. Let him get older, and we can observe from afar."

139

Emerson had not said a word since she left the Hoover building. St. Claire looked at Verduzco and Patch.

"Are you guys buying? We're unemployed now," he said, unable to hold back his grin.

"I'll take care of it, and put on my expense account," Amy teased.

Emerson had a smile forming on her face. "Thanks, guys. I guess my hormones got the best of me?"

St. Claire said. "Are you saying I have hormones too?"

"Yes. Every six weeks since I've known you," Emerson said, lightly pushing her partner's shoulder.

"What are you two morons going to do now?" asked Patch.

"Raise my son. Maybe start an investigative agency. I'm good at that."

"Can I help raise baby Alex and join your new firm?" St. Claire asked.

Emerson leaned over and kissed his cheek. "You're his uncle. We need you. And, yes, you can work at our agency as a full partner," she said.

Verduzco raised her hand. "I might be looking for a new place of employment soon. I've burnt too many bridges at the FBI," she said.

Forest threw his arms in the air. "What am I, chopped liver. Maybe the four of us can start this new agency?" he said.

* * * * *

478

Nine months later, at Emerson's cottage on Coronado Island, the four of them were discussing their first case from a wealthy businessman from Austria. His niece had gone missing.

The four ex-FBI agents read the file he had sent them. They were surprised when they saw her name: Lea Strong.

"The last of Doctor Richards patients he had not killed. I'll bet my life that she's somewhere deep inside the CIA network. I've heard enough rumors about their new weapon," St. Claire said. "I remember that she was pregnant with the doctor's child when she was picked up by the CIA."

Emerson had become agitated, hearing Richards's name. "I'd like to lock all of them up for what they've done to Lea Strong and Conte's women."

Verduzco was shaking her head. "We'll never find out anything about those women. Maybe they're not even in the country."

"Well, whatever it is, we have our first job. Let's not screw it up," Patch said.

* * * * *

Inside Emerson's master bedroom, baby Alex was in his crib. He had been woken up by loud voices, he recognized, that was coming from the living room. He wanted to be with them.

Little Alex had started standing up on his own for the last few weeks. He was distracted by all the photos on the dresser next to his crib.

Today, he was able to stretch his arms and grab a photo that had a picture of his mother with a strange man he did not recognize. He liked it when his mother smiled, and she seemed happy with the man in the picture. So, little Alex was happy too.

The moment he had grabbed the framed print, he lost his balance and fell back, bumping his head. His head hurt, and a lump was forming. But within seconds, the pain and lump had disappeared. He still held the picture frame in both his hands, intrigued with the photo of his mother

479

and a man he did not recognize. Within seconds, his facial structure, like a mound of clay, shaped itself to look like the man in the photo.

Little Alex heard his mother's voice. It caused him to smile and become distracted. He dropped the picture frame, just before his mother leaned over the crib railing. In an instant, his face returned to its normal state.

Jill unaware of what was happening, lifted Alex and carried him to see his two uncles and aunt. Life for everyone had become perfect.

The Faces of Doctor Richards

www.ingramcontent.com/pod-product-compliance
Lightning Source LLC
Chambersburg PA
CBHW022237020726
47496CB00004B/943